PRAISE FOR THE NOVELS OF WILLIAM HEFFERNAN

TARNISHED BLUE

"Superb ... gritty and graphic, a New York smart novel—a winner!"
—Nelson DeMille

"Full of surprises. Heffernan can write a mean page ... a real pro."
—Stuart Kaminsky

SCARRED

"A clever, well-paced thriller. Heffernan lays out his clues and plot twists with a dark glee that amuses and draws one along in his wake."
—*Publishers Weekly*

BLOOD ROSE

"Heffernan builds the fear chapter by chapter ... an enjoyable read!"
—*People*

RITUAL

"Grabs you by the throat in the prologue, and the pressure doesn't let up until the last moment. A major jolt to the nervous system!"
—*Cleveland Plain Dealer*

TARNISHED BLUE

a novel by

William Heffernan

AN ONYX BOOK

ONYX
Published by the Penguin Group
Penguin Books USA Inc., 375 Hudson Street,
New York, New York 10014, U.S.A.
Penguin Books Ltd, 27 Wrights Lane,
London W8 5TZ, England
Penguin Books Australia Ltd, Ringwood,
Victoria, Australia
Penguin Books Canada Ltd, 10 Alcorn Avenue,
Toronto, Ontario, Canada M4V 3B2
Penguin Books (N.Z.) Ltd, 182–190 Wairau Road,
Auckland 10, New Zealand

Penguin Books Ltd, Registered Offices:
Harmondsworth, Middlesex, England

First published by Onyx, an imprint of Dutton Signet,
a division of Penguin Books USA Inc.

First Printing, April, 1995
10 9 8 7 6 5 4 3 2 1

 REGISTERED TRADEMARK—MARCA REGISTRADA

Printed in the United States of America

PUBLISHER'S NOTE
This is a work of fiction. Names, characters, places, and incidents either are the product of the author's imagination or are used fictitiously, and any resemblance to actual persons, living or dead, events, or locales is entirely coincidental.

To Gloria Loomis,
for sixteen years as a great agent,
and an even better friend.

Prologue

The man moved along the macadam walkway. His eyes were down; his hands stuffed in the pockets of an unbuttoned trench coat. The coat was too heavy, out of place in the sun-bathed heat of the park and, together with the downcast eyes and upturned collar, it made the man appear furtive—someone who wanted to pass unnoticed.

Joseph "Little Bat" Battaglia watched him; tried to get a better look at the rough face that remained pointed toward the ground. He wanted to see the man's eyes, see any sudden shift in attention that would scream out a warning. But the man simply continued on, hurrying to one of the park's exits. Then he was gone.

Little Bat shifted his gaze slowly, taking in the rest of the park, moving from one point to another: to each unoccupied bench, to each of the other narrow walkways that crisscrossed the open areas of grass. His breathing had increased as he had watched the man. Now it began to subside. Yet one hand continued to finger the zipper of his lightweight jacket, staying near the revolver tucked in a holster on his right hip. Finally he let the hand fall away, then turned slowly and forced his eyes to roam the traffic-laden street fifty yards behind him.

"What is it, Daddy?"

He glanced down at his ten-year-old daughter and forced a smile. "Nothing, honey. Just checking everything out."

"Cop's eyes?" she said.

His smile widened, became genuine. The child, Amy, his oldest, was precocious even for ten, and for years now she had enjoyed teasing him about being a cop. "You know how it is. Just can't break the habit."

"Gotta case the territory, huh?" she said.

The child was grinning up at him, and he ran a hand against her hair. It was soft and dark and lustrous, just like her mother's. She looked so much like her mother. Both children did. Dark, olive complexions; brown eyes like deep pools. Beautiful. He smiled at the child again. This one, he thought, in a couple of years, oh, will she start to give you worries.

A sharp cry made his eyes rise to the swing area, where his six-year-old, Marie, was playing. His jaw had hardened at the sound; his body had tensed, grown ready. But it had only been exuberance, and he relaxed as he watched her swing wildly, her long hair flowing out behind her. Your tomboy, he thought. Your wild child. The one thing about her that had so disappointed your own father. That she hadn't really been a boy. He looked away, and his mouth hardened almost imperceptibly. Just one more disappointment on a very long list.

Marie jumped off the swing and came running toward him, all arms and legs, limbs flashing in every direction.

"Daddy, can we go get ice cream? Can we? Can we?"

She was breathless, more with the idea than the expense of energy. He reached down and pulled her up into his arms.

"It's late," he said, making a show of looking at his watch. "Your mother expects you guys back."

"She won't mind. I know she won't," Marie chirped. There was a feigned authority in her voice; a certainty she would get her way.

He glanced at Amy, who only shrugged. But her eyes told him she wanted it as well. He hoped what they really wanted was just a little more time with him. And, yes, their mother would mind. She'd be pissed as hell, and would probably start making phone calls. But she was always pissed, no matter what he did. He let out a breath. Divorce sucked. And he had so little time with them. Saturday and Sunday afternoons. That sucked even worse. But it was something he had been forced to accept. So if he stole an extra half hour, tough shit.

"Sure, let's do it," he said. "Besides, I'm getting a Cherry Garcia attack. How about you?"

"Super Fudge Chocolate," Marie squealed.

He made a face, then looked at Amy.

She grinned up at him. "Chocolate Chip Cookie Dough."

"Ugh," he said. It made them both giggle. It always did. He glanced quickly around the park, just to be sure, then took one small hand in each of his, and turned toward the street. Damn those bastards, he thought. But it would only be a few more days now. Just a few more.

Little Bat parked the unmarked car in front of the house, and immediately found a blue-and-white sector car pulling up alongside. He lowered the window and stared at the two uniforms nervously staring back.

"She call the precinct again?" he asked.

The young cop riding shotgun nodded. "About ten minutes ago. Sorry, Cap. Last time she called the P.C.'s office when we ignored her."

Battaglia nodded. It made the uniforms nervous to roust a captain of detectives, but they didn't have much choice. "I'll take care of it," he said. "Sorry you were troubled."

The sector car pulled away, and he glanced at his

daughters and offered a sheepish grin. "Guess I'm in trouble," he said. "Let's go face the music."

The door opened as they were halfway up the front walk, and his ex-wife stepped out onto the small porch. Her eyes were glistening with anger; her mouth a thin, rigid line. Even that way she looked beautiful, he thought. Goddamned dago women, he told himself. He should have known better than to marry one.

The girls kissed him, then ran past their mother. He felt a sudden sense of loss as he watched them enter the house. The house he had once lived in, another life ago. But now only his kids lived there. And his ex-wife. He turned to her. At least the kids knew better than to stay around for the fireworks.

"Look, Angie, I'm sorry I'm late," he began. "We stopped for ice cream." He made another show of looking at his watch, just as he had for the children. "It was only an extra forty-five minutes. You didn't have to call the precinct."

"I told you I'd do it again, if *you* did it again," she said. "They're supposed to be back at four o'clock. I *want* them back at four o'clock."

He looked down at his shoes, rubbed his fingers against his forehead. He was six-two, and two hundred and ten pounds, and he towered over her slender five-four. "Well, at least you didn't call the commissioner's office this time," he said.

"That was next. If you weren't back by five."

He raised his eyes and stared at her. She was still striking, even with the bitchiness spread across her face. Her features were thin and finely etched, accented by her dark eyes and hair, and a wide, sensuous mouth. They actually looked very much alike, and often, at first, people had asked if they were brother and sister. Now they were just strangers who shared two kids. He wished things could be different, easier for each of them somehow. He wished he could still love her the way she wanted. But he knew neither was possible.

He stared at her, willing some kind of peace. "I'd like us to stop this, Angie. God, how I'd like it."

She sneered at him. "You chose your life, Bat. You chose to live like a goddamned animal. Don't put it on me."

"We got kids. We could try for them."

Her eyes blazed, and she spit out her words. "It makes me sick they even spend time with you. It makes me sick what they might see."

He felt his anger rise, and he stood glaring down at her. He forced his eyes away, stared instead at the row of azalea bushes spread across the front of the house. He had planted them himself years ago. Another lifetime. Then he turned and started down the walk. "I'll see you next Saturday," he said over his shoulder.

She watched him go, then turned quickly and stepped back into the house, shutting the door with a sharp crack. She leaned back against it and squeezed her eyes shut. "You sonofabitch," she whispered. "You goddamned sonofabitch."

Joe Battaglia drove the unmarked car across the Queensboro Bridge and back into Manhattan. It was five o'clock and traffic was still light, the Sunday dinner crowds not yet having begun to make their way toward the popular East Side restaurants. He cut over to Third Avenue and headed north. His gym bag was in the backseat. He had planned to stop at his health club. He wanted to work out, and he also wanted to see Leslie. They had argued bitterly the night before, and he needed to set some things straight. But not now, he told himself. He had had enough confrontation for one day; all the turmoil he cared to handle. He turned into Ninety-second Street and headed back toward First Avenue, and found a vacant loading zone only a few yards from his build-

ing. He pulled in and lowered the visor, revealing
the NYPD card that said he was on official business.
It would keep the car from being towed, leaving it
vulnerable only to the city's meter maids, who took
pride in ticketing department cars. But it was Sunday, and he knew they were concentrated in mid-
town, feeding on the tourists from Jersey and
Connecticut. Hey, who knows, he told himself.
Maybe you'll catch just one break today.

The concern he had felt earlier reasserted itself,
and he carefully checked both sides of the street for
any sign of someone waiting, watching. Then he
climbed out of the car and moved quickly to the
front door of the building, key in hand, ready to
open the door that led to the lobby.

His was an older building, lacking the amenity of
a doorman, and the lobby reflected it—a battered
shell, worn by age and neglect. The elevator followed suit, its once proud mahogany paneling now
dull and scarred, and its mechanism rumbled and
groaned as it wheezed its way toward the ninth floor.
But it was the best he could afford. At least for now.
Even a captain's pay didn't stretch to the point of
child support and the hefty alimony payments he had
been forced to accept. And he saw no way out unless
he left the department and entered private practice.
Like his father before him, he had gone to law
school nights while rising in the ranks. His father
had made it to lieutenant of detectives by the time
he was forty, with a law degree. He himself had
made captain by thirty-five, and just two years
later—a short six months ago—had passed the bar.
At least he had beaten the old man at that. He
frowned. But that was as far as it would go. The old
man had left the department and had gone on to
heights his son could never hope to match. Anthony
Battaglia would always be "Big Bat" to those who
knew him. For as long as he lived—perhaps longer.
And his only son, Joseph, would remain "Little

Bat," no matter what he accomplished in or out of the department.

Joe Battaglia drew a long breath. Unless this investigation turns out the way you think it will. Then, even your friends might call you something else. Traitor. Fink. Or, if they find out everything, maybe even . . .

He let the thought die as the elevator doors opened with a jerking, grinding thump, then made his way down the long, dimly lighted hall to his apartment. He stopped before the door, checked both ends of the hall, then scanned the door frame for the telltale he had left earlier. It was still in place, a two-inch length of hair he had plucked from his own head, wetted, and placed across the opening between door and jamb to let him know if anyone had entered in his absence. He closed his eyes momentarily, then wearily inserted the two keys it took to enter the small, cramped studio he now called home. He wasn't looking forward to the rest of the day. There were several hours of work ahead on his computer, going over files he had already accessed and stored on a floppy disk. Then the hours alone with his thoughts, his own recriminations, his own regrets. He drew another heavy breath. Just a typical Sunday night.

Joe Battaglia stepped through the door and moved down the narrow entry hall, and past the enclosed galley kitchen. As he stepped past the kitchen doorway, his peripheral vision caught a flash of movement. Instinctively he began to duck and turn, his right hand moving toward the holster on his hip. But it was too late—he had been too distracted, too slow—and the lead-filled sap caught him squarely behind the ear before he could reach the Smith & Wesson police special. His body sagged, a blaze of light filling his eyes. Then he pitched forward and fell face first onto the cheap shag rug that covered the living room floor.

He awoke a half hour later, his cheek pressed against the unmade sofa bed. He forced his eyes to focus, fighting through the pain that hammered inside his head. He was naked, arms spread out before him. Each wrist was bound by heavy wire to the steel frame of the fold-out bed. He ran a quick inventory of his body. His thighs were drawn up beneath him, and held against his chest by another wire tied behind his knees, then looped up and fastened around his neck, making certain he would garrote himself if he tried to straighten his legs. Two more wires held his ankles to the lower bed frame. He was hog-tied, with his butt stuck up in the air, unable to move.

He carefully turned his head and looked back over his shoulder. A cold chill moved through his body, and he began to sweat. The grinning figure stood behind him, the gloved hands toying with a large, black plastic vibrator.

"Brought you a present, Bat." Long fingers twisted the base of the vibrator, sending a low, steady hum into the room. "I knew you'd really like it." The voice was raspy, softened now by a hint of laughter.

"You motherfucker," Bat growled. "You do this, I'll fucking kill you. It takes the rest of my life, I'll fucking see you dead." He struggled against the wire, and it quickly tightened against his throat. Immediately, he began to choke. Behind him he could hear the man laughing.

"You ain't got the rest of your life. Not unless you tell me something I wanna hear," the man said.

"I got nothing to say to you."

"Yes, you do, Bat. Just tell me where the stuff is."

"Fuck you."

The man laughed again. "Whatever turns you on."

From the corner of his eye, Bat saw a second figure move up beside the first. He turned his head again, gagging against the wire that cut into his throat, and his eyes widened in disbelief. Then pain seared his body, starting in his rectum and spreading up his torso like a sword cutting through his bowels and driving up into his chest. He heard himself howl. It was the sound of a wounded animal, bellowing out rage and torment. He felt the press of something hard behind his ear, and his mind suddenly froze with the terror of what it was.

"Last chance, Bat." The new voice was cold and filled with contempt; a voice he still recognized through the undisguised hatred. The grinning man had moved back, off to his right. Now he began to laugh, and the sound of it sent a chill along Battaglia's spine.

He tightened his shoulders to keep from shaking. "Fuck you, too," he said to the one holding the gun against his head. The words emerged in a croaking gasp.

The second assailant let out a long breath, as one finger tightened on the trigger.

The last thing Little Bat saw was the photograph of his daughters on the bedside table. Then it disappeared in a blinding flash of light that exploded across his eyes. His mind never registered the quiet spit of the silenced pistol.

Chapter One

Eddie Grogan was in love. And, surprisingly, it seemed he was being loved in return. He smiled at the idea. It wasn't something he had expected at fifty-two. In truth, he hadn't expected it at twenty-two. He studied his image in the full-length mirror. Not exactly your classic catch, he thought. He had the flat face of an aging bulldog, and his stocky, fast-fading body featured a stomach that had hung over his belt more years than he cared to remember. His only attribute, as he saw it, was being a detective first grade. And that was something that didn't attract women. Not unless it was accompanied by a good-looking mug, or a great line of bullshit.

Eddie thought about it as he adjusted his tie for the fifth time. Then he stepped back and took in the whole picture, right down to his well-shined shoes. He shook his head. His suit already looked rumpled, even though he had just taken it from the cleaner's plastic bag. But his suits always looked that way. He had them on five minutes and they seemed to crumble and wilt from within. Hey, he told himself, it's like Popeye says, I am what I fucking am.

He glanced at his watch. It was ten o'clock, and he was supposed to pick up Rita in half an hour, so they could do some shopping before lunch. Christ, he thought. Not only was the woman forty-five and still beautiful, but she owned a fucking bar. It was like a dream come true. He gave the tie one more nudge toward his throat, then started across the room, heading for the front door. The sound of the telephone stopped him, and he hesitated; glared at it. He had taken the day off, just to get ready for this date, and he wanted to ignore the call. But he knew it wasn't possible. Not with this new assignment. It was just the two of them—him and Devlin—and he couldn't leave Paul hanging out there alone just because his pecker was twitching.

He picked up the receiver and heard Devlin's voice. "Hey," he snapped, "I was just goin' out for a little romance. You got nothin' better to do than bother a guy who ain't got fucking laid in the last century?"

He waited, listening. "Jesus fucking Christ," he hissed. "Little Bat? They fucking sure?" He listened again, getting the particulars, jotting them down in the notebook he had pulled from his jacket pocket. "Yeah, I can be there in about fifteen minutes, if crosstown traffic ain't too fucked up. I'll make sure everything's secure, and the lid's down tight." He paused a moment. "But I think that'll already be taken care of. You know who's gonna be there, don't you? And he ain't gonna like it when I tell him it's our case." He listened. "Yeah, my sentiments exactly. Right where he fucking breathes."

Eddie replaced the receiver and stared at it for a moment, remembering he had to call Rita, let her know he was stiffing her for lunch. "Jesus Christ," he said aloud, his mind going back to the call. People just didn't ice police captains. It just didn't happen. Even fucking lunatics knew better than that. And that meant this was some really heavy shit. His mind clicked in on Joe Battaglia's father. The Big Bat himself. He shook his head. It's gonna be a fucking circus, he told himself. Shit don't get any heavier than this.

East Ninety-second Street, between First and Second Avenues, looked as though it were under siege by the time Eddie arrived, and he was forced to leave his car double-parked half a block away and hoof it to the front door.

Grogan observed the feeding frenzy that had already begun as he moved as inconspicuously as possible toward Battaglia's building. Reporters, photographers, and television crews were already set up behind a barricade on the opposite sidewalk, and a half dozen uniforms had been assigned to keep them there. Already the mood was becoming hostile, but the bosses weren't taking any chances on this one. No pencil pusher was going to finesse his way into the building, posing as a cop—as they so often did. And whatever information they did get would be minimal at best. Grogan could almost hear them howling already. Just as soon as they found out who'd been iced.

A short distance from the media types, another group was being held at bay. Some thirty or so residents had come out of their buildings to join passersby in the gruesome wait for a body to be wheeled out the front door. They were mostly women and young kids. Several of the women were older, well into their sixties, many wearing their widow's trademark: sturdy black shoes. But others were younger, and equally intense, eagerly sharing their observations with people they had never spoken to before. One woman, perhaps thirty, Grogan guessed, stood in front, still dressed in a bathrobe. Next to her were two street punks, who had wandered into the fun—one black, one Hispanic—each exactly the type the woman would have crossed the street to avoid under other circumstances. But this was different, Grogan thought, a time when New Yorkers were just like people everywhere—ready to stand and gawk at horror wherever they could find it—all their cool and reserve suddenly stripped away. He had always attributed it to some twisted survival instinct. Let's look at what happened to *somebody else,* they were thinking. If for no other reason than to assure ourselves we have escaped again.

The uniforms at the door to Battaglia's building checked his shield and let him pass, and Eddie moved quickly to two detectives standing in the battered lobby.

"The chief here?" he asked.

The two men looked at the shield affixed to Grogan's breast pocket. "Upstairs. Ninth floor," one answered. "But everybody below the rank of captain already got his ass thrown out."

"Shit," the other detective groused. "We didn't even get in the front door. They told us to get the fuck down here and wait for orders. And *we're* the ones caught the squeal."

"Who found the body?" Grogan asked.

"Some guys from Battaglia's unit," the first detective said. "They called it in. But they musta called the chief's office first. Or their boss did. 'Cause by the time we got here, it was fucking brass city. What the hell's goin' on?"

Grogan shrugged. "I'll see if I can find out." He started for the elevator.

"Good luck," one of the detectives called at his back. "Don't plan on staying long."

When he reached the apartment, Grogan found a uniformed captain named Malloy—the precinct commander for Manhattan North—guarding the door.

"You gotta wait downstairs," Malloy barked.

"Uh, uh, Cap. Can't do that," Grogan said.

Malloy stiffened, then straightened, making himself a few inches taller—a typical cop response when his authority was challenged. "You wanna run that by me again, *Detective,*" he snapped.

Eddie raised both hands, palms out. "Whoa, Cap. I'm not breaking chops, here." Grogan's rank, detective first grade, was the equivalent of a lieutenant, and as such subject to the orders of any captain, in uniform or out. But not under the peculiarities of his new assignment. He forced a smile. "You heard about the new unit." Grogan spoke the words as fact, not question. "The one headed up by Inspector Devlin."

Malloy's eyes narrowed. "The one works outta the mayor's office?" His voice wasn't friendly.

"That's us," Grogan said. "And, according to the mayor, from now on this is our case."

The captain stared at him, his eyes even less friendly than his voice. "You better wait here while I get the chief," he said.

"Whatever you say, Cap."

Grogan lit a cigarette and leaned against the wall. It would take time, he knew, before the chief came out. Mario Cervone, the chief of detectives, would first phone the mayor's office to confirm what Grogan had said. Then he would call the P.C. to bitch and moan about being yanked from a case that involved the murder of one of his own men. A small smile formed on Grogan's lips. Then, when the commissioner tells him it's tough titty time, he'll come out and chew your ass for a while. And then he'll take a walk, 'cause he ain't got no other choice.

"What are you doing out here?"

Grogan turned to the sound of Paul Devlin's voice, as he came toward him down the hall.

"I was ordered to wait until Cervone granted me an audience," Grogan said. "I think he wants to polish his ring, so I can plant a good one on it."

"Fuck him," Devlin said. "We go inside. Now."

Pleasure flickered across Grogan's eyes. Unlike most cops, profanity wasn't a normal part of Devlin's speech. It only appeared when he was really hot, or when he came within a mile of Mario Cervone. And the hatred was mutual, which meant the next few minutes would be interesting. This would be the first time Devlin had superseded the chief.

Grogan pushed through the apartment door and started down the poorly lit entry hall, Devlin a few steps behind him.

Malloy turned and saw Grogan approaching. "I thought I told you to wait outside," he snapped. He hadn't seen Devlin coming up behind.

Devlin stepped around Grogan and stared at the captain. Malloy stiffened. As an inspector Devlin outranked him. Working directly for the mayor as he did, he technically outranked everyone in the building. Even Cervone.

"I told him to come in," Devlin said, moving past a now uncertain Malloy. "You got a problem, you lay it on me, not him."

Malloy's jaw tightened, then he lifted his chin toward Cervone, who was just inside the small kitchen, speaking on the telephone in a hushed voice. "You work it out with the chief," Malloy said. "Me, I'm goin' back out in the hall."

Devlin fought off a smile. Malloy was in his midfifties, and an old hand at departmental wars. He knew better than to be in a room when a chief found himself politically embarrassed. Devlin turned to Grogan. "Check the murder scene, and get everybody but forensics and the M.E. *out*," he said.

Devlin emphasized the final word, and Grogan gave him a quick wink. "You got it," he said.

"Forensics and the M.E. aren't here yet."

Devlin turned back to the sound of Cervone's voice. He had just replaced the telephone receiver, holding it gingerly with a handkerchief to avoid obliterating any fingerprints.

"Why not?" Devlin asked.

The two men stood facing each other in the small kitchen. Two sets of hard eyes shooting hatred at each other. It almost made Devlin laugh. But then,

nothing about Cervone could produce that reaction.
Several years ago the man had tried, unsuccess-
fully, to have Devlin brought up on charges in the
death of another cop. Last year, he had pulled every
dirty trick he knew to thwart Devlin's hunt for a serial killer—an effort that had nearly cost the life of
the woman Devlin loved. No, laughter would never
exist between them. Better they should use their
guns, he told himself.

"I said, why not?"

Cervone's jaw tightened. "You'll see when you go
in there," he snapped.

Rising male voices came from the other room.
One said he'd leave only when the chief told him to.

Cervone stepped past Devlin and leaned into the
small entry hall. "All of you. Wait for me in the
lobby. Now!" He turned back to Devlin. "Satisfied?"
he asked.

Devlin stared at the man, as a half dozen ranking
headquarters types filed down the hall behind his
back. The chief was dressed, as always, in a hand-
tailored suit that must have carried a fifteen-
hundred-dollar price tag—although Devlin doubted
Cervone had paid that, or anything close to it. At
fifty-five, his once muscular body was fast sinking
into fat—something his five-foot-nine height only
served to emphasize. He had black hair—
unnaturally so—which he combed straight back,
and a tough, almost brutal face, accented by dark
brown eyes that, right now, made it clear he hated
Devlin even more than Devlin hated him.

"I talked to one of the mayor's flunkies, and to
the P.C.," Cervone said. "They told me it was your
case." He paused a beat. "*I* told *them*, I didn't intend
to be boxed out on the murder of one of my own
captains." He was glaring at Devlin, issuing a challenge. Had this been an old Hollywood western,
Devlin thought, they would each go for their guns
now. The idea had a certain appeal.

"You might get a lot farther if you asked," Devlin said.

Cervone bristled. He drew in a breath. "Okay. So I'm asking."

Devlin offered a cold smile. "I said, might, Chief. For now you get whatever reports the mayor and the P.C. say you *have* to get. And I'll bitch about giving you those. Otherwise, keep your nose the fuck out of it."

Cervone's eyes blazed. "You sonofabitch. Before this is over, I'll grind you into the fucking dirt."

Devlin held his smile. It was more effective than a punch. "You would have tried that anyway, Mario. You wouldn't have been able to help yourself." Devlin took a step forward. At thirty-five he had twenty years, three inches, and ten hard pounds on Cervone, and he knew he'd like nothing better than to use all of it. And he knew Cervone knew it too. "So answer my questions and take a walk," he said. "There's only you, me, and Eddie Grogan here now. You fuck with me, you're the only one who's gonna say you didn't trip and fall."

For a moment Devlin thought Cervone was going to come at him. But the moment passed. The chief smiled. It was the kind of smile a lion would give a gazelle. If lions smiled.

"I'm gonna fucking bury you, Devlin. Deep, down, and dirty. You make book on it."

"I wouldn't expect anything else," Devlin said. "But you already tried that. Remember?"

The two men continued to stare at each other.

"Now, where are the people who found the body?" Devlin asked.

Cervone answered through his teeth. "They're on ice at headquarters. On my orders."

"I want them all in my office. *Forthwith.* On *my* order. You got that?"

No one gave the chief of detectives orders, other than the police commissioner. At least not until

Devlin had taken on this new assignment one month earlier. And that ability was limited to specific investigations dictated by the mayor. The job had been offered after Devlin had trapped a serial killer who had mutilated and killed five women. It was a case Cervone's political manipulations had almost botched, and the chief had barely survived the scandal that had followed.

Devlin continued to stare at him. "I said, have you got that?"

Cervone looked as though he might implode. "I got it. Anything else?"

"Yeah. I want Battaglia's personnel jacket. Tell Deputy Chief Mitchelson to have it ready for me this afternoon. Tell him to be in my office at three. After that you can start sharpening your best knife."

"Count on it," Cervone warned.

Devlin offered his own leonine smile. "By the way, *Chief,* I thought you knew better than to use a telephone at a crime scene."

Cervone's jaw tightened. "I was careful about prints," he snapped.

"You check the redial button?"

"No." The word came through clenched teeth.

"Would have been nice to know what the last call was." Devlin stepped past him. "Take a walk," he said.

When Cervone left, Devlin went to the now tainted telephone and ordered in a forensic team and an assistant medical examiner. As he replaced the receiver, also using a handkerchief, he found Grogan standing in the doorway.

"You have fun dancing with the chief?" he asked.

"You were eavesdropping."

"Not only that. I was already writing my report. About how he tripped and hurt himself."

"He's a clumsy man."

"Yeah, everybody says that about him. But he also has sharp teeth. Everybody says that, too."

"He would have used them anyway, Eddie." Devlin grinned at the older detective.

Despite his rugged good looks, Devlin seemed almost boyish when he smiled, Grogan thought. He was tall and solid, with wavy black hair and dark blue eyes that could be surprisingly gentle or fierce. And there was a two inch scar on his left cheek—the gift of an earlier case—that turned almost white when he was pushed too far. Grogan had seen enough of Devlin's temper to know it was something best avoided. But he had also seen another side of the man—his gentleness and patience with his eight-year-old daughter, Phillipa, and his tenderness toward Adrianna Mendez, the woman he had saved from a serial killer, and with whom he now lived. Grogan fought off a smile, thinking of Adrianna—the daughter of his long dead partner, the godchild he had known since she was wearing diapers. Beautiful, independent, volatile Adrianna. A woman who didn't particularly like cops. He almost laughed. Not the easiest woman for a cop to live with. It was good Cervone didn't know about all that. If the sonofabitch knew, he'd see it as a weakness, a flaw, and he'd figure out a way to exploit it. And this case didn't need any more complications. They had just started, and they were already up to their chins in shit.

Grogan inclined his head toward the other room. "Before you start feeling too good about breaking Cervone's balls, you better come take a look in there. The mayor didn't do us any fucking favors with this one."

Devlin followed Grogan into the other room, and pulled up ten feet short of the body. Little Bat Battaglia lay facedown: wrists and ankles tied to the bed frame, knees drawn up to his chest and held there by a wire encircling his neck. The position had left his buttocks jutting upward, and protruding from the anal orifice was the hilt of a black plastic vibrator. The faint hum coming off the body told them it had been turned on and was still running.

"Jesus Christ," Devlin said. "I wish we could turn that thing off."

"Yeah," Grogan said. "But forensics wouldn't like that. The fucking thing was shoved so far inside, the switch on the base may give us the only latents we're gonna get." He turned to Devlin and shrugged. "Must be Energizer batteries," he added, mocking the popular television commercial. "They just keep going, and going, and going."

Devlin winced. He knew what Grogan was doing. It was something every cop learned early on: Make a joke out of the things that shake you or scare you. And nothing scared a cop more than seeing another cop dead. And dead like this shook you right down to your socks. Christ.

Devlin walked to the head of the bed, pulled a pair of surgical gloves from his pocket, and snapped them on. Carefully, he probed the hair behind the left ear. "Looks like one shot. Small caliber. Deep powder burns, like the muzzle was jammed against his head." So he could feel it, be terrified by it, he thought. He turned back to Grogan, who was jotting what he had said in his notebook. "You see any other wounds when you were in here before?"

"Nothing visible without turning him," Grogan said. "I had a case like this a few years back. Perp did the same thing to the victim. Except he used a fucking cucumber. Turned out they were lovers, and the victim was stepping out on him."

"This look like a homosexual killing to you?" Devlin asked. He had caught a few homosexual murders himself, but each one had involved severe mutilation, especially to the throat and genitals.

"No, it don't," Grogan said. "It's too clean, except for the vibrator. But it looks like somebody wanted us to think it was. Either that, or it was some kind of fucking message. My guess would be contract hit."

Grogan hesitated. He inclined his head toward a framed photograph on the bedside table. It showed Battaglia and two young children—dark-eyed and smiling and beautiful—standing arm in arm on a beach. There were palm trees in the background. "I think those are his kids. I heard he was divorced about a year ago."

Devlin nodded. He didn't buy Grogan's idea about a contract hit. Professional killers did a job quickly and got out, exposing themselves as little as possible. It wasn't a question of being adverse to torture, or inflicting a bit of terror. But when they wanted that, they took their victims someplace where the screams wouldn't be heard. He decided to keep those thoughts to himself; let Eddie pursue his own. At this point the right answer could be anything.

"Soon as the M.E. and forensics finish, I want to go through all his papers," Devlin said. "Address books, calendars, bills. Everything that's here." He looked down at the body again and blew out a long breath. "While we're waiting, I've got to get the deputy commissioner for public information and the D.A.'s office on the phone. We've got to decide what we're giving out to the media. And just how the hell we're going to keep this vibrator out of the M.E.'s report without screwing up any prosecution."

"I think Big Bat will take care of deep-sixing the vibrator," Grogan said. "It'll be contract city as soon as he blows into town."

"Big Bat's gonna keep his nose out of this," Devlin said.

Grogan lowered his chin and raised his eyebrows. He stared at Devlin for several seconds. "Good luck," he said.

The forensic unit and the assistant medical examiner arrived together. The assistant M.E. was Michael Blair, whom Devlin and Grogan had worked with on their last case.

"Jesus Christ. Not him," Grogan said, jabbing a finger toward Blair.

"Fuck you, Eddie," Blair swore as he moved directly to the body.

Devlin fought off a smile. Blair was highly competent, but he and Grogan worked together like oil and water. "You got a problem with Mike?" Devlin asked, goading the older detective.

"Hey, you're the boss," Grogan said. "You use whoever you want. But you ought to know, I've been in this guy's office, and he ain't got no diploma, just a picture of a fucking duck hanging behind his desk."

"That's a picture of you, Grogan," Blair snapped back. "You just don't recognize it, because it was taken before you got so goddamned fat."

Grogan turned away, hiding a smile from Blair. He actually liked the young M.E., Devlin thought. He just enjoyed breaking his chops.

"Why don't you head downtown?" Devlin suggested. "Pull some people from homicide to canvas the neighborhood, then you interview the cops who found the body. By the time you finish, I should be wrapped up here. Chief Mitchelson is due in the office at three."

"You got it," Grogan said. "But keep an eye on Daffy Duck over there. He starts quacking, throw him a fucking fish."

"Go away, Grogan," Blair said. "It's a slow day down at Club Med for the Dead. I might decide to do a post on you. Just for practice."

"Hey, if it meant you'd learn how to do it . . ." Grogan said.

"Go away, Eddie," Devlin said. "I'm gonna need you later. All of you. All in one piece."

Blair carefully removed the vibrator and dropped it into a plastic evidence bag. The hilt of the device had already been dusted by the fingerprint specialist, and both acts had made Devlin queasy; he had turned away each time.

Using equal care, Blair clipped the wires that bound Little Bat, tied twine to each of the severed ends to show where they had been joined, then placed the entire length into a long narrow box, making sure no new kinks were inadvertently made in the wire. The box would be air-expressed to the FBI Laboratory in Washington for chemical and microscopic testing to determine the composition and possible manufacturer. Returning to the bed, Blair slowly turned the now rigid body. Devlin took in the ligature wounds on the ankles, wrists, and neck, the deep discoloration of the skin that had been in contact with the bed. Lividity had left one side of the face, along with the upper chest and knees, a deep purple. Blair pointed to the areas.

"After death the blood settles to the lowest point of gravity," he explained needlessly. "It makes the victim look as though he got a wicked beating."

Devlin nodded. He had seen enough dead bodies, attended more than enough autopsies, to understand the ugly peculiarities of death. But Blair liked to explain things to anyone around him. It was one of his idiosyncrasies that drove Eddie Grogan crazy.

Blair was in his early thirties, and the New York Medical Examiner's Office was his first job out of residency. That, alone, spoke about his competence. The New York City M.E.'s office was considered among the best in the country. Perhaps even the world.

And that also made it a hard road for a young assistant, who constantly fell under the scrutiny of older hands. For Blair it was even harder. He looked younger than his years—blond and boyish, with a short, stocky body that made him seem plump. Only his tired, blue eyes gave a hint of the world weariness the job had already produced. But that wasn't enough for the old hands. Only time and sustained proof of abilities satisfied them. Until then skepticism reigned, and Blair's natural egotism about his medical skills only served to intensify those doubts. But Devlin liked him. And, even more important, Devlin trusted his skills.

He circled the bed, studying the body, while fighting off his own internal discomfort. He and Little Bat had been peers—both in approximate age and rank within the department—and the murder scene imposed an unwanted sense of his own mortality. Like most cops, Devlin despised the indignity of police-attended deaths, and wanted none of it for himself.

But that didn't change the need for the indignities that were still to come. He stared across the body at Blair.

"I need your best shot on this, Mike," he said at length. "We gotta fine-tooth-comb this one. I need information fast. But don't let anyone—even me—push you to the point you might miss something."

Blair gave him a steady look, then inclined his head toward the evidence bag containing the black plastic vibrator. "You worried that might have had some personal significance?"

"You bet. And I want a separate report covering anything relating to it." He watched Blair's eyebrows crease. "We're going to treat it as information known only to the killer, and withhold it from everybody on that basis."

Blair nodded. "You'll get me something in writing from the D.A.'s office? Just to cover my ass?"

"It's already being prepared," Devlin said.

Blair looked down at the body, then back at Devlin. "Is this guy who I think he was? Big Bat Battaglia's son?"

"The same."

Blair let out a shallow breath. "Boy, you didn't do me any favors, asking for me on this one."

Devlin ignored him. "When do you think you'll be starting the post?"

"In about two hours."

Devlin glanced at his watch, then moved to a computer terminal on a desk near the window. The screen was illuminated. It was running a "screen saver" program that showed a group of swans swimming on a dark pond. Very peaceful, very relaxing. "Good," he said. "I want to be there, and it should give me enough time to toss the place first."

Chapter Two

Donatello "Dapper Dan" Torelli sat behind his over-sized desk and stared at the slender, reptilian man who stood before him. His fingers were steepled before his face, the manicured nails flashing under the overhead light. He was watching the man's eyes; looking for any sign of the lies he always expected. The man, appropriately called "Snake," was fighting off a tic that threatened the corner of his left eye. It was a malady that occurred whenever he entered Torelli's office. But then, Mattie "the Snake" Cordino had heard about too many guys who had come into that office and had never been seen again. It was rumored that the basement of the building—which had once been a large butcher shop—still had an old meat locker, complete with hooks from which sides of beef had once hung, and a long cutting table on which they were carved into manageable hunks of meat. It was a rumor promoted by Torelli himself. One that spoke of a long list of victims who had found themselves scattered across New Jersey after an unexpected trip downstairs. It was nonsense, of course. Torelli would never risk such a thing in the basement of his own office. But it had its effect. It spread terror among his men. None of whom wanted to end up as filet mignon just because they had pissed Torelli off.

"So tell me what you think," Torelli said. "This cop was a fucking girl, and his boyfriend whacked him?" He had leaned forward, forearms on the desk supporting his weight. He was a square, blocklike man, whose shoulders looked as though they might burst through his suit coat, and his eyes were hard and cold—never changing—a sharp contrast to his otherwise smooth and slightly round face. Cordino tried to concentrate on the top of the man's head, avoiding his eyes as he spoke. The hair was deep black with only a hint of gray at the temples—unusual for a man of fifty-six, although no one would dare suggest it was colored. People would just say he seemed youthful and fit. Too young and too fit to be the head of one of New York's five Mafia families. That had always been a role left to old men one step away from an iron lung. But those were the old days. And those days, Cordino knew, were long fucking gone.

"I don't know what happened," the Snake said. "I broke in like I was told. To see if I could find that computer stuff." He gestured with his chin toward the stack of disks on Torelli's desk. "And there he was with that fucking dildo shoved up his ass." He shifted his weight nervously. Because of what he had seen, Torelli thought. "He was all trussed up with wire," Snake continued. "And somebody had popped him once behind the ear."

A small smile flickered across Torelli's lips, then disappeared. "I wonder how he liked it?"

Snake smiled for the first time; he knew he could shine up to the boss's joke. "I bet he screamed like a fucking Girl Scout," he said.

Torelli let out a low snort, then eased back in his chair. "Did you get all the shit he had?"

The Snake's mouth twisted nervously. "I searched every inch of the joint. Took all his files and computer stuff. Then I showed it all to our boy and he wasn't worried. Said everything was on these." He waved one hand at the disks on Torelli's desk, and briefly wondered if he should tell him about the marks he had seen on the locks to Little Bat's apartment—slight pick marks that only a pro would notice, but indicating someone else had broken in. He decided against it. It could have happened anytime—even months ago. There was no reason to set the man off.

"You didn't leave a mess, did you?" Torelli asked. "I don't want nobody to know the place was tossed. Better we shouldn't confuse them. Just let them chase this fag thing, right?"

"The place looks like it was just cleaned," the Snake said.

Torelli nodded, the faint smile reappearing, then fading again. "You did good," he said, taking pleasure in the rush of relief that spread across Cordino's face. It was part of his "management technique," something called *creative tension*. He had discovered the idea years ago, while reading a magazine article about an Australian newspaper magnate. The news baron had said he always kept his subordinates under intense pressure; always made them feel their jobs depended on their daily performance. It was something, he had said, that assured extraordinary productivity, that kept everybody working well beyond their abilities. Torelli had liked the idea, had convinced himself it would work even more effectively in his business. After all, his men had a lot more to lose than their jobs.

And the way the families had changed over the years, you needed all the pressure you could get. In the old days you never had to worry about being ratted out by one of your people. Now you could trust no one, not even the guys you were paying to watch your back. And they'd steal from you, given half the chance. It was something that seldom happened under the old dons. You took what they gave you, and you said, *grazie*. And you kissed their fucking hands.

No, those old Mustache Petes didn't have those problems. Their problem was they had no imagination for business. They stuck by the staples—the gambling, the shakedowns, the unions. They had no interest in playing all the angles that were out there. But now everybody wanted to play every fucking angle there was. Everybody who worked for you had imagination. And what they imagined most was you dead—or worse, in jail—and all your fucking money in *their* pockets.

Torelli stared across the desk at Mattie Cordino. The man *looked* like a snake—long and thin, with slicked back hair that looked slimy. And those beady eyes, and that tongue that was always flicking out, licking his lips. He had trusted him with this job because he was good. And because he had to know just what this cop had on him. But it seemed someone had done him an even bigger favor. He had been prepared to have the cop whacked himself, if it proved necessary. But you didn't kill a police captain unless you had to. Not unless you were fucking crazy. And especially not a cop who was Bat Battaglia's kid.

"You sure you got everything? That you didn't leave nothin' that some other jambone cop can use against me?"

Torelli's eyes were glaring across the desk, and Cordino felt his palms begin to sweat as he met that hard stare. But he knew better than to look away. Torelli might become suspicious if he didn't look at him straight. And, when he became suspicious, he did things to people.

"I'm sure, Don Torelli. It ain't a problem. I guarantee it."

"I end up in a court room, you guarantee yourself a fucking coffin. You understand that? You understand *I* fucking guarantee *that*?"

"I understand. I ain't worried about it."

Torelli studied him. No, he was all right. He was scared, but they were all scared when he talked to them. Just the way he wanted them to be. Creative tension. It worked every fucking time.

Torelli eased back in his chair again. "Like I said, you did good by me. Now take a vacation. Some place with fucking palm trees. Let Buster know where you are. But stay there 'til he tells you the heat's down a couple notches." He held up his hand and wagged it back and forth. "It's a precaution." He shrugged. "Just in case somebody saw you near the building. The cops are gonna be running around like a bunch of fucking *melanzanes* on this."

He extended a hand so the Snake could lean across the desk and kiss it as a sign of obedience and respect. The man did it without hesitation, then beat a speedy retreat to the door.

"And don't forget to call Buster," Torelli snapped after him.

Dapper Dan sat back after the man had left, then withdrew a handkerchief from his pocket and wiped his hand clean. He hated the old custom, but it was expected. It was like all the pomp in the Catholic Church. It was bullshit, but the people wanted it. So, just like all the old Mustache Petes, he let them kiss his hand. And who knew where their fucking mouths had been?

Torelli tapped his fingers on the arms of his high-backed leather chair and stared at the floppy disks the Snake had left on his desk. Like anything he didn't understand, they made his skin crawl. He shook his head. Somehow those little bits of plastic held enough information to burn him. They were like little, square bombs. Shit, someday he'd have to learn something about computers. It was a question of survival these days. He continued to glare at the disks. That fucking bastard Battaglia. He'd almost had their boy—almost had everybody. Even the guys who made it possible to beat the last two raps the feds threw at you. And all because of the fucking sex angle. He steepled his fingers again, still staring at the disks. Never should have gotten into that shit. But the profits had been too good to ignore. And the other benefits—all the fucking guys you got to put in your pocket, just because they couldn't keep their dicks in their pants. It had been just too good to pass up. And you gotta admit, you liked watching the movies they took at *the club*. Especially the one of that judge. Sitting in that chair, balls ass naked, that goofy, fucking grin on his face while the broad sucked on his cock. The way he reached out and pulled her head closer, so she got more of it in her mouth. And her only fifteen, even though she looks eighteen, nineteen, easy when she's all fixed up. It was pure gold.

Torelli rubbed his crotch, the star sapphire ring on his little finger sending off flashes of light. A smile spread across his lips. It was no wonder his sainted mother had named him after Donatello. He was a fucking artist. No two ways about it.

He sat forward again and pressed the button on his intercom. "Tell Buster I need him," he snapped. The smile returned. Out in the front room—where everybody was sitting around playing cards and drinking espresso—bodies would be moving around looking for Buster. He loved the Mott Street Italian American Social Club. It was his domain. It was why he kept his office there. And when the big dog barked, all the fucking mongrels stopped licking their balls and did what he said. And thank God he had been tipped off to Battaglia. Otherwise those same fucking mongrels would be sitting out there in a couple of months, trying to figure out a way to put their fucking asses behind *his* desk. The sonsabitches.

Buster Fucci came thought he door, looking hungover. His bloodshot eyes were set like a beacon in his square, flat, prizefighter's face. He had short brown hair that emphasized the boxlike head, a thick neck, and even thicker body. He seemed to be drinking a lot lately, and it made Torelli nervous.

He and Buster had been together since they were kids, breaking heads for nickel and dime handouts from the made guys in their Brooklyn neighborhood. They had come up in the ranks together, and had even been made together at the same ceremony. Buster Fucci was the only guy Torelli really trusted, and it was why he had made him his underboss when he had taken over the family six years ago.

But then, Torelli himself had been the underboss for the previous don, who had trusted him like a son. And he had had the old bastard whacked without batting an eye—had sent the guys who had put six holes in him outside a Manhattan steak house, and then had driven by with Buster to see him lying there with his head in the gutter. It was the thing about trust you always had to remember.

"You look like shit," Torelli said, wondering now if Buster ever thought about running the outfit himself.

"I feel worse," Buster said, falling into a chair opposite his boss. He was fifty-four, two years younger than this man he had worked with all his adult life. But, right now, he felt ten years older.

It was the booze, he told himself. Buster had no idea why he was drinking so much lately. Or, if he did, it was something he wasn't admitting to himself. He just seemed to start, and then forget to stop. And it was killing his stomach.

"The Snake took care of that problem we had," Torrelli said. He reached out and tapped a finger against the stack of computer disks on his desk. "He says everything Little Bat had is on these things. Says he had them checked, like we told him. But I want them checked again. Just to make sure they're what the Snake says they are. Then I want them destroyed."

Buster nodded. He glanced around the office.

There was a lot to lose if what was supposed to be on those disks got out, and the room reflected it. It wasn't a big office, just a little more than average for a guy with a lot of power. The furniture was all good stuff, expensive, and looking every nickel Dapper Dan had spent. The walls were paneled. Not with the class goods, just the four-by-eight sheets of paneling you could buy anyplace. But what was *on* the walls gave you an idea of the kind of power the man had. There were plaques for all the public service stuff he had done, and pictures of him with *everybody*. Politicians, bishops, civic leaders, all high-class shit. They were older pictures, of course. Nobody had been posing with him since all the fucking arrests and trials had hit the newspapers and television. But he knew them all; could pick up a phone and call them. And they would answer; knew they fucking well better. There was even a picture with Big Bat, back from the days when he left the cops and started his climb to all that power he had now.

But then there was other stuff in the office, too—stuff that made him wonder about the man. Like the crucifix that hung right behind his desk—the one Torelli said his wife had put up. But it was a fucking lie. It was like the brown scapulars Torelli had sewn in the sleeves of all his suits, and the one he always wore around his neck—one of those gizmos the nuns had said would get you into heaven if you died wearing it. And there were other things, too. Like the way Torelli made a little sign of the cross on his forehead—making sure nobody saw—then knocked on wood five times whenever he thought bad news was coming. Like doing it would drive the shit away. It reminded him of those crazy niggers they had both made fun of when they were kids—the ones who had floated in from the Caribbean with their little voodoo bags hanging around their necks to ward off fucking devils.

Buster glanced across the desk. Torelli was grinning at him. "Is there somethin' else?" he asked.

"Oh, yeah." Torelli's grin widened. "Somebody did us a favor and whacked Little Bat."

"Jesus Christ." Buster hesitated, then leaned forward. "You sure it wasn't Cordino? Maybe Little Bat caught him inside and he panicked."

Torelli shook his head. "He told me how he found him. This wasn't no accident. This was something that was planned." He told Buster how Little Bat had been killed.

"Motherfucker," Buster said. "I never figured him for no fag."

"Hey, these days who can tell." Torelli tapped his fingers together and let out a small laugh. "Shit, we knew that, we wouldn't of had to worry about him. We could of put him in our pocket."

"Whadda you gonna do about the Snake?" Buster asked, afraid he already knew the answer.

"He's taking a vacation," Torelli said. "I told him to let you know where he was, and to stay there until you told him to get his ass back."

Buster nodded, waiting for more.

"You have somebody keep an eye on him, you find out where he is," Torelli said. "Not one of our people. I don't want nobody to know nothin' about what's goin' on. You use one of the other families. Miami, maybe. Or New Orleans. As a favor to me." He leaned back in his chair, a faint smile playing across thick lips. "We have any problems over this, or if Big Bat ever comes to me, saying he wants the guy who made his kid suffer, I wanna be able to give him the Snake, I have to." He leaned forward again. "In fucking pieces. Everything but his mouth. *Capisce*?"

Buster nodded again. His stomach was churning. "The Snake's a good man, does good work," he said.

"Hey, maybe he'll get lucky and they'll find the guy who did this thing," Torelli said. He nodded toward a statue of the Blessed Virgin set up on a small table, a votive candle burning before it. "I'll say a fucking prayer for him." He let out a low, soft laugh, then his eyes suddenly turned hard. "I didn't go through all those years of shit—taking whatever was handed to me and bowing like a fucking Chinaman—just to see it all in the gutter now." He jabbed a stubby finger at Buster. "You know what it was like. You do what you gotta do in life, and you survive. And when your chance comes, you grab it and you prosper. And you cover your ass, and you don't let nobody take it away from you once you got it."

Buster nodded and let out a long breath. He forced himself up from the chair. "Yeah, you're right. And I'll take care of it," he said. His stomach was killing him. He'd do like he was told. There wasn't any choice. But first he'd get a drink. Maybe two. He started for the door. At least he had never liked the Snake that much. He had only liked the man's work.

"One other thing," Torelli said, stopping him. "Everybody who ratted to this fag cop. I want them fucking dead. And I want them to have time to think about it. *Capisce?*"

"Buster nodded again, wondering if Torelli already knew everyone who had been involved. He also wondered if he knew who had iced the cop. It would be just the way he'd play it. The man never let nobody know what was going on. He didn't trust nobody that much. And if a guy knew something that Torelli didn't want him to know, well . . .

He left the office, and headed for the front door of the club. He needed a drink. And he had to make a phone call. First the call, then the drink, he told himself. And only one this time. Just one.

Chapter Three

Suzanne Osborne stood before a full-length mirror studying her body. She was in her bedroom, naked, fresh from the shower. She turned slowly, first to one side, then the other, offering herself differing views. She paid particular attention to her breasts. They were still firm, even at twenty-seven, still jutted up as they had always done. She knew that men loved her breasts. They were money in the bank. And she had worked to keep them that way. Just like they were ten years ago when the men she worked for had first brought her to New York.

She turned a bit more and ran a hand along her buttocks and upper thigh. You've put on a bit of weight there, she thought. Not much, but enough so those slacks you wore yesterday felt a little tight. So it's back to the health club to sweat it off.

She wondered why she worried about it. Even if her bum were twice its size, there would still be the Arabs. They loved women with big bums. Or little girls who had nothing at all. She thought about the one who had always asked for her when she was fourteen, and had just started working in the house in London. He had kissed you everywhere; licked every part of you. God, he was disgusting, the way he drooled all over you. But the Arabs were all like that. Old pigs, who always thought up the most disgusting things to do. And they always smelled of that spicy food they ate. And half of them, if the truth were known, would rather be with little boys.

She smiled at the thought. And, of course, they were, whenever they could. Paddy's told you about *that* little game—about those special orders they placed with him. And how they always worried about keeping it secret. How their holy book, that Koran thing, said they'd be killed if they did it with a bloody boy, have their bodies thrown from the highest mountain. And served them bloody right, she thought. Buggering little boys, turning them into flaming faggots. Of course the Brits at home weren't much better. Especially the lah-de-dah types—the public school boys. They were so bloody bad she had often wondered how they ever had kids at all. No, back to the health club. Stay away from those bloody Arabs. And the Brits. Stick with the Frenchies, and the Italians. And the Japanese, tiny little sods though they were. She giggled at the thought.

The sound of the doorbell broke her reverie. She glanced at the bedside clock. Bloody hell, she thought, wondering who could be coming by at this time of day.

Suzanne slipped into a flimsy, silk robe and cinched it at the waist, then went to the front door, rose onto her toes, and peeked through the spy hole.

"Bloody hell," she whispered, though not displeased by whom she saw. Must have rolled out of bed needing a soft shoulder this morning, she thought.

Suzanne unlocked the door and pulled it open, her best smile fixed on her face. "Hello, Luv. Now aren't you full of nice surprises today."

The man filled the doorway, his shoulders almost touching each side of the frame. God, he was a big one, she thought, looking up into his handsome face.

He was grinning at her—that bloody, leering grin he sometimes wore. It chilled her; made her think he knew things she didn't want anyone to know. But he couldn't. She'd been careful, very careful.

He reached out and stroked her cheek, and allowed his fingers to toy with her long, blond hair. Then he dropped his hand to the fold of her robe, his fingers spreading it slightly. Wants to see if you're wearing something lacy, she thought.

"Not here, Luv," she said. "Not in the hall." She forced her smile to widen, then turned and walked back into the apartment, knowing he would follow the slight sway of her hips. She continued on through the living room and stepped through the bedroom door.

The blow caught her on the back of the head, propelling her forward, throwing her to the floor next to the bed. She was stunned and dizzy, her head swimming, as rough hands grabbed her; turned her on to her back. The silk handkerchief was forced between her teeth and tied behind her head. Then he lifted her and threw her onto the bed, and began tying her hands and feet to the bedposts with pieces of wire.

Suzanne regained her senses slowly, turned her head to stare at the wires holding her, then looked up at his hovering form. Her deep blue eyes filled with terror. He knew, she told herself. He knew everything. Every bloody thing she had done.

"You little, limey cunt," he hissed. "Like to talk to cops, do you? Well, talk to me, bitch. Tell *me* little secrets."

Suzanne tried to speak through the gag. The muffled sounds made his terrible grin return.

"Sorry. Not good enough," he hissed. He slipped his hand into his coat pocket and withdrew a large, closed knife. His finger hit a button and a long, slender, five-inch blade shot forward.

Suzanne stared at it, then began to shake her head back and forth. She pulled against the wires holding her to the bedposts, and felt them cut into the flesh of her wrists and ankles.

His grin widened, and he glanced around the

room, then walked to the free-standing, full-length mirror, and dragged it toward the bed.

"I want you to watch," he said. "I want you to watch while I cut your tits off. But first a little fun before the pain."

His free hand returned to his coat and withdrew an enormous, black plastic vibrator. Suzanne stared at it. She had never seen anything that large. He twisted the base and a loud humming sound assaulted her ears.

She watched him lower it between her spread legs. Frantically, she began to shift her hips back and forth; struggled to bring her knees together.

He placed the tip of the knife against her stomach, just above her pubic mound, and the tip of the blade cut into her flesh. She gasped; her body froze. He let out a short, harsh laugh, then plunged the vibrator into her vagina. Suzanne let out a muffled scream.

"Oh, yeah. Your cop friend liked it, too, bitch. He *really* liked it."

He climbed onto the bed and straddled her, and Suzanne could see his erection straining against his trousers. She shook her head from side to side, her eyes returning to his face, pleading, begging.

"It's time to cut, sweet cakes." He reached out and grabbed one of her breasts, squeezing and twisting it. "Pleasure and pain," he hissed. "The best of both worlds. Just keep your eyes on the mirror, so you don't miss any of the fun."

Devlin pulled his car into a bus stop on Fifth Avenue, just south of Seventy-ninth Street. He lowered the visor displaying his NYPD vehicle ID and hoped for the best. The area around the Metropolitan Museum was meter maid heaven, and while the car wouldn't be towed, he'd be lucky not to find two or three tickets stuck to the windshield when he returned. The paperwork that would generate

would leave him grinding his teeth for days. He
shook his head at the prospect. Like most cops he
despised the brown-clad *parking enforcement
officers*—as they preferred to be called—and often
envisioned them trading war stories about the cop
cars they'd *busted,* then bitching about their inabil-
ity to call in tow trucks because of visor IDs. He
had no idea if this ever happened. It was simply an
absurdity that slaked his animosity. But then cops
subscribed to several absurdly vindictive theories
about meter maids. One involved the city regularly
kidnapping women from the Department of Motor
Vehicles and men from the U.S. Post Office, and
sending them off to concentration camps to mate.
Meter maids, cops argued, were the offspring of
those couplings.

Leaving his chances to fate, Devlin climbed out of
the car and stretched. The familiar odors of hot dogs
and sauerkraut and onions wafted in from a pushcart
set up in front of the museum across the street.
Somehow—here—the familiar smells seemed out of
place. He stared up at the building he was about to
enter. It reeked as well—of pure, undiluted money.
Like all the buildings along this section of Fifth Avenue, this one would be a co-op—among the most
expensive in the city—with apartments carrying
high-six, or low-seven-figure price tags, and
monthly maintenance bills that would comfortably
support a family of five. He had no idea who
Michelle Paoli was, but she was definitely a long
way from dining on hot dogs.

Devlin had found the woman's name while toss-
ing Battaglia's apartment. The address book had
been taped to the bottom of a table, and Michelle
Paoli had been the only entry that had included a last
name, an address, and a recognizable phone number.
All other entries had been limited to first names, followed by numbers that didn't match any exchanges

in the city's five boroughs. They were either for telephones in other cities, or they were written in code.

Hoping for some element of surprise, Devlin had decided not to call ahead. He wanted to hit the woman cold, without warning. But as he approached the doorman now, he realized the effort might have been wasted. The man stood under a long, green canopy that stretched out to the curb. He was dressed in doorman's livery—peaked cap, shiny brass buttons, gold epaulets, spit-shined shoes—and he had a look on his flat, expressionless face that said: I don't care who you are, you don't get in this building unless I say you do.

Devlin slipped into the blue, summer-weight suit coat he had shed in the non-air-conditioned department car, then approached the doorman, shield in hand. "Michelle Paoli. Which apartment?" He had put all the authority he could muster into his voice, but the doorman had simply stared—first at him, then the shield, then back to his face again.

"If you give me your name, I'll call and see if she's in."

Devlin returned the man's stare and smiled. It was a smile that didn't carry to his eyes. "Have you seen her go out today?"

The man shrugged. "Not that I remember."

"Then she's in. What's the apartment number?"

The doorman looked toward the street. He ran his tongue along the inside of his cheek. "You give me your name. I'll call. And I'll see if she's available," he said.

Devlin wanted to grab the man by the throat. He settled for a growl. "I don't think you're listening to me. Which apartment?"

The man's eyes jumped back. "I'm listening. And what I'm hearing is the board that runs this building. They're saying I let anybody in unannounced, I'm standing in the fucking unemployment line. You got

it? So, you want in, you give me your name, or you
show me a warrant."

Devlin fought off a smile. The man had him. He
was about fifty, he guessed, and about as intimidated
by Devlin's shield as he would be by a sanitation inspector coming to check the incinerator. "What'd
you do before you got this job?" Devlin asked.

"Thirty years on the fire department," the doorman said.

Now it was Devlin's turn to look into the street.
He knew he wasn't about to bulldoze an ex-
firefighter. Or a working one. Firefighters thought
all cops were full of shit, and no amount of bluff or
bluster would cow them.

"Tell her it's Inspector Paul Devlin," he said.
"And tell her I need to see her *now*."

"Happy to," the ex-hose jockey said as he turned
on his heel and headed to a wall phone inside the
vestibule. Devlin didn't have to be told to wait
where he was.

The man returned in less than two minutes. "Seventeenth floor. Apartment A," he said. He didn't offer any regrets. He didn't have to, and he wouldn't
have meant them anyway. He simply took up his
post by the door, and awaited the next *asshole* who
tried to bluff his way inside.

Devlin rode the gleaming mahogany elevator to
the seventeenth floor. The apartment, he was certain,
would have a view of Central Park, and at this location would look down at Cleopatra's Needle, the
Egyptian obelisk behind the Metropolitan Museum.
Devlin pushed the thought away. The obelisk had
been the site, several years ago, of his last official
homicide investigation as a New York cop—the one
the newspapers had called the "Ritual" case—the
one that had also led to his forced retirement from
the department. He hadn't been back to the area
since. He had even refused to go to the Metropolitan
with Adrianna, just as he had avoided the scene of

every subsequent murder that investigation had produced. Instinctively, he touched his upper arm, the spot where the killer's knife had cut him so badly. He still lost use of the arm from time to time. So much so that it had taken an executive order by the mayor to bypass the department's fitness requirements. Now he was back on the job. But he still had no interest in Michelle Paoli's front window. He had no interest in seeing Cleopatra's Needle again. No interest in seeing anything that would remind him of how that last case had ended. Or in remembering the man he had been forced to kill. It had taken two years before he had been able to pick up a pistol again. And he didn't want to relive those terrors. Especially not now.

Apartment A was one of only three apartments on the seventeenth floor, which meant each was larger than the average one-family home. Devlin rang the doorbell and waited. A full minute passed. He was reaching for the bell again, when the door finally opened.

"Yes."

He stared at the woman, momentarily speechless. She was dressed in silk crepe—blouse and slacks— and the material clung to her at strategic points in a loose yet revealing way. She was tall—perhaps five-eight or nine. Her eyes were soft, liquid; the matching brown hair finely sculpted to follow the delicate line of her jaw. The bone structure of her face seemed almost fragile, set off by high cheekbones and slightly pouting lips. It was a face, Devlin thought, that could easily have paid for the apartment had she peddled it to magazine covers.

"I'm Inspector Devlin. NYPD," he said. He felt slightly foolish with the formality, slightly foolish even being there.

"I know," she said. "The doorman explained." She stared at him for several seconds. There was a smile toying with her lips, as though she recognized the effect she was having. "Come in," she said. She turned abruptly and walked away, expecting him to follow. The silk crepe slacks flowed with her, accenting her movements, and Devlin was certain she understood the effect that had as well.

She led him into a large living room, gestured toward a long sofa, then isolated herself in a delicate Chippendale side chair. She crossed her legs, arranged her hands one atop the other, and stared at him again. "How can I help you?" she asked.

Devlin noticed the trace of an accent in her voice that he had missed at the door. French, he thought. But not the usual French. The room he was in was excessively elegant—like the woman herself. It was comfortably furnished, but carefully dotted with antiques, and the impressionist paintings on the walls were either genuine, or very expensive copies. His gut voted for the former.

"I believe you knew Captain Joseph Battaglia," he began.

The woman continued to stare at him. "Knew?"

"I'm afraid he's dead."

Michelle Paoli let out a short breath. Her mouth tightened momentarily with either pain or regret. She was either an excellent actress, or she was genuinely surprised. "I am so sorry," she said. "Joe was a wonderful man. How did he die?"

"He was murdered," Devlin said. "Yesterday."

The breath came again. "God. How terrible."

The early afternoon sun came through the window behind the woman, and it seemed to cast a glow around her body. Devlin wondered if she had selected the chair to achieve that effect.

"How long did you know the captain?" Devlin asked.

Michelle shook her head slightly. "Just a few months," she said. "We met here, at a small soirée I gave." She gestured with her hand, indicating the room they were in. "The party got a bit bigger than

I had anticipated, as those things do. Someone brought Joe, I believe. I'm not even certain who it was."

"And you became friends?"

"Yes." She shook her head, struggling with the reality of the news. "We had dinner a few times. Joe was delightful company. And I enjoy being with handsome and intelligent men."

She stared at Devlin again, as if evaluating him as well. He found himself rearranging his position on the sofa.

"What do you do, Ms. Paoli?" The question was a change in tack, designed to throw the woman off stride; bring out any of the nervous *tells* that would indicate she was hiding something.

"I work at the United Nations. On the secretary general's staff."

"You're a diplomat?"

She offered a faint smile. "I carry diplomatic status, but my work is essentially administrative."

Devlin knew he had to be careful now. As a diplomat, the woman could tell him to take a walk at any time. And walk he would. Like all diplomats she was immune to arrest, or any harassment by police. Christ, he thought. She was even immune to meter maids. She could just toss their parking tickets in the gutter and let the city scream its lungs out.

"I realize you don't have to talk to me," Devlin said. "But I'd appreciate any help you can give."

Michelle waved her hand, dismissing the acknowledgment. "I'll help, of course. But . . . Joe and I . . ." She shook her head. "We really weren't confidants. Merely friends."

"And you don't recall who brought him to the party?"

"No. I am afraid I don't." She shrugged. It was a delicate, slightly helpless gesture. "I can ask some others who were here. But . . ." She let the sentence die.

"I'd appreciate it if you would."

"Of course."

"Did the captain ever speak to you about his work?"

She shook her head again. "It even seems strange hearing him called by his title. I never thought of Joe as a police officer. I knew he was, of course. But we never discussed it. He was interested in art. As I am. Once we went to a gallery together. Another time to a museum."

Devlin allowed his eyes to roam the walls. "You have some interesting paintings here."

"They were my late father's," she said. "He collected. I merely enjoy."

"Is this apartment yours?"

Michelle smiled. "It is provided. As part of my job. So I can entertain in a"—she hesitated; smiled again—"proper diplomatic manner."

"Can you tell me who some of the other people were who were at the party you mentioned?"

She thought a moment. "It's hard to say for certain. I give quite a number. But I may still have the invitation list at my office. I'll have my secretary look." She leaned forward slightly. "But you must remember. Many people came that night without invitations."

"Is that common? At UN functions, I mean."

"This wasn't truly a UN party," she said. "There were some diplomatic people here. But it was more for friends who are interested in art." She smiled again. It was a smile that grabbed your attention, made you want more of it, more of her. "But, of course, you're right. Some parties require a degree of security. But it depends on who will be there. Members of the royal families of some oil-producing states, for example." The smile returned. "Even if they are really lesser members of those families, they often insist on it." Her eyes took on a hint of laughter. "Sometimes I think they do it just to remind us who they are." She offered another helpless shrug. "But at less formal functions, you would be surprised how many uninvited guests arrive. Often with invited guests, of course. But sometimes not. Journalists, for example."

Devlin nodded, then flipped a page in his notebook. "Did Captain Battaglia ever talk about his personal life?"

Michelle looked away for a moment, thinking. "I knew he was divorced. And he spoke about his children, of course." She arched her eyebrows slightly. "Mostly we talked about personal interests we shared."

Devlin hesitated momentarily. "How close a friendship did you have?"

Michelle stared at him. "Are you asking if we were lovers?"

"As delicately as I know how," Devlin said.

The smile toyed with her lips again. "No, Inspector. We were not lovers." Her hands rose slightly from her leg. "How can I explain? I don't think Joe was interested in me that way." She offered her small, helpless shrug, as if to say some things were inexplicable. The gesture was very Gallic, and very accurate, Devlin thought. "I think, in time, *I* might have been," Michelle added. "Interested, I mean. As I said, I am very attracted to handsome and intelligent men."

The woman allowed her eyes to remain on Devlin. It was a clear message. Very distracting, and very agreeable.

He stood and slipped his notebook back in his pocket. "Thank you," he said. "If you can look for that list, I'd appreciate it."

"Of course. I shall."

He took a business card from his pocket and gave it to her. "I can be reached through that first number at any time," he said. He watched her study the card, and wondered if she was pleased that his home number was there as well.

"I may have to get back to you," he added.

Michelle raised her eyes slowly from the card. The smile threatened to appear again. "I hope you will," she said.

"Why do you come here, when you hate it so much?" Michael Blair stared across his desk, taking in the uncomfortable look on Devlin's face. He had just finished the postmortem on Little Bat, with Devlin standing by looking as though he'd rather be tied across a hill of hungry ants. Now they were seated in Blair's small, cramped office, and Devlin still looked as if he'd prefer a turn with the ants.

"It's in the manual," Devlin said. "Says somebody from the crime scene has to be here. So we can testify you didn't autopsy the wrong body." He shrugged. "They don't trust you, Michael."

Blair grinned at Devlin's little game. "Yeah, I know all that," he said. "What I don't know is why you don't send somebody else."

"You never heard a good boss doesn't ask his men to do anything he wouldn't do himself?" He forced a tired smile. "Maybe you'd rather have Eddie?" He watched Blair curl his mouth in disgust. "Besides, the case is too important not to be here myself."

Blair thought about it. "Because he was a cop? Or because of who his father is?"

"All of the above. And because it doesn't feel right, the way they did him. It makes me feel somebody's taking us for a ride."

"Why is that?"

Devlin turned at the sound of the new voice. They had left the door to Blair's office open, and now the frame was filled with the stocky figure of Big Bat Battaglia, the junior U.S. senator from New York. Devlin was momentarily stunned to see him standing there, knew immediately he shouldn't be, knew he should have expected it. Tony "Big Bat" Battaglia had been a bigger-than-life cop, with a reputation for success born of hard, dogged work. Those successes had consistently spread his name across newspapers, and he had parlayed that into a political career. First to a congressional seat from the Bronx. Then, fifteen years ago, into the U.S. Senate. But his meteoric rise hadn't been a fluke, or a question of media hype. He had gotten a law degree while working as a detective, no small feat in itself. And he had waded into the quagmire of New York City politics and had learned it from the bottom up, earning his spurs along the way. And, those who knew, said he had been a good congressman, an effective one for his constituents. And now, an effective member of the senate, despite the rumors of corruption that always seemed to swirl about him. Devlin had always wondered if the rumors came from the fact he had been a cop, or because of his Italian origin. In New York both things seemed to mark you as a latent crook. But the bottom line was that no one had ever caught him with his fingers in the till, and that was the only benchmark Devlin cared about.

"I asked you why it doesn't feel right." It was Bat again, but there was no edge to his voice. He looked battered, beaten. Like a man who had lost his only son should look. But he also looked in control. A cop in harness who had pushed back all emotion.

Devlin stood and gestured toward his chair, indicating Bat should take it.

The man shook his head. "Just tell me. Please," he said.

"I don't think you want to know the details."

"Yes, I do. And I want to see his body."

"Senator, the post has already been done. And we have a positive I.D. I really don't advise it." It was Blair this time. He was standing now, too.

"Please call me Bat. I spent too much time on the job to feel comfortable with my fancy title. Especially with other cops." He tried to smile, but it never quite materialized. "And, what I want is something I have to do. Not anything else. I won't be able to handle this until I know everything. And until I see him."

Devlin shifted his weight; wished he was somewhere else. Battaglia had been a hard-nosed cop for twenty-one years. And even now, at sixty-two, there was a tough edge to him. He wasn't a big man— maybe five-eight or nine—but he had a solid build that still looked fit, a body that contrasted to his more salt than pepper hair and the age lines that etched his eyes and mouth. He was still a handsome man, with a slender, patrician nose, and brown eyes that came across soft but appeared able to look inside you.

Devlin told him how his son had been found. He rattled it off straight, as if giving a report to a commander, only trying to keep his voice soft, rather than cold and dispassionate.

Bat's eyes closed when Devlin told about the vibrator, and his jaw muscles momentarily tightened. Then he stared at Blair.

"Did they do that while he was still alive?" he asked.

Blair's mouth began to move, but the words didn't come.

"Look," Bat said, "I was a cop for a long time. This thing they did. It must have hurt him, damaged him. If he was alive when it happened there would have been bleeding. If not . . ." He let the sentence die.

Blair swallowed. "There was blood," he said.

Bat clenched his fists. "The bastards." He took a minute and stared at the wall, not seeing it. Just composing himself, Devlin thought.

"Can I see my boy, now?" he asked at length.

Devlin let Blair take him in. He wanted no part of it. He had always found victim identifications among the worst parts of the job, even though it was usually done with a degree of delicacy. Normally, relatives were taken to a quiet room upstairs and placed before a draped window. The body was then sent up on an elevator to a small chamber behind the glass, everything but the face covered by a sheet. Then the drapes were opened for as brief a time as necessary. And it was usually done before the post, before the body had been carved up.

What Bat would see, Devlin knew, would be far different. The body would be pulled out of a refrigerated wall unit on a sliding drawer. It would be naked, the wounds from the autopsy held together by coarse black twine in widely spaced sutures. That work was done by a woman—an employee of the medical examiner's office—who was known as "the seamstress." It was her sole function. Sew them up and hose them down—wash off any blood and filth—and it was something that did not require any care or delicacy.

So Bat's final vision of his child would be of a flaccid husk that had been carved like a piece of meat—the chest and abdomen split open in a "Y" shaped incision, the knife going from each shoulder to the sternum, then down to the pubis; all viscera removed, weighed, sectioned, then placed in a plastic bag and dropped back into the body cavity. The face literally peeled off the skull and laid on the chest so the skull cap could be cut away and the brain removed. Then the face fitted back in place and sewn. But never quite right. Never quite fitting the way it had before.

No, he didn't want to watch the man see his son that way.

Bat returned with Blair, face ashen, hands trembling. He looked at Devlin and seemed to force composure upon himself. Just willed it to be there.

"I'd like you to keep me informed about whatever progress you're making," he said. His voice was hoarse now, and Devlin could tell he was fighting to keep the tears inside.

"I'll tell whatever I can," Devlin said. "You know the way these things are played. Pretty close to the vest."

Bat looked at him; held his eyes for several seconds. He had enough power to get whatever information he wanted. But he didn't say that. He simply nodded. Devlin decided he liked the man.

"Is there anything you can tell us—anything your son told you, or anything you know—that might give us a lead into this?" Devlin asked.

Bat was staring at the wall again, and again not seeing it. His eyes looked hollow, drained of everything but pain. "He was a cop. It's the only reason I can think of," he said.

He seemed to come back to himself, and he looked at each man, first Devlin, then Blair. "Thank you," he said. "Both of you."

"I'm very sorry, Bat," Devlin said.

The man offered a weak, fragile smile. Devlin thought it looked like a fissure, behind which everything was crumbling and cracking and falling apart. "I know you are," Bat said. "And I appreciate it."

Devlin's office was located on lower Broadway, two blocks north of City Hall and five west of Police Headquarters, in a building that also housed the department's Organized Crime Control Unit for which Little Bat Battaglia had worked.

Devlin hadn't known Little Bat, but it was probable they had ridden the elevator together. He slipped behind his battered wooden desk. It was two-thirty. George Mitchelson, the deputy chief who headed Organized Crime Control, was due in his office in thirty minutes. The chief had already sent Battaglia's personnel jacket ahead.

Eddie Grogan arrived at two-forty-five, and flopped into a chair opposite Devlin. He glanced

around the large, sparsely furnished room. On a long
table near the window sat Little Bat's computer terminal, still smudged with the gray, resinous, poly-
mer powder they used for fingerprints. There were
some personal papers, bills, cancelled checks, and
the address book Devlin had found, along with what
looked to be a journal.

Devlin noted Grogan's attention drawn to the
items he had had brought from the crime scene.
"The other stuff will be here when the forensics lab
is through with them," he said.

"You find anything?" Grogan asked.

"A bit. Our victim went out of his way to hide
that address book and journal. So far I've only had
time to go through the address book, and it only had
one identifiable entry—a woman named Michelle
Paoli. A diplomat who lives in a co-op on Fifth Avenue. All the other entries are limited to first names
or initials, and the phone numbers are either written
in some numerical code, or are for phones in other
cities."

"No area codes with those phone numbers?"
Grogan asked.

Devlin shook his head. "My bet is they're local
numbers, but that he wrote them down in some type
of numerical variation. That the real number starts
with the third or fourth digit. Something like that.
I'll ask the lab to play with it. See what they come
up with. In the meantime we can have someone
check the numbers against other area codes. Say
from Washington to Boston."

"I'll get somebody on that part of it," Grogan
said. "You get a chance to talk to this Paoli
woman?"

Devlin nodded, then told Grogan about his interview with Michelle Paoli.

"You think there's anything there?"

"I'm not sure. But I think we need to find out
more."

"It'll be tough. Her being a diplomat."

Devlin nodded. "I'll handle it myself. What did you come up with?"

Grogan fished out his notebook. "Two guys from Battaglia's unit in OCC went to his apartment after he didn't show for work, and didn't answer his phone or beeper. It's routine for them to keep close tabs on each other. They're all a little paranoid about the work they do." Grogan shrugged. "Maybe it's macho shit, maybe not."

"Paranoid about somebody coming after them, or about somebody being bought off?" Devlin asked.

"Little of both, I think. But they only talk about the coming after them part." Grogan leaned forward. "Guys I talked to seemed a little wary. Like maybe they thought we were only one step up from Internal Affairs."

"Have to expect that," Devlin said. "We're the only other unit that's outside the chain of command."

Grogan snorted. "Shit. Never thought of myself as a fucking shoe-fly."

"Better start," Devlin said. "Everybody else will." He leaned back in his chair. "These guys, they take anything from the crime scene?"

"They said no. Said they found him just like we did and called it in. Called their unit first. Then the precinct and homicide. There's a lot of talk going around the unit about the way he was found."

Devlin ignored the last part. It was something to be expected. "You notice that his computer was on when we found him?"

Grogan nodded. "So he was workin' on somethin' when he got it."

"There were no computer disks there. Not even blank ones."

"You think the shooter took them? Maybe even turned on the computer himself?"

"Or the guys who found the body," Devlin said.

"It's possible," Grogan said. "If they thought it was stuff from work. They play everything like it was top secret shit."

"I want you to stay when Mitchelson comes. Then I want you to go back and give those clowns a message. Let them know if they took something we don't know about, they'll have us chasing our tails. Tell them I find my tail in my mouth, the guys who put it there can count on working Staten Island next week."

"Why don't you just sic Mitchelson on them? He's their chief."

Devlin shook his head. "He tells them to keep their mouths shut, they'll do a clam on us no matter what I threaten them with."

"Sounds like you don't trust him."

Devlin stared at the computer. "I think the brass is gonna try to make this investigation come out the way they want it to. And Mitchelson's part of their little club."

Grogan gave a small shrug. "Hey, we have to expect that. Especially with the gay angle. Having a commander turn out to be a fruit would make them all choke." He shook his head, grinned. "How'd you make out at the post?"

"No surprises. One shot to the head took him out." He stared at Little Bat's papers spread across the table, at the journal he had found. "The vibrator was jammed into him before he was shot. Blair said it tore up his colon pretty good."

"Jesus," Grogan said. "We gotta nail this fucker. Hard."

"And Big Bat was there." He glanced at Grogan. He was staring back, incredulous.

"For the post?"

"After. But he asked to see the body."

"Christ. How'd he take it?"

"Bad. But he toughed it out."

"Poor bastard." Grogan hesitated again. "But talk about people you don't trust," he finally added.

"Big Bat? Why?"

"I was a young dick during his heyday," Grogan said. "Just six years in the bureau. Word was: Stay away from him. 'Cause he was dirty."

Mitchelson arrived promptly at three. He was a tall, slender, rawboned man, with closely cropped, graying hair, and gray eyes. Devlin thought *gray* was the one word that best described him. Or maybe, somber. Like an undertaker.

"Terrible thing," Mitchelson said. "I've had this command six years, and this is the first man I've lost." He rearranged his lanky body in a wooden visitor's chair that was too small for him. "Whadda ya got so far?" he asked. "My men—ones who found him—said the crime scene wasn't exactly . . ." He hesitated, then added: "Normal, I guess." He shifted his weight again. "Christ, the other bosses—even the P.C.—are off the wall about this. The way he was found, I mean. I hope we can deep-six that part of it."

Devlin ignored him. He knew what the bosses and the police commissioner would want. He also knew that Mitchelson's nuts were being held to the fire for maybe having an undetected homosexual—and a commander to boot—running a big part of his show. He didn't give a damn about any of it. "Tell me about his work," he said.

Mitchelson's gaze fell on the personnel jacket on Devlin's desk. "It's all in there," he said. "He was my exec. Knew the command inside and out. He was a whiz on a computer. Cervone seconded him to me 'cause I needed a guy like that. He could sit there, put together information it would take my men weeks to come up with. Patterns of activity, things like that. It was like he was a magician."

He glanced at the computer terminal on the long

table, took in the fingerprint residue. "That the one from his place?" he asked.

Devlin nodded.

"You find anything has to do with my command, you let me know." It was an order, or at least an attempt at one, Devlin decided. He ignored that, too.

"What was his personal life like?" Devlin asked.

Mitchelson let out a weary breath. "Shit. I wonder how many times I've been asked that question today?" He shook his head. "As far as I knew, it was a typical cop's life. Too typical," he added. "Divorced, less than a year ago. Two beautiful kids. Little girls." He shifted his weight. "His ex wasn't very friendly about it. Kept him broke." He leaned forward. "That's something we watch for. A guy who's got money problems. Just in case." He hesitated again. "But he was clean. I'd bet my career on it."

Devlin nodded again. Decided to let him talk it through.

"Anyway, his wife was being a hardass. He was late bringing the kids back, she'd flip out, call the precinct. Even called the P.C.'s office once, claimed he had snatched them. Christ, he loved those kids. It's all he talked about. That and the job."

"Any threats against him? In this assignment, or from before?" It was Grogan this time, and Mitchelson threw him a look. Like who was he—a *detective*—asking him questions?

"What about it?" Devlin asked, backing Grogan up.

"Nothing he reported," Mitchelson said. "And he would have. It was strict policy."

"So there's nothing from the job you can think of?"

Mitchelson shook his head. "Or his personal life, either. Nothing that anybody knew about." His jaw hardened. "And I don't care how he was found. I don't believe any of this fag shit. The guy was one tough piece of work. And smart. Had everything going for him on the job." He inclined his chin toward the personnel jacket on Devlin's desk. "You read it. He was one helluva cop. As perfect a record as you can get. A captain at thirty-five. A lawyer. Shit, combine that with his political connections, and he had chief written all over him. Unless he stumbled badly, it was just a question of time."

Devlin leaned back; stared across the desk. "I want to send Eddie back upstairs with you. Go through his desk and files."

Mitchelson raised his hands as if warding off a blow. "Our stuff's sensitive. Highly classified because we work so closely with the feds."

Devlin leaned forward, eyes hard on the chief. "I appreciate that," he said. "But this is a murder investigation. A cop killing. I'd hate to have to get a subpoena for department files, but I will."

"Whoa, easy now." Mitchelson's hands were up again. "But I'll have to have somebody there. Make sure sensitive stuff isn't leaving the office."

"Eddie will just take notes, unless it's clearly pertinent. If notes are a problem on some things, he'll just read it." And he'll memorize everything, right down to the punctuation, Devlin told himself. "But he sees it all. Everything in Battaglia's office."

The chief drew a long breath. "Okay, we'll do it your way." He glanced at Grogan, then back at Devlin. "Can I talk to you alone for a minute?"

Devlin nodded to Grogan, who immediately got up and headed for the outer office. "I'll wait for the chief outside," he said.

Mitchelson leaned forward, attempting to add intimacy to his words. "Look, Paul, I know your brief, and I know you've got a job to do. I think we all want the same thing—to catch the scumbag who did this, and to keep the department from being hurt by it." He offered up a nicotine-stained smile that didn't work with his gray demeanor. "Take a word of advice from somebody's been around this place a long

time. Try and be a little less abrasive. You don't
need any enemies in the big building. Especially not
on floors twelve through fourteen."

Devlin forced back a smile. Mitchelson's reference to Police Headquarters, and the floors the
chiefs, deputy commissioners, and commissioner
occupied was too typical. Street cops referred to
the place as the Puzzle Palace, and the top three
floors as the Emerald City—where all the phony
wizards worked. But to the bosses, and the
wanna-be bosses, it was the *big building,* and floors
twelve through fourteen, the sanctum of sanctums.
Cops joked that Catholic commanders had even installed holy water fonts at the elevators. Devlin decided to let the reference go without comment. He
had already made enough waves.

"I'm sorry if I come across that way," he lied.
"But we both know the first forty-eight hours of a
murder investigation is make-or-break time."

Mitchelson raised his hands again. "I understand.
Completely. We all want the same thing, here.
What's best for the job."

Devlin nodded. And for your career, Chief, he
added to himself. If Little Bat comes up tainted,
your career's in the toilet for not spotting it and
stopping it.

Devlin stood and extended his hand. "I'll do what
I can, Chief. And thanks for the advice."

*The children frighten me. In my heart I know
they're all I have. All I'll ever have. I'm afraid
I'll lose them. Afraid they'll never want to see
me again. I have no idea what to do, what to
say, if I'm forced to explain. They're so young.
Too young to even understand what I'm talking
about. Too young to understand any of it. But
they're not too young to hear the hatred and
disgust in other people's voices. Not too young*

*to be told I abandoned them—abandoned
everyone—to do this thing.*

*And what if they don't hear anything at all?
What if through some miracle no one tells them
anything? What do I do then? Just wait for the
day they finally understand? Wait for that look
to come over their faces? That first sign of confusion and disgust? Wait for them to ask me:
Daddy, why did you do this to us?*

*What will I say then? I can't even put the an-
swers down on paper. Because then I'll start putting down all the other words too. All the
excuses. Words like honesty and self-respect.
Words like integrity and acceptance. I can't even
use those words myself anymore. I can't use
words that stab at me like knives. Words I'm no
longer sure I even believe.*

*God, how did this all start? It didn't just
jump out at me. I saw it coming. So why didn't
I just turn and run away from it? Just hide from
it like I've hidden from so many things for so
many years. Hiding is the easy part. You can't
get hurt if you hide. They can't laugh at you,
hate you, abandon you if you're invisible.
There's a subtle safety behind the mask. This is
the real world. This isn't Halloween. People
are only frightened when the mask comes off.*

Devlin was hunched over his desk when Eddie returned an hour and a half later. Little Bat's journal
was set out before him, and he seemed absorbed by
a particular page.

He looked up as Grogan approached; slowly
closed the book. "So how'd it go in the secret world
of Organized Crime Control?"

"Shit," Grogan said. "Even the fucking paper
clips are classified up there." He grinned. "They got
so many wiretaps going, I'm surprised half the
fucking mob ain't been electrocuted."

"Battaglia seem to be concentrating on any one thing?" Devlin asked.

"Yeah," Grogan said. "He seems to have had a big thing for Donatello Torelli." He shrugged. "Which ain't surprising, since he's number one on everybody's hit list ever since he beat those two raps the feds laid on him. Funny thing is, all that interest seemed to stop dead about three months ago—at least as far as Little Bat was concerned. Last three months he seemed to be targeting smaller areas, and concentrating on administrative crap."

"You see anything that made you think somebody told him to stop?"

Grogan shook his head. "Nothing formal. But that kind of order doesn't usually make it to paper. You know what I mean?"

Devlin understood. Bosses didn't like to give orders in writing that showed they had curtailed an investigation. That kind of paper trail had a way of coming back to bite you on the ass. He glanced toward Little Bat's computer, thinking about the missing computer disks. "Maybe he decided to do the work at home. Maybe he found something that made him think it wasn't safe to do it in the office." He drummed his fingers on the desk. "You talk to those guys again?" he asked. "The ones who found the body?"

"Yeah. They say they didn't take nothin'." He offered another shrug. "Who knows? Cops lie sometimes."

Devlin eased back in his chair. "All we've got left is the mainframe of his computer. If there was anything on any of the disks that disappeared, it's probably in there, too. I played with it, but it's loaded with codes and passwords." He shook his head. "One file I was able to open seemed to be written in gibberish. What we need is a hacker who can crack it open."

"You want somebody in the department?" Grogan asked.

"I'd prefer it. Just in case we do find something sensitive. It would be good if we could get somebody assigned here for a week or two."

"I'll ask around," Grogan said.

Devlin glanced at his watch. "Shit," he muttered.

"What's the matter?" Grogan asked.

"I was supposed to take Adrianna out to dinner tonight. But there's no way now."

"How's it goin' with you and my Cuban godchild?" Grogan asked.

Devlin grinned; the boyishness returned to his face. "Hey, she's still doing what she said she'd never do. She's living with a cop." He leaned forward, creating a confidential tone to what he was about to say. "Sometimes—like when I got the call about Little Bat this morning—I hear her muttering in Spanish. I just play dumb, make believe I didn't hear it."

Grogan fought off his own smile. "You're lucky she's crazy about your daughter," he said. "She could throw you out, and keep Phillipa there, she probably would. Hey, look, take her to dinner. I can cover. I already got Rita pissed at me. There's no point both of us bein' in the shit."

Devlin shook his head. He wanted to ask Eddie about Rita, his new girlfriend. But his mind was already too cluttered. "I want to see Battaglia's ex-wife," he said. He ran a hand over the journal on his desk, then placed the personnel jacket on top of it. "Before somebody tells her to keep her mouth shut," he added.

Grogan nodded toward the personnel file and the journal. "Something in that stuff I should know about?" he asked.

"Yeah, lots of stuff," Devlin said. He picked up the personnel folder and pushed it toward the older detective. "This guy was one amazing cop. Just like

Mitchelson said. Tough. Smart. Got about every citation he could get when he was on the street."

"What about that?" Grogan asked, nodding toward the journal as he picked up the personnel folder.

"I haven't read much of it yet. But it looks like it's all personal," Devlin said. "A lot about his kids. A lot about himself. I'm no expert, so we'll have to have it authenticated, but when you compare it to his other personal papers, it seems to be his handwriting."

"So, does it tell us anything so far?" Grogan asked.

Devlin looked down at the journal, then back at Grogan. "It tells us that Little Bat Battaglia was probably gay," he said.

"Jesus," Eddie Grogan said.

Chapter Four

Angie Battaglia stared at the man standing on her threshold, then looked past him to make sure the blue-and-white was still parked in front. Beyond the patrol car a dozen or so reporters were being held behind a line of sawhorses. A cacophony of shouted questions immediately floated toward her, but she ignored them. Only the lights of the television cameras bothered her. She didn't want the bastards taking her picture. Not hers, and not her kids'.

"You must be a cop. Otherwise you wouldn't have gotten this far," she said.

"Inspector Devlin. Are you Mrs. Battaglia?"

"I was."

Devlin was caught short by the response. He glanced over his shoulder, buying time. "Can we step inside? Away from the cameras?"

Angie Battaglia stepped back and Devlin moved quickly past her. When he turned, the woman was closing the door, her back still to him.

"I'm sorry to have to bother you this soon," he said. "But it's necessary."

The woman turned quickly and glared at him. "Let's cut the crap, Inspector. I know the drill. I've had cops in my life for fourteen years." She continued to stare at him, unfazed by his discomfort. "Is it going to take long?"

Devlin shifted his weight. "I'll make it as quick as possible."

Angie lowered her eyes and shook her head.

"That means it will. I should have known better than to ask for a straight answer." She looked up at him. There was no puffiness around her eyes; no sign she had been crying. "We better go into the living room," she said.

The living room was off a central foyer, and took up the entire side of the house. There was a fireplace in the middle of one wall, flanked by two large, blue sofas that faced each other across a round, highly polished cocktail table. Devlin quickly calculated the cost of the house and furnishings. It fell within the parameters of what a police captain should be able to afford. He'd have to check other things, of course—bank accounts, vacation homes, jewelry, gambling losses—but so far, so good.

Angie slid gracefully onto the end of one sofa, and tucked her legs beneath her. She was dressed in black slacks and a black turtleneck, and, given her response at the door, Devlin wondered if the choice of clothing had any significance. She was a beautiful woman, with short, black hair, and striking brown eyes, and the makeup she wore had been carefully applied to make it appear she wore none. But there was no visible sign of grief on her face, only anger, and her eyes were hard on him now, offering no quarter.

Devlin began again. "As I said, I'm sorry for the timing. It just can't be helped."

The corners of the woman's mouth turned up slightly as if mocking him. Only her hands showed any emotion. They were balled into fists in her lap. "It's not a problem, Inspector. It's not like I'm in mourning." She hesitated. Longer than necessary, Devlin thought. "Except for my kids." She looked toward the fireplace. "We were divorced, and it wasn't a very friendly divorce." She turned back to him. "Okay?"

Devlin returned her stare. "You're telling me you no longer loved your former husband," he said.

Pain flashed across the woman's eyes, and for a moment Devlin thought the shell would crack. But she seemed to take hold of herself. "That's right," she said. "Can we talk about something else?"

It was a grudging surrender, and it was what he had wanted. He had to open her up, let her know he could, keep her from thinking she could hold him off, hide anything she didn't want dragged into the open.

"Are the children here?" he asked, throwing her off balance again.

She shook her head, as if clearing it of sudden confusion, "They're in the backyard. With their grandfather."

"Your father?"

She shook her head again. "No. My parents are dead. They're with Joe's father." Her eyes flashed at him. "I divorced Joe. Not his father," she said. A touch of defiance was back in her voice now. He let it pass.

"Did your ex-husband keep any business records, or any personal papers here?" he asked.

"No. Nothing."

"What about any personal property? Anything he had boxed up and stored here? Any weapons?"

She glared at him. "Nothing. He didn't live here. He took everything with him when he left— everything that still belonged to him." The look in her eyes said he had taken some other, less tangible things as well.

"Do you know if he had any enemies?"

"Not while he lived here. He was an administrator. He wasn't a street cop anymore." The line of her mouth hardened. "I haven't kept track of his personal life since he left."

Devlin decided to let the last comment pass for a moment. "What about while he was a street cop? Do you recall any threats?"

"No."

"Would he have told you?"

She looked at the fireplace again. "Joe had his secrets." She kept her eyes averted. "Like all cops."

"What was the cause of your divorce?" Devlin watched her fists tighten. She kept her eyes on the fireplace.

"That's none of your business."

He remained silent. He knew the quiet would force her eyes back to him. When she finally turned her head, he offered a resigned smile. "Everything's my business now, Mrs. Battaglia. And, sooner or later, everything will come out. Better these things come from you, than from someone whose perception might be second or third hand."

She looked down at her lap, saw the fists and relaxed them. "We grew apart," she said. "Stopped loving each other. It happens."

Her eyes remained downcast, but he didn't mind this time. "When did you first suspect he was gay?"

Devlin watched her body jump; her head snap up.

"You sonofabitch." Her voice was little more than a hiss, her eyes a mixture of anger and fear.

"I'm sorry. I have to know."

"There are two children involved in this," she snapped. "Are you going to make them live with filth? Make them think their father was some goddamned pervert?" Her eyes were blazing now; the hands were fists again.

"No, he's not."

The voice had come from the entrance to the foyer, and Devlin turned to meet the hard eyes of Big Bat Battaglia. The man seemed to have a talent for appearing unnoticed, Devlin thought.

Big Bat moved into the room, and as he did, his face softened, almost as though he had willed it. He was dressed in a sport shirt and slacks, and the casual clothes somehow made him look smaller. He sat next to Angie, took one of her balled fists in his hands, and stroked it. Slowly the fist opened.

Devlin knew the scenario wasn't going to work.
He needed to talk to the woman alone; knew he
should insist on it. But he also knew it would only
happen if Big Bat wanted it that way. Otherwise
he'd just be ordered out of the house. Then one
phone call to city hall would ensure he never got
back in.

He looked at Angie. Her whole body had suddenly relaxed. She continued to stare at him, and the
eyes still weren't friendly. But now her body had
sunk back into the sofa, and the line of her mouth
had softened. She looked like a child who had just
experienced unexpected power, one who had just
learned that nothing bad was going to happen to her.

Bat leaned forward slightly. "You were very kind
to me this afternoon, Paul. I'd appreciate it if you'd
extend that kindness to my daughter-in-law." The
words came out smoothly; the voice was soft. The
warning in the words might have been missed if you
weren't listening, Devlin thought. Or if you didn't
understand the game.

Devlin sat forward, bringing himself physically
closer to the pair. There had been no reaction from
Angie Battaglia when Bat had used the term
"daughter-in-law." She hadn't so much as flinched.
Devlin rested his forearms on his knees. "I want that
very much," he said. "No one has any interest in
hurting *Mrs. Battaglia,* or her children." Again,
nothing. "But I have a problem. Finding the people
who murdered your son." He shifted his eyes to
Angie. "To do that I have to know everything about
him. His friends, his enemies, the problems in his
life. Everything."

The woman's mouth tightened; her body
stiffened—the little girl suddenly realizing that no
one ever had enough power to keep all the bad
things away.

She glared at Devlin. "There are children involved in this." She turned quickly to Bat. "Where

are they?" she asked, as if suddenly concerned they
might be in the hall listening.

He stroked her hand. It had balled up again, and
this time stayed that way.

"They're out back. With Jim." Bat turned to Devlin. "Jim O'Brien," he explained. "He was Joe's college roommate at Columbia."

"He's a lawyer," Angie said. Her eyes gleamed
with the imagined threat of the title.

Tell me he's a sanitation man who can let my garbage sit at the curb for a year. Then I'll worry, Devlin thought. He only nodded.

"Look, Paul." Big Bat had leaned closer until he
and Devlin were only two feet apart. He had lowered his voice so it was little more than a whisper.
"This kind of speculation doesn't do anybody any
good. Not Angie. Not the children. Not me. Not the
department."

"But it can't be ignored, Bat." From the corner of
his eye, Devlin could see the woman stiffen again.

"I understand that," Bat said. "I also understand
that things find their way into reports, and eventually get in the hands of defense attorneys. And, before that, they get spread around the big building.
And we both know how some of the brass like to
shoot their mouths off. Especially if they think they
can garner some favor with the media. Or hurt
somebody they don't particularly like." His eyes
hardened with the last statement, then quickly turned
soft again. "All it would take is one 'off the record'
comment, and Angie and the kids would suffer."

And you, too, Devlin told himself. "Are you asking for discretion? Or ignorance?"

"All I'm asking is that this *information* not find
its way into any reports. And that you not push
Angie, or the children on the subject. You can talk to
me. And, I promise, I'll answer your questions."

And make sure I get only the answers you want
me to have, Devlin thought. He nodded slowly. He

was being set up for a fall. If he, or any member of his team failed to file complete and detailed reports, they'd be violating department regulations, and could be brought up on charges. Down the road they also might find themselves accused of suppressing evidence—a situation that would make even an incompetent defense attorney drool all over his three-piece suit.

He sat back. "What I'll do is sit on the reports I get—not distribute them. Cervone and the P.C. will howl, but I expect that anyway." He sat forward again, trying to keep his face as sympathetic as possible. "If this information we're talking about turns out to have no bearing on the murder, I'll lose it. But that's as far as I can ask my people to go."

Angie started to object, but Bat silenced her with a squeeze of her hand. He understood what Devlin was saying. He was giving a flat "no" to obstructing the investigation—which Bat had expected. And Devlin was making sure the members of his unit had their asses covered. He had expected that as well. But he was also offering to put his own tail on the line by agreeing to deep-six information that didn't relate to the killers. That left only one loophole.

"I can live with that," Bat said.

They stood beside a large, backyard swing set. It was made of heavy wood—one of those prefabricated sets you could buy unassembled in any home supply store. Provided you were willing to spend several days putting it together. It was a bitch of a job, and Devlin tried to envision Little Bat building it for his children.

The children were inside now. They had been hustled away by Angie, along with the lawyer, Jim O'Brien, when Big Bat and Devlin had come outside to talk. The kids had stared at Devlin when their mother had led them away, and the older child's eyes had seemed puffy and confused. It was the only sign of open mourning he had seen at the house.

"It's hard on them," Bat said, looking toward the door the children had entered. "But these things always are. Kids in cop families know the job is dangerous. They hear things; feel things. But they never believe it will touch them like this." He turned back to Devlin. "Do you have children?"

"One," Devlin said. "A daughter. Two years younger than your older grandchild."

Bat stared at his shoes, nodded. "Are you close?"

"Yes," Devlin said. "Her mother died in an automobile accident when she was just a baby. I'm all she's ever had."

"My son was very close to his kids. He was a good father to them."

"His personnel jacket says he was a good cop, too."

Bat nodded. "He could have gone far."

There was a sense of regret in the words. One of lost opportunities. But Devlin couldn't tell if the man attributed that loss to his son's death, or to something else.

Devlin let the words hang for a minute. The sky had turned suddenly dark, threatening rain. "Can you tell me what caused the divorce?" he asked at length.

Bat drew a breath and stared at the ground. "Angie discovered he was involved with someone else." He gave a small shrug, his shoulders accepting and minimizing the information at the same time.

"A woman?"

Bat looked toward the house. "She never said." He turned his attention back to Devlin. His eyes seemed harder now, as if drawing from some inner toughness. "She told me he wasn't willing to give it up—wasn't willing to change, was the way she put it—and that she couldn't live with it."

"How did she find out?"

"She found a book—a diary, or a journal. He had written about it in there." Bat lowered his eyes and shook his head. "She'd gotten suspicious. They hadn't ..." He paused, seeming embarrassed by what he was about to say. "They hadn't been intimate in quite a while, I gathered. So she started looking through his things." He shook his head again. "Christ, you'd think a cop would know better than to put things on paper and then leave it around."

Devlin felt the weight of Little Bat's journal in his jacket pocket. He had ignored department regulations and had taken it with him. He had told himself that he wanted to understand the man; read what he had written about himself. But, perhaps—just perhaps—he had wanted to make sure no one else did. "Maybe he wanted her to know, but couldn't tell her." he said. "Maybe, it was easier that way."

Bat's eyes came up and there was a hint of momentary anger. "Let's not assume anything, okay?"

"You're right. We shouldn't. *I* shouldn't," Devlin said. "Did he ever say anything to you?"

Bat's eyes snapped back to him. He struggled with the anger again; won again. "You mean, like was he afraid he might be gay? Hell, no. Christ, the kid played football at Columbia. He wasn't a star, or anything, but hell ..." The words trailed off, as though he had suddenly recognized how foolish he sounded. "No, he never talked to me about anything like that. And neither did Angie."

But you suspected, Devlin thought. Something made you suspect it.

"And nothing when he was younger?" He knew he was being hard on the man, but he needed to be. He didn't think he'd get another chance. The man's vulnerability—and his willingness to answer questions—wouldn't last long.

"No." Already the line of Bat's jaw had hardened. "My son was a man," he said. "In every way. He never gave me any reason to doubt that." A nervous tic came to the corner of his mouth and he rubbed at it with his hand. "I don't care how he was found." He was staring at Devlin now, his eyes hard and challenging. "He was killed for some other reason. I know that in my gut."

Devlin looked away. He didn't want to watch the man's pain any longer. "Does Mrs. Battaglia still have the journal? Or a copy?" he asked.

Bat shook his head, then realized Devlin wasn't looking at him. "No. She said he took it with him." He was silent, forcing Devlin to turn his attention back to him. It was an old cop trick. "You didn't find it?" he asked, when Devlin was again looking at him.

Devlin shook his head. He needed the lie right now. If Bat knew he had the journal, sooner or later he'd put out a contract to have it *misplaced*. It wouldn't be hard. Devlin would simply be ordered to log the book in to the property clerk's office. And, eventually, when he went back for it, he'd find a blank duplicate in its place. It would simply happen, and the brass would be only too happy to look the other way. Hell, hundreds of pounds of heroin had disappeared from the clerk's office. A misfiled, or mislabeled book wouldn't even raise an eyebrow.

Devlin studied the man's eyes. There was a look of relief there, and he knew he had been right about the journal.

"Are you sure Mrs. Battaglia didn't keep a copy? For the divorce?" The question was perverse, but he felt a sudden need for it right now.

"She kept the original. Until the divorce was final." Bat said. He changed his stance, as if suddenly uncomfortable. "It was a very generous settlement. For her. For the kids. But my son insisted he get the book back as part of the deal."

"And that no copies be kept?"

"That's right," Bat said. "At that point he was thinking like a cop again." He tried to force a smile, but it cracked and crumbled.

"Who told you about that? Your son?"

He shook his head. "Angie told me."

"Why? Did you ask to see the book?"

Bat seemed to swallow the question—smother it, along with the anger it produced. He let out a breath, nodded. "I wanted to understand what had made him throw everything away. His family. His home." He waved his hand, taking everything in. "He had a good life here."

"Did you ever ask him why?"

Bat nodded. "I asked. He didn't answer. It was that simple." He suddenly seemed to be fighting back tears. "The past few months we didn't even talk."

Devlin toed the ground. He suddenly wished he had left the man alone. But that wasn't in the cards. He glanced at the swing set. He had built a similar one for his daughter a couple of years ago. It had been a backbreaking, pain-in-the-ass job.

"What about his new assignment?" Devlin asked. "Did he ever confide in you about what he was working on? Any concerns he had for his safety?"

Bat seemed to tense momentarily. Then it was gone. He shook his head. "At first. When he was seconded to Organized Crime Control, he asked me what I knew about the mob families. I'm on some senate committees that touch on those areas. But I knew more as a cop than I do as a senator. And what I did know is pretty outdated. Interesting as history, but not much more."

The answer somehow didn't ring true, but Devlin decided to let it pass. "What about any fears for his safety?"

Again Bat shook his head. Again the tears seemed imminent. He sucked it in. "Nothing scared that kid," he said. He seemed to swell with momentary pride. He turned to Devlin. "His football coach in high school once told me he had more guts than brains." He smiled at the memory, but the smile was forced—brittle, like an old, damaged teacup that was more for display than practical use.

Adrianna was standing before a large canvas, brush in hand, when Devlin returned to their Soho loft at nine o'clock. It was later than he had planned—his daughter, Phillipa, was already in bed asleep, and he could see the remnants of their dinner on the kitchen counter. He had left the Battaglia home at six, had gone back to the office, and had briefed Eddie about his interviews with Bat and Angie Battaglia. Then he had reviewed and approved the investigative team Eddie had hammered together, and had issued marching orders for the next day. As always, the administrative details had taken twice the time he had anticipated.

Adrianna turned away from the canvas as he came toward her. She was dressed in jeans and a baggy work shirt that was spattered with paint. Her raven-dark hair was held back by a bright red headband, and there was a smudge of paint on the tip of her nose. Umber, he thought. An image of Michelle Paoli flashed into his mind. He took in Adrianna's battered work clothes again. Despite it all, she was still the most alluring woman he had ever seen, he told himself.

"Sorry I'm late." He suddenly realized he hadn't telephoned; hadn't done any of the things he should have—like picking up a small bouquet of flowers to say he was sorry about canceling the dinner they had planned over a week ago. "I should have called you," he said. It was a lame statement, made worse by a guilty shrug. His mind had simply been overwhelmed by everything else. Now he was just compounding it all.

Adrianna put down her brush, wiped her paint-

stained hands on a cloth, then came to him and
slipped her arms around his neck.

"I heard about it on the news," she said. "Did you
know him?"

He shook his head. "No. We never met." But I'm
starting to, he thought.

He hadn't told her about the case before he had
left that morning. He hadn't wanted to add to her ag-
itation by mentioning it was a cop killing. But he
should have known better. He should have known
she'd understand. Maybe even sympathize. Her late
father had been a cop—a detective first grade. He
had been Eddie Grogan's old partner, years ago,
which was how Eddie had become her godfather.
Devlin smiled inwardly at the thought. The job was
about as incestuous as anything got. But it was also
why Adrianna hated the fact that he was a cop again.
She had grown up with cops, knew the lives they
led, knew how the job affected them.

They had been lovers in college, more than a de-
cade ago, and he had wanted to marry her then. But
she hadn't wanted a life with a cop, and had walked
away. The rejection had been devastating, but he had
fought it, overcome it, or so he had thought. Then he
had found and married Mary, the wife who had
given him everything he had ever wanted—love,
laughter, the daughter he adored—until a drunken
driver had suddenly snatched her life away. Then
there was just Phillipa.

He had been living in Vermont when Eddie had
come to him years later. Devlin had been forced to
retire from the NYPD when a serial killer had taken
a knife to his arm, leaving him with a partial disabil-
ity and consuming guilt over a dead partner. It had
also left him with the choice of riding a desk, or
finding a new life. So he had taken Phillipa and retreated to the backwoods of Vermont to lick his
wounds and "raise chickens." Or so he had told himself. Within a year, he had found himself running a

small, backwater police department, and facing another serial killer who was leaving a trail of bodies
through the quiet Vermont countryside. When it was
over, he was a celebrity, of sorts. A cop who had
tracked down two madmen. No one ever questioned
the emotional havoc it had brought to his own life.

It was then that Eddie had turned that life around.
Another killer was carving his way through New
York; savagely mutilating, then killing young, successful women in the arts. The detectives working
the case had been rendered useless by a political
quagmire that involved the mayor's office, the FBI,
and the archdiocese of New York. And there was
one final kicker: The next target on the killer's list
was Eddie's godchild, and Devlin's former lover,
Adrianna Mendez.

So he had returned to work the case indepen-
dently, and a third killer had been added to his growing reputation. And he had fallen in love again, and
had stayed. He and Phillipa had taken up residence
in Adrianna's Soho loft. They had added a slightly
battered Bridgehampton beach house to the package,
and retirement had again become the order of the
day.

Then a new mayor had come into office—a result
of the scandal that had rocked the city when that last
serial killer had been caught—and he had promptly
offered Devlin a unique position in the NYPD. He
would fill the unused rank of Inspector of Detectives, and report directly to the mayor. He would, in
effect, be the mayor's safety valve against his own
police department, and would handle all high-
profile, scandal-prone cases. He would pick and
chose his own people, and would have the unprecedented ability to supersede the order of any commander, regardless of rank. In short, he would be
free of the political quicksand that surrounded the
department's chain of command. At least that was
how it was supposed to work. Now, starting his first

case in that job, he was beginning to wonder if it would.

Devlin ran his hands along Adrianna's back, bent down and kissed the drop of paint on the tip of her nose. He ran his tongue along his lips. "Umber?" he asked.

Adrianna wiped the spot with her sleeve and looked at it. "Magenta," she said. "Umber is more brown than purple."

"I'll learn," Devlin said.

She placed her head against his chest. "Never."

"How's Phillipa?"

"Fine. She went to the gallery with me this afternoon. Umberto had a hot prospect who wanted to meet the artist before he bought. She charmed his checkbook right out of his pocket."

"How much?" He listened, then whistled when she told him the price. "I think you should marry me," he said. "I always wanted to be kept by a wealthy wife."

"I think I should just adopt Phillipa, and cut out the middleman," she said. She took his arm and led him farther into the loft. "Have you eaten?" she asked.

"I grabbed a corned beef sandwich on my way back to the office." He slipped his arm around her waist. "I really did want to go out to dinner with you tonight. There was just too much to do."

"Do you want to talk about it?"

"Yeah, I would. But I'm not sure you want to hear."

She led him to a large, overstuffed sofa, pushed him down into one corner, then curled up in the other. "I'll tell you when I've had enough," she said.

He looked across the expanse of sofa, and took in her slender, supple body, her finely etched features and light brown eyes. Suddenly he didn't want to talk at all. He just wanted to lose himself in her. For about a week. He began to move toward her.

She raised a hand. "Talk first. Love later. Maybe," she said.

He smiled and fell back into his place. He realized it was the first time he had smiled that day. It was the real joy of a relationship, he thought. Especially for a cop. Finding someone who could make you smile or laugh at least once each day.

He told her most of it—leaving out only Michelle Paoli and the journal. He told her how the body had been found, and she grimaced and shook her head, driving the image from her mind. But she didn't stop him. He told her about Cervone, and the battle he had promised, but she only shrugged. Cervone's political games had almost gotten her killed in the last serial murder case, and she knew what he was capable of—expected nothing less from him.

The strongest reactions came when he told her about Big Bat's unexpected appearance at the medical examiner's office, then again when he described the confused, lost look on the face of Little Bat's older child. Surprisingly, she didn't react at all when he spoke about Angie Battaglia's response to his questions. He asked her about it.

"She's afraid," Adrianna said. "She's afraid of what people will think of her. And her children."

"What would they think? Even if he *was* gay, it has nothing to do with her."

"But people—some people—won't look at it that way. And she knows they won't. They'll just think she wasn't able to keep her husband sexually interested. That there was something wrong with her. So much so that he even preferred a man to her." She raised her eyebrows at the absurdity of the idea. "But they'll think it anyway, and they'll joke about it. And there will also be gossip that she might have AIDS. That her kids might be infected. She's probably terrified of that herself."

He looked down at his hands, annoyed he hadn't

thought of that himself. "We'll have the blood work back in a few days. Then we'll know."

"You should tell her when you find out," Adrianna said. "I don't think it will change the way she feels about you. But she'll want to know."

He nodded, waited for her to continue.

"What she needs is for it all to just go away," she said. "The marriage ended; now he's dead. She'll want it left at that. She won't want to be hurt any more."

"You think she's in pain?"

"Of course I do. Otherwise she wouldn't still be so angry at him. She's still in love with him, and it will probably take a long time to work through it." She lowered her eyes. "I hope she can. I hope she can come to accept the fact that it wasn't his fault either." She looked back at Devlin. "He couldn't help what he was, Paul. *If* he was. Not any more than you or I can help what we are."

Devlin nodded. "Yeah, I suppose. It would be nice if the brass could see it that way. Then maybe they wouldn't feel a need to bury it all. Somewhere deep. Like the Jurassic Period."

Adrianna offered a quiet snort, more like an exhalation of breath through her nose. "That's about as likely as the Red Sea parting again." She stared at him. "Can *you* see it that way? As a cop? As a man?"

"Yeah, I think so." She continued to stare at him. He felt his discomfort with it growing. "Don't you think I can?" he finally asked.

Adrianna shrugged. "I think you're probably threatened by homosexuality. Like most men are. Maybe more so because you're a cop."

He wanted to tell her to stop the anti-cop dialog; that he didn't need it right now. But he didn't want to fight with her. It was easier just to hear her out. "I'm not sure I understand," he said.

Adrianna leaned forward, and he could tell she

was ready—even eager—for one of the debates she loved to have. "Okay," she began. "Let's forget the everyday gay bashing—the jokes, the put-downs, whatever. Those things exist for the same reasons they exist for blacks, for Hispanics, for Jews, whomever. People simply need to feel superior to other people; other things. So they pick a minority target—a nice, easy one—that will make them feel better about themselves economically, socially, religiously . . . *sexually.*" She ended the sentence with a dismissive shrug. "But sometimes simple, self-serving prejudice turns into fear. Like people who are afraid their daughter might marry a black man, or a Jew, and in doing so somehow taint their own lives, and the lives of their family." She sat back and smiled, looking a bit like the Cheshire Cat, Devlin thought.

"With gays there's always that element of fear because it involves that mysterious, terrifyingly unavoidable drive called sex. Men—some women, but mostly men, because they're less secure about their sexuality—are real patsies for that fear." She made a tough-guy face and began moving her shoulders in a mock swagger. "They've all got that 'Hey, I've got a big dick' complex." She laughed, enjoying herself now. "Some repress it, but it's there. It's inbred from the time they were toddlers sitting on the floor playing cars and trucks." She had enhanced her performance by dropping her voice several octaves.

"Okay, okay," Devlin said. "Get on with it." He was trying not to smile at her little comedy act, but knew she could see through the effort.

"All right. Some fight it fairly successfully. But the reality is that gays truly unnerve men—even if they won't admit it, even to themselves." She raised her hands, holding off any objections. "It's not all their fault. Ever since puberty their value *as* males has been tied to their ability to perform. *'Perform with women.'*" She raised two fingers of each hand

and put imaginary quotes around the words. "It's something that just happened to them. Somewhere back around the time they got together behind somebody's garage and drooled over their first purloined copy of *Playboy*."

She giggled at the image, *really* enjoying herself now. Devlin lowered his eyes and shook his head. "Okay. When you're through having fun," he said.

"Okay. Seriously. Little girls have a similar problem, early on. Usually involving the size of their breasts. But they get over it. Most men never do. They're so tied to their sexuality that any rejection of it—or perceived rejection—is a crushing blow." She sat forward a bit. "So they've got all that baggage. Then, suddenly, they're confronted with the unimaginable prospect that somebody can be sexually attracted to a person of the same sex. It mystifies them. Challenges their strongest pubescent value. And it scares the hell out of them. What if they turned out to have '*those feelings*?' " Again the quotation marks. "What if a son or daughter did? Or, even worse, what if they fell in love with a woman, and she turned out to like other women better? The whole concept challenges their very essence, which for men, sits about eight inches below their belt buckles." She rolled her eyes. "And if they happen to be cops, the extension of that essence—their badges and their guns—is also suddenly endangered." She sat back and stared at him. "So, yes, I wonder if somewhere deep down, maybe you wouldn't like to see the whole question buried, too." She offered a sympathetic tilt of her head. "And I know that puts you in a box. Because you can't ignore it. Because maybe it's the key to the whole thing."

Delvin ignored the sympathy. Her premise had produced a big, inner squirm, and he didn't like the way it felt; needed to challenge it. "So what is Angie Battaglia feeling? Isn't it the same thing?"

"No. Anyone—man or woman—would feel rejected, devalued, in the same situation. But that's on a very personal level. For men even the hypothetical is threatening. It's a more visceral response. Women guard their sexuality, too. Some to a greater degree than others. And mostly because of religious or social pressures. That's why the anti-ERA fanatics, and the anti-feminists have been able to scare some women off. When feminists accepted lesbians as part of their cause, they opened a very scary door for some women. They made those women fearful that they'd be accused of being gay. And some women—especially those in tightly restrictive religious or social settings—became frightened that they'd have to live with prejudice they didn't deserve. Perhaps even be rejected because of it. So they backed away."

"You don't paint a very pretty picture of what I've got to deal with," Devlin said.

"No, I guess I don't." The look of sympathy returned. "And I'm afraid Big Bat may be right." She paused a moment. "God, what a nickname. It sort of personifies the whole thing. Especially if he sees himself that way." She stared at her hands a moment, thinking about it. "But he's right about the media. If they ever get hold of this gay thing . . ." She shook her head, letting the sentence die.

Devlin thought about Little Bat, about his journal, about the fears he may have lived with—the department itself, his peers, his father. He recalled how Big Bat had quoted his son's high school football coach saying he'd had "more guts than brains." He wondered if the man would ever be able to put that statement in perspective. If anyone in the department would ever understand it that way. If *you* will, he added to himself. He decided he wouldn't tell Adrianna about the journal. He would keep it to himself.

"What are you thinking about?" Adrianna asked.

"Lots of things," Devlin said. "And I'm wondering about my offer to Big Bat. About deep-sixing all the gay evidence if it turns out to be irrelevant."

"You think maybe you're subconsciously trying to protect the department?"

His decision to remove the journal came to mind. "Who knows?"

"Maybe you just want to be decent to his family. At least that's what I'd like to think."

And maybe I don't think it matters, Devlin thought. Maybe I don't think it's anybody's business who the man slept with. Except it might. It could even be the reason somebody killed him. Or, at least some part of the reason.

He leaned his head back against the sofa and stared up at the high tin ceiling. "What's funny, in a ridiculous sort of way, is that if the guy had simply been whoring around—chasing other men's wives, or whatever—we'd be all over it like holy on the pope. And nobody would have cared. But because he might have been putting his dick in less acceptable places, we're all tiptoeing around it like cats in a dog pound."

"My, you're waxing poetic tonight."

"Yeah, that's me. Poetry personified." He raised his head and turned toward her. "I think we should talk about something else," he said. "Anything else. I think I'm gay'd out."

Adrianna winked at him. "We don't have to talk at all, sailor."

Devlin raised his eyebrows, affecting shock. "Hey, did I ever tell you I have a big dick?"

She smirked at him. "No, you haven't. But then, I've seen it, haven't I?"

"We could always pretend."

"You're just like all cops," she said.

"How's that?"

"You think it's the size of the weapon that counts. What really matters is whether or not you can hit the target."

He put his hand on his chest, and grunted as
though he had just been shot.

"What the hell," Adrianna said. "Let's pretend
anyway."

Michelle Paoli moved through the gathering of elegantly attired men and women. She was dressed demurely in a simple black sheath, adorned by a single
strand of pearls. It was a failed effort not to detract
from the other women in the room. She walked with
her head erect, as she stopped to smile and speak
with individual men, thereby placing herself slightly
above her surroundings. She ignored the women entirely.

The room through which she moved was a reflection of her own elegance. It was a large drawing
room, with a small bar at one end, manned by an el-
derly Hispanic dressed in a red doublet and black
bow tie. The furnishings were antique, intending to
reflect a subtle urbanity, rather than provide comfort,
and thereby mirrored the city's better private clubs.
The lighting was subdued, and soft, classical music
played on a well-concealed stereo system.

"Ah, *Mademoiselle. Bonsoir.*"

Michelle turned as a hand gently touched her arm.
A small, silver-haired man beamed up at her. He was
well past sixty, dressed in a gray, double-breasted
suit that accented his frail body, but his blue eyes
held the gleam of a young boy's. Michelle's smile
made them even brighter.

"*Bonsoir, Monsieur Vallery. Etes-vous seul?*"

"*Non, non. Je suis avec*"—he raised his chin,
searching the room, until he found a young woman, dressed in a provocatively low-cut, yellow dress.
—"*Evetta,*" he concluded, smiling.

Michelle eyed the woman, not pleased with what
she saw.

"*Très bien,*" she said. "*J'espere que nous nous
reverrons bientôt.*"

She gave the man another smile, then moved away, her own eyes searching the room now. She spotted Leslie Boardman off in one corner, speaking with an Arab diplomat. Boardman was dressed in a fawn-colored Armani suit that emphasized his slender frame and tanned, model's face. She raised her chin, then watched as he disengaged himself and came to her.

"A problem?" he asked.

"Monsieur Vallery, from the French delegation, is being entertained by that new girl, Evetta."

Boardman seemed nonplussed. "So . . . ?"

Michelle kept a smile on her lips; her voice pleasant. "It's her clothing, dear. She's dressed like a cheap slut."

"Dear, she is a slut," Boardman said. He, too, was smiling for the benefit of their guests.

Michelle fought to keep anger from her eyes. "It's the cheap part I'm concerned about. Speak to her."

The room had begun to thin, some members of the gathering having already moved to other rooms upstairs. Paddy Rourke would be up there now, tending to his duties. She suddenly found the entire evening distasteful. Discreetly, she moved toward the doorway, in the direction of her office. She would occupy herself with other work, she told herself, and put everything else out of mind.

Chapter Five

"I want somebody inside this fucking investigation."

Mario Cervone sat behind his desk, toying with an old sap he had once carried as a street cop. He lifted the six-inch leather tube and allowed the leaded end to fall into his open palm. It hit with a dull, flat thud, and he glanced at it appreciatively, then tossed it onto a stack of papers. Saps were against regulations now, and he used his as a paperweight. And as a reminder of older, better days.

George Mitchelson shifted his lank body in the institutional visitor's chair. "I've got a man in my unit we could use. But I can't promise Devlin will take him."

It was seven A.M., early enough to keep their meeting private, and Cervone swiveled his chair so he could look down at the oddly angled streets that crisscrossed the government buildings in front of One Police Plaza. Only a scattering of people moved along the sidewalks now; the real crush wouldn't begin for more than an hour when thousands of city, state, and federal employees poured out of the subways and headed for their offices.

"Don't worry about that." He turned back, picked up a sheet of paper, and handed it to Mitchelson. "That's a list of the people Eddie Grogan requested, and that I approved. You'll notice I also authorized two unnamed transfers that Grogan didn't ask for. One from your unit, and one from Internal Affairs."

Mitchelson stared at the list, then looked back at

Cervone. "Internal Affairs?" There was something close to shock in his eyes. No one invited the department's anticorruption unit into an investigation. The "shoe-flies," as they were known, were based in an out-of-the-way building on Hudson Street, and, except for specific matters mandated by department regulations, their investigations were never encouraged. Instead, they were dreaded and avoided by senior commanders, whose careers could be threatened by their secretive probes. Few in the department even knew the identities of the men and women assigned to the unit.

"Yeah, that's the clincher," Cervone said. "That's why Devlin will take who we offer." Mitchelson still looked confused, and Cervone leaned back in his chair and grinned at him. "It will put him in a box. If he turns down a suggestion that Internal Affairs be involved, and it leaks out . . ." The grin widened. "And he knows it will. Well, then it looks like the mayor's new supercop might be planning a little cover-up. And he can't afford to let that happen."

"So he'll take anybody you offer," Mitchelson said.

"Not quite anybody. But he'll take Internal Affairs, because he doesn't have a choice. And he'll take somebody from the *very sensitive and secret* unit his victim worked for, because it would look just as suspicious if he didn't."

Mitchelson glanced at the list again. "I know most of these people. Except for this Sharon Levy and this Ramon Rivera."

"They're just like the others," Cervone said. "A pair of fucking misfits. The whole crew they picked are fucking clones of Eddie Grogan. Not a team player in the bunch."

Mitchelson knew exactly what Cervone meant—that none of the people Grogan had chosen would cooperate with the brass. They'd listen respectfully to any approach, then do a tap dance and report right back to Devlin.

"This Levy broad," Cervone continued, "the woman's a fucking dyke. Came out of the closet right after she was promoted to homicide." Cervone spoke the last line through his teeth. "I wanted to flop her straight back into the bag and stick her in a patrol car in the Bronx." He glanced down at the sap on his desk. "The chief of department almost wet his fucking pants. Said we'd have the Gay Officers Alliance League all over our backs."

Mitchelson nodded sympathetically. "And probably every fag on Christopher Street demonstrating in front of City Hall."

Cervone picked up the sap and began playing with it again. "Christ. Used to be the Irish and the Italians and the Jews had their official organizations to push their people along. Then the fucking niggers and spics had to have one, and everybody had to live with that. Now the fruits got one. Shit, ten years ago, we found a cop was taking it up the Hershey highway, we dumped his fucking ass. Or at least put him in a job so miserable, he'd quit. Today we're supposed to celebrate the fact we got faggots on the force." He shook his head. "Hell, we've even got a gay liaison officer in the chief of department's office. And we publicize the fact. What's next, a gay detectives' association? Then they wonder why civilians don't respect the job anymore." He jabbed the sap at Mitchelson. "Just wait'll they find out we had a captain who was a goddamned fruit."

"Hopefully, nobody will find out," Mitchelson said.

Cervone stared at him. "George, you better hope to hell nobody does. Or some people around here"—he waved his arm to take in the upper floors of the building—"they're gonna start asking why they didn't know. And when they start asking those questions, they start looking for somebody to blame."

Mitchelson nodded, then rearranged himself in his chair.

"Now, which guy from your unit do we shove down Devlin's throat?" Cervone asked.

"Federici," Mitchelson said without hesitation. "He's the best, and most trustworthy guy I've got. I just hope they don't box him out."

"He's a detective," Cervone snapped. "He's supposed to find out things people don't want him to know." He jabbed the sap at Mitchelson again. "You tell him to pay special attention to the work they're doing on Little Bat's computer."

Mitchelson leaned forward, lowering his voice. "My guys—the ones who found the body—they checked it before anybody got to the scene. They said it was clean."

"Yeah. And maybe it was. But this other guy on Devlin's team—the other one you didn't know—this little spic, Rivera. He's a computer whiz from administration. And, if he finds something your boys couldn't, we need to know. You tell Federici that. *Capisce?*"

Mitchelson nodded. He was beginning to look a little frightened, Cervone thought.

"Look, George, the only way we can cover everybody's ass on this is to know what the hell is coming down. We don't want any surprises. I already got that word straight from the first deputy's office, old Mac Brownell, himself."

"There won't be any," Mitchelson said. "I'll see to it."

"Good. I'm already working on it from this end." He put one finger through the loop at the end of the sap and began twirling it. A satisfied smile threatened the corners of his mouth. "I called in a chip at the D.A.'s office, and arranged to have the case assigned to somebody we can work with," he said. The smile appeared. "Remember. Evidence isn't evidence until the D.A.'s office says it is."

Dapper Dan Torelli's face turned bright red, and Buster Fucci sat back in his seat and awaited the explosion. They were in Torelli's car, headed away from his surprisingly modest home on Brooklyn's Ocean Avenue. The car was equally nondescript—a three-year-old Buick, painted banker's gray. But the car was much more than it seemed. It carried four thousand pounds of armor plate, and its bullet-proof windows could withstand anything up to a fifty-caliber machine gun. And, despite the three-piece business suits they wore on Torelli's order, the driver and bodyguard who occupied the front seat carried enough armament to hold off a company-sized military assault. Thereby both house and car followed the Mafia chief's most often repeated rules: "Don't draw no attention to yourself. And always cover your fucking ass."

"What the fuck you mean, files could still be in the computer? What is this shit? And now our guy says the stuff we got shows maybe there's other stuff we don't got? The Snake said our boy told him he got everything. So who fucking took the other stuff?" Torelli's shout filled the car, strong enough to make the heavy windows rattle.

Buster raised his hands defensively. "He did. He got all the disks Battaglia had. And the disks had all the stuff about us on them."

"Then what the fuck are you talking about?"

Buster made a helpless gesture. "Our guy says the disks are just copies of the work inside the computer. And that some of the stuff on them says maybe there were other disks, too. But he don't know for sure." He held up his hands again, begging for time to explain. "The stuff that might still be in the computer, it's just the way those fucking machines work. I don't understand it, but it's what our guy says. It wasn't nobody's fault." He pushed his palms toward Torelli, fighting off another outburst. "Look, we knew Battaglia was taking work home, and we sent the Snake in to snatch the disks so we could find out what he had on us. And to see if it would give us a handle on who was ratting us out. The Snake did all that. But he doesn't know shit from computers. He didn't know the computer might of had all the same shit stored inside. And, even if he did, he wouldn't know how to get rid of it, except maybe take a fucking ax to the thing."

"So he should of done that," Torelli snapped. His voice was slightly softer now, but his face was still purple with rage.

Buster kept his hands up. "Hey, we told him not to make a mess. Not to tip nobody that he'd been there. We didn't know Battaglia was gonna get whacked, and all his shit was gonna end up as part of a fucking murder investigation. We thought we'd have time to deal with whatever it was he had on us. Take out whoever we had to before they climbed onto a fucking witness stand. Steal the fucking evidence. Even take out Battaglia, if we had to." He leaned forward; his eyes pleaded for reason. "Look, I'm worried too. But it wasn't the Snake's fault. He did what he was told. And now at least we know what Battaglia had on us. We can go from there."

Torelli's color deepened even further. "I want that fucking computer whacked," he shouted. "You tell our boy downtown to see to it. You tell him I said it could mean his fucking ass as well as mine. What's the point of having some fuck cop in your pocket, you can't get things done. Tell him I don't give a fuck, he has to blow up the fucking building. He just does it."

Buster raised his hands again. "Okay. I'll tell him." Jesus, he thought. Now he was putting out contracts on fucking machines. "But it's dangerous.

As your underboss it's my job to tell you that. You gotta understand."

Torelli sat back and stared out the window. "Just do it," he said.

Buster nodded, then turned toward his own window. Like hell he would, he told himself. In a few days he'd tell Torelli that Devlin's office was too well guarded. He'd fucking scream, but then he'd accept it. And another crazy, fucking idea would be dead. That was the bottom line. Buster Fucci had no intention of doing anything that was fucking stupid. Especially something that might turn around and bite him on the ass.

The car was moving along a commercial section of Flatbush Avenue, headed toward the approach to the Brooklyn Bridge. The storefronts looked old and battered here, like down-at-the-heel relatives of their Manhattan cousins across the river. Torelli noted that the people walking along the sidewalks looked the same way.

"I hate this fucking place," he mumbled, his voice soft now, introspective.

"What's that?" Buster asked. He was relieved to hear the change in tone, the change of subject.

"Brooklyn. Fucking Brooklyn. It reminds of growing up here with holes in my fucking shoes."

"There ain't no holes there now," Buster said.

Torelli turned toward him. His eyes were suddenly feral again. "And there ain't never gonna be," he said. "Even if it means we gotta pile the bodies knee-deep all around us."

Buster nodded, then turned and looked out his own window again. Brooklyn didn't look that bad to him. In fact, it was looking better to him each day. He understood what that meant. And he also understood there wasn't a fucking thing he could do about it. He wasn't sure which part of that personal message scared him the most.

Devlin pointed at the gibberish on the computer screen. The characters stared back at him like some ancient message carved into a Mayan temple:

$$\text{⚑☜⍓☟&} \quad ◆⬜ \quad ◆☝⬜⍓ \quad ⬧◆⬜⬜⍓♏ \quad ⌘■ \quad ⬧☝⌖⍓◆☒$$

$$\triangle⍓⬜⬜◆⌘◆ \quad ♫⬜☒☝♐ \quad ☝●⬜■⍓⅄ \quad ◆⌘◆≈ \quad ■☝⬟⍓◆☐ \quad ⬧☝◆⍓◆$$

$$☝■⬜ \quad ⬜●☝⍓♍◆ \quad ●⌘◆◆⍓⬜ \quad ♫⍓●⬜◆⍫$$

"You mean those are words?" he said.

Ramon Rivera sat before the terminal with an elf-ish grin on his twenty-eight-year-old face. He was a small man—no more than five-six—and rail slender. His large brown eyes and black curly hair, together with his size, made him look like a teenager, and the constant smile affixed to his handsome features marked him as one who could not stay out of trouble.

"It's called 'Wingdings,'" Rivera said. "It's a computer font that assigns symbols to letters in the alphabet."

"So it's a language?" Devlin asked. There was a hint of excitement in his voice.

"Just like any other," Rivera said. He swiveled his chair and grinned up at Devlin. "He was using it to hide information, and he was being really cool about it."

"How so?" Eddie Grogan asked. He was standing next to Devlin, both men ogling the incomprehensible computer screen in bewilderment.

"He had this set up under the games window on his program manager screen. It was tricky getting it there, but he did it." Rivera inclined his head in admiration of a fellow computer expert, then caught the lack of understanding on the faces of his two new bosses.

"The games window is the place where computer games are stored—chess, solitaire, space invaders, stuff like that. High-tech toys for kids and adults. Battaglia must have put this there so anyone searching his program files would think it was something his kids were playing with, and just pass it by without paying much attention. He was cool. He had it right out in the open, but made it look like something else. But his whole setup was cool. He was a very cautious man."

"How do you mean?" Devlin asked.

"Well, you got this terminal set up just like it was in his apartment, right?"

"Right," Devlin said.

Rivera pointed at the system. "He had backups everywhere, man. The whole system was one failsafe after another." He pointed to a small, rectangular box on the floor. "That's an uninterrupted power source," he said. "If the power goes, that thing kicks in and operates the computer on batteries for up to twenty minutes. It gives you time to shut the system down. Otherwise a power failure would wipe out everything on your hard drive. All the files. All the programs. Everything. You'd end up with zilch—a piece of worthless metal that couldn't do shit until you reinstalled all your stuff.

"Then, according to the log he kept, he backed up all his files on computer disks, so if anything was lost through a program error, he could still reinstall it from them." He pointed to an empty slot on the front of Little Bat's machine. "On top of that he had a tape backup system that automatically copied all his files and programs, so if the disks were lost, or if somebody swiped them—as they obviously did—or if anybody accidentally, or intentionally erased his stuff, he could reinstall it all from the tape in one, quick, easy operation." Rivera's grin widened. "Shit, the whole system reminds me of this broad I knew in my old neighborhood. She loved to fuck, and she was on the fucking pill. But every time she decided to do it, she used a diaphragm, too. *And* she insisted the guy use a condom. The woman was a fucking fortress against sperm."

Grogan waved his hand, dismissing the sexual anecdote. "But the disks *were* stolen, and I don't see any fucking tape. So where the hell is all this backup supposed to be?"

Rivera turned his chair back to the terminal and tapped a finger against the screen. "Right here in the Wingdings," he said. He began running his finger under each block of symbols, reading them as one would a different language.

"Backup tape stored in safety deposit box, along with code key to names, dates and places listed below." He spun his chair around, still grinning. "Under that there's a list of names in code, with dates and locations next to them. There's also a final message that says: 'I knew a good cop would find this.' " Rivera tapped a finger to his chest and offered a quick bow. Then he inclined his head back toward the screen. "Then it says: 'I just hope it's the right cop.' "

"You read that shit like it was English," Grogan said.

Rivera stared at him, clearly offended by the remark. "Hey, man, computers are my thing. Besides, I dig Wingdings."

"You are a fucking wingding," Grogan said.

"Hold on," Devlin said. "You can translate the whole thing, right?"

"I can do better than that," Rivera said. "I can change the font and print it all out in English."

"Do it," Devlin ordered.

Rivera turned back to the screen and rapidly tapped out a series of commands. The laser printer came to life, and began spitting out sheets of paper. Devlin picked them up, one sheet at a time, and began reading with Eddie Grogan looking on over his shoulder.

"Shit," Grogan said. "It doesn't tell us where the

safety deposit box is, or under whose name. Or who's got the fucking key."

"Just another safeguard," Rivera chirped. "He expected you to find it, and get a subpoena to open it when you did. With or without a key. I'm telling you, the man was a fucking fortress."

Devlin picked up the remaining sheets and began reading the coded list. "Cop one, April third, Money Club." He glanced at Grogan.

Eddie inclined his chin toward the list. "The Judge," he read. "With Lolita. May seventh, Money Club."

Devlin picked up the next item. "The Politician, June seventeenth, 123 Restaurant, with Bagman."

"Sounds like we're talking about a fucking pad, here," Grogan said. "You think that's why he started keeping the work at home? He knew he couldn't trust his office?"

"Smells that way," Devlin said. "But let's not forget it's in code. And that the man liked to make things appear as though they were something they really weren't."

"A fucking fortress," Rivera said.

Devlin glanced down at the short Hispanic cop, whom they had seconded from the chief of administration's office. "I want you to keep at this thing," he said. "Find anything else he may have hidden in there. Especially anything that will give us a clue about the location of the safety deposit box." He turned to Grogan. "And let's get two of our people checking banks. Given the way this guy played things, I doubt the box was rented in his name. But we'll check. All five boroughs, Nassau, Suffolk, and Westchester counties."

Grogan let out a breath.

"I know," Devlin said. "Too many banks, too little time. But after we finish those, we'll start on Jersey, then Connecticut, if we have to. And, as we start coming up with the names of Battaglia's friends and associates, we'll run their names, too."

"Ugh," Grogan said. "I'll give it to Cunningham and Samuels. They're fucking moles. They love that shit."

"Tell them they hit, I'll buy them the best dinner they ever had," Devlin said.

"What about me? For this magnificent work I just did?" Rivera griped.

"What, you want a fucking taco?" Grogan snapped.

Rivera ignored the slur and inclined his head toward the outer office where the other members of the new team had gathered. His eyes had latched on to Sharon Levy, a tall, striking redhead. She was seated on the edge of a desk with one shapely leg crossed over the other. "Just give me an introduction to *her*," Rivera said.

Grogan glanced at Levy, then turned back to Rivera. "She's almost six-feet fucking tall," he said. "She ever rolled over in bed, she'd crush you like a fucking bug."

"I like big women," Rivera said. "I like their big, long legs—"

Grogan cut him off. "Never mind. You wouldn't like this one. And she wouldn't like you. The woman's gay," he added. Grogan watched the look of surprise, then horror on Rivera's face. "It ain't no secret," Grogan said. "She's very up-front about it."

Rivera's face suddenly returned to its ever-present grin. "That's only because she ain't had me," he said. "I can fucking cure her, man. Fucking guaranteed. Shit, they don't call me 'Boom Boom,' for nothin'."

Devlin turned away to hide a smile, then turned back to face the man. "Well, look, *Boom Boom.* You just romance that computer, and get into its knickers first."

"Yeah," Grogan added. "And after you get everything you can out of it, then I'll tell Sharon what you wanna do to her body. But I'll wait, 'cause you ain't gonna be no good to us after she kicks the living shit outta you."

Rivera's grin widened. "Man, the lady's gonna take one look at what I got to offer, she's gonna forget all about any women she's been humping."

Devlin jabbed a finger at the computer terminal. "Hump that," he said. "With all your inimitable charm and skill. And what you just gave us?" Devlin held up the computer printout. "This stays with just the three of us. Got it?"

Rivera let out a weary breath. "Yes, sir," he said. "But that other thing. I gotta tell you, that's a fucking shame, man. You are denying that lady the chance of a lifetime."

"Yeah, I know," Devlin said. "I hope she forgives me someday."

"She won't, man. She *definitely* won't."

Devlin led Grogan back to his office and flopped down behind his desk. He spread the printout across the already cluttered surface and stared at it for a moment. "You tell Cunningham and Samuels to keep what they're doing close to the vest, too," he said at length.

"You worried about our two new friends?" Grogan inclined his head toward the outer office. "Internal Affairs and Organized Crime?"

Devlin stared through the glass panel in his door. New desks and file cabinets had been moved into the area overnight to accommodate his hastily assembled staff. The room looked chaotic and makeshift, and those who hadn't been given overnight assignments were busy trying to settle themselves in. He had a ten-member squad now, Devlin thought. Not including Eddie and himself. Two more than he had asked for thanks to the byzantine mind of Mario

Cervone. It was a no-win trap that he couldn't avoid.
But he could play within it.

"So how you gonna deal with that pair—Federici
and Jones?" Grogan asked.

Devlin spun his chair around and stared out the
window. Outside a steady rain was beating the city
into submission, slowing traffic into angry, horn-
blaring knots, and sending up clouds of steam from
the July-baked pavement. All across the city now,
salespeople would have inexplicably appeared on
street corners, selling cheap umbrellas for five bucks
a pop. The umbrella people seemed to materialize
out of nowhere. Devlin had always envisioned them
living in underground caves and miraculously
emerging when the first raindrops hit the sidewalks.
He spun back to face Eddie.

"I'm going to assign them to each other," he said.
"Internal Affairs and Organized Crime. They just
seem to go together." He smiled at the older detective. "Then I'm gonna take each of them aside and
suggest the other one can't be trusted—that he's
been pushed down my throat and has to be watched.
Federici won't buy it, but Jones will."

Grogan grinned in appreciation. "Yeah, that'll get
the shoe-fly's blood up for sure. He'll have his nose
up Federici's ass like a mutt in heat." He paused.
"And you're right. Federici will catch on, because
he knows the game that's being played. But there
won't be fuck-all he can do about it. He's the one
you're really worried about, right?"

"You got it," Devlin said. "Jones was just a Tro-
jan horse—to make sure I couldn't turn Federici
down. Cervone knows the bosses can squash anything Jones comes up with that they don't want
made public. Shit, they've been hiding corruption
for so long they're masters at it. The old 'Blue Wall
of Silence' doesn't have many holes in it." He
picked up a pen and tapped the printouts on his
desk. "I want you to very quietly let the others know

that Jones and Federici are to be kept out of the loop on anything we develop. They'll understand. They've all been around long enough to know how the game is played. And I'll make sure the dynamic duo is out doing something else any time we hold a general briefing. You can brief them later on anything we *want* them to know." Devlin stopped tapping and raised the pen in front of his face. "One other thing. I want an extra uniform assigned to night duty here. To watch the place when everybody's out working."

"You don't trust the one we already got?" Grogan asked.

"It's just harder to reach two guys than it is to reach one," Devlin said. "One more thing. I want you to work with Sharon Levy, whenever you're not working with me. Did you pick her because she was gay?"

"Yeah, that was part of it," Grogan said. "I thought it might help. But she also happens to be one helluva homicide dick. She's a fucking pit bull when she gets her teeth into something. You worried about her being gay?"

"Not at all," Devlin said. "I think it was a good pick. We need somebody who knows that scene. I just don't want her hassled in any way that might make her hold back. And I don't want us spending too much time on this gay thing. You make sure *everybody* understands that."

Grogan raised his eyebrows.

"No, the bosses haven't gotten to me," Devlin said. "We're gonna push that part of it as much as it needs to be pushed. I just don't want our guys concentrating on it so much, they miss other stuff that's staring them in the puss. Tell them to treat it the same way they would any other case that had a sex angle. A heterosexual sex angle." He tossed the pen on to the desk. "Our shooter may have had an entirely different reason for offing Battaglia. And, just maybe, at the same time he knew he was gay, and had a hard-on for people who are. Get it?"

Grogan nodded. "Or maybe he just wanted to point us in that direction."

"Right. Just make sure everybody understands that."

Grogan nodded. "I'll make sure Federici hears it, too. It'll get the word back to the wizards in the Puzzle Palace, and maybe take some of the heat off us. You think Cervone's got any more curve balls coming our way?"

"He's already thrown one," Devlin said.

Grogan raised his eyebrows again.

"The assistant D.A. who's been assigned to the case, is Jenny Miller."

"Never heard of her," Grogan said.

"Neither has anybody else. I made some calls this morning, when I heard about it. She's new and she's nervous. First time in their homicide division. Up to now she's handled mostly shit work. Arraignments, traffic, all the crud nobody wants. The only experience she's had on murder cases is making court appearances for other assistants when somebody was copping a simple plea that had already been worked out."

"Jesus," Grogan said. "Ripe for plucking."

"Yeah. I'll bet Cervone has already invited her out to dinner." He grinned. "But I'm meeting her for lunch this afternoon. Right after I see another bozo lawyer."

"This guy, O'Brien? The one at Battaglia's house last night?"

Devlin nodded. "He avoided me like the plague. And I want to know why. I've never known a lawyer who could keep his nose out of anything that smelled like a courtroom."

"Or a hospital," Grogan added. "You got anything else for me?"

"Did the canvass on Battaglia's building turn anything up?"

"Naw. Nobody saw nothin'. There's an old broad, named Miriam Goldstein, they haven't been able to reach. Seems she's away, and was probably away when it happened."

"Have somebody keep checking back on her, just in case. And send Sharon Levy in. I want her to do a fast check on any health clubs Battaglia might have belonged to. There was that gym bag in the backseat of his car. And I want to know if he had any special friends there. Gay friends. Then I want her to look through his stuff; see if he went to any other places that are popular with gays. Places we might not recognize."

"You got it," Grogan said. He glanced back over his shoulder as he headed for the door. "I hope she ain't gonna take *me* to those joints," he added.

"You'll love 'em, Eddie. It'll broaden your horizons."

"My horizons are as broad as I need 'em," Grogan said. "Besides, shit-shooters make me nervous."

"No disrespect, sir. But I don't wanna be the house fruit inspector."

Sharon Levy sat with her legs majestically crossed. Her strong nasal twang identified her as working-class Queens; something Devlin would have recognized even without the benefit of her personnel jacket. Everything else about her said "Manhattan." From her well-tailored suit, to her coifed hair, to her subtle use of makeup, she was a class act.

"You can drop the 'sir,' " Devlin said. "And fruit inspector isn't what I have in mind." He leaned forward and stared the woman down. She was ready for a fight he had no intention of offering. "Look, you're the only gay cop I've got in the squad—at least the only one I know about—and I intend to use every resource available. Okay?"

A small smile flickered, then faded from Levy's mouth. It wasn't because she knew other gay cops in the squad, Devlin decided, but simple satisfaction that he had acknowledged it was possible.

"I just wanted to be up-front . . ." She paused, consciously deleting the "sir." "I'm a good detective, and I just want a chance to show it."

Devlin leaned back in his chair, the confrontation over. "You wouldn't be here if you weren't." He grinned at the woman. "And don't worry. I'll work your buns off. And, if I don't, Eddie Grogan will."

The smile returned to Levy's face and remained, the combination of Devlin's own smile and his words finally putting her at ease. She was a striking woman, with vivid red hair, emerald green eyes, and a wide, sensuous mouth. Her other features were soft—not beautiful—but clearly attractive, and younger than her thirty years. She was tall, easily five-ten, maybe more; large-boned, yet slender, and Devlin thought she would have made him look twice upon entering a room.

"Are we sure Captain Battaglia was gay?" she asked, all business now.

"I'm not sure of anything," Devlin said. He hesitated, thinking about Little Bat's journal and tried to decide if he wanted to discuss that yet. He decided against it. "Outside of how he was found, there's nothing definitive." He sat forward. "I want this case handled like any other homicide that has sexual undertones. Nothing more, nothing less. I want the possibility of a gay lover checked thoroughly. But if you get something that points in another direction, you jump on it and run it into the ground. I'll give you a lot of slack, unless I think you're off in outer space."

"I get the feeling you think this gay thing could be a red herring," Levy said.

"What I think is that the shooter pointed us in that direction. And that makes me nervous," Devlin said. "I also think the bosses at the Puzzle Palace want us to avoid the whole issue; just stick our heads in the sand. So, whether he was—and more importantly, if it means anything—I just don't know. But we're gonna look at it." He tapped a finger against his wristwatch. "Right now, all I want is to get this guy fast. Before the political shit gets any deeper."

"I'll start with the health clubs," Levy said. "And I'll look for any close relationships. Male or female."

Devlin nodded. "You'll be teamed up with Eddie, when he's not working with me." He grinned again. "If the case does take you into any gay bars, or bathhouses, be gentle with him. Those places make him nervous."

"They make me nervous, too," Levy said.

Devlin watched the woman rise from her chair. She moved like a large, graceful animal. "One other thing," he said, "be prepared for Rivera. I think he has designs on your body."

"Yeah, I know," Levy said. "The little bastard's been leering at me from behind his computer terminal." She smiled at the idea. It was obviously not the first time she had dealt with the situation.

She started for the door, then threw a final line over her shoulder. "He puts his hands on me, I'll make him a fucking soprano."

Devlin fought back another smile. He felt a sudden sympathy for Boom Boom. His machismo appeared headed toward some minor devastation.

Chapter Six

I don't know what Angie has told my father.
What's worse I'm afraid to ask. She's liable to
say anything. She tells me anything, just to see
me squirm. So why not him? She's the only one
who really knows how much his disapproval ter-
rifies me. But would she do it? Hurt him just to
get at me? And does it really matter? Things are
coming to a head. Soon I'll have to deal with
him. Talk to him about it all. I won't have any
choice. Then everything will come out. The hurt,
the rage. And, if he knows anything about my
life, that will come out then, too. So now I have
to wonder—if it comes to that—if he'll see it as
a point of vulnerability. Of course he will. He
won't be able to help himself. But would he try to
use it? God, I hope not. He can't win that way.
Not the way he has in the past. Not this time.

So it doesn't matter whether he knows or not.
But I still want to find out. I want that small
edge. Just in case I need it. And I can get it. I
can ask Jim what my father knows. Except for
Angie, he's the only other person I can ask.
He's the only one my father would have gone
to. And, Christ, if anyone should understand,
it's Jim. But can I still trust him? God, if I can't
there's no one. No one at all.

Devlin closed the journal and sat back for a moment. Then he got up slowly, took his coat and hat

from a clothes tree in the corner, and headed for the door.

Jim O'Brien's law office was in the Woolworth Building, diagonally across City Hall Park from Police Headquarters, and four blocks south of Devlin's own building. Devlin cut into the park to get what shelter he could from the overhanging branches. The rain was still beating down, and the temperature had dropped. Gusts of wind came off the East River, pinning scraps of sodden paper, and other debris against the trunks of the sickly looking trees. He was wearing the overly long trench coat and the wide-brimmed hat that Adrianna always laughed at. She insisted it made him look like an out-of-work Indiana Jones. But he liked his rain outfit. It was less cumbersome than an umbrella. It kept his head dry. And more important, it left his hands free. Only British cops—at least in books—carried umbrellas. But the Brits seldom carried guns, or needed them.

Despite the rain, a homeless old harridan sat on one of the park's benches, her legs spread wide, a sodden sheet of newspaper covering her head. There was a greasy bag tucked under her splayed legs, and she had placed another piece of newspaper across her lap to protect its contents.

"You got any change, Mack?" the woman hissed as Devlin reached her.

He stopped, dug a hand into his pocket, and withdrew some folded currency. He peeled off a dollar bill and handed it over.

The woman sneered at him. "Hey, a big, fucking spender," she hissed. "What are you? A goddamned social worker?"

"A cop," Devlin said.

The woman let out a loud snort. "Then you probably stole the fucking money, anyway."

Devlin winked at her and moved on. After a

dozen more steps, he stopped, dropped into a crouch, and affected tying his shoe. The brief visit with the bag lady had let him pick up the tail twenty yards behind. The man wasn't very good at it. He was dressed in a blue pea coat and watch cap, and each time Devlin had stopped, he had pulled up and quickly turned away. As discreetly as possible, Devlin slipped his revolver from its holster and into the pocket of his trench coat.

Picking up his pace, he moved rapidly to the southern tip of the small, triangular-shaped park—a man trying to outrun the rain—then darted through a break in traffic on Broadway, and jogged diagonally across to the intersection at Barclay. Out of the corner of his eye he could see Pea Coat break into a trot, struggling to keep up. When he reached the sidewalk, the man was only five yards behind.

Devlin slowed at the intersection, then abruptly spun around and took two quick steps back toward the street. Pea Coat almost ran into him. Devlin's left hand shot out and grabbed him by the throat.

"Freeze, motherfucker. There's a thirty-eight pointed at your belly."

Pea Coat's eyes darted to the bulge in Devlin's coat pocket, where his right hand was. Then he looked back into Devlin's face with a sick grin.

"What is this? A fucking stickup?"

Pea Coat was medium height, maybe five-ten, but built like a young bull. He had a flat, street fighter's nose, thick lips, and dark eyes that showed no sign of fear. His five o'clock shadow was already at work at eleven A.M.

Devlin jerked him toward the side of the Woolworth Building, laid his revolver against his back, and kicked his legs apart.

"Assume the position, asshole." A quick pat down found nothing but hard bulging muscle. Pea Coat started to push himself from the wall, but Devlin forced him back. "Stay there. You move when I *tell* you to fucking move."

There was a squeal of brakes behind him, and Devlin glanced back at the blue-and-white patrol car that had pulled to the curb. He yanked his gold, inspector's shield from his pocket and held it up for the two uniforms to see. "On the job," he called back.

"Hey, what is this shit?" Pea Coat growled.

"Show me some I.D., and do it slow."

Carefully, Pea Coat pulled his wallet from a rear pocket and handed it back to Devlin. The two uniforms had moved up beside him.

"What is it, sir?" one asked.

"I need you to take . . ." He paused and glanced at Pea Coat's driver's license. "Mr. Vincent Maribucci here, down to the precinct and hold him. Devlin handed the wallet to one of the cops, then pulled a business card from his jacket pocket. "Then call Detective Grogan at this number, and tell him I want him to come down and have a little conversation with Mr. Maribucci."

"Hey, fuck that shit," Pea Coat snarled. "What's the fuckin' charge?"

"Following a police officer, dressing like a mope, and being a general asshole," Devlin snapped. He glanced back at one of the cops. "Cuff him," he ordered.

"Fuck you, Devlin," Pea Coat snapped back. "Nobody was fuckin' followin' nobody. I was on my way to my fuckin' barber."

"Yeah, jerk. And you just guessed my name, right?"

Pea Coat hesitated a moment. "Hey, you're a famous fuckin' cop. What can I say?"

One of the uniforms had just finished cuffing Maribucci's hands behind his back. "Take him in," Devlin said. "And tell your sergeant I'll be there in about an hour. Keep him away from everybody except Grogan."

"I wanna call my fuckin' lawyer," Pea Coat growled.

"Sorry, Mr. Maribucci. All the phones are out. Terrible storm." Devlin grinned at the man as he was hustled toward the patrol car. Then he adjusted his hat and headed toward the entrance of the Woolworth Building. Indiana Jones, my ass, he told himself.

Devlin entered the lobby and found himself—as he always did—overwhelmed by its elegance. Completed in 1913, the once "tallest building in the world" had set the tone in its theatricality for the great skyscrapers of the 1920s and 30s. The style was pure Gothic, the lobby evoking the feel of a medieval church, the central axis a massive nave with elevator banks replacing side chapels, the marble walls, allegorical murals, and mosaic ceiling set off by crockets and tracery unabashedly stolen from the great ecclesiastical buildings of medieval Europe. It was lost splendor, no longer affordable in contemporary buildings here, or in any other place in the world.

Jim O'Brien's office was on the seventeenth floor, overlooking the park and the East River. The reception area was masculinity personified—complete with leather furniture, hunting prints, and a receptionist who offered a gratifying visual diversion for waiting clients.

Since his visit was unannounced, Devlin had expected to wait, and was surprised when O'Brien agreed to see him immediately. An equally attractive secretary came out, collected him, and needlessly explained that "Mr. O'Brien's eleven o'clock canceled."

O'Brien was standing behind an oversized, antique desk when Devlin entered. The office continued the hunting-print/leather-furniture motif, then one-upped it with a stuffed Bengal tiger rug laid over a wall-to-wall red carpet. Devlin wondered how O'Brien had overlooked the obligatory mounted sailfish. It was all that was needed to complete the he-man image.

"Have a seat," O'Brien said, gesturing toward an overstuffed leather club chair. "I was sorry I didn't have a chance to speak with you yesterday. But it was a difficult time. How is the case going?"

Devlin took the offered chair, sunk into the plush leather, and ignored the question. O'Brien was running a bit at the mouth. It could be nerves. If it was, Devlin wanted to keep them on edge.

O'Brien was at least six-two, with a lean, strong body. It was obvious he worked at keeping the fat away. He had thinning blond hair, blue eyes, and a meticulously trimmed mustache. The only flaws in his otherwise handsome face were the capillary bursts on his cheeks, marking him as someone who enjoyed his before, during, and after dinner drinks a bit too much. His clothes, like the office, shouted money—pinstripes, fitted silk shirt, a ninety-dollar foulard necktie—but the jacket was now hanging from a coat tree, and the cuffs of his shirt were turned up, adding to the *just one of the guys,* he-man persona. Devlin instinctively disliked the man. But that, he decided, could simply be his natural distaste for lawyers.

"I understand you and Little Bat were roommates at Columbia," Devlin began.

"Let's call him Joe," O'Brien suggested. "He hated the name, Little Bat."

Devlin stared at the man, forcing more.

"He grew up with it," O'Brien explained. "It put him in his father's shadow and never let him climb out."

"How did he and his father get along?"

O'Brien shrugged. "Hard question. I think he

loved his dad. I mean, really loved him. Respected him. *And* was scared to death of him."

"Why scared?"

"Usual reason. Afraid he'd never measure up. The senator throws a big shadow."

Devlin crossed one leg over the other and studied the tip of his shoe. "I noticed the name on the door when I came in. O'Brien & O'Brien. Father? Brother?"

"Father," O'Brien said. "He started the firm. He's retired now, but he's still a partner, even though the practice has changed since his day. Now we do a lot of corporate work—for clients who are fighting their way through the federal bureaucracy. But my associates and I still carry on with the children of my dad's original clientele." He smiled. "My father makes sure of that. We do tax work, trusts, that sort of thing. Wealthy clients. Some northshore WASP, a lot of lace curtain Irish." He smiled at the latter term, then added: "Those with enough money to raise lace curtain to the tenth power."

He didn't explain the smile. He didn't have to. Devlin had been raised shanty Irish, and had once asked his father the difference between the two classes of Irishmen. The old man had snorted. "There's only one small difference," he had said. "*Lace curtain* never fart in the presence of clergy."

"So you and Joe had a lot in common. With your fathers, I mean."

O'Brien sat back in his red leather, executive chair and smiled. "Very perceptive, Inspector." He toyed nervously with the end of his necktie. It was a schoolboy gesture—a kid in the headmaster's office, awaiting the ax. "Yeah, we had that. Some other things, too." He paused, then leaned forward. "But we also had a different perspective of *his* father. You see, you might say I work for the senator. I managed his last reelection campaign, and I intend to do it again in two years." The line of his jaw hardened. A bit defensively, Devlin thought. "I happen to think Anthony Battaglia is one helluva U.S. senator." He hesitated again, then smiled. "And his continued success hasn't worked out badly for me." He shrugged. "It's put me on the party's national committee. And that's brought this firm some of the corporate clients I mentioned earlier."

Devlin digested the information. "So Joe didn't confide much."

"About his father?" O'Brien shook his head. "Not in the past few years."

"Were your wives friendly? Did you socialize much?"

"I'm not married." O'Brien waved his hand, taking in his successful surroundings. "This is wife and mistress all rolled into one. You see, Joe and I were different in other ways, too." He clasped his hands in front of him. "I don't love my father. I hate the old sonofabitch. I just live in his shadow, and fight every day to prove I'm better at all this than he ever hoped to be." The smile returned, then disappeared. "I think Joe tried that for a time, but gave it up. I'm not sure why. Maybe he just loved Big Bat too much to compete. Or maybe he realized the gap between them was too great, too insurmountable."

Devlin sat forward and clasped his own hands, imitating O'Brien's gesture of intimacy. "Maybe there was another reason. One you'd understand." He stared at the man. "When did you first realize Joe Battaglia was gay?" he asked.

The question hit O'Brien like a soft slap in the face. He blinked several times, then sat back and began worrying his necktie again. "You think I'd understand that?"

"Yes, I do."

"You been investigating me, Inspector?"

Devlin didn't answer. He just continued to stare at the man.

"What you're really asking is if we confided in each other. About being gay."

Devlin nodded. "Yeah, that's what I'm asking."

O'Brien drew a deep breath; sat forward again. "Okay," he began, "I'll level with you. Not because I want to, but because I want the rotten bastard who murdered one of the most decent men I've ever known." He tried to smile, shook his head, then looked back at Devlin. Tears seemed to be somewhere behind his eyes. Or maybe it was just an act. "Hell, I loved the man," O'Brien continued. "And, no. Not in *that* way. I don't know if Joe ever *had* a lover." He began playing with an expensive fountain pen on his desk, keeping his eyes fixed on it. "Joe was the first person *I* ever told. Oh, I told my father later. He treated me like some piece of shit. Insisted I get psychiatric help, and then threatened to bounce me out of the firm if I ever told anyone else my *dirty little secret*."

"Why'd you pick Joe to tell?"

"You mean did I suspect he'd be sympathetic?"

Devlin nodded.

"Yeah, I suspected. And I also knew I could trust him. We grew up together. Played football together in high school, then in college. We were like brothers back then." He stopped, took in Devlin's stare, then smiled. "I know what you're thinking. Two fags on the same football team." His own stare hardened. "But we're everywhere, Inspector. We're like the commies the rednecks used to see under everyone's bed." He tossed the pen aside, and clasped his hands again. "There are usually about seventy guys on a varsity football team. So if you take the accepted average of gays to straights—about one out of ten—then I figure there were at least six more of us slapping asses and hugging each other before and after every game." He continued to stare Devlin down. Pure defiance. "Five, if Joe was one, too."

"You say *if*. You're not sure?"

"I know he was struggling with the fear. I don't
know if he ever found out."

"The fear?"

"You bet your ass, the fear." He stood and began
pacing toward one wall, then back. "You're a kid,
when you first start to wonder. Suddenly you're getting these feelings about other guys that you *know*
you're not supposed to have. Hell, you've been
taught that all your life. In every subtle way possible. And, sure as hell, from your peers. Hell, the ju-
venile fag jokes alone tell you that." He raised his
arms in a helpless gesture. "But there they are. Your
feelings. And they scare the living shit out of you."
He turned and began staring at Devlin again. "And
you sure as hell don't want anyone else to know."
He returned to his chair and slumped back into it.
"So you finally get up the guts to tell somebody.
Somebody you think you can trust, and you pray to
God he won't spit in your face."

Like your father did, Devlin thought. "So you and
Joe confessed your concerns to each other. In college?"

"Yeah. In college."

"But Joe wasn't sure."

"No, he said he wasn't. He was just scared."

"But you were sure about him."

O'Brien shrugged, sighed. "Let's just say I felt if
you had those feelings they were there for a reason.
Then Joe joined the cops, got married, and had kids.
For a time I wondered about it. I thought: Maybe he
was just trying to be kind, trying not to hurt my feelings. He was like that."

"What about after he left his wife? He didn't talk
about the reasons?"

O'Brien shook his head. "When gays come
out—or at least try to live a life that doesn't contra-
dict who they are—it's not uncommon for them to
back away from friends in their former life. It's just
safer for them if they do."

"And that's what Joe did?"

"We saw each other. But we didn't talk about those things. I recommended a good divorce lawyer when I heard he had left. But he just used his wife's attorney. Waved the white flag. Guilt does that to some people."

"So you never knew. Not for sure."

O'Brien laughed. It was a coarse, brittle sound that contradicted everything else about the man. "I knew, but I didn't. Okay?"

"Did the senator suspect?"

A helpless shrug. "I have no idea."

Devlin digested the information, then switched tack again. "Did he ever mention a woman named Michelle Paoli? Or something called the Money Club?"

O'Brien stiffened, almost imperceptibly. If Devlin hadn't been staring at him, he would have missed it. O'Brien shook his head. "Never. Not that I recall, anyway."

"You're sure?"

"Positive."

"You have any idea who might have killed him? Did he ever express any fears about anyone in particular?"

"Joe wasn't afraid of any living being." O'Brien was back in control now. He stared at his desk momentarily, then back at Devlin. His eyes had become hard. "And if I knew who killed him—if I was sure—you wouldn't have to worry about finding the sonofabitch."

Devlin nodded. He wondered about that last part. He believed most of O'Brien's story. As much as he could allow himself to believe anyone, or anything. But first he had to find out why O'Brien was lying about Michelle Paoli and the Money Club. And maybe about what, if anything, Big Bat had known about his son. He stood. "I may be back to talk to you again," he said.

O'Brien nodded. "Look, what I told you. I hope it doesn't have to find its way into any public record like an official report."

"You didn't tell me anything that needs to be reported," Devlin said.

O'Brien's body seemed to sag imperceptibly. "Thanks," he said.

The First Precinct, one of the city's oldest, is located near the exit of the Holland Tunnel, and the constant flow of tractor trailers rattle the windows and shroud the building in a thick, blue haze of exhaust fumes. The interior isn't much better. Like most precinct houses, it looks battered and beaten, its decor and upkeep best described as nouveau squalid. But the men who work there don't seem to mind. As a post it is one of the city's safer precincts. Here, they claim, more cops die from carbon monoxide than from bullet wounds.

Devlin wondered about that bit of precinct humor as he sucked in a breath of fetid air. Vincent Maribucci was in a shabby, third-floor interrogation room. He had endured the air, along with a half hour of Eddie Grogan's browbeating and looked no worse. At present he was picking his nose, holding up his finger, and studying the rewards of his search.

Devlin watched him through a two-way mirror, shook his head in disgust, then turned to Grogan. "So what did you find out?"

"From Mr. Suave? Not a fucking thing," Grogan said. "From his rap sheet? All we have to know." He handed Devlin a computer printout, then waited while he read it.

"Officially, he's a member of the longshoremen's union. But the only dock that hump ever saw is one he threw somebody off of. Unofficially, he's a fucking leg breaker for Peter 'the Bunny' Rabitto."

"Capo in the Torelli family, right?"

Grogan nodded. "Supposed to run Torelli's porno

operation. Strip clubs—gay and straight—movies, sex stores, massage parlors, you name it. The asshole fancies himself a film director. Goes around wearing a fucking ascot and sunglasses. Anyway, our nose picker in there, he's just muscle. Gets sent around if somebody ain't doin' what he's supposed to. Like sending in the loot on time." Grogan glanced through the two-way mirror. Maribucci was holding up his finger again, studying it intently. "Ooo," Grogan said. "Looks like he found a keeper."

Devlin fought to keep a straight face. "Rabitto reports directly to Torelli?" he asked.

"No. Supposedly he goes through Buster Fucci, Torelli's underboss. But it's the same thing. Our OCC reports claim that Rabitto runs a little film operation for the family. All porno stuff, or course. They also claim that Torelli thinks the bunny rabbit likes little boys. Calls him Bunny the Fag. Doesn't like to deal with him directly." Grogan shrugged. "Whether he is—or if it's because of some of the gay flicks he makes, I dunno."

"But he lets him work for the family," Devlin said.

"Hey, all Torelli cares about is how much scratch comes into the kitty. And he's the kitty. Which, if you think about it, makes the Mafia a more socially conscious employer than the fucking U.S. Army."

Devlin glanced in at Maribucci again. "You let him call his lawyer?"

"Yeah. Guess who?"

"Larry Matz."

"You got it. Torelli's own personal shyster. Supposed to be on his way down right now."

"Cut Maribucci loose," Devlin said. "And tell the desk sergeant to give Matz the runaround when he gets here. Keep him cooling his heels as long as possible. Then call for some backup. You and I are gonna pay Dapper Dan a visit at his clubhouse."

Grogan glanced at his watch. "I thought you were breaking bread with our new assistant D.A."

"I'll call her and set something up for later. Right now I feel like eating Italian."

Sharon Levy watched the man sweat. She was not the only one watching. The man's own eyes were fixed on a floor-length mirror as he pumped away on an abdominal exercise machine. He seemed pleased with what he saw.

He had reason to be, Levy decided. Leslie Boardman was beautiful by any standard. He was tall and slender and fit, with a hard, sinewy body, and perfect features—long blond hair, blue eyes, square jaw, and a perfectly straight nose. The floor supervisor at the health club had described him as a male model, who had been featured in a popular Marine Corps TV commercial. She had also snickered, and said he was "a flaming poof"—her words—and that he had been a "special friend" of Joe Battaglia, that the two had often worked out together.

The health club had been only the third in Battaglia's neighborhood that Levy had visited. There had been no membership card in the captain's personal effects, only the gym bag in the rear seat of his car. The floor supervisor had explained that he had used the club as Boardman's guest for ten bucks a pop. That also told Levy something about Battaglia's finances. They had been stretched too thin to afford several hundred dollars for even a limited membership. It also told her that Boardman had met the captain somewhere else.

Levy waited until Boardman finished his exercise. His face was buried in a towel, mopping up the sweat, and when he looked up, he found Levy and her gold shield standing before him.

"This is about Joe, I guess," he said. Levy thought she detected a hint of nervousness, maybe even fear in his eyes. But then, a lot of people dealt with cops that way.

"I need to talk to you. The floor supervisor said we could use one of the empty offices."

"Does it have to be now?"

"Afraid so."

Boardman shook his head, rearranging his long blond hair, then ran his hands through it, pushing it back over his ears. He didn't say anything else, just offered a dramatic gesture indicating he would follow.

Levy led him to a small office, where Boardman dropped onto a sofa, folded one leg over the other, and cupped the knee with both hands. His attitude had become world-weary and defiant.

"This really cuts into my time," he said. "These workouts are necessary for my career, and I take them quite seriously."

Levy perched on the edge of a small desk and stared at the man, letting her silence, and her eyes, cut into him. "We take things seriously, too, Mr. Boardman. And the murder of a police captain is way up on the list."

Boardman looked away. It was a gesture of exaggerated exasperation, but Levy noticed telltale movement in the fingers cupping his knee.

"What do you do for a living, Mr. Boardman?"

He turned back to face her. "I'm an actor, and a model. I can give you the name of my agent if you want to confirm that."

"That would be helpful," Levy said. "Also your home address and phone number." She jotted the information in a notebook, then stared at him again. Boardman's fingers continued to play against his knee.

"Look," he said, cutting through the silence. "I was shocked when I heard about Joe. But I have no idea who killed him, or why."

"How long had you known Captain Battaglia?"

Boardman closed his eyes momentarily. The look of exasperation was back. "Six months. Maybe seven."

"Which?"

Boardman shook his head—openly nonplussed by the need for such precision. He seemed to count back mentally. "Six," he said at length. "We met at a party. Sort of an impromptu thing after a show at an art gallery. I didn't know the people, and I doubt I could even find the apartment again if I tried."

Levy took down information about the gallery, the artist, the approximate date of the show; that the party was on the East Side "in the sixties somewhere," and that both Boardman and Battaglia had gone to the exhibit alone.

"Was the captain interested in art?" Levy asked.

Boardman wagged his head from side to side. "I think he was just trying to meet people. He was recently divorced, you know."

He offered the final bit of information with a touch of contempt. Levy wondered if it was contempt for marriage, or with the fact that someone would live with a woman. "So you and Captain Battaglia became close friends?"

"I suppose."

"How close?"

Boardman seemed to stiffen. He sat more upright and stared at Levy with one eye slightly narrowed. "If you're asking about my sex life—or the lack thereof—it's none of your business."

Levy smiled. What she really wanted to do was reach over, grab Boardman by his T-shirt, then slap him silly.

The smile was misinterpreted, and Boardman sat even straighter. "Yes, I'm gay," he said. "So, if you're a gay-bashing cop, bash away."

Levy's smile remained fixed. "I don't get involved in gay bashing, Mr. Boardman. I'm gay, myself."

Boardman stared at her, then cocked his head to one side. "Well, enlightenment in the police department. How encouraging."

"We're trying."

Boardman sneered, then looked away again.

Levy slipped off the desk and leaned forward, forcing Boardman's eyes back. "Mr. Boardman. Don't piss me off. You won't like me if you piss me off."

Shock registered slowly. "Are you threatening me?"

"Consider it advice," Levy said. "Now answer my questions without any wise-ass bullshit."

Boardman's intertwined fingers twisted nervously against his knee, but his eyes remained defiant. Gay macho, Levy decided. "What do you want to know?" Boardman asked.

"How close were you and Captain Battaglia?"

"Close. We saw each other two, sometimes three times a week. Dinner, a movie, that sort of thing."

"Were you sleeping with him?"

Boardman hesitated. Deciding whether to lie, or not, Levy thought.

"No." A pause. "I don't think Joe was quite there yet. In his sexuality, I mean."

"Did he express any fears? Tell you about any threats? Ever discuss what he was working on?"

"Never."

Levy stared at the man, convinced he was lying. She just wasn't sure why, or to what degree.

"Thank you, Mr. Boardman," she said. "I'll probably be in touch again."

"What is this shit? You just walk in like you own the fucking place? Get the fuck out of here."

Dapper Dan Torelli flexed his shoulder muscles, and rotated his head. It was a move prizefighters made before the bell rang to start a round. Coming from Torelli, seated behind his oversized desk, it looked mildly absurd.

Three patrol cars—the backup Eddie had called for—were waiting when they arrived at Torelli's Mott Street clubhouse. Four men from two of the units entered with them to keep the family members in the outer rooms at bay. The other two uniforms were stationed outside to keep everyone else out. Devlin and Grogan went straight to Torelli's office and barged in, followed immediately by Buster Fucci, who took up station behind Torelli's high-backed chair. Devlin knew their time was limited. By now someone was already on the phone reaching out for Larry Matz. They'd get little information now; even less when Matz arrived. But at least the message would be sent.

Grogan jabbed a finger toward Torelli's face. "You answer the questions here, or we lock your fat guinea ass up, and ask 'em then. You got that, mouth?"

Torelli jabbed his own finger back. "You watch your fucking ethnic slurs, you Irish prick."

"Shut up," Devlin snapped, "or we drag your ass out from behind that desk."

Torelli sneered at him, then sat back in his chair and grinned. "Ask your fucking questions, then get the fuck out."

Devlin put his fists on the desk and leaned forward. "One of your boys—a beat-up piece of shit named Vincent Maribucci—was following me today. I don't like it."

Torelli glanced back at Fucci. "You know anybody named Maribucci?" He looked back at Devlin as Fucci shook his head. "I never heard of the guy. Happy? Now get the fuck out."

"He works for another one of your assholes," Grogan said. "Bunny Rabitto. You know. Bunny the Fag."

Torelli extended his hands to each side. "Hey.

This guy—what's his name?—he works for this
Bunny guy, you go talk to him. Why bother me with
this shit?"

"Why are you so interested in this Battaglia
case?" Devlin asked. "You a little nervous about
what we might find out?"

Torelli sneered again. "Who's interested? Whadda
I care some fag cop gets himself whacked?"

"Fag cop?" A small smile played across Devlin's
lips.

Torelli's jaw clenched momentarily, then he
smiled. "Just an expression. You're all fags as far as
I'm concerned." He snapped his eyes to Grogan.
"Fat guinea ass, huh?"

Grogan laughed in his face. "You're in the shit,
Torelli. And we're gonna bury you in it."

"Whadda you know about the Money Club?"
Devlin asked. He had thrown the question out on the
spur of the moment. Now he kept his eyes on
Torelli's face, watching for the tells. It was an old
gambler's term cops used to describe a subject's response to questions. Some giveaway sign—a gesture, a change in speech pattern, any indication the
question had struck home. Torelli's jaw had tightened almost imperceptibly.

"Whadda ya talkin' about? Some investment club,
or somethin'?" Torelli shook his head in disgust. "I
don't have time for this bullshit."

The door to Torelli's office opened, and a short,
pudgy man marched in with the attitude of a general.
He was dressed in an expensive, double-breasted
suit that only emphasized his girth, and Devlin noticed that he wore a star-sapphire ring that was
smaller, but almost identical to the one Torelli wore
on his little finger.

Devlin turned and smiled. "Hello, Counselor," he
said. "You get Mr. Maribucci out of the slam?"

Larry Matz glared at him with pale blue eyes. He
had a round, fat face under a sharp widow's peak of

thinning brown hair, and he looked about as threatening as the local butcher. But cops and prosecutors regarded him with serious dread. Especially when faced with his courtroom talent for cross-examination. They referred to it as being "Matzed."

Devlin had little respect for lawyers. Most, he had found, couldn't find their dicks with both hands. But Larry Matz was one of a handful of exceptions. You crossed him at your peril. He could throw enough inventive and complex paperwork before a judge to keep a cop handcuffed for weeks while the department's attorneys sorted through the legal mumbo jumbo.

"What's the purpose of this invasion?" Matz demanded. He was puffed up like a bantam rooster. Just playing out a role for his best-paying client.

"We had a few questions for Mr. Torelli. But we got what we came for. Sorry we can't stay and chat."

"A few questions?" Matz asked. His eyebrows were arched now. "So you invade the gentleman's office with eight armed men?"

"What gentleman?" Grogan asked.

Devlin pushed on before Matz could respond. "You know how it is, counselor. You can always find a cop when you don't want one."

"I'd like to know what questions you had for Mr. Torelli," Matz snapped.

"I'm sure he can fill you in." Devlin offered a regretful shrug. "You know what it's like in the department these days. Constant manpower problems. I've gotta get these men back on the street."

Matz leveled a finger at Devlin as he and Grogan started for the door. "This happens again, you'll find yourself before a judge, Devlin."

Devlin turned and stared at Matz's protruding finger, then into the man's eyes. The small scar on Devlin's cheek had turned white. He gave Matz a cold smile. "I knew a man once," he said. "He had to pick up his teeth with broken fingers. He had a helluva time."

Matz's face reddened. He puffed himself up a bit further. "You threatening me, Inspector?" Matz, it was said, lived a fantasy that he was really part of the mob—the unofficial *consiglieri* of the Torelli family. When the delusion overcame him, he liked to play the tough guy.

Devlin laughed. "Purely informational, Counselor." He winked at him, then continued out the door.

Grogan took Devlin's arm when they reached the street. "You notice that picture on the wall in Torelli's office?" Grogan asked. "Arms around each other, all buddy, buddy."

"I noticed," Devlin said. "It was an old picture. Maybe twenty years."

"Yeah," Grogan said. "Little Bat was probably in high school when Poppa was doin' photo shoots with the mob."

Devlin looked off into the street. The shit was getting a lot deeper than he wanted. He wondered how Big Bat would react when he found out about Torelli. "I think we may have to slap a tail on the senator," he said. "Somebody he doesn't know."

"Having a police inspector followed wasn't smart," Matz said. "It just draws attention that you don't need." The lawyer made certain he was looking at Buster Fucci when he spoke, making sure his words fell there, not on Torelli.

Torelli waved away the mild rebuke. "Buster was only doin' what he was told. I gotta know what these cops are after. What they mighta got out of this fag cop's apartment."

"There are other ways," Matz said. "Safer ways."

"Fuck safer!" Torelli shouted. "I wanna know fucking now!" He jabbed a finger into the top of his desk, then spun around to face Fucci. "You find out everything you fucking can about this fucking cop, Devlin. I wanna know every weak spot that prick has. I wanna put his fucking balls in my pocket. *Capisce*?"

"I'd hold off on that—" Matz began. The look he got from Torelli stopped him from going on.

Torelli jabbed a finger up at Fucci. "You just do it, Buster," he snapped. "And I want it fast."

Chapter Seven

"Boardman was lying through his teeth," Sharon Levy said. "All the tells were there."

Devlin could see the satisfaction in the woman's eyes. He glanced at Eddie. The man was like a cat who had eaten a particularly tasty bird. It was almost five o'clock, and they had gathered in Devlin's office to run through the results of Levy's day. "You two gonna tell me about it? Or is it a secret?" Devlin asked.

Levy leaned forward. "About three o'clock—right after he left you—I put out a call to Eddie for backup, and we tailed Boardman when he left the gym. First he went back to his apartment on East Eighty-second. Then, about a half hour later, he comes out all spiffed up like he's headed for work, so we stay on him." Levy glanced at the notebook in her hand. "He hoofs it straight down to East Fifty-second Street, and he goes into this converted town house—one of those big old suckers just a few doors from Sutton Place. So we set up a watch, but he doesn't come out again."

"What's in the building?" Devlin asked.

Grogan spoke through a wide grin. "Somethin' called the UN Committee for Monetary Equality," he said. He waited for Devlin's response.

Devlin raised his eyebrows. "The Money Club?"

"Sounds like it could be," Grogan said. "But there's more." He glanced at Levy.

"Well, this place gets some pretty heavy traffic

while we're eyeing it," she continued. "First was a thug named Paddy Rourke, who Eddie knows from a couple of other cases he worked."

"The Westies Gang, right?" Devlin said.

"You got it." Grogan said. "Same outfit that's supposed to do a lot of heavy work—including contract hits—for the Torelli family."

Levy flipped a page in her notebook and continued. "So we hang on to see what's next, and we start getting this line of high-class ladies—some who I recognize from a stint I did with Public Morals. They're all top-of-the-line pros who used to work the class cafés like the Oak Room at the Plaza, and the old Sherry Netherland. Most of them I thought had left the game—or at least the city—because I haven't seen 'em around in a couple of years."

Devlin looked from one to the other. "Anybody check out this committee?"

"Oh, yeah," Grogan said. "I never heard of it, so I tapped an old homicide dick I know. Threw in his papers about eight years ago, and signed up with UN Security. He said the committee was set up back in the late sixties to study third-world monetary problems. Said it's run out of the secretary general's office by a Greek diplomat named Ari Popolis. But, get this. The executive director is none other than Little Bat's friend, Michelle Paoli."

Devlin let out a low whistle.

"Yeah," Levy said. "Curiouser and curiouser."

"I think we need Rivera in here," Devlin said. "Tell him to bring the file he pulled out of Little Bat's computer."

Devlin jotted down a name on the last of nineteen index cards. "Let's take another look at this Wingding file." He attached the last card to a display board he had set up behind his desk. Then he jabbed a finger at each one and ran through them.

Cleopatra	The Politician	Fed 1	123 Restaurant
The Greek	Friend 1	Fed 2	The Spider
Cop 1	Friend 2	The Lover	The Watcher
Cop 2	The Judge	The Boss	The Money Club
The Bagman	Lolita	Boss 2	

"Okay," he said. "Now, let's run through them
again. And let's put our best guesses on what, or
who each might be. The Money Club seems easy."
He stared at each in turn. "I emphasize *seems easy*.
Just so we keep in mind we could be off base. But
for starters, lets ID this as this UN Committee on
Monetary Equality. What about The Watcher?" All
three, including Rivera, remained silent. "Okay. The
Spider?"

"We're assuming this Money Club—if it's this
UN committee—has something to do with sex. At
least peripherally." It was Levy, and all eyes—
especially Rivera's—turned to her. She made an uncertain, somewhat helpless gesture with her hands.
"Well, spiders lure victims into webs. So my guess
would be whoever's running the place, or shilling
for them."

"Okay," Devlin continued. "Let's put down this
Paoli woman and this diplomat, Popolis, and a question mark for a possible shill."

"We got some other names that might fit Popolis
and Paoli," Grogan interjected.

"Yeah, I know," Devlin said. "But let's keep them
here, too. At least until we get somebody harder for
this slot." He jabbed his finger at the next two cards.
"Next we got The Boss, and Boss Two. Best guess
would seem to be Torelli and his underboss, Fucci.
Anybody have a problem with that?" There was a
round of shaking heads.

Devlin turned to the next card, but was stopped by
a soft knock on his door. The door swung back and
Ralph Federici stuck his head inside.

"Sorry, Inspector. I didn't know you were tied up. I just wanted to check something with you."

Devlin moved his body in front of the display board to block as much of the Organized Crime cop's view as possible. "Unless it's urgent, it'll have to wait until tomorrow morning," he said.

"No, no. No problem. I'll catch you then," Federici said.

Devlin stared at the man as he idled in the doorway. He was only average height, and lean, with a narrow face and almost black eyes, and combined with his long nose and slicked back hair it gave him the look of a predator. Like a ferret, Devlin thought. "Anything else?" Devlin asked.

Federici smiled. "No, I'll catch you then."

When the door closed behind him, Devlin shot a look at Grogan.

"Sorry," Eddie said. "I thought the little prick was out with his shoe-fly buddy. They musta come back while we were in here."

Devlin inclined his head toward the display board. "Let's make sure we remember to lock this thing away so he doesn't get a chance to eyeball it."

He turned back to the board. "Okay. Next we got Feds One and Two. Any ideas?"

"We think Torelli's tied into this somehow. Right?" Grogan said. "That's why he was having you tailed." He watched Devlin nod agreement, then went on. "I'd like to find out who the federal prosecutors were on the last two raps he beat in court. And who the agents were who put those cases together. See if we can tie them back in to this some way."

"To the Money Club?" Levy asked.

"Yeah, that, too," Grogan said. "But mostly to Torelli and the dates and places listed on this Wingding printout. He beat the shit out of the feds in court. The best way to do that is to have some flaws in the evidence the prosecution is using, and to know about it ahead of time so you're ready to shoot it down."

"Good idea," Devlin said." He tapped the next card. "Let's do the same with this one, The Judge. Let's find out who the judges were on both cases, and if *they* tie back somehow."

Devlin moved up the board. "Next we have Friend One and Friend Two."

"One of them could be Boardman," Levy said. "And the other could be someone we haven't come across yet."

"Maybe this lawyer, O'Brien," Grogan added.

"Okay," Devlin said. "We'll put them down. But they also come after The Politician—and I think we have to go with Big Bat on that one—so we want to check and see if any of his senate friends might have something to do with this Money Club. Okay?" He waited while everyone nodded.

"Next. Cops One and Two."

"Best bet's gotta be OCC," Grogan said. "It's where Little Bat was working, and it ties into the Torelli thing. *If* we're right about that."

"What about The Greek?" Devlin asked, moving on.

"Gotta be Ari Popolis," Levy said. "He's the only Greek we got so far. So he gets his second slot on the list. The spider *and* the Greek." She stared at the board a moment. "On the next one—Cleopatra—I'd give a second slot to the Paoli woman."

"Why?" Grogan asked. "Paoli's not an Egyptian name, is it? Sounds dago to me."

"Just some old high school history," Levy said. "I just remembered how Mark Antony got his dick in a wringer with the Roman army when he couldn't keep his tunic zipped around Cleopatra. If she's running this money place, and it involves sex somehow, I think it fits."

"Okay, we'll put her down," Devlin said. He hesitated. "But let's remember this is all speculative.

Just a starting point. When we find out more, the names will probably change. So, what I want you to do now, is compare and check these names against the other stuff on the printout—the dates and places one was with another." He picked up the list. "For example, we've got The Politician with Boss Two last April second at 123 Restaurant. We've got The Politician at the same restaurant again on June 17, with The Bagman. So somebody see if Big Bat was in town on that date, and check to see where he likes to eat. Also which restaurants Fucci likes to go to. Then see what you can put together."

"Hey, if you can get me their credit card numbers, I can hack into the card company computers, and pull out those dates and restaurants for you," Boom Boom said. "Shit, I could probably even get their numbers. It would just take some time."

Devlin stared at the man. He had been silent throughout the meeting—almost like a fifth wheel. Now he was the center of attention. The grin that spread across his boyish face said he liked it that way. "You can really do that?" Devlin asked.

"Shit." Boom Boom's grin widened. "American Express, Visa, Diner's Club, nothing is safe from these fingers." He held up his hands and fluttered the digits.

"Then do it," Devlin said. "If we can get the numbers we will. But get started as though we can't. I'd just as soon not tip anybody off that we're looking." He let his eyes roam the long list of contacts on the printout. "We'll have to do it on every one." He glanced at Grogan. "So divide it up among everybody except Federici and Jones and get started."

"You got it," Grogan said. "What's your next move?"

"After you get this work parceled out, you and I are going over to this UN building on East Fifty-second, and see if Michelle Paoli works late. I think the lady fed me a line of shit the first time, and we need to talk to her again."

Sharon Levy sat at her desk, studying the computer printout, until Devlin and Grogan had left. Then she decided to steal some time just to think. The best way, for her, was to clean her weapon. It was a mechanical job—like doing the laundry, or washing her hair—and it freed her mind and allowed it to roam without distraction.

Levy removed her .38 Chief's Special from her purse, emptied the shells, and stuck them in her jacket pocket. Then she closed the cylinder and laid the weapon in her lap while she searched her desk for the cleaning kit she had brought from home.

Out of the corner of her eye, she saw Boom Boom Rivera swagger into the detective's bullpen, perch on the edge of an adjacent desk, then throw a quick wink at Stan Samuels, the only other detective still in the office.

Levy glanced up at him. Boom Boom was staring at her. His soft brown eyes were large, almost doelike; his smile revealed rows of whiter-than-white teeth. He was still feeling his oats from the meeting, she decided. Sharon rolled her eyes, and went back to her search.

"Sha-*ron*," Boom Boom crooned, "let me say that you look absolutely fine *to-day*."

Levy raised her eyes slowly. "Thanks, *Boom . . . Boom*." She offered up a slow, false smile. "Now get the fuck out of here."

"Sha-*ron*. Don't *be* that way. I'm here to offer you delights you ain't even *dreamed* about."

Levy leaned forward and let her smile widen into a threatening grin. "Listen, you sawed-off little shit. Get back in your hole and take your pathetic little dick with you. You keep bugging me, I'm gonna squash you like a fucking cockroach."

"Baby, baby, baby."

"I'm not your fucking baby, asshole."

Boom Boom reached down and grabbed a handful of crotch. "Lady. You ever saw what I got for you in *here,* you would give up women for-*ever.*" Boom Boom raised his hands in a helpless gesture and allowed a look of pure innocence to spread across his face. "It's the truth. I swear to you."

Levy leaned back in her chair, and dropped her hands to conceal the empty revolver in her lap. "You don't say? It's that big, huh?"

"It is truly *magnificent,*" Boom Boom said. "A wonder of the *fucking world.*"

"Well, why don't you just whip it out then, and give me a *fucking look.*" She shrugged her shoulders. "Who knows? I could be so overwhelmed, I might convert on the fucking spot."

"Baby. Let's have a little privacy." He inclined his head toward Samuels, then lowered his voice to a stage whisper. "I don't wanna make my man, Stan, over there, feel inferior."

"Hey, whip that sucker out," Samuels shouted. "Just let me get my glasses on, so I don't miss none of your teeny fucking weenie."

Boom Boom smiled, inclined his head again toward Samuels, then shook it slowly. "Man, the jealousy us Spanish dudes live with." He winked at Levy. "Let's go someplace we can do this right," he offered.

"Naw, naw," Levy said. "I don't buy nothin' sight unseen. Whip that sucker out. I promise you, I won't fucking faint."

Boom Boom stood, then lowered one hand to his zipper, a slow grin spreading across his lips.

Levy's hand came up from her lap, holding the revolver. She closed one eye and, using a two-handed grip, leveled the weapon at Boom Boom's crotch. "Come on, sweet cakes," she crooned. "I bet I can take four inches off that sucker. *If* you got four inches."

Boom Boom's smile flickered, but held by force of will. "Baby, four inches ain't nothin'." The grin was weak now, but still in place, as his hands hovered near the zipper. "You ever seen those new urinals they got in men's rooms now? The ones they put up so they're down lower to the floor? Hey, everybody thinks they're for kids, you know? But they're really for the Spanish brothers. So our dicks don't hang in the water."

"Yeah, yeah," Levy said. She squeezed one eye tighter as she sighted over the barrel. Her tongue was protruding from the corner of her mouth as if helping concentrate her aim. "Just whip that little weasel out. I'll put it out of its misery."

Boom Boom hesitated, but only until his machismo kicked in. He pulled the zipper down, and began to slip his fingers inside.

Slowly, Levy cocked the revolver. The three clicks of the hammer filled the room. Boom Boom pulled the zipper closed and took a quick step back. "Man, you are one crazy fucking dyke," he snapped. "Blow a guy's cock off, just 'cus he offers you a little."

"And don't you ever forget it, scumbag," Levy said. "Now take your shriveled up little dick the fuck out of here, before I decide to shoot it off *through* your tight, little pants."

Boom Boom turned to Samuels and jabbed a finger back at Levy. "You see what that woman did? She's fucking crazy. Points a loaded fucking gun at another fucking cop. What is that shit?"

He turned back to Levy and glared at her. Levy pointed the revolver at the ceiling and pulled the trigger. The hammer hit the empty chamber with a loud snap.

Boom Boom's jaw dropped, as Samuels' sudden laughter assaulted his back. He sneered at Levy. "Hey, I knew it wasn't fucking loaded. I was just playin' wit' you."

Levy jerked her thumb toward the computer cubbyhole. "Go play in there," she said. "With your dick, or any other useless piece of shit you can find."

Chapter Eight

The building on West Fifty-second Street had been one of the city's great turn-of-the-century homes. It was a wide, Georgian-style, brick row house, five stories in height, accented by floor-to-ceiling windows on the first three levels, each hung with heavy, brocade drapery. The high stone steps that would normally have led to the second floor had been removed, replaced with a bastardized and more functional entrance at street level. Through the new glass-front door Devlin could see a reception area manned by an attractive young woman. Behind her a fixed security camera scanned the room with a wide-angle lens.

The woman smiled warmly as Devlin and Grogan approached her desk. She was petite—nineteen or twenty, Devlin guessed—and had long blond hair, blue eyes, and a sweetly innocent face. Her large breasts rested provocatively on the edge of the desktop, and she greeted them with an equally provocative Scandinavian accent.

Out of the corner of his eye, Devlin could see the grin spreading across Eddie Grogan's face. Devlin removed his shield and identified himself.

"We'd like to see Ms. Paoli," he said.

The woman's eyes fluttered nervously, and her smile faded. "Do you have an appointment?"

"I spoke with her yesterday," Devlin said. "She knows what it's about."

The woman's uncertainty faded—slowly. "Just a

moment," she said, then stood and moved to a set of double doors off to her left. She was wearing a form-fitting knit dress that hugged every curve of her body.

Grogan's eyes followed her until she had disappeared through the door. He let out a breath. "Oh, Ingrid," he said. "You make my little heart go pit-a-pat." He grinned at Devlin. "I'll bet you the pension she ain't wearin' a thing under that pecker-pulsing frock."

"Try to control yourself."

"Hey. I'll try," Grogan said. "But I ain't promisin' nothin'. I ain't seen my friend Rita in days."

The woman returned within a few minutes, smiled bravely, and directed them through the double doors to the first office on the left. When they entered, they found Michelle Paoli seated behind a Louis Quatorze desk. She looked very businesslike and efficient, and slightly nervous, Devlin thought. To her right, a man was casually sprawled in the corner of a stripped sofa. Devlin recognized Paddy Rourke from the mug shot he had seen earlier. He also knew the man was licensed to carry a Glock automatic as part of the bogus bodyguard service he supposedly ran.

Michelle stood as they entered, and gestured toward two delicate chairs in front of her desk. She was dressed in a simple, but elegant black skirt, and a white silk blouse that was demurely closed at the throat, held in place by an antique silver brooch.

"I didn't expect to see you again so soon, Inspector." She glanced toward Eddie Grogan.

"This is Detective Grogan," Devlin said. "We came up with a few more questions." He glanced toward Rourke, imitating her curiosity.

Michelle made a delicate gesture toward Rourke, her long, slender fingers moving with the grace of a dancer's. "This is Mr. Rourke," she said. "He's consulting with us on some security matters."

"We know Mr. Rourke," Devlin said. "What we didn't know was that the UN hired thugs to solve security problems."

Michelle's eyes widened slightly. A short, derisive laugh came from the sofa.

"You've been talkin' to Grogan," Rourke said. "Hello, Eddie. Long time."

Grogan fixed his eyes on Rourke. "Hello, punk. Break anybody's legs lately?"

Rourke returned Grogan's glare, but limited his reply to a smirk. He was a large man, slightly over six feet, with broad shoulders and two hundred pounds of well-packed muscle. He was what Devlin's father had called "black Irish." He had dark, curly hair, blue/black eyes, and a sallow complexion that seemed almost Spanish. He also had a nose that had been broken more than once, and there was a jagged scar across his forehead—the kind made by broken glass—and a tattoo on the back of his right hand that intoned: Irish Justice. Except for the well-tailored blue suit, he could have been typecast as one of the hoods in *Guys and Dolls*.

Michelle sat forward in her chair. The slight shock was gone now, and her eyes had become severe. But she was still nervous, Devlin thought. He wondered if it was due to Rourke's presence.

"Are we here to discuss personnel practices, or did you have some questions?" she asked.

"Both," Devlin said. He kept his eyes on her face, wondering when diplomatic privilege would kick in, and jettison him to the street.

"First, I believe you have another employee named Leslie Boardman."

Michelle nodded, but said nothing.

"Seems he was a friend of Captain Battaglia's," Devlin said.

"If he was a friend of Boardman's, then Battaglia musta been a fruit."

The comment had come from Rourke, and Devlin

slowly swiveled his head and pointed a finger at his face. "Shut up," he snapped.

"Please, Paddy. Let the inspector continue," Michelle said.

Devlin turned back to face the woman. There was a tightness around her mouth now. Not anger. Nerves.

"Mr. Boardman tells us he met Captain Battaglia at a private party after a show at an art gallery. Sound familiar?"

"It's possible they met at my home. I can't be certain."

"And, in the six months that followed, you never knew anything about their friendship? Even though Boardman worked for you, and you and Captain Battaglia had also become friends?"

"I'm afraid not."

The lie was blatant, and it brought a new tightness to Michelle's mouth. Boardman had also lied about where he had met Battaglia. He had told Levy it was at a party in the East sixties, but that he couldn't recall the name of the host. For some reason Boardman and Michelle Paoli were working very hard to conceal a three-sided friendship with a dead police captain.

Devlin leaned back in the chair and studied the woman. "We've also noticed some of the other *employees* who work here. Women we recognize from other activities. Like prostitution." He inclined his head toward Rourke. "Combine that with our sweetheart over there, and we have to wonder what's going on."

"You don't have to talk to these clowns," Rourke snapped. "Tell 'em to take a walk."

Devlin glared at Rourke again, but his attention was stolen by Michelle suddenly rising from her chair.

"I think Mr. Rourke has a point, Inspector. If you have any questions regarding the committee's personnel, I feel you should take them up with the appropriate people at the secretary general's office."

Devlin glanced at Grogan, then stood. "Just one more question." He paused, and allowed his eyes to bore into the woman's face. "Does the term 'The Money Club' mean anything to you?"

Michelle's jaw tightened. "Nothing," she said. "I'm afraid I'll have to ask you to leave now."

Headed back toward the office, Grogan stared across the car seat and grinned. "Some broad, that Paoli woman," he said. "Makes the one in the reception area look like fucking boy."

"And she was lying through her beautiful teeth," Devlin said.

The car fought its way through late rush hour traffic on Second Avenue, slowing to a crawl as it cut across Forty-second Street and the looming art deco facade of the Daily News Building. There was a lone, ragged man marching in front of the building, one of the city's endless supply of streetcombers. He was waving a blank placard above his head. It had been hammered out of a piece of scrap wood and the side of a cardboard box, and the man was yelling obscenities at passersby, the building, the world. Devlin wondered why there was nothing written on his placard, or if the man even knew.

"You notice how she kept glancing at Rourke?" Grogan asked.

"Yeah. Like maybe he was there to make sure she didn't say anything," Devlin said.

"A watcher? Could be. If he is, maybe she'll talk if you get her alone."

Devlin nodded. "It's worth a shot." He glanced at Grogan. "And she can't stop us from talking to the women who work there. I doubt we'll find any diplomats in that crew."

"Sharon and I can look some of them up in the

ay-em." Grogan grinned again. "I'll leave Ms. Paoli to you. What the fuck. Rank does have its privileges." Grogan glanced at his watch. "Hey, it's almost seven. You want me to drop you at home?"

"Let's stop back at the office first." He wondered what time Michelle Paoli faced the world in the morning. Not too early, he thought. Although she might not like even a late morning visit. She just might not be sleeping too well tonight.

Michelle picked up the phone and punched in a series of numbers. "Mr. Popolis," she said, when the call was answered. "This is Michelle Paoli." She waited, then tapped her fingers nervously on the desk, as Popolis greeted her with a series of banal pleasantries.

"We have a problem, Ari," she said when he had finished. "The police were here asking questions again. I need to see you as soon as possible." She listened with growing anxiety. "I'll be there in one hour," she said.

When she replaced the receiver, Rourke was staring at her. "You don't need the fat Greek," he said. "Just stay cool, and stay away from the cops. I'll handle it."

"How?" Michelle asked.

Rourke grinned, but his eyes remained cold, mirthless. Just looking into them could sometimes send a shiver down Michelle's back.

"I'll talk to our little fairy, Boardman, and to some of the girls. Devlin won't get shit from them, he comes around."

"I don't want anyone abused," Michelle said.

Rourke stared at her. "Lady, I know my job. And this part of it don't include taking orders from you." The grin returned. "So, I don't give a fuck what you want. *Capisce?*" He started for the door; tossed a final line over his shoulder. "But right now you can relax. I got some other business to take care of."

Marie asked me today why we couldn't all live together, "like before." I've expected the question for a long time now. But it still stopped me cold. I'd thought about it. Figured what I'd say when one of them finally asked. I had it all planned. The words I thought would work. "Your mother and I just don't make each other happy anymore." But, when the time came, I couldn't say it. The lie just jumped out at me. Angie had nothing to do with it. And I couldn't make her carry part of the blame. Not with our kids. And that's the big joke in all this. How easy it is to lie to yourself. But not to your children. Even if lying is what we do from the first moment we have them. Just by presenting ourselves as that safe, all-knowing haven they can always count on, always find refuge in. Maybe they should know from the beginning just how weak and frightened and insecure we really are. Would it diminish us as parents? My father would think so. But would it? I wonder.

"Dad, are you listening?"

Devlin came back to himself. "Yeah, honey. Sorry."

Phillipa used the chopsticks like a child raised in Hong Kong rather than Queens. She popped a piece of orange chicken into her mouth, chewed furiously, swallowed, then continued her story.

"So, anyway, this geek comes up to us—like he's panhandling, or something—and all of a sudden he makes a grab for Adrianna's bag."

"This is in Union Square?" Devlin asked.

"*Yes,* Dad. Just like I told you." Phillipa rolled her eight-year-old's eyes, exasperated with the interruption. Devlin fought back a smile. His daughter had the same expressive blue eyes her mother had had, the same blond hair, the same field of freckles across her nose. And everything excited her. She seemed to have flowered anew since they had returned to New York. She loves this city, he thought. Just can't get enough of it. Just like her father.

"Sorry," he said.

Across the table, Adrianna hid her own smile behind a napkin.

"Well, Adrianna lets out this growl, like she's suddenly turned into a Rottweiler, or something, and she kicks the geek in the shins." Phillipa was bouncing in her chair, animated by the story. "And the geek lets out this yelp, and starts hopping around on one foot, and Adrianna takes her bag and whacks him across the face, and starts yelling at him." She glanced at Adrianna and started to giggle. "I won't tell you exactly *what* she said. Because if *I* said those words, I'd be in serious trouble."

Devlin looked across the table and raised his eyebrows. "What *did* you say?" he asked.

"You don't want to know," Adrianna replied. "It comes from living with a cop." There was a hint of color in her cheeks.

Devlin rolled his eyes in a poor imitation of his daughter, then turned back to the child. "So what happened next?"

"Well the geek is hopping around, trying to cover up, and Adrianna is still whacking him, and there's blood dripping from his nose, and he turns and tries to run, and Adrianna kicks him again. This time in the tush. And she tells him to get out of there—which he's already trying to do, except she won't let him. But she adds a few *more* words to it. Words that *I'm* not allowed to say." She stifled another giggle. "And then the people sitting on the benches near us all start to clap."

Devlin stared across the table again. "Did you take a bow?" he asked.

The color in her cheeks had deepened, but Adrianna nullified it with an imperious tilt of her head. "As a matter of fact, I did," she said.

"So what happened to the geek?"

"I think he's still running." Adrianna made a face at him and returned to her dinner.

Devlin inclined his head to one side as if digesting the story. He turned back to Phillipa. "Maybe I should give her my extra set of handcuffs," he said.

"Can we talk about something else?" Adrianna said. She shot a glance at Phillipa. The child covered her mouth and giggled again.

The telephone interrupted them, and Phillipa leaped from her chair and raced across the loft.

"Of course you can be excused," Devlin called after her.

Phillipa ignored him, and breathlessly answered the phone. A moment later she was back. "It's for you, Dad," she said. "Your office."

Adrianna winced, and Devlin offered her a helpless shrug. "Sorry, Babe," he said.

"Don't call me 'Babe,' " she said. "Remember what happened to the geek."

Devlin listened as one of the uniforms assigned to his office passed on the message.

"When did she call?" he asked. He listened again, jotting a number on the pad next to the phone. "Okay. Thanks," he said. Devlin disconnected, then dialed the number he had been given. It was answered on the fourth ring by the soft, slightly accented voice he remembered so well.

"Thank you for calling me back," Michelle Paoli said. "I would like to see you. Alone, if possible."

"When?" Devlin asked.

"Could it be tonight?"

Devlin thought he detected a note of fear in the voice. The kind that could make people change their minds if they were given enough time. "Forty-five minutes," he said. "Your apartment?"

"Thank you," she said. "I'll tell the doorman to expect you."

Devlin walked back to the table, placed his hand

on Phillipa's shoulder, and offered Adrianna another look of regret. "Gotta go," he said. "But it shouldn't take more than a couple of hours. Wait up for me?"

Disappointment was etched in Adrianna's eyes. Then it turned to resignation, then concern. "Be careful," she said.

He winked at her. "Maybe I should bring you with me," he said. "There's lots of geeks out there."

It was almost nine when the cab dropped him off at Michelle Paoli's building. The afternoon rain had turned the evening sultry and stagnant, raising the specter of more heat and humidity for the coming day. The night doorman—a gracious, well-spoken black man—was helping an elegantly dressed couple into a waiting cab. The man was silver haired and pushing sixty; the woman easily thirty years his junior. By the way Silver Hair savored the woman's legs as she slid into the cab it was obviously not a father/daughter dinner date.

The doorman smiled pleasantly, checked Devlin's I.D., then passed him through without the ritual telephone call upstairs. But, despite the courtesy, the effect of the building was still the same, and as he rode the elevator to the seventeenth floor, the tan, off-the-rack, summer suit he had worn throughout the day suddenly seemed rumpled and ill fitting and out of place.

Michelle Paoli answered the door almost immediately, and Devlin wondered if she had been pacing the small, marble-floored vestibule waiting for him to arrive. She was dressed in a white silk blouse and slacks, and again—like the silk she had worn the previous morning—the fabric seemed to flow with every movement, offering subtle accent to every line of her body.

"Thank you for coming," she said. "I wasn't sure you would."

"It's my job."

She looked down momentarily, then raised her eyes to meet his. There was a hint of regret, perhaps even fear on her face, a nervous movement at the corners of her mouth. If it was intended, Devlin thought, it offered an image designed to melt the hardest heart.

"I appreciate you coming alone. In this ... less official manner." She shook her head. "The way you were treated at my office ... I wasn't sure you would."

Devlin fought to keep his face flat, unmoved. "What is it you wanted?"

Michelle reached out and tentatively touched the sleeve of his coat. "Please. Come inside."

He followed her back to the same room they had used the previous day. Michelle indicated he should sit at the end of a small sofa, then she took the other end for herself. They were only two feet apart, and the positioning felt suddenly intimate, reminding him of the way he and Adrianna often sat together.

Michelle held the fingers of one hand in the other, making no attempt to hide her nervousness. "There are things going on at my office that frighten me. Things I think you should know about."

Devlin stared at her, offering neither surprise nor concern. "Have you talked to your security people?" A vision of Paddy Rourke flashed in his mind. "I mean UN security."

"I can't do that," she said.

"Why?"

"I'm not sure what would happen. I only know it might be dangerous."

Devlin rearranged himself on the sofa so he was facing her more directly. "You better tell me about it."

"Yes, I will," she said. "But you have to understand there isn't a great deal you can do. All of it, everything it involves, happens on UN property. Foreign soil to you."

"Yeah, I know the drill. But tell me anyway. I'll worry about the problems later." Devlin understood the complexities of diplomatic immunity. He had dealt with them before. He had no more right to officially enter a UN building uninvited than he had a foreign embassy. No matter what crime might have been committed.

Michelle let out a hollow laugh. It, too, held a note of fear in it. "How to begin?" she said. She gave a small shake of her head, drew a deep breath. "The Committee for Monetary Equality—the Money Club, as you called it today—has nothing to do with Third World monetary problems." She hesitated, looking for some element of surprise on his face. "It's what it was always intended to be. A house of pleasure, a place where diplomats can safely indulge their libidos." She studied his face again, as if trying to see if she were telling him things he already knew. There was nothing there. "You may already know these things. The Money Club, as you call it, has existed for years with the quiet acquiescence of the city and the police department." The hollow laugh returned. "It's existed so long many of the people running the city—perhaps even important police officials—may not be aware of it."

Now she had gotten the look she had been waiting for. "I don't understand," Devlin said. "This club was approved, authorized somehow, but people who should know about it, may not?"

"Oh, someone knows. I'm certain of that. In part because we are left alone. But with all the changes in personnel that have taken place over the years—with retirements, new administrations—I can't be certain who knows and who does not. Certainly Washington knows. Certainly people in your government's intelligence apparatus."

"How long has this . . . club existed?"

"It began in 1968, I believe."

Devlin stared at her. "You better start there," he said. "This is becoming a little hard to follow."

Michelle nodded. "Yes. It's the only way for you to understand."

She rose from the sofa and walked slowly to a set of French doors that opened onto a terrace. Behind her, the lights of the city accented her tall, slender figure, making her appear almost frail.

"As I said, it began twenty-five years ago, in the late 1960s." She turned to face him. "The exact date is unimportant, but if you need it, I'm certain I can get that for you."

"Go on," he said.

She gave another small shake of her head, as if clearing her mind, organizing her thoughts. "There had been a rash of attacks—muggings I think you call them. They all involved diplomats who had procured prostitutes on the streets. For the most part the victims were lower-level diplomatic personnel from smaller nations. But, you must remember, those were very tense times. Everything was a source of propaganda. Everything a source of outrage. The great powers were all struggling to align support wherever they could. No one wanted incidents of any kind, and Washington was pressing your city officials to put a stop to it. But there was little the city could do."

Michelle returned to the sofa, hesitated, then sat facing him again. Her features were tense, as if pleading with him to understand. She lowered her eyes, then began again, her French accent even heavier now. "In most citys in the world where the UN operates to any significant degree—especially in Europe—prostitution is more open. Often it is even condoned and regulated. Because of that it isn't surrounded by other criminal activities as it is here. People are rarely attacked. Those involved in it don't want any problems with government officials that will adversely effect their business, cause it to be made more restrictive."

"And someone wanted it that way here?"

"Yes. I'm not certain if the plan was inspired by someone at the UN, or within your government in Washington, or even by some city official. But somehow it was decided that the UN would be allowed to operate its own place of prostitution in the city. A club, so to speak, on UN property, one that catered only to foreign diplomats, and did not spread beyond that limited use."

Devlin raised a hand, stopping her for a moment. "A legal whorehouse that the city would keep its hands off." There was a hint of incredulity in his voice. But what she was saying wasn't really a surprise. It was something that had been the subject of rumor and speculation among cops and the news media for years. But ultimately, it had always been dismissed as a figment of overactive imaginations. He continued to stare at her. "That's what you're describing, isn't it?"

A hint of color came to Michelle's face. "I didn't mean it to sound quite that crude," she said. "But I suppose it is." She offered a very Gallic shrug. "From the beginning, the women were to be paid through rather expensive membership dues, and per visit fees that were to be masked as the cost of meals in the committee dining room." She forced a weak smile. "But, of course, that was always an illusion. Intended to protect the egos of everyone involved, I suspect—the diplomats who were members, and those who oversaw these activities." She lowered her eyes, studied her hands for a moment. "But it was always, in reality, what you termed it. And it was the responsibility of the UN—or rather, certain of its employees—to see it remained discreet." She raised her eyes and offered him another weak smile. "Not only to avoid difficulties here, but in the members' home countries as well. You see it was always understood that dues and other charges would be paid out of the personal resources of individual members, never by the UN itself. Or by the nation the diplomat represented. But, of course, everyone realized that in many cases those expenses would find their way back to the treasuries of member nations."

She paused, allowing Devlin to soak up the information, before offering an even more sobering dose. "And that, of course, is where your government's intelligence apparatus stepped in."

Devlin stared at her, unable to hide his surprise this time. But it was so obvious—the potential for blackmail so blatant. "Which agency?" he asked.

"At first, I'm told it was the FBI." She stood again, started toward the terrace, then turned back. It was as though she needed to push away her fear with movement, Devlin thought. And it was fear, he decided. Not some act she was using to gain sympathy.

"What I'm telling you is what *I* was told when I became involved five years ago." She returned to the sofa again and clasped her hands in her lap. "Very sophisticated cameras and listening devices had been installed in certain rooms, and members who had been ... targeted, I guess you would say, were then directed there for their assignations." Her hands were twisting together now. She noticed Devlin looking at them, and forced herself to stop. "Then, in the early seventies, the FBI pulled out. Its director, Mr. Hoover, had died, and I'm told the agency had come under some unwanted scrutiny about its domestic intelligence activities."

"So who took over?"

"One of your other intelligence agencies. I'm not certain which. You have so many of them."

The statement—her ignorance about which agency—didn't ring true, but Devlin let it pass for the moment. "But why would the UN go along with any of it?" he asked instead.

Michelle shook her head again. "You have to remember this was all run from the secretary general's office. U Thant held that position then. He was Burmese, and, despite his public image, he, like most Southeast Asians, was very fearful about the political climate in his part of the world. He was, shall we say, easily persuaded to work with your government."

"But he retired," Devlin said. "In the early seventies, I think."

Michelle nodded. "And then Waldheim took his place. I can't be certain he knew—the system was already in place, and run by others. Others who were then being *compensated* by your government." She smiled at the choice of word, and shook her head again. "But, given recent disclosures, Waldheim was certainly susceptible to pressure."

"What about the current secretary general?" Devlin asked.

"I'm certain he doesn't know. Not about the intelligence activity, at least. But then it's no longer being run the way it was—by an official agency of your government."

"How so?"

Michelle's hands began twisting in her lap again. "About four years ago I was told things were to change. That intelligence gathering activities had been turned over to a private source. Or, at least, that is how it was described to me."

"And that's when Paddy Rourke showed up?"

Michelle nodded. "And a man named Rabitto. Although I seldom see him."

And Rabitto works for Torelli, Devlin thought. He ran a hand through his hair. It wouldn't be the first time the government had used the mob to do its dirty work. Especially when it wanted to hide its own involvement. "How else did things change?" he asked, certain he suddenly knew the answer.

"Other people were allowed to come to the club," she said. "People from your government. From Washington, and from the city."

"And they were directed to those special rooms?"

"Yes."

Devlin's mind flashed to the list they had found hidden in the Wingdings file on Little Bat's computer. The Politician, Cop 1 and Cop 2, The Judge, Fed 1 and Fed 2. He let out a slow breath. What a boondoggle it had been for Torelli. What a way to ensure he could beat any rap that came down.

He stared at Michelle. The vision suddenly seemed tarnished. She was little more than a very upscale madam, one who happened to carry a diplomatic passport. "How do you know all this? The history of it all, I mean?"

"You mean why would they tell someone who ran a place like that?"

Devlin felt suddenly embarrassed by his bluntness. The woman didn't deserve it. He pushed his embarrassment aside. "Yeah. That's what I mean."

Michelle looked down at her hands, and again stopped their nervous twisting. She rubbed her palms softly against her thighs. "When the club was first started, my mother was the person who was asked to run it." She raised her eyes, then elevated her chin slightly. Devlin couldn't decide whether it was defiance, or pride. "She was Corsican," Michelle continued. "From Marseilles. And her background made her suited to the work." She paused a moment, her chin rising a bit more. "She was offered the job by my father, who was an Italian diplomat on the secretary general's staff. He had been put in charge of the club, and she had been his mistress for many years."

"They weren't married?"

"No."

"And your father? Is he still involved with the club?"

"No. He died seven years ago. His assistant, a Greek diplomat named Ari Popolis, took over at that time. When my mother died two years later, he offered the post to me."

"And then, shortly after that, these private contractors took over the intelligence activities?" Michelle nodded. "And Popolis knew?"

"Yes. I assume he, too, was being paid, but I can't be certain."

"Like your father was paid?"

"Yes. That I know about."

Devlin sat quietly for a moment, allowing it all to sink in. His eyes fixed on one of the room's many paintings—expensive paintings from her father's collection—the ones they had discussed on his previous visit. Paintings that now belonged to her. He leaned forward, eyes hard on the woman. "And you think Captain Battaglia found out what was going on and was killed because of it?"

"I think he found out. I'm not certain how. And I think that is why he became friendly with me, and with Leslie Boardman." She shook her head. "Perhaps Leslie told him. Perhaps they were lovers. I don't know. I haven't discussed it with him. I've been afraid to even try. I do know that Paddy Rourke and this Rabbito man were very nervous, very watchful during the past month. And now, since you have become involved, it has gotten even worse."

"And that's what has you frightened?"

"Yes. That and the woman who was killed."

"What woman?" Devlin asked. He had leaned forward, bringing himself to within a foot of her. The subtle scent of her perfume filled his nostrils.

Michelle's eyes widened. "Suzanne Osborne. One of the women who worked at the club. I assumed you would have known about it."

"Where was she killed? And how?"

"At her apartment. I think the detectives who came to my office said it was in Greenwich Village." She looked momentarily confused by his lack of knowledge. "It was right after your first visit here. The detectives came to my office that same day." She gave a small shiver, hugged herself. "They said it was a particularly brutal murder, and asked if she had had any difficulties with anyone at work."

"They knew she worked there?"

Michelle nodded. "Most of the women who work at the club are formally employed as receptionists, and are paid a modest salary from club funds. The other money they earn is paid to them in cash. It was set up that way originally to avoid problems with your government's tax laws." She shrugged. "Should one of the women's incomes ever come into question. Most actually spend some time at the reception desk."

Devlin thought back to the woman he and Grogan had seen earlier that day—the form-fitting clothes she had worn, the seductive way she had walked.

"Do you remember the names of the detectives?" he asked.

Michelle shook her head. "I thought you knew. When you came to my office today, I was certain that was why you had come." She rubbed her thighs again, more vigorously this time. "Paddy thought so, too. He was angry when he learned I had spoken to those other detectives. That's why I behaved so badly toward you today. I was afraid of what he would do." She shook her head again. "But the other detectives, I just can't remember their names. I have one of their business cards at my office, I can—"

"It's all right. I can find out. This woman— Suzanne Osborne, the one who was murdered—did she know Battaglia?"

"I don't know. She could have. But I can't be certain. He never came to the club."

"Was she involved with any of the Americans

who started coming to the club? Did she help set them up?"

"I don't know."

Devlin's eyes hardened. "How could you not know? You run the place."

Michelle's lip began to tremble, and she visibly fought back tears. Devlin sat back, giving her time.

"When it started . . . when United States officials, and other Americans started coming, I questioned it, and was told it was a new policy. I objected, and demanded to know who had changed the old policy." She crossed her arms, hugging her shoulders again. "I was told not to question it, just to mind my own business. It wasn't advice. It was a warning. And since then I've concentrated on the finances and business side of my work, and have ignored what takes place inside the club."

"Then who oversees the women, and what they do, or don't do?"

"Paddy Rourke. And ultimately Mr. Rabitto."

"Were they the ones who threatened you?"

"It was Rourke. But when I complained to Ari Popolis, he advised me not to interfere, and to concentrate on other matters. He said it might be dangerous to oppose them."

"And now you believe it."

"Even more than before." She stared at him, then looked away toward the terrace. She had released her shoulders and was softly rubbing her thighs again. "I'm terrified by the things that are going on all around me."

Devlin leaned forward again, and placed a hand on top of hers. "I can see that you get protection. Here, and at your office. With your help I could even get someone inside."

Michelle shook her head vigorously. "No one works at the club without their approval. And if they knew you had men watching me here . . ." she let the sentence die.

"We could wire your apartment, and your office. Even you yourself. Then have people nearby who could get to you if you appeared threatened."

She shook her head again, even harder this time. "They check the club for listening devices—ones that aren't supposed to be there—at least twice a week." She waved her hand, taking in the room. "There are no devices here. Yet. I've had it checked myself. But they could put them here if they became suspicious. Nothing stops them when they want something." She took his hand and squeezed it. "If I thought I could get away from them, I'd simply resign and go back to France. But I'm afraid they'd never allow it."

"Then you have to help stop them if you want out. It's the only way." He could feel her hand trembling in his. After several moments she nodded. "But only you must know," she said. "No one else. Even the officers who work for you. Otherwise I'd be too afraid they'd find out."

"All right," Devlin said. "But we'll have to find a place to meet. I can't keep coming here. And it's obvious I can't go to your office."

Michelle nodded quickly. "I have a friend who's traveling in Europe," she said. "I go to her apartment several times a week to make sure her maid has taken care of things, and to forward any important mail. I have a set of keys I keep in my office, and the maid is only there one day a week while my friend is away."

"Do you have an answering machine for your phone here?"

She nodded.

"We'll set up a code, and you can check your machine several times a day. When I need to see you I'll call, say my name is Roger—make it sound like I'm a friend—and that I'll call back at a certain time. You meet me at the apartment two hours after the time I give you. If you can't be there, call my of-

fice from a public phone, and leave a message that
'Miss Jones' has to cancel her appointment. Then
you give a time, and be there two hours after that.
My office will find me and tell me."

"But what if someone follows me there, and then
sees you leave?"

"You'll leave from here each time we meet. Even
if you have to come here first from your office. I'll
be nearby, watching, and I'll follow you to the other
apartment. Just to be certain no one else has."

Michelle Paoli slumped back against the sofa.
"Oh, God," she said. "I don't know if this makes me
feel better, or even more frightened."

Devlin felt her squeeze his hand again. "It'll be
all right," he said. "I promise you."

She looked at him, her eyes soft and vulnerable. It
made him feel as though he should reach out and
hold her, comfort her.

"I want very much to believe you," she said. "To
believe it will all work."

Paddy Rourke stood in the center of the loft. The
woman was asleep on a sofa, a biography of Salva-
dor Dali on the floor beside her. He looked around
at the paintings stacked along one wall, at the one in
progress on a large easel. He rolled the knife in his
hand between his fingers. He wanted to take the
blade to some of those paintings, leave a little message for Devlin, and the bitch he lived with. But that
wasn't what he was there for.

He had followed Devlin home from his office,
then waited until he left again. Then he had waited
still longer, until only one faint light remained on in
the loft. He had picked the lock on the downstairs
door and quietly climbed the stairs. There had been
no sound from inside the loft. He had checked the
door frame for any telltales he'd have to bypass—a
small hair, a piece of transparent tape, that would let
Devlin know the apartment had been breached.

Then, again, he had carefully applied the picks to the two interior locks.

Rourke moved silently across the loft. He wore a black tuque, pulled down over his face, with holes cut for his eyes and mouth. He touched the Glock in his shoulder holster. At least Devlin wasn't asleep inside the loft; the knife would be enough if the woman woke.

He went to the foot of a stairway that led to a second, half floor. There was a single door at the top. He climbed the stairs and eased the door open. A child lay sleeping in a single bed. The child stirred, and Rourke flattened himself against the wall. Nothing. He drew a long breath, then made his way back to the lower level, and went to a desk in one corner.

The search proved fruitless. Nothing but bills and personal papers. Not a thing about the fucking murder, he thought. Nothing that would pinpoint any of the cop's weaknesses, like they had told him to find. A small smile spread beneath the tuque. He glanced toward the stairs that led to the second level, then at the woman on the sofa. Well, that wasn't completely true, he told himself.

Chapter Nine

Adrianna had been asleep when Devlin had gotten home shortly after midnight. He had lingered at Michelle Paoli's apartment, tried to ease her fears—or at least that's what he told himself he had been doing. Adrianna had been curled up on the couch when he had finally made it back. She had been wrapped in an old terry-cloth robe that bore faint traces of paint from early morning assaults on her work, and he had sat quietly for several minutes, looking at her, telling himself how much she meant to him. Then he had awakened her gently and had led her—still half asleep—to bed.

Devlin still hovered at the edge of sleep the next morning, when he felt her hand slip around his waist. Adrianna's fingers played along his stomach, then moved up and began toying with the hair on his chest. He felt her body close against him, her lips barely touching the back of his neck.

"I like the way your fur feels," she whispered. "Are you awake, sailor?"

"Mmmm."

The contented purr produced a smile, and she slowly moved her hand lower until it was barely touching the other patch of fur six inches below his navel.

"You sound like someone's fat, happy pussycat," she whispered.

His hand slid back and began to lightly stroke her

thigh. She could already feel the soft, wet pleasure at her own center, and his touch increased the delightful anticipation. Her fingers moved lower, and began to lightly explore the shaft of his semierect penis. She paid particular attention to the sharp ridge at its head. She knew it was most sensitive there; would bring a quick and satisfying and intense pleasure.

She had known many men in her thirty-one years—most now blending into a maze of bodies and faces and personalities—but she had never loved one with the intensity she felt for this man. She fleetingly thought of a question a foolish friend had once asked her: "Which one was the best?" The answer, which she had laughed off then, came to her now. The one you loved the most.

He was fully erect now, and so very hard, and as he turned toward her, she felt her own legs part, as if commanded by some voice outside her. His hand slipped between her legs, as she continued to play with him, fingers tightening about him, stroking faster now, enjoying the rocklike feel of his need.

His fingers found her clitoris, and her legs parted even more. Her own contented sigh—nearly a gasp—filled his ears. Pleasure rushed to her in waves, converging at the soft center of his touch, and she suddenly wanted him inside her, unwilling to wait, wanting that overwhelming sense of fullness, that initial thrust of his hard cock penetrating deep inside her.

She urged him back, then climbed on top, and used her hand to gently guide the head of his penis to the tip of her clitoris. Slowly, she used him to momentarily stroke herself, then, unable to wait longer, carefully guided him inside, and eased down the length of him, feeling a hard, swollen, hungry need that matched her own.

"Oh, yes, baby," she hissed. "Yes. Yes. Yes. Yes."

* * *

Adrianna struggled out of bed at six, made coffee, and sat with him. She was slightly tousled and languid, still barely awake, but not from lack of sleep. Paul explained that he had an early breakfast meeting with Jenny Miller, the assistant district attorney he had blown off the previous day. Then he told Adrianna about the second murder victim, Suzanne Osborne. The words jarred against her lingering pleasure, made her wonder how men could rush so quickly back to their brutal worlds, and deny themselves that soft, quiet afterglow. But her mental complaint evaporated with his next words, replaced now with another. She listened to him explain that his leave-early-get-home-late routine would probably continue for several more days. It wasn't unexpected, simply jarringly inappropriate. And the tone of his voice offered no hint of regret.

"Then maybe I should take Phillippa out to the beach house," she said. "We won't be seeing much of you anyway, and at least she'll get some beach time." There was a barely concealed edge in her voice.

Devlin was initially startled by the idea, then agreed—reluctantly, he thought. Adrianna simply stared at him. She seemed angry. He studied her face, then dismissed the notion. Adrianna nodded, more to herself than him, he thought. "We'll go this afternoon. Before rush hour." She paused. "I hope you'll miss us," she added. The edge was back in her voice, then her eyes seemed to soften. She reached out before he could answer, and took his hand. "I know how important this case is. And I know you've begun to admire Little Bat—for lots of reasons," she said. "Just don't lose your perspective about him."

He asked her what she meant.

"Just that you seem to think he was some kind of exceptional cop, maybe even an exceptional man.

But maybe—just maybe—he wasn't as heroic as you think."

He just stared at her, waiting for more.

She gave him a small shrug. "Maybe he wasn't such a hero, that's all. Maybe heroes don't walk away from the people who love them, just because they think their sex lives will be better." She repeated the shrug. "I just want you to think about that."

Devlin made his way to the small coffee shop where he was to meet Jenny Miller. Adrianna's words played over in his mind, mixed there with other images he tried to dismiss—Michelle Paoli, dressed in soft silk; Adrianna curled up on their comfortable, old couch in a paint-spattered, terry-cloth robe. He pushed the images away, told himself to stop being an idiot. Just do the damned job, he told himself. You've got a butcher out there who's already killed a cop and a hooker. Just get him. Just nail his ass to a wall and get back to your life.

He entered the restaurant, already filled with people delaying their arrival at work a few minutes longer. It was a solemn, somewhat sullen crowd—mostly government employees—and typical of New Yorkers in the pre-workday hours. Most sat alone, many perusing newspapers still held in the half-page vertical fold preferred by subway riders. Bagels, spread with cream cheese, or Danish pastries adorned most tables. Only a few showed the greasy remains of heartier fare. Devlin searched the gathering for a smiling face, found none, then asked the hostess if a Jenny Miller had already arrived, and was directed to an isolated table at the back.

As he crossed the room, he still hadn't decided just how much he would tell this new A.D.A. He had called the Ninth Precinct and had gotten the names of the detectives who had caught Suzanne Osborne's murder. He had reached one of them, Stan

Mikowski, at home. Mikowski had filled him in, and had agreed to have the file and all his case notes at Devlin's office later that morning. There was no question the cases were related. The vibrator that had been found in Suzanne Osborne's body had sealed that fact in Devlin's mind. That and the wire used to bind her body. But there was still the question of what to tell this assistant district attorney. And what to hold back.

Jenny Miller was in her early thirties. She was a small woman with short blond hair and nervous blue eyes, and she was dressed in a severely cut business suit that seemed designed to hide both her age and the fact that she was attractive. Devlin noticed she wore neither wedding nor engagement rings.

"Sorry about yesterday," he said, as he took a seat opposite the woman. "Things were moving pretty fast. I assume you've read the initial reports."

The woman nodded. "Every word," she said. "Pretty gruesome stuff."

She was trying to remain cool, professionally detached, Devlin thought. But she couldn't keep herself from leaning forward, and that body language and the eager look in her eyes told him how excited she was. It's her first murder, he reminded himself, wondering how that might impact on how well they worked together. But it was a moot point, he decided. The only real question was how much he would tell her. Slowly, he began running through the crime scene, what had been found there, and later on the computer. Then he moved on to the autopsy and the initial interviews with Big Bat, Angie Battaglia, Boardman, and Michelle Paoli. He was leading up to Torelli, and his connection with the UN—still trying to decide how far to go, whether he would get into his last interview with Michelle, or hold it back.

"We've got some delicate areas," he said as a preamble. He was trying to lead into the Money Club, the questions of diplomatic immunity, and the sex club that had been operating on UN territory for the past twenty-five years. He was still feeling his way when Jenny Miller interrupted him.

"I already know about that. Chief Cervone gave me a thorough briefing." She shook her head. "This whole homosexual thing is going to be hard to avoid, but I'll do what I can."

Devlin's blood immediately turned hot. The woman was assuming what those *delicate areas* were, based solely on her conversations with Cervone. He gave himself time to let the anger pass. "Cervone's not running this investigation," he finally said. "In fact he's been told to stay out of it. So let's forget anything he told you."

The woman stiffened. "Told to stay out by whom?" she asked. Her voice had turned hard, trying to show who was in charge. It also reignited the cooling temperature of Devlin's blood.

The small scar on Devlin's cheek turned white. "By the P.C., by the mayor, and by me."

Jenny waved a hand at him, dismissing the information. "Look, I'm not interested in department politics. I—"

"No, you look, lady." Devlin glared across the table as he cut her off. "This isn't politics, and it isn't traffic court, either. It's a murder investigation. And Cervone's not running it. I am. If I win, you get to prosecute—maybe. So, if you want to help, great. You want to play patty cake with Mario Cervone, you get your goddamned information from him."

Devlin had pushed himself away from the table and now stood. "Just a damned minute," Jenny snapped. "Who the hell do you think you're talking to?"

Devlin stared down at the woman. Her anger was feigned, and it couldn't quite overcome the nervousness in her eyes.

"Not to you, lady. Not until I'm sure I can trust you."

The woman began to stammer, as Devlin turned abruptly and walked out of the restaurant.

Detective Stan Mikowski laid the crime scene photos on Devlin's desk, and tapped his finger against the obscene wounds on Suzanne Osborne's chest. "Cut 'em off and tossed 'em on the floor," he said. He jabbed a stubby finger toward another photo, a solitary shot of the woman's severed breasts. "I had one other case with mutilation like this," he said, as he slumped back into his chair. "Couple of years back. Woman who got iced by her lady lover." He grimaced. "Found the perp sitting in the corner, crying, when we got there." Mikowski shook his head. "We get a couple of gay murders a year in the Ninth," he said. "Goes with the territory, I guess. Some of them get real ugly."

Some in the straight world get pretty ugly, too, Devlin thought. Mikowksi was an older cop, who easily had his thirty years in. Just an old bull, Devlin told himself, sizing up the man. Someone who had stayed on the job because he didn't know what else to do with himself. Like Eddie Grogan, he thought. Except Eddie still cares. This guy, if you're reading him right, has seen more than he ever wanted to, and now just wants to look the other way.

"You figure this for a gay murder?" Devlin asked.

"Looks like it could be, yeah," Mikowski said.

"What about the vibrator?" Devlin asked. He tapped a finger against one of the photos, which showed the vibrator still inserted in the victim.

"I figure it was a toy they used—you wouldn't believe some of the stuff we find in fag apartments. Or, maybe this lady was bi, and her girlfriend lost it when she found out she was having it off with a guy." He made a face, as though it didn't matter either way.

"Tell me something," Devlin said. "I didn't see

anything about it in the reports. Was the vibrator still turned on when she was found?"

Mikowski looked surprised. "Yeah, it was." His face suddenly clouded, as though anticipating a reprimand for leaving that fact out of his report. "How'd you know? I was kinda holding back on it. You know. One of those things only the perp might know sort of thing."

The excuse was lame, but Devlin let it pass. "Just curious, that's all," he said.

Mikowski continued to stare at him. So now he'll decide you're some kind of sex freak, Devlin thought. So, let him.

"Were the wires used to bind the woman sent to the FBI lab?" Devlin asked.

"Yeah. Right from the scene," Mikowski said. "It's s.o.p."

Devlin nodded; made a mental note to check with the FBI to see if the wires matched. "Okay," he said. "We've got some information that this woman had some contact with Captain Battaglia. So we're taking over this case as part of our investigation." He stood, effectively dismissing the detective. "I want you to keep that between yourself and your immediate superior. But you come up with anything on the street, you pass it on to us, okay?"

"You got it, Inspector," Mikowski said.

Devlin decided the man looked relieved to have one less case to worry about. Or, maybe, it was just this one, now that it had been tied to a political hot potato like Little Bat Battaglia. But, in any event, he doubted he'd get anything more out of Mikowski. He also doubted the man would keep his mouth shut, which meant that everything would find its way back to Mario Cervone. But there wasn't anything he could do about that now.

Chapter Ten

Leslie Boardman stood in front of the living room fireplace, one hand resting on the mantel. It was a dramatic pose, designed to conceal the rush of fear that was threatening to take control of his body. He drew a deep breath of feigned irritation. With his free hand he brushed back his hair, inadvertently revealing the slight tremor in his fingers. Paddy Rourke grinned at him. He was seated on an oversized sofa, and his suit coat was spread open so Boardman could see the butt of the pistol strapped under his left arm.

"What was I supposed to do? Refuse to answer her questions?" Boardman ran his hand through his hair again. "Look, you weren't there. That dyke detective would've just run me in and kept asking until I answered. This way I didn't tell her anything she didn't already know."

"And what did you tell her?" Rourke's voice was a soft, threatening hiss.

"Nothing. Just that Joe and I knew each other. Socially. I didn't even tell her we met at Michelle's apartment."

"She ask if you fucked him?" Rourke grinned again. "Or if *he* fucked *you*?"

Boardman's jaw tightened, but he fought off the flash of anger. "She asked," he said. "I told her we weren't that close. Christ, I told you all about this, right after it happened."

Rourke ignored him. "That true? That you weren't that close?" He laughed.

"What difference does *that* make." The words had come too quickly, before Boardman could control the tone. He ran his hand through his hair again. "I wasn't about to tell her anything that would get me more involved than I already was. That's all."

Rourke's grin widened, but his eyes remained hard, unforgiving. Boardman was dressed in jeans and a white T-shirt emblazoned with a large pink triangle. Just like all the fags wore now, Rourke told himself. All the ones who had crawled out of their fucking closets.

He kept staring at the man. The little faggot was well built, in a thin, health-club sort of way. He had a hard, well-defined upper body that looked strong, and probably was. Just like all the fucking poofs who worked their little buns off on fancy weight machines. But as strong as he probably was, he'd be easy meat, Rourke decided. Muscles didn't mean shit, unless you knew how to use them. He knew skinny little shits, and fat slobs who could pound a fucking weight lifter into the earth. What mattered was experience. And pure, fucking meanness.

Rourke pushed himself up from the sofa and walked slowly toward Boardman, stopping when there was no more than a foot between them. "So you didn't tell this dyke cop, nothin', huh?" He shrugged through his grin. "Okay, let's say I believe you. Now tell me what you told Battaglia. There's a man down in Little Italy wants to know. *Capisce?*"

"About what? What would I tell him?"

"About our little enterprise, that's what. About our little cameras, maybe."

"You know that's not true. That's ... that's ... crazy." Boardman shook his head violently. "I told everybody who Battaglia was just as soon as I found out. And I was told to stay close to him, and find out what he was after."

"But you never found out shit. Did you?"

Boardman's face contorted, taking on the look of a small boy who was about to burst into tears. "Because he never asked me about *anything*. Never once. What do you think I am, a mind reader?"

Rourke's right hand shot out and grabbed Boardman by the front of his shirt. "I think you're a fucking little faggot, who doesn't know when to keep his mouth *or* his asshole shut. And I think you're dead fucking meat, you don't learn very fucking fast."

Rourke's fist began twisting the T-shirt, bringing his knuckles up against Boardman's throat. Boardman's hand instinctively shot out, grabbing Rourke's wrist, and the bigger man was momentarily surprised by the strength of the grip.

A slow smile spread across Rourke's lips, and he glanced down at Boardman's hand. Then he leaned slightly back, dropped his chin to his chest, and drove the crown of his head into the smaller man's face.

Boardman let out a yelp, but it was cut short by the sharp, hooking left that followed immediately, driving Rourke's fist up into his liver. Boardman doubled over and sank to his knees, his head falling forward against Rourke's thighs.

Rourke reached down, grabbed a handful of hair, and yanked Boardman's head back. Slowly, he withdrew his automatic and pressed the barrel against Boardman's forehead. Blood poured from the man's shattered nose, as Rourke grinned down at him. "You little faggot. You ever touch me again, I'll fucking blow your brains out."

Rourke could feel Boardman begin to tremble, and his grin widened. He released Boardman's hair, kept the pistol pressed against his head, and moved his hand to his zipper. Boardman's eyes followed the movement and Rourke began to laugh.

"Open your fucking mouth." Rourke's voice was

soft now, almost a purr. "I had a little girl like you in the joint. Used to cop my dick every night after lights out."

Boardman began to shake his head, but the barrel of the pistol pressed forward, stopping him.

"I find out you told the cops *anything,* the next dick in your mouth is gonna be your own. I'll cut it off and watch you fucking choke on it." He jabbed the pistol against Boardman's head, snapping it back. "Now you got work to do, faggot. So do it!"

Someone's watching me, and there's nothing I can do about it. There's no one I can go to. No one I can trust. They know about me. Everything. Maybe it will make them feel safe. If it does, it will give me the time I need. I've been stupid. I've made the one mistake I fought against for so long. But it's too late now. It's over for me, no matter how it turns out. I just have to make sure it's over for them, too.

I asked him why he did it, and he just looked at me as though I were insane. I wanted to grab him by the throat, but it wouldn't have done any good. Wouldn't have changed anything. Did I really expect him to be different? Was I really that stupid?

But it doesn't matter. I'll take him down with the others. And then I'll live with it. The only question now is if I have enough time.

Devlin let the words in Little Bat's journal play across his mind. He was standing in the large outer office, awaiting word that the mayor was ready to receive him. The call had come a half hour earlier, stating that His Honor wanted him immediately. So, he had come. And then, as usual, he had waited.

"Why don't you sit," the secretary suggested. "He's on the phone with Washington." She paused, raised one hand, and imitated a jaw opening and closing. "There's no telling how long."

Devlin glanced at the row of chairs along one wall, then back at the woman. Ellie Cohen was still trim and attractive at forty, and she possessed the smooth, mollifying manner of a professional ombudsman. She had been with the mayor throughout his long tenure as Brooklyn borough president, where she had perfected one major talent: how to keep people happy and content while Howie Silver simply kept them waiting. It was a role of tactful office wife to boorish husband—one Silver had come to depend on more and more. And it had led to the inevitable rumors about just how close their relationship had become. But Devlin dismissed that speculation. It wasn't a question of loyalty, or even that he liked them both. Howie Silver was a pure politician and, as such, Devlin wouldn't put anything past him. But he wasn't a stupid man. If someone wanted to catch him in a compromising position, they'd have to work harder than that. And Ellie Cohen? Well, she was simply too shrewd to give up the one thing she had worked so hard to achieve: the pure, unadulterated dependence of a powerful boss.

Devlin smiled. "It's okay," he said. "Even Howie can't talk forever."

Ellie Cohen rolled her eyes. "Don't bet the pension on that one, Inspector."

Forever lasted another fifteen minutes.

When Devlin entered the office, he found Silver stretched out in his chair; feet propped up on the desk. He was in shirt sleeves, tie slightly askew, and he already looked battered, even though it was still an hour before noon. The green-tinted, bulletproof glass in the windows behind him only added to the image; it cast a sickly pallor over his normally sallow complexion.

"Boy, you do know how to stir up shit," Silver began, as he unfolded his slender body, and forced himself into a sitting position. He raised one hand and patted the side of his head—satisfying himself that every silver-streaked hair was still in place—then stared at Devlin over the dark, ever-present smudges beneath his eyes.

"Two calls. One from the first assistant D.A. One from some flunky at the State Department. Both of them wanting your ass drawn and quartered. Is there somebody you haven't pissed off today?"

Unlike most politicians, complaints never bothered Silver until they reached the level of a personal threat. Until then they only amused him. Right now he was amused.

"How do *you* feel about me?" Devlin asked.

A wry smile crossed Silver's lips. "Right now I just want to know why so many people want your balls in their pocket. So tell me." He motioned toward a visitor's chair and waited.

Devlin led him through it step by step, leaving nothing out. He watched Silver's eyes widen, until he finally fell back in his chair, shaking his head.

"That cocksucker. That little shit."

Devlin fought off a smile. Despite the polished image he offered up for public consumption, Silver slipped easily into his own past—back fifty years, when he was a poor Jewish kid growing up on the hard streets of Flatbush. "Which cocksucker?" Devlin asked.

"That prick from the State Department. He never said anything about a goddamned whorehouse. All he said was that you were infringing on diplomatic immunity."

"He probably thought you knew. Or, maybe, he doesn't know himself."

"Sonofabitch." Silver stood, hitched up his trousers, and began pacing. "This is great. I'm in office seven months, and I've got a city-approved cathouse operating under my nose. I've got a dead police captain—one who happens to be Big Bat's kid. And, just maybe, I've got a bunch of politicians, cops, and prosecutors in Donatello Torelli's goddamned pocket." He turned and stared at Devlin. "You have any other good news?"

"Just that somebody in your police department has to know about the cathouse."

"You sure about that?"

Devlin nodded. "I'm just not sure who. Or how much they know. Or if it means anything. But somebody has to know about the Money Club. And they have to know the feds are running a honey trap. They may not know it was turned over to Torelli. And they may not know that Little Bat found out about it. But I have to assume they did. On both counts."

"But this was set up twenty-five years ago. Maybe nobody knows. Maybe all that information got lost as people retired."

Devlin shook his head. "Information like that had to get passed down. The feds would make sure it was. And at a pretty high level. It's the only way they could guarantee the operation stayed safe." Devlin read the uncertainty on the mayor's face. "Look, Howie. We're talking about a very safe operation. It's on UN territory. It has a very elite clientele. It's all wrapped up in diplomatic immunity. But, no matter how safe it is, somebody can still drop a dime on it. Some hooker who used to work there, one who gets busted later and wants to buy her way out. Whatever. So, let's say that happens, and some low-level commander tumbles to it. But because it's the UN, because it involves diplomatic immunity, it's got to be run up the chain of command. Right up to the P.C. if nobody below him kills it. Right to *this* office, even. And the feds weren't about to take a chance that some politician might approve a raid just for the publicity and votes it might get him. So they had to have *somebody* who could stop it before it got that far. And they'd never take the chance of letting their protection slip away through retirement."

"But wouldn't that boss—whoever the hell he was, or is—tell his boss?"

Devlin shook his head. "Secrets mean power." He grinned. "And, in case you haven't noticed yet, cops love power."

Silver let out a breath, returned to his chair, and fell into it. "So what do I tell this clown when he calls back?"

"Tell him you've got a murdered police captain, and he should kiss your ass."

The ghost of a grin flickered across Silver's lips. "It's not that easy," he said. "It's a fun idea. But not easy. You'd be surprised the pressures Washington can bring to bear. One department contacts another, and suddenly there are delays in federal aid. All of a sudden I get a call from the national committee, telling me future political support has become very questionable. All kinds of shit."

"So tell them it's taken care of. Tell them your cops are keeping hands off. I've got somebody inside their operation now. So I don't have to go back to their little club. You did what you could do. You ordered me to stay away. If they bitch about me interviewing U.S. citizens who work there, well . . . ?" He shrugged. "There's no law against that, and they'd be putting their political asses on the line by trying to interfere with a murder investigation. Especially a cop killing."

Silver nodded, thought about it. "When it all comes out, they'll still be pissed."

"But you can warn them ahead of time. Give them time to start covering ass, to distance themselves from the people who are going to take the fall. They can't expect you to do more than that."

Silver nodded again. "You sure you can trust this Paoli woman?"

Devlin shook his head. "But, if I can't, it'll be an easy way to find out."

"What about the D.A.?"

"You climb on Cervone, and let the D.A. know you have. That should take care of it. Jenny Miller will get the message." Devlin inclined his head to one side. "And, in the meantime, I'll keep her running in circles until I'm sure I can trust her. I don't think she'll complain again. She's ambitious, and this is her big shot. She won't want anyone to think she can't handle it."

The mayor nodded. "That I can do." He rubbed his hands together. "And when you find out which one of your bosses has been keeping this little secret, I want to know. The sonofabitch is going to retire."

Don't bet on it, Devlin thought. But he could end up in jail.

Chapter Eleven

"I'd like to take a knife and cut his heart out." Leslie Boardman raised his fists, slammed them against his thighs, then looked away.

It was an act, nothing more. And it was bred by impotence, Michelle Paoli thought. Leslie's eyes were now fixed on a small sailboat struggling against the outgoing tide of the East River; not really seeing the boat at all. Or, perhaps, wishing he were on it.

They were seated on a bench in the small park just north of the UN General Assembly Building, partially hidden from strolling tourists by a tall, evergreen hedge. You could always tell the tourists in New York, Michelle thought. Even more so than in Paris or London. Even without the small, inexpensive cameras dangling from their necks, there was an attitude, a demeanor that separated the two. New Yorkers seemed to have been born with theirs. When she had first arrived in the city years ago, a friend had described it as a *don't fuck with me* approach to life. She had laughed then, but had soon found it was true. Tourists in the city carried with them a wide-eyed charm, people looking for adventure and in great expectation of a good time. New Yorkers, meanwhile, moved about expecting disaster and dementia as part of their daily encounters. And the invisible barriers they erected about themselves were truly impregnable. But there were other differences as well. Few native New Yorkers wore plaids with stripes, and even fewer white belts with white shoes.

Dismissing the moment of reverie, Michelle took one of Boardman's fists, opened it, and placed her other hand on top. Leslie had called her an hour ago, his voice a mixture of desperation and rage. Too close to panic, she had decided, and she had asked him to meet her on the grounds of the UN, one of the few places she still considered safe to use.

"There's nothing you can do. Nothing either of us can do. We both know that." She stroked his hand. "But it will be over soon, I promise you."

His eyes snapped back. Anger showing through the fear. "How? How can you promise *that*?"

"I can't tell you. Just trust me. We'll be rid of Rourke, all of them, very soon."

He let out a derisive snort. "That's what I thought when Battaglia got involved. But it didn't work. *That* didn't turn out too well, did it?"

His voice was sharp, accusatory, and it raised her own level of anxiety. His fear was becoming contagious. She replaced hers with anger. "*That* was your plan, Leslie. Never mine. Never." She freed his hand and glared at him. The man had dragged her deeper than she had ever intended to go. She should never have trusted the simpering fool. When he had come to her; told her what he had done, she should have washed her hands of it, gone straight to Ari and told him. Let *him* handle it. But he would simply have gone to Fucci, or Rabitto, and that would have made things even more difficult. And, in the end, nothing had changed. Except that Joe Battaglia was dead and Leslie was still alive.

She let out a long breath, composing herself. "I don't want anything to happen to you. So I want you to do just as Rourke said. Speak to no one. Especially the police."

"And how am I supposed to do that? You don't know anything about the police here, how they can hound you, bring you in for questioning, do fuck-all whatever they want." His voice had turned into a whine. He didn't try to fight it, and that undisguised weakness disgusted her. He leaned closer, and she could smell the sickly scent of his cologne. "A police captain's been murdered. The rules don't apply anymore. You don't seem to understand that."

"I'll see they leave you alone." Her words were tight, clipped; she was fighting off anger again.

"And just how the hell are you going to do that?" he demanded.

"That's not your concern," she snapped. "If they come to you, just tell them you have nothing more to say."

He snorted. Then her eyes made him look away.

"Otherwise, you can handle it yourself. Would you prefer that?"

He kept his face turned toward the river. His hands closed into fists again. But it wasn't from anger. It was to keep her from seeing them tremble.

"No, I don't want that." His shoulders sagged, as if something that had kept him erect had suddenly been taken away.

Michelle reached out and took both fists; held them until they opened again. "Then just do as I say. And trust me."

Eddie Grogan pushed the photographs away. Belatedly, he inclined his head toward one showing a vibrator still protruding from Suzanne Osborne's body. It was as though he had wanted it as faraway from him as possible.

"I checked the reports. It was the same model as the one used on Little Bat," he said. He looked up at Devlin perched on the edge of the desk.

"We contacted the manufacturer, to get a list of retailers. I put Levy on it, but Jesus, Paul, you wouldn't believe how many vibrators get sold here every year." Grogan gave himself a small shake.

"Sometimes this fuckin' job makes me feel like I'm still a snot-nosed kid." He stared at Devlin. "What's happening in this fucking city, so many women gotta rely on plastic. There's even a store on First Avenue that specializes in these things. Levy told me that last Easter they even had a fucking window display with the fucking Easter Bunny carrying a basket full of them." He widened his eyes for emphasis. "Vibrators instead of Easter eggs, get it? The fucking gift that keeps on giving." Rita, the new love of his life, flashed through Grogan's mind, and he wondered if she, too, had one tucked away in her night table drawer. Maybe found it in her fucking Christmas stocking. A gift from jolly, old Saint Nick. He'd have to ask her. No, he decided. If she did, he didn't even want to know about it.

Devlin fought off a smile, then shook his head, dismissing Eddie's outrage. He tapped a finger against the photograph. "Let's forget the Kinsey report. We've got to assume it's the same perp, and that means he used both of these things within a few hours. It also means he probably bought them at the same time. So maybe we'll luck out and some clerk will remember somebody who did."

There was no conviction in Devlin's voice, and Grogan knew why. Salesclerks in New York wouldn't notice if you walked in and asked for two pregnant elephants. "I'll keep Levy on it," he said. "What about the wire?"

"The Fibbies say it's the same. Probably even from the same spool. But it's too common to trace. You could pick it up in any hardware or building supply store." Devlin glanced at a pad filled with notes. "What about this neighbor of Little Bat's? The old lady we haven't been able to locate?" he asked.

"Still among the missing," Grogan said.

"Keep somebody on it. Anything else come in?"

Grogan shuffled some papers on his desk, found what he was looking for, and handed it to Devlin.

"Final lab report from the M.E.," he said needlessly. "No drugs or alcohol in his blood."

And no diseases, Devlin noted, as he looked the report over. He reminded himself to let Angie Battaglia know.

"He had a hot dog, a Coke, and some ice cream a couple of hours before he died," Grogan continued. "Musta been when he was with his kids."

Devlin nodded. "Anything else?"

"Yeah. The M.E. released the body. Funeral's set for tomorrow. We got a memo from the chief of department's office. No viewing. Just a ceremony at the church his ex goes to, then the burial."

Devlin looked up from the M.E.'s report. "Full department funeral?" he asked. It was an honor given to all cops killed in the line of duty, and Devlin had wondered if the bosses would find a way to weasel out of it.

"Yeah. The mayor, the P.C., all the chiefs. Everybody in dress uniforms. He gets the full shot." He gave a small snort. "If he hadn't been Big Bat's kid, the bosses would have been falling over each other trying to be someplace else. But they'll all be there. Unless they're in fucking intensive care."

At least the man would have that final dignity, Devlin thought. He wondered if what he uncovered over the next few days would take it all away again. He tried not to think about it.

"Okay. I want you to do a couple of things for me. First, I want Suzanne Osborne's telephone number put in the computer and run against that list of numbers we found in Little Bat's apartment. We'll see if Boom Boom can use it to break the code, if that's what the hell it is. Next, I want you to speed up getting the court records on both of Torelli's trials. I need to know all the players as fast as you can get them: the judges, the prosecutors, and the cops. And

I want to know who in Washington would have gotten advance information on the evidence they were going to use against him. I also want photographs of every one of the bastards." He paused a minute, keeping his eyes on Grogan. "And I need it all tonight. And I need you to do it yourself. Don't farm it out."

Grogan raised his eyebrows. "Sounds like a photo lineup. What's goin' on?"

Devlin leaned forward. "This is between you and me, Eddie. Nobody else. I'll put it all in a report. But that report's going in my safe, and it's gonna stay there for now."

Grogan's eyebrows rose again at the willful violation of department procedures. It was something *he* might do. But normally not Devlin.

"Yeah, I know," Devlin said, answering the unspoken concern. "But we've suddenly got an informant inside the Money Club. And it may be the only way we can keep her alive."

"Her?"

"Michelle Paoli." He watched surprise register on Grogan's face. "She called me last night. Scared shitless." Quickly, he ran down what Michelle had told him, leaving nothing out.

"Jesus," Grogan said, when he had finished. "And she thinks you're the only one who knows."

"That's right. And if she finds out I told you, she just might dive behind her diplomatic passport and tell us to take a walk."

"Hey, I wouldn't blame her."

"It does solve one problem, though," Devlin continued. "I've been worried that sooner or later we'd have to talk to this Ari Popolis, who oversees the whole show. There's no question he'd tell us to take a walk, and that we'd find ourselves behind the eight ball as far as their little whorehouse goes."

Grogan shook his head. "You ever get the feeling we're slowly inching out on a limb with a fucking saw in our hands?" He hesitated a minute. "But it all fits."

"What fits?"

"Levy came up with somethin' on Boardman today. Seems our little sweetheart started out as a porno star in gay flicks. Then he turned legit. A couple of Off-Broadway plays, some heavy-duty modeling jobs. But it all went down the tubes about three years ago, when somebody dropped a dime on him. The advertising execs, and the producers didn't like the image. Cute, huh? Advertising guys and producers objecting to a cocksucker." Grogan tapped his nose. "I'll bet the pension those porno flicks were made by one of Bunny Rabitto's companies. And that Bunny dropped the dime when Boardman tried to walk away."

"And Boardman ended up working for Rabitto again. This time at the Money Club." Devlin digested the idea.

"Yeah," Grogan said. "And if Boardman even suspected that, it would be a helluva motive to pass on information to Little Bat. Especially if he thought he had Rabitto by the balls. If your little canary, Paoli, was a part of that, she'd have a reason to be scared shitless. Boardman, too."

Devlin stood, thought about it. "Lot of coincidence there, Eddie."

"Yeah. But I've seen worse. And this Paoli broad could have been involved. She sure as hell is now."

Devlin nodded. "Yeah, she is," he said at length. "We better check Boardman out again. And I think it's time to have a little, private talk with Paddy Rourke. Get somebody to pay him a visit this afternoon."

Grogan snorted. "I can hear that tune, now." he said. "Hear no evil, speak no evil, see no evil. And where's my fucking lawyer?"

Devlin turned toward the door. "We'll try it anyway. And try to have that other information and the photographs by five."

"You gonna see this Paoli broad tonight?"

Devlin nodded again. "But first I'm heading home. Adrianna's taking Phillipa out to the beach house for a few days. I want to see them before they leave."

"Yeah, you better. I just broke another date with Rita for tonight. As the Brits say, she was not amused. And, Paul. Watch yourself with this Paoli broad." Grogan gave him a steady look. "You're gonna have to spend a lot of time with her without any backup. Just remember what she is. Even if she don't turn tricks herself, she's still nothin' but a high-class, fucking hooker. And you don't ever trust a fucking hooker."

Devlin returned Eddie's gaze and fought off a smile. The man was speaking as Adrianna's godfather now, not just as his partner. "I know that, Eddie." The smile fought its way through. "I'll give Adrianna your best."

"Phillipa, too," Grogan said.

The smile widened. "I won't forget Phillipa either," he said.

Adrianna and Phillipa were packing when he returned to the loft. Outside, the humidity was beating the city into wet, irritable submission, and Devlin had a sudden vision of throwing his own bathing suit into the pile and going with them.

"Looks like the idle rich are heading for the good life," he said, as he made his way across the loft.

Phillipa grinned at him, then raised her chin imperiously. "Someone has to do it."

"And it might as well be us," Adrianna chimed in. "We'd love to have you come with us."

Devlin sat on the edge of the bed, where their clothing had been arranged in neat piles. "It's the curse of the working class," he said.

"I meant so you could carry our bags," Adrianna added.

He glanced around the bed. "Looks like you need someone. What about all the clothes you already have out there?"

"This is new stuff," Phillipa informed him. "To add to our collection."

"Yikes. Just remember, I'm only an inspector, not a chief."

"But you have a rich girlfriend," Phillipa said. "*She* bought them."

Devlin inclined his head toward Adrianna. "Thanks, rich girlfriend. Any new stuff for me?"

"Not a thing." She turned her head away from Phillipa. She didn't want the child to see the irritation on her face. "But there could be. *If* you found some time for us."

Devlin felt the tension in her words. "Doesn't look likely." He offered up a look of regret. "Little Bat's funeral is tomorrow. *And* I think we may have a break. But it's going to take some slogging."

Adrianna didn't know if he was trying to be evasive. But she decided to change the subject anyway. "Will you need your uniform?" she asked. "That battered old thing you've got hanging in the closet doesn't even have your new shield or rank on it."

"I'm working the case. Nobody will expect me to wear it."

She glanced at Phillipa again. "Maybe you should. Let's take a look at it." She ran a hand over Phillipa's shoulder. "You finish packing. Okay, honey?"

"Sure," Phillipa said.

Adrianna took Devlin's arm and led him across the loft to a large storage closet. It was a ruse to get away from his daughter, and Devlin understood that. He suspected Phillipa probably did as well.

Adrianna opened the walk-in closet door and drew Devlin inside. Then she turned and placed her hands on his shoulders. "I'm sorry. I'm just angry you won't be with us."

Devlin stared at his shoes, refusing to rise to the bait.

"Be careful," Adrianna said. "Please be careful."

He leaned forward and kissed her forehead. "Don't worry," he said. "Nobody in the department can even *remember* the last time an inspector got hurt on the job. Unless it was a paper cut."

Adrianna stared at him. It was a steady gaze, not unlike the one Eddie Grogan had given him. "This ceremony for Little Bat tomorrow. What do they call it?"

He lowered his eyes and shook his head. "I never should have fallen for a cop's daughter," he said.

"What do they call it?" Her voice was insistent.

"You know what they call it."

"What?"

"An inspector's funeral."

"Okay. I went to one for my father. I don't ever want to go to another one for someone I love." She leaned her head against his chest. "And I never want to take Phillipa to one."

"I'll be careful. I promise."

Adrianna and Phillipa left at three, trying to beat the madness of rush hour on the Long Island Expressway. Devlin, soaked with sweat after wrestling their bags into the car, was just changing his shirt when Eddie Grogan called.

"You want I should bring everything by the loft?" he asked.

"No. I'll be back at the office in about an hour. Did you get somebody to roust Rourke?"

"Yeah, I sicced Cunningham on him. It was like I thought. He don't know nothin'. He never even heard of Little Bat, or Donatello Torelli, or nobody. I think he was probably at a Boy Scout meeting—

with his fucking lawyer—when everything went down."

"Did Boom Boom have any luck with Suzanne Osborne's telephone number?"

"He's still working on it. I'll goose him a little."

Devlin left the loft and drove his department car north into Greenwich Village. He pulled to the curb at a bank of pay phones, climbed out, and dialed Michelle Paoli's home number. He had no idea if her telephone was tapped, or not. But with new telephone technology that could automatically identify a caller's number, he had decided never to chance a call from his office or home.

Michelle's answering machine connected on the fourth ring, and Devlin immediately went into their prearranged routine.

"It's Roger. Just calling to see if you could join me for dinner. I'll call back around six."

Devlin replaced the receiver. If Michelle followed their plan and checked her machine for messages—if she hadn't gotten cold feet—she would leave her building at eight, and head for the friend's apartment they had agreed to use. All he could do now was set himself up and hope for the best—and make sure she wasn't followed by someone else.

"What do you mean there's no such thing as date rape, you little piece of shit?"

Sharon Levy looked as though she might come out of her chair and strangle Boom Boom Rivera right in the middle of the squad room.

Rivera grinned at her. "It's bullshit, and you know it. Gloria Steinem, and all those other uptight, liberated chicks invented it to make sure nobody ever got laid. What, you never heard the expression: 'Her lips may say no, no, but there's yes, yes in her eyes'?" He jabbed a finger at Levy's reddening face. "Hey, let me tell you somethin'—"

"Don't tell me shit, asshole," Levy snapped.

"Hey, I know, I know. You want every guy who does it, without an engraved invitation, to get his balls chopped off."

"No," Levy sneered. "I don't wanna cut their balls off. I'll tell you what I fucking want. I want every one of those assholes thrown in a cell with a six-foot, four-inch, two-hundred-and-fifty-pound gay biker. That's what I fucking want. Then I wanna take 'em out, after about two weeks—after their fucking assholes are about the size of the fucking Taconic Parkway—and then I wanna ask 'em if they've changed their fucking minds about consent."

Rivera stared at her. "Jesus," he said, rearing back in disgust. "You are one sick, fucking chick."

"You're not feeling well, Levy?"

The two cops turned to the sound of Devlin's voice.

"I'm fine, sir," Levy said. "It was just a private discussion."

Devlin noted the faint hint of a growl in Levy's voice. He stopped in front of Rivera, keeping his face as expressionless as possible. "I guess you finished checking that phone number," he said. "Otherwise you wouldn't be out here raising Detective Levy's blood pressure."

"Yes sir," Rivera said. "It turned out just like you thought. I gave the info to Detective Grogan."

"Great. I bet you could goose some credit card information out of that computer, you went back in and played with it a while."

"Yes, sir. I'm sure I could do that."

"That's nice." He turned, took a half step away, then stopped. "It's also nice, because then"—he reached out and placed one finger against the center of Rivera's forehead—"Detective Levy won't be tempted to put a small hole right about here."

"Yes sir," Rivera said.

"That isn't the place I had in mind," Levy said.

Devlin inclined his head to one side. "Whatever," he said.

Eddie Grogan's office as the squad's whip was about half the size of Devlin's, but about twice as neat. It always amazed Devlin that Grogan could walk around looking like a rumpled bag of wet laundry, yet have an office—and an apartment—that always looked freshly cleaned.

"Boom Boom tells me he had some luck," Devlin said, as he reclaimed his earlier perch on the edge of Grogan's desk.

"The kid's a fuckin' wizard," Grogan said. "And I'll tell you something else. Little Bat was one cautious sonofabitch. It's a wonder anybody ever got to him."

"So, Suzanne Osborne's number was in his address book."

"Plain as day," Grogan said. "Except you'd never recognize it unless you knew how to read the numbers." Grogan scratched out a series of seven numbers on a piece of paper, then turned it toward Devlin. "What he'd do, when he wanted to conceal a phone number, is he'd start here." He took a pencil and taped the fifth number in the series. "He'd write down the fifth, sixth and seventh numbers, followed by the first four. Then, when he put it in his phone book, he'd reverse the whole thing. So, let's say, in his book, we find the number: 432-7846. The first thing we gotta do is reverse it to: 648-7234. Then, if we want the real number, we start at the fifth digit, then add the first four to the end. And we end up with 234-6487." Eddie grinned at him. "Boom Boom tells me a seven digit code can produce a few million variations, and if we didn't have a number to start off with—one that was already in Little Bat's book—it mighta took the computer a week to figure it out. But since he had a number that was already in the book—even though it was in code—all he had to do was feed the number into the machine—along with every other number in the book—and ask the computer to figure out if the first number appeared in the others in a different sequence. Then, once the computer had the coded number isolated, it could tell you just how the code was put together."

He picked up another sheet of paper on his desk and handed it to Devlin. "These are the phone numbers in Little Bat's book, and the real numbers beside them. Ma Bell says we oughta have names to go with them by tomorrow."

"Good. We'll get people out to interview them as soon as we get the list."

"You gonna run the names by the Paoli woman when we get them?" Grogan asked.

Devlin thought about it, then shook his head. "Not yet. Right now I just want to find out what *she* knows. We can go back to her later, if we have to."

Grogan picked up a large manila envelope and handed it over. "In there you got all the players in the two Torelli trials. There were different federal judges, but the same prosecution team in the U.S. Attorney's office. Ditto on the Attorney General's office in D.C. But the guys in Washington—the ones who would have had advance access to evidence and trial strategy—are pretty high on the fucking totem pole. Makes it look like Washington wanted his ass pretty bad."

"Yeah. Mafia dons, terrorists, and big-time drug dealers," Devlin said. "The high-profile busts that make the feds wet their pants. Lets them stand in front of the microphones and tell the public there really is a war on crime."

"So you don't think the intelligence agency that set Torelli up with this honey trap scam would've gone to the attorney general and asked him to back off."

Devlin shook his head. "I think they would've taken whatever Torelli gave them, and said: *grazie.*

But if he got his ass in a jam, I think they would of taken a walk. Don't forget, Lucky Luciano did some heavy work for the OSS and the CIA, and the feds still deported his ass back to Italy. But that doesn't mean they wouldn't have looked the other way if Dapper Dan set up some people who *could* help him."

"Like a judge, or a prosecutor," Grogan added.

"Or a cop," Devlin said.

"As far as the cops go, it was a mixed bag of feds and guys from our Organized Crime Control unit, who worked both cases."

Devlin glanced up at the ceiling. "Which means if it was one of our guys, it would have been somebody pretty high up."

"Yeah," Grogan said. "You can bet the feds didn't share a lot with the grunts working the case. They never do. But a chief? That would be different."

Devlin picked up a pencil and began playing with it. "So we're looking at Mitchelson. Or somebody even higher, who he would have reported back to." Devlin tapped the pencil against his leg. The logical assumption was Mario Cervone. But, even though he despised the man, he couldn't imagine Cervone playing pattycake with the mob. "Who's Mitchelson's rabbi in the department?" he asked.

"Supposed to be the first deputy commissioner, Mac Brownell."

Devlin conjured up a mental image of the man. It came across as tall, physically rigid, and professionally severe. Brownell had been chief of department under the previous administration. Then he had retired, only to return as first deputy when the new P.C. had taken over. Devlin knew little about him, other than his reputation as a tough administrator with an exceptionally low tolerance for error.

Devlin pondered the possibilities. "It doesn't fit," he said at length. "But nothing about the case does. All we can do is look at the trial transcripts, see what evidence blew up in the prosecution's face, then trace it back and see who knew what before-hand."

A grimace spread across Grogan's face. "I'll ask for a hurry-up on transcripts of both trials. It should give us some nice bedtime reading."

"Yeah. But don't expect to spend too much time in your bed. And do it as quietly as you can." Devlin added. "The last thing we want is to tip anybody off."

"One other thing," Grogan said. "The press is hounding us. We keep passing them on to public information, but they keep calling back. Sounds like they're losing their sense of humor."

"Just keep sending them back to the P.R. types. Blame it on me. Tell them I'm a stickler for rules and regs."

"Oh, yeah. They'll believe that one," Grogan said.

Chapter Twelve

A dirty, bearded man of indeterminate age struggled up the avenue, shuffling from litter can to litter can, stopping at each to rummage inside, then moved on. The trash man was dressed in baggy trousers and a tattered, ancient sports coat, and each—like the man himself—was covered with filth. Another man approached from the opposite direction. He was wearing a blue blazer with brass buttons that flashed in the fading evening light, sharply creased tan slacks, and tasseled loafers that looked as though they had just been shined. He was walking a white toy poodle. The dog had on a red leather collar encrusted with rhinestones, and it trotted along with its short tail held erect, the small pom-pom of fur at its end bobbing with each step.

The dog walker wasn't watching the dog. His eyes were fixed on a young woman who had just exited a building across the avenue. She was long and lithe, with flowing auburn hair, dressed in white slacks and a pale peach blouse. There was a Gucci scarf draped casually across one shoulder, the cost of which would have fed the trash man for several weeks.

The dog walker's attention was brought back when the dog—now opposite the trash man—began to strain at its lead, barking and snarling. Slowly, the trash man raised his head from the litter can he was working, and offered up a filthy toothed grin. The little dog leaped against the lead, yapping and snap-

ping, as though it might tear the man apart. The
trash man leaned closer, then casually extracted a
filthy fork from a pocket, raised a finger, and beck-
oned to the dog. The dog walker yanked on the lead
and hurried past.

Devlin sat behind the wheel of his car, watching
this perfect tableau. It seemed the sum total of everything the city meant to him. His head dropped
back against the headrest and he smiled with a mixture of humor and regret.

Michelle Paoli came out of her building at exactly
eight o'clock, waited while the doorman hailed a
cab, then headed south on Fifth Avenue.

Devlin was parked a block and a half up the avenue, just below the main entrance to the Metropolitan Museum. He ran a loose tail, a half block behind
the cab. He already knew where Michelle was
headed. Now he wanted to see if anyone else was
tracking her there.

The cab followed a circuitous route, stopping
once at a florist—as Devlin had directed—before finally reaching the apartment of Michelle's vaca-
tioning friend. It was located on the short, dead-end
block of Seventy-second Street, between York Avenue and the East River. No one had followed.

Devlin turned into York, pulled into an illegal
loading zone, then backtracked to the building.
Michelle was still in the lobby, collecting her
friend's mail from a lock box.

Her eyes snapped up as he was accosted by the
doorman, and she moved in quickly, explaining they
were together. Once inside the elevator, she simply
stared at him. Almost imploringly, he thought.

"No, you weren't followed," he said.

"Are you certain?"

"Positive."

Her body sagged slightly with relief. Then she
seemed to catch hold of herself and forced a smile.

Confidence returned to her eyes. Perhaps it, too, was forced. Devlin couldn't tell. She was dressed simply, but elegantly, in a pale blue blouse and tan slacks. A lightweight, blue-checked jacket was fitted loosely over her shoulders. Devlin's mind flashed to the woman he had seen earlier—the one who had captured the dog walker's attention. Everything about each woman said they knew who they were, and what they were about. He wondered if it was true of either—or merely a facade.

"I'm sorry if I seem nervous. Something happened today." Michelle hesitated, bit her lower lip. "I found out that Leslie Boardman was . . ." She struggled for the right words. "Roughed up, I guess you'd say. By Paddy Rourke."

"At your club?"

She shook her head. "At Leslie's apartment. He called and asked to meet me."

"Where?"

"We met in the park on the grounds of the UN. It was the only place I could think of where I could see anyone watching. Leslie wasn't badly hurt. Just frightened."

Devlin decided not to tell her that parks were prime locations for watchers. They were open, easy prey to binoculars and directional microphones. But she hadn't been followed tonight, so she had probably gotten away with it. He kept his voice soft, unconcerned. "I don't think you should meet anyone like that again. If you have to, find someplace in the building, away from your office." He looked at her; asked his next question as casually as possible. Almost as if it didn't matter. He didn't want the woman any more rattled than she already was. "What made Rourke go after him?"

"He wanted to know what he had told Joe Battaglia."

"And?"

"He told him he never told Joe a thing."

"Is that true?"

She hesitated again, stared at the elevator door. "He says it is."

Devlin thought she was lying. But he expected it. The woman didn't know how much she could trust him. Not yet.

The elevator opened into a small foyer with two widely separated doors, the main and service entrances to a single apartment.

"Who lives here?" Devlin asked.

"A friend who owns an art gallery on Fifty-seventh Street. She'll be in Europe for several more weeks."

He followed her into a massive living room with a commanding view of the East River. He knew he shouldn't be surprised, living as he did with a successful artist. The art world, when it paid off, did so with heavy bucks for its favored few. But for someone raised in a poor, Irish neighborhood in Queens, it was still difficult to fathom.

"I want to check the rest of the apartment," he said.

Fear jumped to her eyes. "Why?" she said. He could hear a slight tremor in her voice. Her eyes darted toward a small hall on her left, concerned now someone might be hiding there.

"Just procedure," Devlin said, trying to calm her. "We'll do it each time we come here."

She followed him down a hallway, looking in each room. One they found locked, a dead bolt cylinder fitted into the door.

"My friend stores valuables in there when she travels. Things she's afraid might be broken by a house sitter."

Devlin looked at her, eyes curious.

Michelle laughed. It was the first time she had done so since they arrived. "No, not me," she said. "She usually has a graduate student in art history stay here while she's away. This time the plan collapsed at the last minute, and she asked me to keep an eye on the apartment, instead. But everything had already been locked up by then, so she just left it."

"I thought, maybe she didn't trust you."

She laughed again, and Devlin decided he liked the sound of it. "Perhaps she doesn't. Perhaps the story about the student isn't true," she said.

When they returned to the living room, Michelle slipped out of her jacket and dropped it across a fragile-looking chair, then slid into the corner of an oversized sofa. Devlin took the middle of the sofa. He placed the manila envelope he had brought with him on an intricately carved coffee table.

"I have some photographs I want you to look at," he said.

"Of what?" she asked. There was a touch of nervousness in her voice again.

"Just some men. I want to know if you've seen them at the club."

She moved closer to him, so she could look down at the photos as he spread them on the table. "I won't be able to tell you if they used any of the rooms," she said. "As I told you, I'm not directly involved with that." She let out a breath. "And, it's done rather discreetly. Members gather in the lounge, and other common rooms. Then they go off with whomever they choose, whenever they choose." She offered her small, Gallic shrug. "But I'll be able to tell you if they were in the building. And possibly which member brought them."

Devlin arranged the photographs in two rows. Michelle ran her fingers through her hair, her upraised arms causing her breasts to be outlined against the thin fabric of her blouse. The soft, subtle scent she was wearing made him even more aware of the proximity of her body. The woman was very beautiful, and she was frightened. It was a dangerous combination.

"I want you to take your time; tell me if any of

these people look familiar." He turned to watch her as she concentrated on the pictures. Her slightly pouting lips were more pronounced in profile, the delicate bone structure even more so. She ran one hand—the one nearest him—through her hair again, and he found himself struggling not to look at the swell of breast it offered.

"Do any of them ring a bell?"

Michelle glanced at him, momentarily confused by the idiom. "Oh, yes." At first he didn't know if she meant she understood what he was saying, or if she was referring to the photographs. Slowly, she reached out and delicately touched the edge of one of the pictures. It was of a man in his early sixties, balding, with a wide, smiling mouth. "This one," she said. "He has been there several times." Her hand moved to a picture above and to the left of the first. "And this one, I think. I can't be certain, but I believe so."

Devlin looked at the second photo. The man was in his late forties, with short, dark hair, graying at the temples. It was an official photograph, one distributed to the media, and the man's eyes and mouth looked hard, intimidating, almost as though he were trying to cast himself as someone to be reckoned with.

"Why can't you be sure?"

"He looks so severe in this picture," Michelle said. "People seldom really look that way." She hesitated. "Except my father. He always looked severe. But he was an arrogant man, who wanted to control everyone—in every way. My mother. Even his only child." She turned to him, tried to smile, then raised her head slightly, as if hoping he would understand what she meant. Devlin thought he did.

She turned back to the pictures. "But I believe it was him. If so, both of these men came with another American—though at different times. And each time they were guests of an Italian diplomat."

Devlin put the two photos aside, picked up the others and placed them on the sofa. Then he withdrew another batch from the envelope and spread them across the table. "How about these?" he asked.

Michelle's hand went out immediately to one of the pictures. "This one," she said. "This is the American the other men came with." Her eyes scanned the remaining photos. "These I don't recognize."

Devlin stared at the photo she had selected. He felt a twist in his stomach. He had included the picture on a whim, a hunch. He put the other photographs away, and spread the three she had picked on the table. "Do you know the names of any of these men?"

She touched the first two photographs. "I was introduced to them, but I don't recall their names."

Devlin placed a finger against the photo of the balding, older man. "This is a federal judge named Oliver Rockwell. Next to him is Walter Silverberg. He's a deputy attorney general from Washington."

Uncertainty flashed across Michelle's eyes. "Those aren't the names I was given." She shook her head. "Perhaps I'm wrong. But I was so sure. At least about the older man." She hesitated a moment, making up her mind. "No, I'm certain he was there. Several times, in fact. And always with this other man." She pointed at the third photograph. "I remember *his* name. It was Fiorelli. I remember it because, as a child in Corsica, we had a neighbor by the same name."

Devlin stared at her; watched her eyes. He was looking for a tell that would let him know she was lying. "This third man, the one who brought the others. Fiorelli wasn't his real name." He continued to watch her. "His name is Anthony Battaglia. He's a United States senator, and he was Joe Battaglia's father."

Michelle's eyes widened, then seemed to slip behind a glaze as she digested the information. "But . . ." The sentence died in her throat, as she grasped what it all meant. Her mouth remained slightly open, a disbelieving circle.

Paddy Rourke adjusted the lens on the camera, then stepped back and stared through the two-way mirror. The middle-aged man was hunched over the boy, doggy style, grunting with each thrust, sweat staining his face and back. The woman, also naked, sat on the edge of the bed and watched. Her fingers idly manipulated the tube of jelly she had earlier used to lubricate both males.

The man slapped the boy's rump, then commanded in a breathless voice: "Lick her! Lick her!" His voice held a distinctly Middle Eastern accent, and had the tone of someone used to being obeyed.

The woman, who was young and blond, and not much older than the teenage boy, dutifully positioned herself, legs spread, beneath the boy's head.

Rourke listened to the man grunt more loudly as the boy did as he was told, and as the woman, too, began to moan with pleasure.

The man ejaculated with a loud roar, then collapsed against the boy's back. "Don't stop. Don't stop," he hissed. Then gradually—recovered from his own exertion—he slid down, positioning himself between the boy's still splayed legs, and assaulted him with his mouth.

Rourke grinned into the mirror, recalling how the man had earlier rejected Leslie Boardman as the object of his lust. Boardman was circumcised, and while the Arab insisted he did not question Boardman's honesty about not being a Jew, he had been unwilling to take the chance, and had asked Rourke to find him a "suitable, non-circumcised penis." Rourke fought back laughter, thinking of the man's ever so precise words.

"Faggot," he hissed. Maybe he'd see about having

the film doctored, he thought. Maybe they could splice in a circumcised dick, and make the bastard pay even more to keep it out of the wrong hands. He liked the idea, he decided. He'd have to remember to ask Bunny if it could be done.

Devlin picked up the phone on the first ring. He had called Eddie as soon as he had gotten home, and had asked him to have a computer check run on Big Bat.

"Yeah, it was in his department file," Grogan said. "Fiorelli was his wife's maiden name. She's dead now. Passed away about five years ago."

He filled Eddie in.

"Sonofabitch," Grogan said.

"Yeah. Sonofabitch. I'll see you tomorrow." Devlin replaced the receiver. Like many people, Big Bat had chosen an alias he wouldn't easily forget, one that had some meaning in his life. He decided not to speculate on why a man would use his late wife's name when visiting a whorehouse. Better to leave that one to the shrinks, he told himself.

Chapter Thirteen

I keep asking myself how I really feel about him. If it's really worth risking everything I have, everything I've always told myself I wanted. Angie. The kids. Even being a cop. At least the kind of cop I've always tried to be. No, that doesn't matter. I could give that up. I could live without it. But not without Amy and Marie. Not them. And not Angie, either.

That's the crazy part. Not wanting to give her up. She deserves better than this. Better than having a man who can't be what she expects; who can't love her the way she needs to be loved. The way I promised to love her all those years ago. And I meant it then. I really meant it. I keep looking back, trying to see if I was lying to myself, just telling myself what I needed to hear. But I can't find the lie, even though HE tells me it had to be there. Hidden away with all the other lies I forced myself to believe.

He's a great one to talk about lying, when his whole life is a lie. But that really doesn't matter. Those are his nightmares, his consequences. What matters is what I'm going to do about my own problem. If I'm going to face up to it, or run away. And, if I don't run, how I'm going to deal with all the people it hurts.

Devlin closed the journal as Eddie Grogan entered his office. It was six-thirty in the morning, and Devlin had already been at his desk for half an hour. The squad wasn't due to start its shift until eight, but neither man was surprised to see the other. In fact, neither would have been surprised to see the entire squad at their desks—had they known about the new turn the investigation had taken. It was the nature of the beast. Good homicide detectives were like sharks. The scent of vulnerable quarry produced an inexplicable hunger.

"Ah, the smell of blood must be in the air," Grogan said. He ambled across the room, glanced at the journal on Devlin's desk. "You getting anything out of that?"

Devlin stared at the journal, shook his head, then surrendered to a shrug. "I'm not sure. I've read through it twice. Now I'm starting at the beginning again." He sat back, steepled his fingers. "That part goes back a couple of years. In fact, almost all of it does. I *think* it's what his wife must have found. The stuff that led to his divorce." He watched Grogan raise his eyebrows, and shook his head again in response. "It doesn't say anything specific. No names, anyway. I'm hoping, if I keep going over it, something will jump out at me."

"But nothing yet, huh?"

"No. Nothing." Devlin sat forward. "Except a picture of a guy who didn't like his life very much."

"You want me to take a crack at it?"

Devlin stared at the journal, and again shook his head. "Let me keep at it a little longer. Then we'll see."

"So what's the next step? You gonna confront Big Bat?"

"I'll wait for him to come to me. Ask how the investigation's going."

"He might do that today. At the funeral."

Devlin nodded. "But I'm just gonna drop some names on him. Torelli. The Money Club. Then we'll

see what he does. Who he goes to see." Devlin
leaned back and stared at the ceiling. "Right now
I'm planning a little burglary."

Grogan grinned down at him. "Anybody I know?"

"You know the burglar." He sat forward. "That
guy we used last year to break into the art gallery."

"Willie the Gimp. How could I forget?"

"Think we could talk him into another job?"

Grogan grinned. "You see the report on that ice
job a few weeks back? The one in the diamond district?"

"Willie?"

"Had to be. There ain't nobody else that good."
Grogan raised both hands, palms up. "They'll never
nail the little weasel. But I think Willie could be
talked into a favor. Who's the target?"

"Our friend, Michelle Paoli, had one other bit of
information," Devlin said. "Seems that Paddy
Rourke changes the film in his little cameras on a
regular schedule. Mondays, Wednesdays, and Fri-
days. They have a room upstairs with a safe."

"We're gonna rob the UN?" Grogan's eyes had
gone wide.

Devlin shook his head. "They also have a couple
of VCRs. Before the films are put in the safe, they
get copied. Then, like clockwork—every Monday,
Wednesday, and Friday—Bunny Rabitto shows up
with two little attaché cases."

Grogan grinned again. "One copy for the feds.
One for Torelli."

"That would be my guess."

Grogan shook his head. "So we rob the Mafia, instead of the UN. I'm not sure the Gimp will feel a
lot better about that."

"Let's see where Bunny takes the films first. Just
have the Gimp primed and ready. We'll have Levy
stake out the Money Club. Follow the little Bunny
Rabbit wherever he goes." Devlin rubbed his palms
together. The smell of blood was indeed in the air.

"You still have Samuels and Walker tailing Big Bat?"

"Eight ayem to eight pyem. He's pretty much been staying put, so I haven't put a night team on him yet. You wanna change that?"

"No. Just make sure Samuels and Walker are outside the cemetery today. We'll see what happens and play it from there."

"We're gettin' a little short on bodies. You want I should find some more people?"

Devlin shook his head. "Let's keep the group tight. If we have to, you and I can pick up some of the slack."

The remainder of the squad straggled in shortly before eight, along with one unexpected visitor— Assistant District Attorney Jenny Miller.

"I'm here to make peace, Inspector." The words were out before her rump hit the visitor's chair facing Devlin's desk. "I didn't understand the situation. I just assumed . . ." She drew a breath. "Look, it's been explained to me. This is my first homicide case. I just want to make good on it."

Devlin stared at her. "Hey, I'm in your corner on that one." The woman still looked nervous. She knew if she didn't make peace, she'd be out. The mayor would see to it if asked. But that wasn't all of it. That she hadn't been replaced already meant the game was still being played. Devlin wondered if he could turn that to his own advantage.

"Who do you report to on this? What I mean is, who gets to see whatever I give you?"

She twisted in her chair. "The head of the homicide bureau."

"And he reports back to the first assistant D.A., right? The guy who gave you the job?"

She nodded. "Or to the D.A. himself. If he asks. But you're right. Usually the first assistant." She waited, as Devlin continued to stare at her. "I know what you're thinking," she said. "They picked me because I'd do what I was told. That I'd be afraid not to."

"And because they didn't think you'd hold back information if I asked you to. Will you? It may be the only chance we have of winning on this thing."

Jenny Miller bit her lower lip. "I do that, it could be my neck. You know that."

"Yeah, I know it." A smile toyed at Devlin's lips. "Mine too. So answer the question. But don't bullshit me. You bullshit me, the last body I leave behind will be yours."

Jenny Miller took another deep breath. "You won't ask anything more than holding back on information."

"That's right. And, if they find out and break your chops, you can say I withheld whatever it is from you."

"And you won't deny that?"

"You got it."

A smile crossed Jenny's lips. "Then you've got a deal," she said.

Devlin sat forward and rested his forearms on the desk. "Good. Then there's some stuff you oughtta know."

Jenny drew a long breath. "God, I wonder if I'm gonna wish I never heard of this case."

Devlin's smile finally found its way home. "You only *think* you might feel that way. Fifteen minutes from now you'll just wish you listened to your mother. And went to medical school."

The mournful wail of bagpipes floated across Greenlawn Cemetery, across its hills and knolls, its quiet, hidden glades, and tree-lined walkways. It was a sound heard there many times before. Greenlawn was among the oldest burial grounds in New York, and the sad wailing of the pipes that danced past the intricately carved gravestones of forgotten statesmen

and Mafia dons, stevedores and grocers and petty
thieves was no stranger there. It was a song sung
many times, the lament to a fallen cop, filled with
regret, and intended as such—a sad and mournful
balladry of death arrived too soon.

More than four hundred cops—replete with con-
tingents from upstate New York, Connecticut, New
Jersey, and Pennsylvania—flanked each side of the
flag-draped coffin. The police were in dress uniform, their shields bearing a thin band of black cloth
to honor a fallen brother. At the foot of the casket,
Angie Battaglia huddled beside Big Bat and her two
daughters. They stood alone and isolated. Behind
them—only a few feet away, yet distant—were a
somber melange of city and state officials, members
of congress, the hierarchy of New York's Catholic
Church, and the vice president of the United States.
Even farther back, but separated from the dignitaries
by a single row of uniformed officers and secret service agents, was the remainder of Little Bat's family
and friends.

A nervous, young priest stood at the head of the
casket, attended by two altar boys. Behind him, and
off to his left, Devlin and Eddie Grogan stood alone.
And still farther back, held behind a sawhorse barricade by yet another line of cops, were rows of reporters, photographers, and TV crews.

"Jesus, I hate these fucking things," Grogan
whispered, as the last whine of the pipes drifted into
silence. "Especially those goddamned bagpipes.
Promise me. If some creep ever nails me, there
won't be no *fooking* bagpipes."

Devlin kept his eyes just past the casket. "No bagpipes," he whispered. He was watching Angie
Battaglia. He had telephoned her the previous day,
and had told her about the medical examiner's find-
ings. He had done it simply. "The final autopsy report is in," he had said. "Mrs. Battaglia, I just
wanted you to know there was no sign of any dis-

ease in Joe's body." There had been silence. Then a
soft intake of breath. "Thank you," she had said.
There had been nothing else, just the quiet click of
the disconnecting line.

He watched her now. All the anger was gone. She
seemed stunned; there was an almost undetectable
sway to her body as she gripped her children's
hands—that lingering part of what was now gone.
The children, like their mother, stared at the coffin,
as if trying to comprehend the body of their father
lying inside. They were motionless, pinned in place,
their pale faces waiflike, two small, sad flowers vulnerable to everything about them. Big Bat stood beside the older girl, the side of his coat brushing her
shoulder. But his hands touched no one. They hung
at his sides. Father and grandfather, he seemed apart,
alone. His face was slack against clenched jaw. He
had taken on years, and his shoulders were hunched.
As the priest began his final prayers, his eyes never
left the flag-draped bier, and Devlin wondered if his
mind was going back in time—to some earlier place
in the life of his only child. Or were his thoughts
perhaps more current—hovering among the very
things that had brought his son to this final place.

The priest moved forward, sprinkling the coffin
with holy water, then sliced the air in the sign of the
cross, a final blessing. There was a look of relief on
his face, a man soon to be away from so many
watchful and powerful eyes. Then the honor guard
stepped in. Crisp and starched, they folded the flag,
laying it in the hands of the sergeant in charge, who
pivoted smartly and, in turn, rested it in the waiting
arms of a woman, not truly a widow, but a widow all
the same.

The bodies jumped—mother and children, father
and priest; the children clinging to their mother's
arms, as three, successive explosions from seven rifles filled the air. Then the mournful dirge of a single bugle sounding taps, and it was done. Thank

God it's done, Devlin thought. He felt a weight he
hadn't known was there slowly leave his body.

"Impressive," Grogan said. "But it still don't beat
the alternative."

They were watching the line of dignitaries pass by
the bereaved, stopping briefly to offer quiet words of
condolence.

"What doesn't?" Devlin asked. He was watching
the vice president, flanked by two secret service
agents. He said something to Big Bat, took his hand,
then spoke to Angie Battaglia. The children stood silently, the younger's face pressed against her mother's hip.

"Being fucking dead," Grogan said. He shuffled
his feet. Even the sound of the word disquieted him
when applied to a fellow cop. "You gonna talk to
Big Bat?"

Devlin shook his head. "Later, I think."

They turned into a path that would skirt the lingering crowd, only to find the first deputy police
commissioner approaching quickly, cutting them off.

Mac Brownell was tall and lean and forbidding, a
man who carried himself with the self-imposed se-
verity of a Southern Baptist minister. Behind him,
Devlin could see Martin Boyle, the police commissioner, watching—a large, bluff man, with a scarlet
face that always made him seem two steps away
from a stroke. Boyle was a career politician, who
had made a name for himself as the city's investigation commissioner, charged with ferreting out corruption in city government. During his tenure, he
had found a great deal—though mostly at lower
levels—a task, Devlin thought, only slightly more
troublesome than finding shit in a sewer. But Boyle
had cleverly parlayed each success into a glowing
headline, then modestly demurred all praise, thus becoming an instant darling of the media, which
promptly cloaked him in a mantle of incorruptibility.
So when the police department—embroiled in yet

another scandal—found itself in need of a new head, Boyle was a logical and politically popular choice. That he knew nothing about the day-to-day operation of a major police force seemed only a minor obstacle. He had brought Mac Brownell with him. And as former chief of department, Brownell knew it all.

"The senator would like a word before you leave," Brownell said without preamble. The request—being the errand boy who delivered it— seemed to embarrass him. It was something Boyle had not wanted to do, so he had passed it on.

"Sure, Chief," Devlin said. He had been told previously, by Eddie, that Brownell preferred the old title, as opposed to the new. Devlin glanced toward the dwindling parade of mourners. "We'll hang around until the senator's finished."

"You better do it alone." Brownell's eyes hardened and he gave a quick glance at Grogan, reaffirming his message. "But before you speak to him, *I'd* like a quick briefing. I feel like I'm out in left field on this. And I don't like it."

Devlin understood it now—the first deputy suddenly running messages this way rather than sending one of his own innumerable lackeys. Big Bat had asked for an update, and neither the commissioner nor Brownell had been able to provide one. It had been a political embarrassment for both. And the commissioner had issued this duty as punishment. Now, Brownell wanted to make sure it didn't happen again, so he was playing errand boy for another politician. And in doing so he was sending Devlin a message: *You're not making friends by putting me in this position.* The message was received.

"We haven't got a lot," Devlin said. "But things are pointing to the captain's work, not something personal." He saw the surprise, the sudden sense of relief on the man's face.

"You mean it was a hit? Not some homosexual thing?"

"I can't rule anything out just yet, Chief. But that's how it looks."

The first deputy quickly shifted his weight, first to one side, then the other. It was almost a little dance, and it challenged the image of physical control he tried to project. "Yes, of course," he said, after a moment. He nodded to himself; his eyes glittered. "I never bought this homo angle. I don't care how the hell he was found. And I appreciated not seeing anything about it in the reports I read."

"There was no reason for it to be there," Devlin said.

"Exactly. Exactly." He nodded again. "We have to stick together on this." His eyes bored in on Devlin. "I understand you've had some problems with the D.A.'s office. You need any help there?"

"I think it's been resolved," Devlin said.

Brownell did another little dance step, and Devlin wondered what kind of dance he'd do when he learned just where the investigation *was* headed; that it might even track back to one of his own chiefs.

"Good. Good." Brownell was nodding again. "I want you to know I've told Chief Cervone to back off," he added. "His interest is understandable. Little Bat was one of his boys. But I know your brief. And I've impressed that on him. I assure you he won't interfere." He didn't mention the call from the mayor, telling him to do it.

"That's great, Chief." Devlin accepted a "one of the guys" squeeze of his upper arm. He had a mental image of the first deputy's conversation with Mario Cervone—one he would probably repeat again within the next hour. It went something like: "Keep an eye on that sonofabitch Devlin. I don't trust the back-stabbing bastard."

"I'll tell the senator you'll wait to speak with him," Brownell said. "And keep me posted on what's happening. I know we don't want too much on paper. But stop in the office. I'm always available to you." He glanced at Grogan. "You, too, Detective."

"Thanks, Chief. I will." Devlin said.

"Yeah, me, too. You can count on it, Chief," Grogan added.

They watched Brownell make his way back toward the line of mourners.

"Helluva guy," Grogan said. He was fighting off a smirk.

"That's what everybody says about the man," Devlin said.

"Watch your fucking back," Grogan said.

"Always," Devlin answered.

Big Bat made his way to Devlin as a uniformed sergeant accompanied Angie Battaglia and his grandchildren back to a waiting limousine. Devlin had already sent Eddie to their own car.

"Walk with me," Bat said. "I don't want to leave Angie and the kids too long."

They walked slowly. The limo was parked about one hundred yards away.

"The first dep tells me you'd like an update," Devlin said.

"Everything you can tell me," Bat said. He threw Devlin a sharp look. He wanted him to know he meant everything, *period.*

"Right now we're concentrating on two areas. One is your son's personal life—which doesn't seem to be panning out. The other is Donatello Torelli, and a little operation called the Money Club."

There was a slight start in Bat's body, one that would have gone unnoticed had Devlin not been watching for it. Bat pulled up and turned toward him.

"The Money Club? What are you talking about?" Devlin noticed he had passed right over Torelli. His face had gone pale.

"It's part of the UN," Devlin said. "But it's not

what it's supposed to be." He watched small beads of sweat form on Bat's upper lip. "And it ties back to Torelli. Under the table. We think he's been using it to compromise people." He paused, letting it sink in. "People in *our* government." He explained what they had found—how Torelli had become involved, how he'd been using it.

"A legal whorehouse," Bat said. His voice had gone soft, distant.

Devlin thought about the term. It was probably correct. It was happening on UN property—foreign soil—where they could make their own rules, their own laws.

"Yeah. But we think Torelli used that information to beat the last two raps the feds hit him with," Devlin said. "And that's not legal, Senator. That's blackmail. Plus a few other things."

Bat's breath was coming short and fast. It was hitting him for the first time, Devlin thought. That he had played a part in his son's death. Or, maybe, that his own ass was about to be caught.

"So you think Torelli had my son killed?" The words came out in a rush, a gulp of air.

"I'm not saying that. It could have been somebody who was being blackmailed *by* Torelli. It could have even been somebody in the department who knew about it, knew your son had tumbled into it."

"Cops?" Bat's face was ashen now, and his cheeks had gone slack. There should be anger, Devlin told himself. Rage. But it wasn't there.

He reached out and took Bat's arm. "Look. You're the only one who knows about this, outside of my team. Not the commissioner, the first dep, nobody." The mayor knows, Devlin thought. And Jenny Miller. But you don't have to know that, Senator. You only have to know what I want you to know.

Devlin paused, watching the man's eyes. "I need you to keep this to yourself," he added. "I know you understand that."

Bat nodded. It was a slow, unnatural movement. Like a puppet.

"Thank you," Bat said. "I appreciate you telling me."

Devlin watched him turn and move off to the waiting limo.

"How'd he take it?" Grogan asked, as Devlin slid into their car.

"Like a man who'd just been hit with a hammer." He glanced out the rear window and spotted Samuels and Walker parked fifty yards beyond the cemetery entrance. "Now we'll see what he does, who he goes to," Devlin said.

Chapter Fourteen

Bunny Rabitto climbed out of the black Buick Ultra and ambled toward the front door. He was carrying two briefcases—one leather, one metal. Halfway to the front door, he stopped and looked back. His driver had come out from behind the wheel and was leaning against the front fender, watching the street. The engine of the car was still running.

A small smile played across Bunny's lips. It was just like when he was a kid. He'd be standing on the corner with the guys, watching some heavy hitter come to one of the neighborhood restaurants, or to see somebody, or to buy a fucking pack of cigarettes. Whenever it happened, there was always a torpedo standing by the car, eyeballing the street. And always with the fucking engine running. It was the way it was done, and it had always made his mouth water; made him want the same thing for himself. And now, even though he'd had it for years, he still liked to see it. Fucking A Right. Just like in the fucking *Godfather*.

Bunny continued toward the front door. There was a slight sway to his overweight body. He was dressed in an iridescent sharkskin suit that looked like a glimmering tent from the rear. It spread from his thick neck, across broad shoulders padded with fat, down to a wide bottom, all of it forming an enormous inverted *U;* all held up by two rumpled, stubby stalks of pantleg. He was still smiling when he pulled open the door. Had he seen himself from the rear, that smile would have faded, for Bunny was a surprisingly vain man. What also would have killed the smile was something neither he nor his bodyguard had noticed—the car parked half a block from the entrance to the Money Club, with Sharon Levy slouched down in her seat, watching every move the fat man made.

Bunny let out a soft grunt as a rush of cool interior air struck him. It was late morning, but the heat outside already hit like a hammer, and the short walk from his air-conditioned car had left his forehead coated with sweat. He smiled at the young receptionist, laid one briefcase on her desk, then took a handkerchief from his pocket, and gently patted the moisture away. He did it with care. He was balding badly, and each day he combed long strands of hair from the side of his head across the vast emptiness. From then on, throughout the day, touching his head became a delicate act. You had to be careful not to dislodge the hair. Otherwise it lost its position, hung down, and made you look like a fucking geek.

Finished, he glanced back at the receptionist and smiled, his fat cheeks creasing, causing his eyes to squint. She was fucking beautiful, a fucking jewel, with big, heavy tits and a pouty little mouth that he'd just love to have nibbling on his pepperoni.

"Hey, sweet lips. You got no idea what you're doin' to my blood pressure. What say we find a quiet place and make nice-nice?"

The receptionist smiled at him, then shook her head slowly, regretfully, he thought. She had thick blond hair and wide, almost innocent eyes. She was no more than nineteen or twenty, but the slight, permanent curl at the corners of her mouth said she understood the effect of each look, each gesture better than most women twice her age.

Bunny shrugged. "Hey, into every life," he said. He picked up the second briefcase and waddled toward another door.

The receptionist reached under her desk and pressed a button that released its electronic lock.

Rabitto went directly to Michelle Paoli's office and entered without knocking. He took in the room quickly. Rourke was seated on the sofa; Michelle behind her desk. She stood and extended her hand as he came toward her.

"Mr. Rabitto," she said. "How nice to see you."

Bunny's eyes flashed to Rourke. "Don't get up," he snapped. "I don't want you should hurt yourself, showing some respect."

Rourke remained seated. "Hey, Bunny. You know I love you."

"Yeah, I know," Rabitto said. "You and the police commissioner both." He placed one briefcase on the desk, and took Michelle's hand. He looked her up and down. "God, you're gorgeous. If only you *really* worked in this joint."

Michelle felt repulsion course through her body, but she smiled into Rabitto's fat, creased face. Rabitto had never been with any of the women who did work in the club. Torelli had established that rule at the outset. His people were to leave the women alone—were to leave the club as it appeared to be: a safe haven for diplomats and their friends. "Do you have time for an espresso?" she asked.

"Naw. I wish," he said. "But I got an appointment." He turned to Rourke, then inclined his head toward the briefcase on the desk. "Let's get the stuff," he said. He turned back to Michelle. "You, I can't wait to see again," he added.

Michelle forced another smile. "I hope next time you'll be able to stay longer," she said.

When Rourke and Rabitto had left, Michelle sat back in her chair and drew a long breath. Then she picked up her phone and buzzed her secretary. She wanted to get out, find a public phone, and call Paul. Let him know Rabitto had made his regular pickup. But first she had to contact Ari Popolis. She'd been trying to see him for two days now, and she had to pin him down to a specific time.

"I'm going out," she said, when her secretary answered. "But first, get me Mr. Popolis, please." She replaced the receiver and stared at it. She had no idea why Ari was avoiding her, or if he really was. But his apparent reluctance to see her was playing havoc with her nerves.

Rourke moved directly to the large wall safe and began entering the combination. Rabitto moved up directly behind him and read the numbers over his shoulder. He already knew the combination, so was gaining nothing by doing so. But it was instinctive, something he couldn't help. Like studying a tout sheet at the track—on a race he already knew was fixed.

"You get anything good since my last visit?" he asked Rourke's back.

"Nothin' we can use," Rourke said. "All diplomats. Stuff for the files, for future reference." He swung the heavy door back. "There's a tape of Boardman sucking off a little Iranian shit," he added. "Maybe Torelli will get a kick out of watching it."

"He don't watch that fag stuff," Rabitto said.

Yeah, but you'll watch it, Rourke thought. Everything gets you fucking off. "We're supposed to have a congressman coming in tomorrow night."

"From where?" Rabitto asked.

"Florida. Miami."

"What's he like?"

"Young stuff. Just like all those old humps."

"You want I should send Tina by? We get some good shit, the boss, maybe, could sell this congressman to our friends down in Miami."

Rourke shrugged. "Couldn't hurt. But the Panamanian diplomat who's bringing him says he's fucking crazy about blondes. I got a little chick here should send him up the fucking wall." Rourke grinned. "And he ain't gonna be hard to put in our pocket. He's got a rich wife—an old broad—keeps him living like a fucking Rockefeller. He ain't gonna want her to see him getting his rocks off with some chick young enough to be her daughter."

Rabitto nodded. "I'll send Tina by anyway," he said. "The boss is gettin' a little nervous about these chicks here; about who they might be fuckin' talking to." He gave Rourke a steady look. "You find out anything for us on that?"

"Hey, I told you. All the fucking leaks are plugged."

Rabitto jabbed a finger against Rourke's chest. "You better be fucking sure they are. This Devlin's gettin' somethin' from somebody. And Dapper Dan don't like it." He watched Rourke shrug. "You check out this Paoli broad like I told you?"

"She ain't talkin' to nobody. Trust me."

"You better be fucking sure. Somebody's talkin' to that prick cop. You wire her phones here, and at her apartment, like I said?"

"It's all taken care of. Two days ago." Rourke said. "She ain't talkin' to nobody. I even got a wire in her fucking living room and bedroom." He grinned. "She ain't even gotten laid in the past two days."

"What about Boardman?"

"Him I'm still watching. But I don't think so."

"You don't *think* so? You get even a fucking hint, I want him whacked. *Capisce*?"

"Don't worry. I talked to him. He knows he's dead fucking meat, I get even an idea he's flappin' his gums. Hey, maybe you should have a talk with this fucking cop. Find out what he fucking knows, then whack *his* fucking ass. Then your problems are over."

Rabitto stared at him. "Yeah, maybe I should whack the fucking pope, too. But don't *you* worry.

This cop gets too close, he can kiss his fucking ass good-bye." He jabbed another finger at Rourke's chest. "For now, you just keep your fucking eyes open. Dapper Dan don't want no surprises."

"There won't be any. I guarantee it," Rourke said.

The Buick Ultra pulled into a loading zone in front of a Long Island City warehouse. Sharon Levy had followed the car across the Fifty-ninth Street Bridge and into the industrial maze that made up Manhattan's prime gateway to the Borough of Queens. As the Buick came to a stop, she drove past it and pulled into a parking lot across the street, then watched through her rearview mirror as Bunny and his driver entered the warehouse.

A tall, skinny black kid, with a reversed baseball cap and Walkman earphones attached to his head, ambled up to the car. He was wearing a black T-shirt with a picture of Malcolm X on it, and orange shorts that hung below his knees. He started to hand Levy a parking claim check. Levy flashed her shield and told him to take a walk. The kid muttered something unintelligible, but distinctly unpleasant, then spun around and bebopped back to his glass-enclosed booth.

"Yeah, fuck you, too," Levy said, as she adjusted her side and review mirrors to keep the warehouse entrance in view.

She had volunteered to take the detail without a partner, to ease the unit's manpower problems. But Devlin's okay of the lone surveillance had included instructions to stay in her car and avoid any confrontations. Levy pushed open the door. The instructions hadn't said anything about stretching her legs.

She moved quickly across the street and into the warehouse. There, she found herself in a small entrance foyer, leading to another locked door. But the directory attached to the wall gave her what she wanted. Four companies occupied the building. Last on the list was Spider Films, and it appeared to occupy the entire top floor.

Back in her car, Levy settled in to wait. There was a small Greek diner next to the warehouse, and she desperately wanted a cup of coffee, but her instincts told her to sit tight. Maybe she could con the parking lot attendant into getting her one. Fat fucking chance, she told herself.

Twenty minutes later her instincts proved correct, as Bunny Rabitto exited the warehouse and made his way to the diner, metal briefcase in hand. Five minutes after that, a distinctly government issue car holding two men, pulled up to the curb—one man exiting and entering the diner, while the second remained behind the wheel.

Levy picked up a camera from the seat and trained a telephoto lens through the rear window. The car's license plate came into view, and she clicked off three shots, then settled back to wait. Ten minutes later Rabitto and the visitor left the diner, the metal briefcase now in the other man's hand. Levy clicked off five more shots and settled back to wait for more.

At twelve-fifteen the black kid with the Walkman strolled up to her car again and tapped one long finger against the glass. Levy lowered the window and stared at him. "What?" she snapped.

"Hey, lady cop," the kid began. He was dancing from one foot to the other, not out of nervousness, but to the beat of the music still flowing into his ears. "I was jus' talkin' to my main man on the phone. An' he says he don' care nothin' 'bout yo motha fuckin' badge. *He* says you gonna sit here, you gonna pay like ev'body else."

Levy lowered her head, shook it, then looked back up at the kid. "Okay, asshole. You go tell your *main fuckin' man* that I get any more static, I'm gonna count the number of fucking cars he's got in this lot and see if it jibes with how many his license says he's *supposed* to have. And you tell him, I'm gonna keep coming back until I find out he's got too many, and then he's not gonna have that fucking license anymore. And, one more thing, asshole. You talk about my *motha fuckin' badge* one more time, I'm gonna slap some cuffs on your ugly fucking ass, and toss it in the backseat. *You* got *that*?"

The kid took a quick step back. "Sheet," he said. "Yo one mean, fuckin' momma. You know *that*?"

"And don't you forget it, fool. Now beat it."

An hour later Rabitto's driver and another goon exited the warehouse and took up stations on either side of the entrance. Levy wondered if the parking lot owner was one of Torelli's people, and had alerted Rabitto to an ongoing surveillance. This concern vanished ten minutes later when Buster Fucci pulled up in a silver Cadillac, and entered the warehouse, leaving his own two goons to stand watch with Rabitto's.

Levy slouched down in her seat and propped her telephoto lens against the headrest. Fucci came out twenty minutes later, a small, brown paper package in his hand. His image was captured on five rapid exposures.

Levy started her car as Fucci's pulled away. She had decided to break off the Rabitto surveillance and see just where Torelli's underboss was taking his brown paper present. As she backed out into the street, the parking attendant stepped from his booth and waggled his fingers in an exaggerated farewell. Levy tossed him the bird.

Fucci's car moved like a homing pigeon across the Fifty-ninth Street Bridge, onto the FDR Drive, then down to Canal Street—the long-standing demarcation line between Chinatown and Little Italy.

The car made a quick right onto Bowery, then left on Broome, and a final left onto Mott Street, before

pulling to a stop before Torelli's red-brick fortress.
Shit, Levy thought. The worst place in the world to
try and conduct a surveillance—a street dominated
by a Mafia clubhouse, and populated by more
wiseguys per square inch than ants on a fucking ant-
hill.

Fucci's car sat in front of the clubhouse with the
driver seated on one fender. All she could do, Levy
decided, was to park her own car down the street,
and play lady cop out doing some shopping. There
was no way she could hope her car wouldn't be
I.D.'d for just what it was.

Fuck it, she thought. She swung open the car door.
Sometimes the best way to hide, is not to hide at all.
She pulled down the visor, displaying her department vehicle I.D., crossed the street, and followed
two black-clad grandmothers jabbering in Italian
into a bakery. Can't be more obvious than this, she
told herself. Maybe if I flaunt it, nobody else will
worry about seeing me.

The ploy apparently worked. Twenty minutes later
Fucci left the clubhouse, reentered his car, and
headed back toward Canal Street. Levy had time to
amble out of a small butcher shop—a package of
braciola now joining her loaf of bread—get to her
car, and pick up the tail in the maze of perennially
stalled traffic.

Buster Fucci's car turned into a battered Brooklyn
street, a mix of warehouses and tenements that
marked the lower end of Park Slope. It was foreign
territory, of sorts, an area controlled by the Colombo
family, and it had been chosen, in part, for that very
reason.

The neighborhood was also the boyhood home of
Alphonse Capone, the place where he had learned
his trade in the early days, long before he was
shipped off to Chicago, after proving too enthusias-

tic about putting small holes in the heads of wiseguy rivals.

The car moved past Monte's, one of Fucci's favorite restaurants. But it was not the place for the meeting he was about to attend. Its clientele was dominated by cops and politicians, judges and bookmakers. A meeting there would be tantamount to standing on Times Square with a sign around his neck. Instead the car moved three blocks south, turned into a narrow, tenement-laden street, and pulled up before a hole-in-the-wall, storefront restaurant with the name Angelina's scrawled across the front windows.

Fucci climbed out of his car, noted that the CLOSED sign was already on the restaurant door as requested, and entered, leaving his two goons to keep all unwanted visitors at bay.

Fucci accepted warm greetings from the owner, a short, fat, balding man, who became even more effusive when a fistful of bills was thrust into his hand "for his trouble." He then settled into a rear table—a glass of Chianti before him—to await his guests.

Ten minutes later, Big Bat Battaglia and Jim O'Brien came through the door, and Fucci rose from his chair, moved forward, and warmly embraced the senator.

"Bat," he began—his face marked with as much grief as he could muster, "Donatello asked me to tell you how sorry we were to hear of your son's death. He said to say he would have been at the funeral, but . . ." He offered a shrug of resignation mixed with regret. "He thought it wouldn't be good for you if he did."

"Thank you, Buster," Bat said. "And thank Dapper Dan." His eyes turned hard. The two men were equal in size, and approximate in generation, but Bat's stare made Buster suddenly feel smaller, less significant than he really was.

"I brought something for you," Buster said. "A gift to show our sorrow, and our respect."

Bat glanced toward the table, his eyes stopping at the rectangular, brown paper package. "Thank you," he said. "But that's not what I'm here for."

Buster shrugged again, then gestured toward the table. "Let's sit and eat. And you'll tell me what you need. I ordered for us—I hope you don't mind. Some clams. Some veal piccata. They make it here like your mother made it."

When they were seated, the owner scurried forward with wine and bread, then retreated quickly to his kitchen, well out of hearing.

Bat picked up the brown package that had been placed in the middle of the table. "The films?" he said.

Buster nodded. "With our regret. But it was business. I know you understand."

Bat placed the package in front of O'Brien. He stared at Buster for several, long seconds. "I don't give a shit about the films," he said. "You can tell Dapper Dan he can take his copies and send them to Channel Five. It doesn't matter to me anymore."

"There ain't no copies. You got our word," Buster said.

Bat turned his head away, his eyes filled with disgust. "Don't bullshit me, Buster. I've known Dapper Dan since I was a snot-nosed patrolman. If he had something on his mother, he'd keep a copy." He turned back to face the man. "But I don't give a shit. Understand that. All I want is to know *who* killed my boy. And, if it was one of your people, I want him fucking dead."

Buster shook his head. "It wasn't us. We had a problem with your boy. That's no secret. But we had it under control. We had no reason to hit him. If it was one of our people that did this thing—even through some kind of mistake—I promise you, that person's heart would already be in your hands. I give you my word on that."

The owner started through the kitchen door—plates of *ostriche arreganato* balanced on his arms and hands—as Bat leaned forward, eyes gleaming. The owner stopped in midstride, turned and quickly retreated to his kitchen.

Jim O'Brien reached out and placed a hand on Bat's arm. Bat brushed the hand aside. His eyes remained on Buster. "Then you find out for me who it was."

Buster glanced at the brown paper package in front of O'Brien. "We're trying to show our friendship," Buster said. "I dunno if we can do this other thing you ask. I dunno if it's in our power."

O'Brien had reached out for the package containing the tapes, and was sliding it back, preparing to put it in his pocket. Bat's hand went out and stopped him. He pushed the tape across the table to Buster.

O'Brien's face flushed. "Bat. Let's consider this—"

Bat raised a hand stopping him in midsentence. Then, to Buster: "This means nothing to me. If exposing my own foolishness would get me this killer, I would do it tomorrow."

Buster stared at him. "That would hurt everyone."

Bat nodded. "This thing I ask you for means that much to me."

Buster let out a long breath. He picked up the package and slid it into a side pocket. "I'll tell Dapper Dan what you need. What can I say to you, but that we'll do everything we can."

"I'm telling you, we almost fell over each other," Sharon Levy said. "I felt like I stumbled into a meeting of the Detectives Benevolent Association when Samuels and Walker rolled in behind Big Bat.

It was a fucking traffic jam of cops and wiseguys and politicians."

They were gathered in Devlin's office—Samuels, Walker, Levy, Grogan, and Devlin—as the detectives explained the results of their dual surveillance.

"I can't believe nobody made you guys," Grogan said.

"I can't either," Levy said. "If I'd been a leper with a bell around my neck, I couldn't of been more obvious."

"So we lucked out," Devlin said. "Once in a blue moon we're entitled." He inclined his head toward the large, flip-sheet display board behind him. The first sheet held the list of coded names from Little Bat's computer, with some additions Boom Boom had pulled out in his continued search.

Cleopatra	The Politician	Fed 1	Boss 2
The Greek	Friend 1	Fed 2	The Spider
Cop 1	Friend 2	123 Restaurant	The Watcher
Cop 2	The Judge	The Boss	The Money Club
Lolita	The Bagman	The Lover	The Hooker

"Okay," Devlin said. "Let's see what real names we can add to our list." He extended a finger toward The Spider. "Looks like Spider Films and Bunny Rabitto are our best bet."

"And Angelina's for the 123 Restaurant," Samuels chimed in. "The joint's street address is 123 Norris Street."

"Right," Devlin said. "And Fed 2 could be the guy Levy saw picking up the briefcase from Rabitto. We'll have to wait until we get the photos developed and get a make on the car he used. But let's add him anyway."

Devlin pushed himself up from his chair and turned over the first sheet on the board. A second list appeared with suspected I.D.s noted beside each entry, several of which had been added over the past few days. He jotted in the new candidates, then stepped back.

Cleopatra (Michelle Paoli?)

The Greek (Ari Popolis?)

Cop 1 (Mitchelson?)

Cop 2

Lolita

The Politician (Big Bat)

Friend 1

Friend 2

The Judge (Oliver Rockwell)

The Bagman

Fed 1 (Walter Silverberg)

Fed 2 (Bunny's contact?)

123 Restaurant (Angelina's)

The Boss (Donatello Torelli)

The Lover (Leslie Boardman?)

Boss 2 (Buster Fucci)

The Spider (Bunny Rabitto)

The Watcher (Paddy Rourke)

The Money Club (UN Committee)

The Hooker (Suzanne Osborne?)

"Okay," Devlin said. "First we work to eliminate the question marks we've put next to some of these people. That means some third party corroboration that they either dealt with Little Bat or The Money Club. At the same time we work to fill in some of the blanks." He jabbed a finger at the board again. "I'm betting that Friend One and Two are some congressional buddies that Big Bat dragged into the club. So, the most important ones to me are Cop Two, the Bagman and Lolita. My gut tells me that somewhere, among those three, we've got the key we need to bust this thing open. So when you go back at the question marks, keep those three items in mind. Push for anything that'll give you a name."

"What about this O'Brien guy?" Samuels asked.

"Yeah, he's right up there on top of the list," Devlin said. "We just don't know where. But, keep in mind, he could just be a political flunky who's completely out of the loop on this. Anyway, for now we drop all surveillance on Bat and Rabitto, go back to hammering at the people we know about. We check them inside out. Look for any paper trails, and see if we can tie them back to anyone else." He turned to Levy. "I want you to work Boardman. Hard. Also this dead hooker, Suzanne Osborne. Boardman just man know something about her. Especially any ties she had to Little Bat."

He turned to Cunningham. "Joe, I want you to get me everything you can on Judge Rockwell, and this deputy attorney general, Walter Silverberg.

"What about me and Walker?" Samuels asked.

"You guys divide up the rest of the list. But one of you put in some time on this O'Brien guy. I wanna know if he's been seen with anybody else on this list except Big Bat. And I want one of you to sit on him tonight, the other tomorrow morning. Just to see if this meeting today forced any big changes in his plans. And, in any spare time, keep checking back on Miriam Goldstein, this lost neighbor of Little Bat's that we can't seem to find."

"What are you an Eddie gonna work on?" Levy asked.

Devlin grinned at her. "You keeping tabs on us, Sharon?"

"I just don't wanna trip over your feet," she said. "One more traffic jam'll give me a nervous breakdown."

"Don't worry," Devlin said. "We'll be doing something where even you won't find us."

"You told me this Federici guy was so good. So far he's come up with shit." Mario Cervone leaned across his desk. "So what gives?"

George Mitchelson twisted in his chair. Cervone was standing, and even though he was on the other side of his desk, it made Mitchelson feel as though he was hovering over him, ready to pounce.

"It's this shoe-fly he's gotta work with. He can't shake the guy. Federici thinks Devlin told this I.A.D.

guy to bird dog him. Says this guy's been sniffing his ass steady since day one."

Cervone ground his teeth, returned to his chair, and leaned back. "I got Mac Brownell on my back every day. He wants to know what Devlin's got, and he wants to know yesterday."

"We just gotta get rid of this internal affairs guy you slipped in on Devlin. Then Federici can do us some good."

Cervone stared across his desk. He was looking for some sign Mitchelson had intended the remark as a personal criticism. The Organized Crime Control chief's face remained a blank.

Cervone stood, paced a few steps, then returned to his chair. "You know how it works," he said at length. "I can request the guy be put in, but there's no way in hell I can order him out. You know that." He drummed his fingers on the desk. "But Mac Brownell can. He can order Internal Affairs to pull him back for manpower reasons. He can even say he wants this guy for something that's come to his attention. Something that needs investigating post haste. Shit, he knows how the game is played. He watched commissioners and deputy commissioners play games with Internal Affairs for thirty years."

Mitchelson saw a chance to get off the hook. "Getting rid of this guy is the only way it's gonna work for us," he said. "If Brownell can do it, we're home free."

Cervone rocked back and forth in his chair. "Brownell was your rabbi back in the old days, am I right?"

"That's right," Mitchelson said. He felt bad news coming, portents of trouble. "We haven't had a lot of contact since he came back as first deputy commissioner." Mitchelson shifted his weight again. The portents were growing worse; he could feel it. "It's been a question of propriety," he added.

"But you're still friends, right?"

"Yes. Sure. We're still friends."

Cervone sat forward and jabbed a finger toward the deputy chief. "Then I want you to go see him. Tell him what the problem is. Tell him we need this shoe-fly yanked."

Mitchelson knew exactly what Cervone was doing. He was distancing himself from a request that could come back to bite someone. You, Mitchelson thought. You're the one it'll bite if you do this. "You think that's a good idea?" he asked, taking a final shot at avoidance.

"I think it's the only idea," Cervone snapped. "Unless *you* can figure out another way."

Mitchelson let out a long breath. "I'll try to see him later today."

Chapter Fifteen

The woman was naked except for a sheer, silk blouse. Slowly, she unfastened the buttons, spreading the blouse slightly. Her breasts, small and erect like a young girl's, had been faintly visible through the fabric. Now the opening offered a hint of flesh along their sides as well.

A small smile played at the corners of the woman's mouth as she watched the man watching her. His eyes lingered on her breasts, then dropped slowly to the tuft between her legs. She had red hair, and the color carried to her pubis, which she had carefully trimmed and groomed until it was in the shape of a small heart.

She moved to the man, her steps slow and provocative. One hand went to the necktie that seemed to be strangling the loose flesh beneath his chin, as a single finger of the other hand gently stroked his upper thigh—close to, but not quite touching the visible bulge in his trousers.

"You're wearing too many clothes, Ollie." Her voice was catlike, almost a hiss, and she leaned against him and flicked her tongue against his ear.

"I've told you not to call me Ollie." The man's voice was a croak, a near gasp for air.

The woman leaned back and stared at him. The fingers of one hand spread the open blouse further, revealing one childlike breast.

"If you're not a good boy, I'll have to be mean to you. You know that."

The man let out a low groan and his head plunged toward her exposed breast, tongue extended as if reaching for some prize.

The woman gently pushed against his shoulders as she took a quick, dancer's step back. She laughed.

The man lunged again, and again she retreated.

"First your clothes, *Ollie*," she hissed.

The man quickly began to shed his clothing as the woman stood, hands on hips, head cocked, watching with approval.

At last he was naked, his bony, loose-fleshed body extraordinarily pale, his erect penis thrusting from a clump of tangled gray hair like some aging toy soldier on parade.

The woman backed toward the bed, eyes on his erection, tongue moistening full lips. She slipped onto the bed and lay back. Her hands moved along her body, from beneath her breasts down to the small scarlet heart. Her legs parted, fingers descending, carefully spreading the labia, until she revealed a bright, vibrant pink that seemed to leap from the flame-red hair.

"I want you to lick me, Ollie." Her voice was almost a moan, her eyes pleading. "Lick me and make me come in your mouth."

The man stumbled forward and fell before the bed, his face dropping between her spread legs. The woman's hands went to the back of his balding head, fingers entwining in the thinning hair above his neck, as she forced his head harder against her.

"Oh, yes, Ollie. Lick it, lick it, lick it." She draped one leg across his shoulder, pressing him even closer, and her head began to thrash back and forth, as his hands went to her breasts, cupping each, fingers finding the nipples, manipulating, stroking.

"Oh, your tongue, your tongue. Your fingers." The woman arched her back, holding herself above the bed, her hands pressing his head harder against her. She let out a long, shuddering moan, her body fighting to sustain its position, until finally collapsing back, her hands and legs dropping away from him.

She slid back and stared down at him, the small smile again playing at the corners of her mouth. "Oh, you were so good, Ollie." She extended one hand, and he reached for it. "Now it's your turn."

She took his hand and guided him up beside her, then gently pressed him back with both palms, as she rose to kneel above him. Slowly, one at a time, her fingers encircled his penis, the movement reminiscent of a violinist manipulating the strings of his instrument. The fingers closed and stroked slowly, gently, as her head descended, her tongue sliding between smiling lips as she began to lick the head of his penis, a small child savoring a long-awaited lollipop.

The man began to groan; the flesh under his chin shook. He reached for her hair as she raised her head, her hand stroking him faster now, her mouth spread in a wide smile. He moaned again, and a white, milky liquid shot from him, spreading out over her fast-working fingers.

The woman continued to stoke him, but the smile was gone now, the eyes distinctly severe.

"Oh, Ollie. That was naughty. Very naughty."

"I know. I know." The man had squeezed his eyes shut, and small tears appeared at the corners. "I'm sorry. I'm sorry."

The woman reached out and lightly slapped his cheek, forcing his eyes to open. He stared up at her, his face a mixture of embarrassment and expectation.

"I have to punish you now," she said. "You know that. We said if you were bad, I'd punish you."

"I know. I know."

The man's eyes had become eager. His shoulders shook. His hands flew to his face, covering it.

The woman rose on the bed, and stepped across

his body, straddling him. "You were bad. *Bad!*" Her voice rose sharply.

"Yes, I know."

The man's hands were still covering his face, and the woman squatted, reached out, and roughly removed them. His eyes remained squeezed shut.

"Watch!" she snapped.

The eyes opened—squinting at first, then full. The woman remained squatting, her hands on her knees. Slowly at first, then heavily, a stream of urine splashed onto the man's chest. He threw back his head and let out a roar of ecstasy. "Oh, yes. I'm bad. Bad!"

Devlin reached out and hit the stop button on the VCR.

"Jesus H. Christ," Eddie Grogan hissed.

"If she'd suck my cock, she could piss on me, too."

Devlin and Grogan turned to stare at Willie the Gimp. He was short, skinny and grungy, a battered looking elf, who seemed even smaller slouched down in an overstuffed chair, one skinny leg draped over the arm. They were in a windowless screening room in the warehouse studios of Spider Films. Earlier, the Gimp had bypassed two alarm systems, picked the locks on three doors, and deftly opened a massive, freestanding safe—"These old Moslers suck," being his sole comment. Now, he shrugged.

"You're not only a thief, you're a fucking pervert," Grogan snapped.

Another shrug. "Hey, what can I say." He grinned with nicotine-stained teeth—a dying testament to his four-pack-a-day habit. "I ain't exactly Robert Redford. A flute player like that, she wants to honk on my horn, she can do any fucking thing she wants to me."

Grogan shook his head, then turned to Devlin. "Sometimes I'm sorry I ever busted that hump and put him in my pocket." He looked back at the blank screen. "You know, I testified before old *Ollie* once. Somehow he looked different, sitting in federal court all wrapped up in his judicial robes." Grogan shook his head again. "He has a rep as a *hang 'em high* judge. The fibbies just love his ass. I wonder what those FBI jarheads would think, they saw him playing bedpan to little Miss Bleeding Heart Pussy."

"Hey, play that part where he dives into her fucking muff again."

Devlin glanced at the Gimp. "Shut up, Willie," he said. He pushed the eject button on the VCR, then collected the tape. "I want to take this with me," he said. "We'll label a blank tape the same way this one is, and stick that one back in the safe."

"There were two copies, right?" Grogan asked.

"Yeah, but I don't want to take any chances that somebody'll spot one missing. This way, if they find the second copy is a blank, they'll just figure somebody screwed up."

"You gonna play this for the judge?"

"First I'm gonna play it for our lady friend. See if she can I.D. the flute player."

"How 'bout you make a copy for me?" It was the Gimp again.

Devlin jerked his thumb toward the door. "Time to go, Romeo," he said.

"Shit," the Gimp groused. "It ain't like you stiffs are payin' me for this job."

"You just keep your mouth shut about it," Grogan snapped.

"You kidding?" The Gimp widened his eyes. "After you told me who owns this fucking place, you think I'm gonna talk about cracking it like a fucking sardine can? And after all the heavy names I seen on those tapes in that fucking safe? Shit, if the fucking wiseguys didn't plant me in a cornerstone someplace, the fucking good guys would arrest me, prosecute me, sentence me, and bury the fucking key in fucking Iowa."

"And don't forget it," Grogan said, as he pushed the Gimp through the door that led to the main studio.

Devlin found a blank tape, labeled it to match the one he was taking, then handed it to the Gimp and told him to close up the safe.

The room they were in was a small sound stage, illuminated by soft night lights. It held several sets decorated in battered, cheap furniture—a bedroom, a living room, and a Jacuzzi that had suspicious-looking scum floating atop its stagnant water.

Grogan glanced at each set in turn. "I didn't know Kmart had a fucking decorating service," he said. He drew a breath, then held his nose. "This place smells like a fucking sperm bank. Kinda puts you off getting laid."

"I thought you said you hadn't done that in the last century," Devlin said.

"Hey, I do it. It just ain't like it used to be."

"How's that?"

"Your body just lets you know you're getting older, that's all," Grogan said. "Like when you crawl between the sheets with a really great chick, you're not sure anymore what you like best—the getting laid part, or that nice little nap that comes after."

"Eddie, you're breaking my heart," Devlin said.

"Just wait," Grogan snapped. "Someday even you're gonna be fat and old and short of breath."

"Hey, like Mark Twain said: given the alternative, that doesn't sound too bad."

"Yeah? Well, it doesn't matter anymore, anyways," Grogan said. "At least not for me."

"Why?" Devlin asked.

"I broke another date with Rita last night. And she told me to take a fucking hike." He shook his head. "And the woman *owned* a fucking bar."

Chapter Sixteen

Michelle sat on the edge of the bed, staring at the television screen. Devlin stood just inside the doorway, leaning against the frame. There was an antique dressing table set against the opposite wall, a large, gilded mirror hanging above it, and he studied the woman's reflection as the VCR played out Judge Oliver Rockwell's humiliating sex life. There wasn't a great deal to see. She seemed captivated, her eyes never leaving the screen; only the slight, almost imperceptible twist of her lips showed her discomfort.

As urine began to splash down on the judge's writhing body, Michelle stabbed the remote, shutting it off. Then she lowered her head, eyes closed. Devlin wondered if it was due to embarrassment, or disgust, or from somehow having been a party to what she had just witnessed—even if far removed.

"Her name is Tina," Michelle said. She had opened her eyes, but her head remained downcast. "I was never told her last name. She was brought in for . . ." She hesitated. "Special projects, I imagine."

"What else can you tell me?" Devlin asked. He wanted to move to her; sit next to her on the bed. But he was afraid it might be misconstrued.

Michelle looked up. She seemed surprised to see him standing so far away. She raised her chin. Toughing it through, Devlin thought.

"I was told by Paddy Rourke that she was Bunny Rabitto's friend. I assumed he meant his lover." She blinked at the idea. "I don't know if it's true, or just something Paddy said to see if he could shock me."

"Did it shock you?" Devlin asked.

"Very little shocks me anymore. Some things just make me want to hide. By myself. Away from everyone."

"That would be a waste," Devlin said. The words produced a small smile at the corners of her mouth. The smile reminded him of Tina's. He pushed the similarity away.

"Thank you, Paul." Michelle drew a breath. "Sometimes what I do—what it's turned into— makes me feel very dirty. It helps to believe you don't think of me that way."

Devlin wondered how he did think of her. No, that wasn't it. He wondered how he would think of her if she wasn't so incredibly appealing. If she wasn't so beautiful and so obviously vulnerable to everything around her.

Michelle stood, and moved toward him. "May we go into the other room?" she asked. Her voice seemed almost demure.

"Sure." He stepped back to let her pass, then went to the VCR, ejected the tape, pocketed it, and followed her into the living room.

They were in her friend's apartment. Michelle now stood before a living room window. Her arms were folded across her body as if warding off a chill, and she was staring down into Seventy-second Street, watching the miniature human stream fourteen stories below. Devlin came up behind her, closer then he normally would.

"I'm sorry I had to ask you to watch that," he said.

Michelle's shoulders seemed to stiffen, and he wondered if she sensed the lie in his words. He thought about telling her it was just part of the job— wading through the filth so you could beat the bastards.

"Sometimes . . ." he began. She had turned to face him; the movement was so abrupt it stopped him. She stepped forward and leaned against him, her head against his shoulder.

"I understand," she said. "I just don't want you to think of me that way. As a part of all that . . . that. . . ."

He ran a hand along her upper arm, trying to offer comfort. He realized he wanted to put his arms around her; hold her, but he fought the impulse.

She seemed to sense his discomfort and stepped back. "Can we talk about something else?" She forced a smile, but her eyes seemed to be pleading with him. "Just for a few minutes?"

He knew what she wanted. She wanted some normalcy. A temporary escape from it all. She was still very frightened; she knew she was still a potential target, because of what she was doing. "That's a good idea," he said. He took her arm and led her to the sofa.

When they had settled in, she offered another melancholy smile. "Tell me about yourself?" she asked. "About your family?"

He told her about Phillipa, about their life together since her mother's death. He told her about Adrianna—how they had parted years ago, before his marriage—and how they had found each other again, and now lived together.

"Will you marry?" Michelle asked.

Devlin looked down at his shoes and smiled. "I don't know," he said. He looked back at her, still smiling. "I don't think she's ready to marry a cop. Her father was a cop."

"But *you* would marry *her*." It was spoken as fact, not question.

Devlin shrugged. "I guess I haven't thought about it very much. There hasn't been much point. In a lot of ways we're still feeling our way along. Kind of slow dancing to fast music. Trying it out, I guess."

He looked away momentarily, as if considering what he had said. When his eyes came back to her, he was smiling again. "She's crazy about my daughter, and my partner claims if she could keep Phillipa, and get rid of me, she'd jump at the chance."

Michelle returned his smile, her own more genuine this time. "I doubt she feels that way," she said. "You're a very appealing man, Paul."

He tried to dismiss her words. "But I have a lousy job," he said.

This time Michelle looked away. "As do I," she said.

He stared at her for a moment. "Will you leave it? When this is over?"

Michelle kept her eyes averted; her lips appeared to tremble, but she quickly fought it off. The idea seemed to frighten her, and when she looked at him again, the melancholy was back in place. "I would like to say yes. But I don't know if it's possible."

She's saying it depends on you, Devlin thought. On whether you can beat the bastards. She just won't lay it out that blatantly.

"When this is over, you'll have that chance," he said. He knew he might be lying again; knew she might know it as well. When it was over—if Torelli found out she had turned on him—it would only be a new phase of the same nightmare. She might be safe back in the mountains of Corsica, but he didn't think it was the life she wanted. Her only real chance was to be kept out of it when they finally nailed the bastards. And that was still a real question mark. Until then, he had to concentrate on just keeping her alive.

"Can you tell me anything else about Tina?" he asked.

"Back to work?"

"Afraid so."

Michelle forced another smile, weaker this time. It made her seem suddenly younger and more vulnerable, and he felt the urge to comfort her again. But that's not in the cards, he told himself. She isn't a kid. She's been playing in the big leagues a long time. And you've got to use her, and everything she knows. Whether you want to or not.

"I can't tell you a great deal," she said. "I overheard her talking to Paddy once. She was telling him about her apartment in Brooklyn. I don't know very much about Brooklyn. I've never even been there. But I recall her saying something about walking along some promenade that looked out on the Statue of Liberty. Paddy laughed at her, and she seemed offended. She's really very young."

"That would be Brooklyn Heights," Devlin said. "If she lives there, we'll find her. If she's really Rabitto's girlfriend, we'll find her even quicker."

"I wish I could tell you more."

"It's enough. For now," Devlin said. He stood, excused himself, then went to the phone and called his office.

"I have to leave," he said, when he finished the call.

Michelle's eyes filled with disappointment. "Thank you for telling me about yourself, Paul," she suddenly said.

He smiled down at her. "Next time it's your turn."

She returned the smile, weakly this time. "Perhaps I've already told you too much." She offered a Gallic shrug, and the smile became stronger. "But I do wish we could have more time like that. Just talking about innocent things."

Devlin nodded. "Yeah, me too." He suddenly wasn't sure how innocent he felt. He pushed it away.

Michelle was staring at him, but said nothing.

Devlin shifted his weight. "But right now I have to check on a lawyer who wouldn't know innocent if it came up and bit him."

Michelle smiled again. "That shouldn't be difficult. I'm told all American lawyers are like that. But perhaps next time," she said.

He returned the smile, then reached down and took her extended hand. "Yes. Definitely next time."

Devlin turned off Fourteenth Street onto Seventh Avenue, and into the noontime crush of Greenwich Village traffic. The uniformed dispatcher at his office had given him a message from Eddie Grogan, asking that they meet post haste. He turned into Christopher Street, drove two blocks, spotted an unmarked department car in a loading zone, and pulled in behind it.

"So, what's up?" he asked, as he slid into the rear seat.

Samuels and Grogan turned to face him from the front.

"I'll let Samuels tell you," Grogan said. "I just dragged my ass down here after he called it in."

Samuels was grinning as Devlin turned to him. "Looks like your idea to sit on O'Brien paid off," he said. "I was on him, outside his apartment this morning, but he never sticks his nose out 'til ten-thirty. And he ain't dressed for any kind of lawyerly business. So I follow him, and he beats his ass down here. Gets here just in time for this joint to open." Samuels inclined his head across the street, toward a storefront bar and restaurant with blackened plate glass windows. The name, Matchmaker, was written in pink script across the darkened glass.

"And?" Devlin asked, prodding him.

"So I sit. And lo and behold, about eleven-fifteen, our friend Leslie Boardman shows up, goes inside. So I call it in and wait. Boardman stays about half an hour and leaves alone." Samuels grinned again.

"So now, I figure I'll take a look inside. Just to be sure old F. Lee O'Brien ain't scrammed out a back door. Or is maybe lying in a pool of blood somewhere. So I go to the bar and order a drink." He rolled his eyes. "Man, it's a fruit peddler's convention in there. But I play it cool, eyeball the place, finish my drink, and beat it. Our boy's just sitting back in a corner slugging down silver bullets. Looks like he's had three or four already."

Devlin turned to Grogan. "You let Levy know? Boardman's her baby."

"I called her on a land line soon as I found out," Grogan said.

Devlin sat back and thought for a moment. "Maybe it's time to get the pot bubbling a little bit," he said at length. He turned to Samuels. "You head back uptown. Eddie and I will take this from here. When you get there, tell Levy to climb on Boardman's ass, if she isn't already doing it. Tell her to let him know his little tête-à-tête didn't go unnoticed. I think maybe we should inject a little paranoia into his game."

The Matchmaker was dimly lighted, struggling for that feigned sense of intimacy that so many meeting place bars strive for, but seldom achieve. The silky voice of Mel Torme crooned from an in-house stereo, and there were framed travel posters—primarily of Greek islands and Parisian street scenes—intermingled with pictures of show business personalities mounted on every wall. A badly hand-painted portrait of Judy Garland hung behind the bar.

Devlin and Grogan moved slowly past the horseshoe-shaped bar, giving their eyes time to adjust to the poor lighting. Off in a far corner at the rear, they could just make out a lone man hunched over a table.

"Can I help you gentlemen." The voice of the bartender—nasal and mildly suspicious—halted their progress.

Devlin tossed him a wink, and inclined his head

toward the rear. "Here to meet a friend," he said. Heads at the bar—all male—turned to watch them.

"Get the feeling they think we don't belong?" Grogan said sotto voce.

"I think they're only worried about me," Devlin said. "You seem to fit in just fine."

"Fuck you, Inspector," Grogan hissed in reply.

James O'Brien, Esquire, sat hunched over a half-filled martini glass. His eyes seemed fixed on the clear, slightly oily liquid, as if awaiting a divine message from an oft-consulted oracle. He was dressed in jeans and a tight-fitting, pale blue pullover that accented his well-toned body. A lightweight, tan sports jacket was hung over the back of his chair.

"Drowning olives, Counselor?" Devlin asked, as he and Grogan pulled up chairs and sat, uninvited.

Slightly glazed eyes rose slowly from O'Brien's drink. He looked at each in turn. Only the slight jerk at the corner of his mouth betrayed his surprise.

"You don't mind us joining you, right?" Devlin asked.

"Would it matter if I did?" There was a mild slur in the man's voice; his eyes had become suddenly cautious.

"Not really," Devlin said. "We can talk here. We can talk a few blocks south. Me? I'm thirsty."

O'Brien sat back in his chair and tried to stare Devlin down. When that failed, he let out a soft chuckle. "You tailing me, Inspector?" he asked.

"Part of our new police state tactics," Devlin said. "You know how it is."

"I'm afraid I don't," O'Brien said. "I don't practice much criminal law."

"Pity," Grogan said. "It might come in handy."

Devlin inclined his head toward Grogan. "Oh, excuse me, Counselor. This is Detective Grogan."

O'Brien offered Grogan an exaggerated grin. "Charmed, Detective." He turned back to Devlin, his eyes struggling for a harder cast. "So, what can I do for you?"

"Tell me about Leslie Boardman," Devlin said.

O'Brien looked away momentarily and shrugged. "He's a friend. What else do you want to know?"

"Start with what you two talked about," Devlin said.

O'Brien smiled again, but it failed to carry to his eyes. "Sorry, Inspector. But he's also a client, so I can't do that."

"You usually conduct business down here in the fruit belt, Counselor?" It was Grogan this time, and the remark brought an angry sneer to O'Brien's mouth.

"It was at his request," O'Brien snapped. "As I'm sure you gentlemen know, he's been under a little pressure lately."

Conversation stopped as the bartender approached the table. O'Brien's eyes shot toward him, exposing the first hint of nervousness.

"Everything okay here, Mr. O'Brien?" the bartender asked. He was a tall, slender man, no more than thirty, with close cropped hair and a neatly trimmed mustache. He, too, was wearing jeans with something like a twenty-eight-inch waist, Devlin guessed, and a wide net tank top that revealed a hairless torso.

"Everything's fine, Geoffrey," O'Brien said. "I'd like another martini. Up."

The bartender looked at Devlin and Grogan. His eyes were still suspicious.

"Nothing for me," Grogan said.

"Just a Coke," Devlin added.

"I'll have the waiter bring your drinks over," the bartender said, then turned away with a final, unfriendly glance at the two interlopers.

Grogan leaned forward, resting his weight on his forearms. "Protective. And he seems to know you."

"I've met Mr. Boardman here before."

"I'll bet," Grogan said.

"Listen—"

"You seem to do a lot of lunch meetings," Devlin said, stopping him.

O'Brien's eyes snapped around. "You have been following me, haven't you?"

"Tell us about Buster Fucci," Devlin said. He was staring at the lawyer, eyes hard, the rest of his face blank.

"We happened to see him in a restaurant yesterday. An old haunt of the senator's. Bat pointed him out to me."

"So what'd you talk about?" Devlin watched O'Brien's jaw tighten; his fingers begin to move along his long-stemmed glass—classic tells.

"He came over to our table and said hello. That was it. Happens to the senator all the time."

"Especially in restaurants with CLOSED signs hanging in the window." Devlin grinned at him, shook his head. "So what'd you and the senator talk about?"

"That's none of your business."

"Why don't you let us decide that, sweet cakes?"

It was Grogan again, and O'Brien glared at him. "I don't think I like you very much, Detective."

"I'm fucking crushed," Grogan said.

"What about it, Counselor?" Devlin, too, leaned forward, adding physical motion to match Grogan's pressure.

"The senator's also a client," O'Brien said. "Same professional privilege."

"You sure do have a long client list," Grogan said. He offered up a death's-head grin. "Tell me, Counselor. The senator know you're a nancy boy?"

O'Brien's teeth ground together, then his eyes snapped to Devlin. "I thought we had"—he hesitated a beat—"an *understanding*." He continued to stare across the table. "I had hoped your word was worth something."

Devlin studied his fingernails. "It usually is, Counselor." He raised his eyes slowly. "Until somebody fucks with me. And, right now, you're fucking with me."

O'Brien picked up his drink and tossed the last of it back. "I've told you what I can," he said.

Devlin pushed himself away from the table and stood. The move was followed by Grogan.

"We'll be talking again, Counselor."

The waiter approached the table, O'Brien's martini and Devlin's Coke on a tray. Devlin reached into his pocket and withdrew some folded bills. He peeled off a ten and tossed it on the tray.

"Drinks are on me," he said.

Grogan extended one hand. The fingers were folded into the shape of a gun. He lowered the thumb like a hammer and winked. "Ta ta, Counselor," he said.

"How'd you like my Charles Bronson imitation?" Grogan asked.

"A classic," Devlin said.

"Yeah, it was, wasn't it?" He was grinning. "And I think we shook our boy up a little bit. He seems a little tight about his sexual orientation. Like he's afraid we're gonna open his closet door." He let out a soft chuckle. "Whadda the gays call that now?"

"Outing," Devlin said. He had cut back to Seventh Avenue, which would lead him into West Houston, and finally over to their office on Broadway. Traffic was bumper to bumper, and the temperature in the non-air-conditioned car was stifling. Heat rose off the pavement, causing the air to shimmer in an exhaust—tainted blur.

A half block ahead of their car, two cab drivers stood in the middle of the street screaming at each other. As they moved slowly past, Devlin could see that one cab had clipped the rear of the other. He also noted that both drivers were Arabs, and were shouting threats in their native tongue. He wondered absently how many English-speaking cabbies were left in New York.

Grogan ignored the scene. "You gonna use the fact he's gay to turn him?" he asked. His mind was still fixed on O'Brien.

"Only if I have to. I want to give him some time to think about it. See how he responds when things start coming down around everybody's ears."

"You think he'll call? Try to shop a deal?"

"If things get hot enough." He glanced quickly at Grogan. "He's a lawyer. Trading for an edge is what he's all about."

"You think maybe he was involved with Little Bat? Or maybe Boardman was, and O'Brien's playing nice-nice, and holding his fucking hand. Maybe even looking to pick up on the action. Shit, maybe they had one of those ménage à trois things going."

Devlin threw Grogan a sharp look. "I don't care who humps who. Past, present, or future. All I wanna do is shake everybody's little house and see where the dust settles. Somewhere in there is our shooter. If it had anything to do with where somebody's dick went, we'll find that out later."

"So whose house do we shake next?" Grogan asked. "Big Bat's?"

"Not yet," Devlin said. "I want to wait. See if he pays us a visit first. Right now I'm gonna drop you at the office. I want you to get us a small truck. We'll need it first thing in the morning. Then, when it's all set, I want you to find somebody." He filled Grogan in about Tina, her possible relationship with Rabitto, and her apartment somewhere in the vicinity of Brooklyn Heights.

"Hey, she's as good as found," Grogan said. "What are you gonna do?"

"I'm gonna drop in on Jenny Miller at the D.A.'s office," Devlin said. "I think it's time she started earning her keep."

* * *

Jim O'Brien's knuckles whitened as he clutched the telephone in his hand. "Don't tell me not to panic," he snapped. "I'm telling you, Devlin knows about the lunch meeting yesterday. He knows about today. He's all over me like stink on dog shit, for Chrissake."

He was standing at a pay phone in a small hallway at the rear of the Matchmaker. A young man came out of the nearby restroom, offered him a coy smile, then moved on. O'Brien gritted his teeth as he listened to the voice on the phone.

"We need to stop him. That's what we need to do." His hand tightened even harder on the receiver. "Shit, listen to me. We need to bring whatever pressure to bear that we can. Set him up, if we have to. I don't care. But this thing is starting to unravel. Just like it did with Joe." He listened to the voice again; squeezed his eyes shut. "Hell, this is your area. You're the one who can make the pressure happen. I'm just the fucking lawyer, the fucking negotiator."

He listened again, staring at the blank wall to his right. His face had gone slack. "All right. All right," he said. "I'll leave it to you. Just understand. We're close to going down on this. Just like before."

O'Brien dropped the receiver into the cradle and slumped against the wall.

Another young man passed him, headed for the men's room. He stopped and turned. "Are you okay?" he asked.

O'Brien's eyes shot up. "Fuck off," he snapped. "Just fuck off."

Jenny Miller's eyes widened. She cocked her head to one side, then slowly shook it. "That's not the way things are done around here. Young, aspiring A.D.A.'s don't go off getting search warrants without clearing it with the first deputy. Not if they want to continue being young, aspiring A.D.A.'s."

Devlin leaned back in his chair; steepled his fingers. "I told you, there isn't time. This is an extraordinary situation. As the ranking officer in charge, I'm telling you lives may be at stake, and the evidence we're after could disappear." He grinned at her. "Besides, your first deputy isn't available. And he won't be until well after four o'clock, when the courts will be closed."

"Judges can be reached at home. It's done all the time."

"It may be too late if we hold off that long."

Jenny twisted in her chair. "How do you know the first deputy isn't available?" Jenny demanded.

"Trust me."

Jenny stared at him for several moments. Her consistent efforts to make herself appear unattractive had reached a new plateau today, Devlin thought. She was dressed in a mousy gray business suit, a white ruffled blouse with a klunky, grandmother's cameo at the throat, and sensible black shoes. Her blue eyes were hidden behind horn-rims, too small for her face, and her short, blond hair looked as though it had been washed in Borax, then combed out with a Brillo pad. Oh, Jenny, Devlin thought. To be so pretty, and to be so protected from admiring eyes, 'tis surely a pity.

Jenny picked up her telephone and punched out a series of numbers, then asked for her boss. She listened, asked when he'd be back, then said, "Thank you," and hung up.

She stared across the desk again. "How *did* you know?"

Devlin smiled again. "I arranged it."

The woman's eyes widened. "Where is he?"

"Cooling his heels outside the mayor's office." Devlin ostentatiously consulted his watch. "He'll be there until well after four."

"What's going to happen with the mayor?" she asked. Her beautiful blue eyes had developed a nervous tic, and her fingers were worrying a pencil she had picked up from her desk.

"The mayor's going to tell your boss what a splendid chap he is—how pleased he is that our investigation has suddenly become so fruitful—and that he intends to write a letter to the D.A. praising both your boss *and* you—splendid woman that *you* are, as well—and how if either of you ever decide to try your hand at city government, or perhaps have designs one day on a judgeship, he would certainly be in your corners." Devlin extended his hands to the sides, like a priest offering a blessing to his congregation, then brought them back to their steepled, prayerful pose. "When your boss comes back, and finds out you took the initiative in his absence, I don't think he's going to be terribly pissed."

She shook her head again. "I suppose you have a judge picked out, too."

"I do, indeed."

Jenny blinked her eyes. "Has anyone ever told you you're a very evil, manipulative man?"

"Many and sundry people," Devlin said.

She let out a breath. "This scares the shit out of me, Devlin. And I'm not sure I really like you anymore."

Devlin grinned at her. "Day after tomorrow, when the newspapers are talking about a young, mob-busting, assistant district attorney, you'll probably want to kiss me."

"I doubt that." She hesitated. "You think they will?"

"I can almost guarantee it."

Jenny sat back and blew out a long, long breath. "Oh, God, why am I doing this?" She shook her shoulders, as if fighting off a shiver. "I guess we better get started," she said.

"Forthwith." Devlin rose from his chair. "And Jenny, one other thing."

"What?" Her eyes had widened again, expecting yet another unwanted problem.

"Lose that suit, that shirt, and that Godforsaken cameo."

Michelle sat across the desk from Ari Popolis. Behind his high-backed chair a row of floor-to-ceiling windows revealed the skyline of Manhattan stretched out to the Hudson River beyond, the towering buildings brightened only by faint glimmers of sunshine. Popolis was dressed impeccably as always—a double-breasted, Savile Row suit in a gray pinstripe, a pale gray silk cravat, a pocket handkerchief folded in four precise points, a starched, white linen shirt, revealing exactly one half inch of cuff, and black, Bally shoes, polished to a mirror shine—all of it accenting his sleek, patrician face, uncharacteristic blue eyes, and mid-length dark hair, appropriately gray at the temples. He was a dashing figure, Michelle thought. For a man approaching sixty, even an imposing one. She tried to smile, and failed. She found Ari Popolis utterly detestable.

"I think you underestimate our problem," she said. "This murder investigation is leading straight to Donatello Torelli. And, if he is still involved with us when he's arrested, it will expose our activities as well."

Popolis shook his head. "*If* he's arrested." He shrugged, indicating he thought that unlikely. "So what do you advise?"

"I urge you to tell your friends in Washington. Suggest they end his involvement. Perhaps even terminate their own, at least temporarily."

Popolis waved a dismissive hand, the sunlight behind him reflecting the high gloss of his recently manicured nails. "You worry too much." They spoke in English—his heavily accented. "And, if you think Washington is going to back away from an operation of twenty-five years because of some local police official, I fear for your faculties, my dear."

Michelle's jaw tightened, but she forced away any sound of rancor. "Then just suggest they rid themselves of Torelli. *Before* he panics and begins killing more of our staff."

Ari's eyes hardened. "There is no evidence he has killed anyone," he snapped. He glared at her. "And what do you think would happen to me if he learned I was trying to have him ousted from this little enterprise?" He jerked his head forward, indicating the other side of the UN Building. "My new home would be out there with the fishes of the East River." He shook his head. "No. The proper solution is for you to get *closer* to this police officer. Find out what his plans are. Then we can alert Washington, and they can stop him before he causes any of us any harm."

"Including Torelli," Michelle snapped.

Ari waved his hand again. "I don't care what happens to Torelli. I can live with him, or without him. I would prefer without. But I am not a fool." He leaned forward. "I'll warn Washington, and I will advise them Torelli may be becoming a problem. But I expect you to do a little work with this policeman. So we know what to expect."

"I'm not one of the whores, Ari."

"No one said you were, my dear. And I also know that your wiles far exceed any need for dependence on mere sexuality."

Michelle glared at him. "And I also have no intention of leading this man into any traps you, or your Washington friends may devise."

Ari let out a long breath and turned his chair. In profile he appeared almost majestic, chin elevated, his nose more Roman than Greek. He spoke to the far wall. "We have worked together a number of years now. Our liaison began out of respect for your father, and the fact that you had done well working with him. And your work has continued to be more than satisfactory." He turned back to face her. "I hope that is not about to change."

"Are you threatening me, Ari?" Michelle's eyes bore into him, and it appeared to make him momentarily nervous.

"Threats are for amateurs," he said. "I am a diplomat, and a professional." He drew another long breath. "Michelle. Follow my advice. If you do not, I cannot say what will happen. It may well be taken out of my hands."

Michelle stood abruptly, her demeanor both elegant and distant. "Thank you for your time, Ari," she said. "And your counsel."

When she had left, Ari stared out the window for several minutes. A lone window washer worked on a scaffold high above First Avenue. It seemed to fascinate him. Finally, he rubbed his thumb and index finger against his eyes, dismissing the scene. He had two telephone calls to make. One was to his handlers in Washington, to let them know trouble was on the horizon and closing quickly. But the other call was more important, and had to be made first.

He spun his chair back to his desk, removed his private phone from a desk drawer, and punched in the number he had been given. When the call was answered, he fought back a sigh.

"May I speak to Mr. Buster Fucci, please?" he said.

Sharon Levy rang the doorbell, awaited a response, then pressed it again, holding it in this time. She heard a rustle behind the door, a mumbled curse.

"Who is it?" a voice called out.

"Detective Levy, Mr. Boardman. Open up."

There was a hesitation. "I'm afraid I'm indisposed. Can you come back another time?"

"Open the door, Boardman. It's either that, or I

get the super to open it, and I drag your sorry ass downtown."

The door opened and a red-faced Leslie Boardman stared back at her. He was wearing a black silk kimono, emblazoned with gold Japanese characters. His hair was in disarray, and a quick comb with his fingers did little to help. He looked as though he was about to stamp his foot.

"This is harassment," he snapped. "You are embarrassing me in front of my neighbors."

Levy glanced past him. From an open bedroom door a young man, perhaps eighteen, perhaps not, was peeking out.

"Get rid of the chicken," Levy said. "I need to talk to you. And you'll want it to be private."

Boardman drew himself up—like some self-inflating doll, Levy thought. "Now you want to order people out of my home? This is intolerable."

Levy lowered her eyes; shook her head. When she looked up again, Boardman still looked adamant. "You want I should come in; check his I.D.? Especially his date of birth?"

Boardman's lips twisted. "I don't know his date of birth," he said. "I just met him a few days ago. This isn't a long-term romance."

"Well, we could find out together," Levy said. "Or maybe it's something I *don't* have to know. It's up to you."

Boardman turned stiffly. "Warren, I'm afraid you'll have to leave. Please get dressed."

Levy waited on a white leather sofa while Warren struggled into his clothes in the adjoining bedroom. When he finally emerged, he glanced at her furtively, said a quick good-bye to Boardman, and beat it out the door.

Levy squeezed her eyes shut. Christ, this lifestyle sucks, she told herself. And here you are, as gay as a fruitcake yourself, making it even harder for this poor twit.

"Are you satisfied?" Boardman asked. He was glaring at her, but he looked as though he was about to cry.

Levy ignored the question. "Tell me about Jim O'Brien," she began. "Tell me about his relationship with Captain Battaglia. And tell me what you talked about at lunch today."

Boardman's hands began to tremble. His eyes were wide and disbelieving. Now she was certain he would begin to cry. At that moment Sharon Levy didn't like herself very much.

"So he stonewalled you," Devlin said.

Levy nodded. They were in Devlin's office, reviewing her intentional harassment of Boardman.

"Do you think he'd been warned you might be stopping by?"

"Not unless he's a helluva better actor than I think he is." She shook her head. "No, he's scared shitless," she said. "But he's still not ready to crack. Not yet. But I don't think it will take much more to get him there."

Devlin studied her face. "You don't like this very much, do you?" he asked at length.

"Not very much," she said.

"Because he's gay?"

"Yeah, that's a big part of it." She hesitated, knew he was waiting for more. "Look, Inspector. I'm a cop, and a damn good one. I do whatever it takes. Just like we all do."

"Nobody's questioning whether you're a good cop, Levy."

"Yeah." She hesitated again. "Well, I'm also a good, gay cop. And in a lotta ways being gay is like being a leper. Sometimes all you've got are your own kind."

"Sounds like what it's like being a cop," Devlin said.

Levy inclined her head, smiled. "I never thought

of it that way, but you're right. It is." She let out a breath, then continued. "Anyway. I got no problem going after Boardman. He's a jerk, and he may be up to his eyeballs in this thing. It's just the way we have to do it. Using his sexual orientation to make him twist in the breeze, well, it's just hard."

"Like busting another cop," Devlin said.

Levy lowered her eyes and smiled again. "I get your point." She looked up. "You went after another cop once, didn't you? Everybody knows that story."

Devlin studied his nails a moment. "Yeah, once," he said. "A few years back. Before I left the department that first time."

"How'd you handle it? Afterwards?"

Devlin leaned back in his chair. "Badly. I handled it badly, Levy."

Levy nodded, then shrugged. "So whadda you want next with Boardman?" she asked.

"Stay on his ass," Devlin said. "Stay very tight on his ass."

When Levy had left, Devlin picked up his phone and punched out a long-distance number, then the number of his personal telephone credit card. He needed some sanity in his life, he had decided. Even if it was only fleeting. Adrianna answered on the fourth ring.

"Did I pull you in from outside?" he asked.

"No, it's pouring rain out here. Phillipa and I are baking cookies."

"What kind?"

"Your favorite. Want to come out and have some?"

"I wish."

"Want to come out and have anything else?" Adrianna had lowered her voice to a near whisper.

"I wish even more," Devlin said.

Several seconds of silence passed. "Are you sure about that, Paul?"

Irritation flared. "Dammit, of course I'm sure about it," Devlin snapped. "I'm not on some damned picnic here."

More silence. Then, "How's the case going?" Her voice was aloof now.

"We're slogging, but we're getting there. I think." Devlin's own voice was still sharp, irritated.

There was another pause. "Are you okay?" The words were softer now.

"I just miss you. Both of you. That's all." Devlin let out a long breath. "It doesn't make it any easier having you think I don't."

Seconds of silence passed. "Well, we found a couple of guys out here, so we're just fine."

Her voice had been suddenly light, and it forced a smile to Devlin's lips. "Just remember, I have a gun."

Adrianna laughed. "You want to talk to my assistant chef?"

"Very much."

"Hold on a sec. And, remember, I love you."

"I love you, too."

Devlin switched the phone to his other ear. He glanced out his window. The sun was beating down like a furnace in Hell. And only seventy miles east it was pouring rain. Somehow it made them seem ever farther away.

"Hi, Dad."

"Hi, baby. What's happening?"

"Nothing much. Just enjoying the life of the idle rich. Adrianna's only kidding about the two guys, by the way."

"I know."

"It's really four guys." Phillipa giggled.

"So long as they're all under eight."

"Don't worry. We miss you. Are you coming out?"

"Not right away. I hope soon. But I can't say when yet."

"Pooh!"

Devlin looked up. Eddie Grogan had just stuck his head inside the door. "Look, sweetheart, I think something just came up. Let me talk to Adrianna. I'll try to call back tonight."

"Okay, Dad. Love you."

"Love you, too, honey."

Devlin raised one finger to Grogan, then waited for Adrianna to get back on the line.

"Hear you gotta run," she said, without preamble.

"Yeah, but I'll try to call back tonight."

"Paul." She hesitated a beat. "Are you okay?"

"I'm fine."

"Are you eating?"

"Of course I am."

"Something besides corned beef sandwiches and coffee?"

Devlin looked down at the remnants of the corned beef sandwich and container of cold coffee on his desk. "I'm eating like a king," he said. He heard her sigh. "Look, I gotta go. But I love you, babe. I'll try and call tonight."

"I love you, too," she said. "'Bye."

Devlin hung up the phone and looked at Eddie. There was a smirk on his face. "Don't say it," he warned.

"I wasn't gonna say nothin'." The smirk widened. "What's up?"

"You got a call from the first dep's office. A command performance. Forthwith, and all that shit."

"Mac Brownell?" Devlin smiled and raised his eyebrows affectedly. "Curiouser and curiouser," he said. "I just better get my sweet Irish ass over there."

Mac Brownell's office was in the very heart of the Puzzle Palace—in the middle of floors twelve to fourteen. The Emerald City as street cops called it— the palatial home of the phony wizards. Devlin approached One Police Plaza with the same trepidation as most street cops who worked outside its confines—the entering of foreign territory where one would find few friends, if any, a place governed by careerists, and where self-interest and self-preservation were the essential rules of order.

The building was a massive, red brick square, squat despite its fourteen floors, and remarkably sterile. Its main approach led past a rusting steel sculpture that lent dominance to a brick courtyard. It had been intended to represent the city's five boroughs, but had been dubbed—again by cops—as "Lindsay's Revenge" in honor of the mayor who had commissioned it. The outsized lobby, which rose two full stories, was a once-intended atrium where nary a tree had grown. It was dominated by a large circular counter where credentials were supposedly checked. Devlin flashed his shield toward it and moved on to a far bank of elevators. So much for security, he thought, as he punched the button that would summon his ride into the Holy of Holies on the thirteenth floor.

Mac Brownell's office was suited to his station. It was large, faced the East River, and had an outer office replete with two secretaries, both middle-aged, civilian women. When he introduced himself, he was told the first deputy would be with him *shortly*. It was as he expected, just part of the game played out now for generations. A *forthwith* command to a superior's office was intended to let the supplicant know he was pissed. The length one was forced to cool one's heels, told him—and everyone else—the degree of that displeasure. The exercise accomplished two things. It ground the work of as many people as it affected to a screaming halt. And it reaffirmed the authority and elevated the ego of the superior who employed it—the latter being of far greater concern than the former.

After a half hour had passed, Devlin was ushered

into Mac Brownell's private office. Here the game continued. Brownell allowed Devlin to remain standing before his desk, as he continued to peruse, shuffle, and apply ink to various pieces of paper. Once a suitable time had elapsed, he looked up with hard, blue eyes, a scowl of displeasure affixed to his slender, aesthetic face.

"Take a chair, Devlin," he snapped.

Devlin did as he was told.

"I've got to yank one of your men."

Devlin leaned forward, prepared for a fight.

Brownell eyed him malevolently. There would be no debate. "Jones, the lad from Internal Affairs," he went on. "There's an IAD investigation he's needed on. I can't discuss what, of course, but you can second somebody else to replace him if you want. But from a different command. IAD can't spare anyone."

Devlin eased back and nodded. "I'll get by for now," he said. "Is that it?"

Brownell's scowl deepened; his piercing blue eyes became even harder. When he had been chief of department, it was said that glare had sent mere mortals into states of instant catatonia.

Devlin smiled. "What else can I do for you, Commissioner?" He hadn't forgotten that Brownell preferred to be addressed by his old title—chief—rather than the newer, more proper one, which labeled him a civilian. He deliberately withheld it now, a choice that was not lost on Brownell, given the further deepening of his scowl.

He leaned forward. "You can ease up on the senator a bit," he said. "The man's had enough grief. And you certainly don't consider him a suspect."

"What's your interest in the senator, Commissioner?"

The question seemed to rock Brownell. His eyes blinked. It was not because he feared the question, Devlin knew, but simply that he had dared to ask it.

"Humanitarian, damn it," he snapped. "The man's

suffered enough. He's lost his only son, and now has to live with the fact that the boy turned out not exactly as he had hoped."

Devlin leaned forward again. "I'm not sure how he turned out, Commissioner. Other than dead at the hands of a cop killer."

Brownell waved a dismissive hand. "Oh, let's not play word games, man. We all know what young Battaglia was. Now all we need to do is spare his family—and the department—the public humiliation of it." His stare darkened again. "Is that understood?"

Devlin let out a breath, counting away his anger. "No, let's not play word games," he said softly. "And let's not play at intimidation, either. I'm not buying."

Brownell blinked again. "So you want to take me on, do you?"

"Only if I have to, Commissioner. Mostly I want to be left to do my job."

"You know, you have a strange brief, Devlin. But mayors come and go."

"So do the commissioners they appoint."

"But not the administrative chiefs. They're here for the duration. And they are *my* people."

Devlin smiled again. "I'm here for the short ride, Commissioner. I've already got my pension. When the stink gets unbearable, I'll head for a sweeter-smelling climate."

Brownell sat back, the scowl slowly changing into an unpleasant smile. "So you think that's checkmate, do you?" He looked off to the side and offered up a slight shake of his head. "Ahh, you're a hard man, Paul Devlin. And they tell me you're one helluva good detective." He brought his eyes back. "So good, they say, we probably would have drummed your ass out of the department, had you come to notice earlier." The smile widened. "Definitely not a team player, are you?"

"Depends on whose team, Commissioner."

"Ahh, but there's only one team, isn't there? When all the bullshit falls away, there's just us."

Devlin studied the man. He was only a bit younger than his father had been when he had died. He wondered what the old man would have thought of Mac Brownell. He could almost hear his voice. *He's nothin' but a fooking commercial traveler.* "I guess I take a simpler view, Commissioner," he said at length.

"And what is that?"

"That the public pays us to catch criminals. And let politics and favoritism be damned."

Brownell laughed. It was a cold, harsh sound. "Spare me, Devlin. You're a cagier character than that. Look at the nest you've feathered for yourself." He waved his hand again. "But let's not bicker. Or insult each other's intelligence. Certainly you can cut the senator a little slack."

"Again, Commissioner, what's your interest? Your *personal* interest?"

Brownell let out a weary breath. "Big Bat and I are friends. We were in the academy together. Went in after our stints in the Korean War. And, a few years later, we were partnered together in the Seven-Eight." He tapped his fingers on his desk, his look slyer now, a bit deprecating. "But I thought you would've known that. That you would've pulled Bat's old personnel jacket by now."

Devlin's stomach tightened. The man was right. They should have. But they hadn't. "And you kept up your friendship."

"We did. Oh, we parted. Bat chose the detective bureau, then politics. I followed the career path into uniformed administration. But you know how old partners are. Always brothers, no matter what. We touched base."

Devlin wondered if Brownell's reference to old partners was an intended cruelty, a comment on his own former partner, whose death still rested heavily at his feet. "I'm afraid I can't afford the luxury of sentiment, Commissioner."

"Damn it, man. I'm not asking for sentiment. I'm talking about decency and consideration and respect for someone who was one of our own."

Devlin leaned forward again. "He'll get decency and consideration, Commissioner. But he won't get a pass in a murder investigation—a cop killing. Not because he's a U.S. senator, or a former police lieutenant, or your old partner."

Brownell's face had gone scarlet. "Find your damned fag killer," he shouted. "Just don't drag his damned father through the dirt. It's not needed."

Devlin shouted back. "Does that include his involvement with Torelli and the Money Club?"

Brownell blinked again; his body stiffened. "I don't know what the fuck you're talking about." He stood abruptly and leaned forward until his chest was hovering above his desk. "Just get your killer and leave the rest of it alone. There's none of it that's any concern to you."

Chapter Seventeen

Donatello Torelli threw the glass across the main saloon, shattering it against the richly paneled bulkhead. "What the fuck you mean they took the tapes."

Buster Fucci watched orange juice run down onto the thick, sea-blue carpet. They were on Torelli's forty-five-foot sports fisherman, heading out of its dockage in Sheepshead Bay.

"Better we should wait on the details until we're a little farther out," Fucci said.

Torelli spun on him. His hand lashed out, slapping Fucci across the face. "Don't tell me what the fuck to do," he snarled. He caught hold of himself, realizing what he had done. "You're right," he snapped. He turned and walked quickly to an internal telephone, pressed a button, and issued a terse command to the bridge. "Get us the fuck out of here. Fast."

Bunny Rabitto felt his legs tremble. He kept his eyes away from Fucci, afraid to acknowledge his humiliation with even a glance. From the corner of his eyes he could see Fucci's rage, the redness swelling up from his collar, spreading across his face. A few feet away, Larry Matz stared blindly at his shoes.

There was a surge in the boat's engine; the forward thrust of movement threw everyone momentarily off balance. It also intensified the quiver in Bunny Rabitto's legs. They were headed out to sea, where no one would know who returned and who didn't.

The New York mafia, under the wisdom of the

late *cappo di tutti capi,* Carlo Gambino, had begun using seagoing vessels in the mid-seventies as a way to combat new technologies in government surveillance. "You can't bug the fucking ocean," Gambino had reportedly told his underlings, also pointing out that directional microphones were only successful when they couldn't be seen. "On the ocean you can see forever," the boss of all bosses had intoned.

One of those underlings sitting at Gambino's knee was a much younger Donatello Torelli. Years later—when he had arranged the untimely demise of Gambino's successor, and had seized control of the family—one of the first things he did was buy a seagoing yacht. Besides, the man loved to fish.

When they were two miles offshore, with no other vessels in sight, Torelli ordered the three men out onto the aft deck. The engines slowed and he directed them to the aft rail, where the gurgling roar of the boat's twin screws would further obscure their conversation. Several months earlier he had read an article about the sophisticated satellite surveillance being employed by the National Security Agency, and he was not at all certain the feds weren't bugging him from outer space.

"So tell me how the fuck this thing happened," he shouted.

Fucci stared at him, still burning inside from his slapped face. Torelli had simmered quietly as they had made their way out to sea. Now he was back in a full-blown rage. The man could turn it on and off at will, he told himself. And that made the slap even worse. No one—*no one*—slapped Buster Fucci's face.

"Answer me!" Torelli roared.

Torelli's shirt was partially unbuttoned, and Buster could see the edge of the brown scapular he wore—the thing that was supposed to get him into heaven if he croaked wearing it. All Buster wanted to do right now was to tear the fucking scapular off his throat, stick a shiv in his gut, and feed him to the fucking sharks. Instead, he turned to Rabitto, afraid even to speak to his boss. "Answer his fucking question."

Rabitto, who in a deluge of sweat was fast staining the fifteen-hundred-dollar silk suit he wore, began to stutter.

"I d-d-d-dunno, Boss." He swallowed hard. "I get this call at seven in the fucking morning from the building super. And he tells me there's cops all over the fucking place. Says they got a search warrant and they kicked in the fucking door." He swallowed again, looked at Matz for support, got none, and continued. "I call some of my boys, and I jump in my fucking car and race down there. I dunno if it's fucking cops, or not. I think, hey, maybe it's one of the other families, or some freelance assholes highjacking us. But when I get there it's this fucking cop, Devlin, and his whole crew, loading all our tapes, and all my fucking business papers into a fucking truck."

Torelli was glaring at him, and Rabitto felt a sudden threat to his bladder. "I called Larry right away, just like I'm supposed to." He glanced at Matz again. "But, by the time he gets there, the fucking cops are gone, and all I got is a copy of the fucking warrant, and my dick in my hands."

Torelli's face was almost purple. Buster stared at him, wondering if he'd have a stroke. He does, I'll throw him to the fucking fish, he told himself. He turned to Matz. "This warrant legal?" he asked.

Torelli turned to Buster, as if just comprehending his question, then to Matz. "Well?" he snapped.

Matz fished the warrant from an inside pocket, held it up. "I'm afraid so. The affidavit supporting it mentions a confidential source." He shook his head. "But that doesn't mean much. It's signed by a judge who'd okay anything the cops threw at him."

"What fucking source?" Torelli grabbed the document from Matz's hand, pulled it open, and began running his eyes over it. The words seemed to fuse in legal gibberish. "What fucking source?" he shouted again.

"It doesn't identify anyone in particular," Matz said. "It never—" He was stopped by the shock of seeing Torelli begin to rip the affidavit to shreds.

Torelli threw the savaged document to the deck. The wind caught the pieces, sent them dancing against the gunwales, taking some up and over the sides into the sea. Matz stared after them in disbelief.

Torelli rounded on Rabitto again. "So who told this fuck, Devlin?" he shouted. "And how'd he get into the fucking safe? I paid thousands of dollars for that fucking safe. What'd you do, leave the fucking thing open?"

Rabitto shook his head violently. "No, Boss, no. We always lock it. I do it myself. He musta had the combination, or somethin', 'cause there wasn't a mark on it."

Torelli's eyes widened; he looked as though his head might explode. He lunged at Rabitto, grabbed him by the neck, and forced him back over the rail. The sound of the twin screws pounded in Rabitto's ears like the oncoming hoofs of Death's own chariot. His arms flailed helplessly.

Torelli reached down and grabbed a gaff, affixed by metal clamps to the rail. He brought the enormous hook to Rabitto's throat. "Tell me!" he screamed. "You gave him the fucking combination, didn't you? Tell me! Tell me!"

Fucci jumped forward and grabbed Torelli from behind. Matz, hesitating at first, uncertain what to do, finally joined him. Together they pulled him back, as Fucci forced the gaff away from Rabitto's throat.

"No, Donny, no," Fucci soothed. He was using Torelli's boyhood name; his face was pressed against

Torelli's head, crooning in his ear. "We ain't got nothin' that says he done it. Wait. Wait."

Rabitto's body slid from the rail; slumped to the deck. He was gasping. Torelli kicked out savagely, catching him in the ribs. Rabitto fell back, groaning.

Fucci dragged Torelli back. The resistance was gone now; the anger spent. Torelli threw the gaff to the deck. Fucci released him, ready to jump back if he rushed Rabitto again.

Torelli began to pace in small circles. "We ain't dead yet," he said. "I still got my copies of those tapes—the important ones at least." His eyes shot to Fucci. "You get them outta the basement," he said. "Put 'em in a bank vault someplace. This fucking Devlin's liable to show up at the clubhouse with another fucking warrant."

He resumed pacing; jabbed one finger at the deck. "We gotta find out who sold us out, and take care of that fuck. This Devlin, he knows too much. We gotta find out what he knows. He's got a free hand in this thing. Too fucking free. We gotta whack him, then whack him." His eyes shot back to Fucci. "Shove a fucking dildo up *his* ass. And I want anybody who can tie us to this operation gone. That means the fucking Snake disappears, *capisce*? And anybody else we can't trust."

Across the deck, Rabitto was struggling to his feet. Torelli went to him; gently slapped his cheek. "I'm sorry, Bunny. No offense."

He turned and stared at Fucci. The look was hard and cold. It told Fucci all he had to know about Rabitto's future.

When Torelli had turned away, Fucci looked down at his hand. Entwined in his fingers was Torelli's scapular, pulled away during their struggle. He rolled it up in his fist and stuffed it in his pocket.

"Remember back in the sixties . . . ? Shit, no. How could you remember? You were in fucking diapers back then. Well, anyways, back in the sixties there was this big push against pornography. Every asshole politician in the city wanted to shut down porno theaters. But, before they could padlock the fucking doors, somebody had to go to the theater, watch the fucking film, then say, 'Yeah, this is a dirty fucking movie.' I mean, these movies, everybody's fucking and sucking to beat the fucking band. That's the whole point, right? I mean the bozos who go to see these skin flicks and play with themselves, they ain't there for any redeeming fucking social message, right? But, anyways, somebody's gotta go and watch. So all of a sudden there's all these cops and prosecutors and fucking judges sitting around watching some broad suck off a guy who's got a dick like a fucking elephant. And it's all in the name of fucking justice." Eddie Grogan shook his head. "Man, I was just a young fucking cop then. And, I'll tell you, I wanted that job more than anything in the fucking world." He jabbed a finger toward the television screen in Devlin's office and grinned. "And now I fucking got it."

Devlin looked away, fighting off a smile. "I'm glad I made your whole career, Eddie."

"Hey," Grogan said. "Who deserves it more?" He glanced back at the television screen. "Jesus Christ," he said. "Look at this Tina broad. She's got a tongue like a fucking boa constrictor."

Devlin turned back to the screen. Walter Silverberg, deputy attorney general of the United States, was seated on a bed, his back against the headboard. Tina was kneeling at his side, her red head bobbing between his legs, her tongue flicking out along the shaft of his penis.

Silverberg's face was pure delectation. His eyes seemed ready to pop from his head. Sweat had formed on his upper lip. At the bottom of the screen, his toes wiggled.

Devlin studied his fingernails. He wondered how

the man would remember the scenario in a few days' time. His career would be over. Perhaps his marriage, if he had one. An old line his father had used, about "thinking with your dick in your hand," came back to him. He gave up on his fingernails. At least Silverberg hadn't opted for one of Tina's golden showers.

"I want eight-by-ten glossies made from these other tapes," he said. "Just like we made on the judge. Something graphic we can show these people when we talk to them."

"We better bring a defibrillator, too," Grogan said. "I think we're gonna need one. Just to get their fucking hearts started again."

"Yeah." Devlin shook his head; ran his fingers through his hair. "I want to move on Tina now. We got somebody outside her apartment, right?"

"Cunningham," Grogan said. "He's supposed to call us, she starts to leave."

Grogan reached down next to his chair and lifted a small carrying case to his lap. "I got something here for her," he said.

He opened the case and withdrew a laptop computer. There were wires dangling from the rear with round tabs on the ends. It reminded Devlin of an electrocardiograph.

"What the hell is that?" Devlin asked.

"It's my version of a lie detector," he answered. "And I'm the fucking operator. I'm betting she never saw one—or will think it's just some new computerized version. She thinks we know she's lying, maybe we can break her."

Devlin shook his head again. "Where'd you come up with this idea?"

"An old boss of mine," he said. "Way back when I was a kid, working vice. He usta pull scams like this all the time. Claimed you could make anybody believe anything, you went about it in an official way." Grogan laughed. "I remember this one time, it's Christmas Eve, and things are slow. We're all sitting around the squad room making fucking paper airplanes.

"Then this black hooker comes in. Dumb as a fucking rock. She's all in a snit. Claims this john *violated* her." Grogan wiggled his eyebrows. "Well, the lieutenant listens to her beef, and it's clear the only thing she's pissed about is she didn't get paid. Guy took the money back after she gave him some head.

"So the lieutenant—crazy fuck, he was—he's bored. So he plays along with her. Asks her if she can describe the guy.

"Well, she starts, and he says, 'No, not his face. Tell me what his dick looks like. We got a special mug book on dicks,' he says—'a special one we use for rape cases—and maybe, we look, we can find a picture of this guy's schlong.'

"So the hooker, she starts describing this guy's shwantz—how long it is; how thick; whether he's circumcised; any fucking tattoos, pimples, whatever. Then the lieutenant, he comes over to one of the guys in the squad, hands him a fucking pad and pencil, and says he's just been promoted to police artist."

Devlin started to laugh, but Grogan waved him off. "So they sit there for maybe a half hour; this hooker working her buns off trying to describe this guy's dick. The detective, he's drawing; he's erasing; he's working *his* buns off trying to get this guy's pecker right. After a while I'm thinking even he believes in what he's doing.

"So, anyways, they finish the sketch, but the lieutenant, he ain't had enough fun yet. He tells the hooker to wait, and he goes into another squad, and puts the con on seven guys. Then he leads the hooker into the identification room and sits her behind the two-way mirror.

"Then in come the seven cops, and on the lieutenant's command they drop their fucking shorts, and all seven of them are standing there with their dicks hanging out. And we have a fucking lineup."

Devlin was laughing so hard, tears were streaming down his cheeks. Grogan joined in, barely able to finish his tale.

"So, then, this hooker, she takes in everybody's dick. She stares. She fucking studies them. Then she starts screaming and she points at one fucking guy. 'That's him. That's the motherfucker done ripped me off,' she says."

Grogan wiped his tears away. "And, you know what? It fucking was. The fucking cop she I.D.'d had snuck out for a little Christmas Eve horn honk. We had solved the fucking case."

"So what happened to the cop?" Devlin asked, barely able to speak.

Grogan wheezed out the reply. "The lieutenant made him pay her. Then he told her, 'Merry fucking Christmas.'"

Tina Grimaldi's apartment took up the bottom floor of a renovated, four-story brownstone on Henry Street. To Devlin, Brooklyn Heights had always been a bastardized neighborhood with no central defining character of its own. In part it was Yuppie heaven, with a smattering of celebrities that included novelist Norman Mailer. Then there was the industrialized quadrant, dominated by the main offices of the *Watchtower,* the official publication of Jehovah's Witnesses. Then the headquarters of Brooklyn's Borough government and its courts. And finally, a few blocks west, it suddenly became Carroll Gardens, a hard-core Italian enclave once controlled by murdered mobster Crazy Joe Gallo. And now there was Tina Grimaldi, flute player to the political stars.

Tina answered the door on the third ring, dressed in a miniskirt and a lacy, low-cut camisole. She had been doing her nails, and now held one hand—fingers half finished—away from her body to dry.

"Whadda ya want?" she said, clearly not pleased by the interruption of her toilette.

Devlin and Grogan each flashed their shields and received only a roll of Tina's eyes in response.

"So?" she said. She had cocked one hip, and was rapidly tapping the toes of one naked foot on the carpet. And careers were about to be destroyed over this bimbo, Devlin thought.

"So, you're under arrest. Get your shoes on," Devlin snapped.

"Arrest! What for?" Tina shouted.

"Prostitution and extortion." Devlin snapped back. "Move it."

Devlin and Grogan stepped forward, forcing her to retreat inside.

"What is this?" she continued to wail. "Who says I'm a hooker? Whadda ya mean, extortion?" She was clearly frightened; her eyes darted around the garish living room, as if searching for something, anything that would lend credence to her words.

Devlin extended a hand to Grogan, who promptly produced a manila folder. Devlin shoved it at Tina.

The woman stared at the folder as if it were a snake, then finally took it. Her eyes widened as she gaped at the eight-by-ten photographs depicting her ministrations to Judge Oliver Rockwell. When she looked up, her eyes were still frightened, but defiant.

"So I screwed the guy. So what?" she hissed.

"Oh, you screwed the judge, all right," Eddie Grogan said. "Then your pimp, Bunny Rabitto, screwed him. Made him pay through the nose because of the pictures you and your friends took."

The photographs fluttered to the floor. Tina's eyes had become enormous ovals. "He was a judge?" Her mouth had also become a large circle. "Nobody told me he was a judge."

Grogan snorted. "Yeah, you thought he was

maybe a traveling salesman. Or here for a fucking Shriner's convention, right?"

"He was just a friend of Bunny's. I was just doin' him a favor."

Her voice had gone up several shrill octaves, and Devlin realized he had guessed right. They hadn't told Tina whom she was setting up, or why. She wasn't telling the complete truth, but in her panic she had already fingered Rabitto, and would probably spill the rest of what she knew if they played her right.

"Sure, Tina," Devlin said, his voice laden with sarcasm. "And the films they took, they were just gonna send them to the judge later as a little memento of you pissing on him, right?"

"Look, I told you, I didn't know he was a judge. I just thought he was some john—" She stopped herself, bit her lip. "Just some guy Bunny knew. Like it was some joke they were playing, or something."

"That's bullshit," Grogan growled.

Devlin held out a hand, stopping him. It was time for him to become the *good cop* now, to offer Tina some hope. "Why should we believe you?" he asked. "We got *those*." He jabbed a finger at the photos scattered at their feet. "We got the original film you posed for. We got the judge's testimony about how they shook him down afterwards, threatened to make the film of *him* with *you* public." He let her digest that final lie, then continued. "Hell, we got everybody cold. Bunny'll do ten years in the slam. You, too, plus a couple more for prostitution." He closed his eyes, shook his head. "How old are you gonna be when you get out, Tina? Thirty, maybe? Except you'll look forty, 'cause the slam isn't too good on your looks. Hell, your teeth will be rotten—because they don't take very good care of you in there. Your skin will look like you've been washing it in lye. And, maybe, you'll have some scars from some of the hard cases who live in the joint."

"Yeah," Grogan hissed. "And some of those hard cases in there, they're just gonna love that little, heart-shaped snatch of yours. They'll be all over you like flies on shit. So why should we listen to your fucking lies? Your ass belongs to us."

"Because it's the truth," Tina screeched. She was staring at Grogan's sneer, trying to plead it away. "I didn't know he was a judge. I just thought he was some old geezer they were running a game on." She caught herself again. "Like a joke, ya know?"

Eddie snorted again, turning his head away in disgust. Devlin held up another mollifying hand.

"If you could prove that, maybe it would be a different story," he said.

Her eyes snapped to his; locked on hopefully. "How?" she asked.

He shook his head. "No, there's no percentage. We already got all we need."

"How?" she said again. Her voice had a whining quality to it now.

Devlin turned to Grogan. "Whadda ya say? You wanna try?"

"What the fuck for?" Grogan snapped. "It's a waste of time. She's dead meat."

"What?" Tina pleaded.

"Go on," Devlin implored him. "What can it hurt? At worst you get some practice. And you show me how this new gizmo works."

"You're getting fucking soft between the ears," Grogan said. He looked away again, obviously disgusted with Devlin now.

"What?" Tina begged again. She was moving from one foot to the next, doing a little dance.

"Go on, Eddie. What the hell."

Grogan raised his hands, then threw them down in disgust. "You want it, I'll do it. But it ain't gonna do no good." He glared at Tina. "She'll just lie through her fucking teeth."

"Just get the machine," Devlin said. "We'll give it a shot."

Grogan turned away and stomped off toward the front door.

"What machine?" Tina asked. Her eyes were wide, wild.

She probably thinks we're going to torture her, Devlin thought. She was that scared, that dumb. "It's a new kind of lie detector," he said. "Runs through a computer. Eddie's an expert with it. Now sit down and shut up. You open your yap again, he won't even do it."

"Ain't I supposed to have a lawyer with me when I do somthin' like that?"

Devlin's eyes widened. He turned in a full circle. "I don't believe this shit," he said. "You want a lawyer? Okay, get your shoes on. You have the right to remain silent. You have the right to an attorney—"

"Wait a minute! Wait a minute!" Tina wailed. "I was just askin'. Don't go off the deep end."

Devlin jabbed a finger toward her face. "Then just sit, and shut the hell up," he snapped.

Tina did as she was told. She sat on the edge of a large, aquamarine sofa. Her palms were pressed together prayerfully, and held between her knees. Devlin sat across from her in one of two large, white fuzzy chairs that seemed to grow out of a matching white, furlike carpet. The remainder of the room was decorated with similar flair—chrome end tables, holding large, bulbous, orange lamps; a matching cocktail table with a bowl of plastic fruit at its center; an Italian provincial desk sporting an antique, French telephone, laminated in gold; a massive home theater television set; and a glass-fronted stereo, flanked by the largest speakers Devlin had ever seen. There were two portraits facing each other from opposite walls—one an overused rendering of a naked woman lying on her side, her back to the room as she peered over one shoulder; the other, a large print of the Sacred Heart of Jesus.

Devlin nodded toward the picture of Christ. "You religious?" he asked.

Tina shrugged. "I guess," she said.

Devlin pursed his lips. "Maybe it'll help," he said.

Grogan returned, his cloth carrying case slung over one shoulder. He pulled the chair away from the desk and set it before Tina, grumbling all the while that he was wasting his time. Then he removed the laptop computer, and began attaching the bogus wires to her body.

Devlin fought off a smile as Grogan placed the first in the center of her forehead.

"Brain waves," he snapped.

The second went to the center of her chest—more for his own pleasure than the effect, Devlin thought.

"Heart rate," Grogan said.

Two more went on either wrist, followed by the intonation: "Pulse."

And, finally, the last pair—one on the inside of each knee. Devlin eagerly awaited the explanation.

"To see if your fucking knees shake," Grogan offered.

Devlin was gratefully surprised he hadn't tried to slide one up her thigh to measure any leakage. He was certain Eddie had thought about it.

Grogan settled into the chair, facing her. The laptop was on his knees, screen pointing away from her. Normally, lie detector tests required nothing but yes and no answers, but Grogan was sure Tina was unaware of that fact. He doubted many soap operas had lie detector scenes. He tapped in some gibberish, then stared at her.

"What's your name?" he snapped.

"Tina Grimaldi."

"Did you boff a judge named Oliver Rockwell?"

Devlin stared at his shoes.

"I didn't know he was a judge," Tina said. Her voice held a high whine.

"Just answer the question," Grogan snapped. "And don't whine. It makes funny lines on the screen. "Did you boff him, or not?"

"Yes," Tina said. She sounded cowed now.

"Did you know Bunny Rabitto was making a fucking movie out of it?"

"No."

Eddie hit a key on the computer, as Boom Boom had earlier showed him. The laptop let out a sharp beep. He turned to Devlin and sneered. "She's fucking lying already," he said.

"Okay, I knew," Tina said. "But I didn't know they were gonna blackmail him."

"But you suspected, right?" Grogan said.

"No!"

Beep.

"All right. But I didn't know he was a judge."

"Okay," Grogan said. "Finally a little truth here." He stared at her. The woman's shoulders had sagged in relief. "And this happened at this club the UN runs?"

"Yes. Then later at some apartment."

Grogan kept his face blank, trying to hide his surprise. "Yeah, I was gonna ask you about that," he said. "Where was the apartment?"

"I dunno, exactly. On the East Side someplace. I didn't pay attention to the address. Hey, it's been a long time. Okay?"

"How come you switched places?' Grogan asked, ignoring her complaint.

"I dunno. Mr. Fucci told me we had to do it again. In a different place this time. I just did like I was told."

"This happen with any other people?"

"Yeah. A couple."

"Who?"

"I dunno. They never told me anything but first names."

Beep!

"Look, I ain't lying," Tina screeched.

"Yeah, but you ain't tellin' the whole truth," Grogan snapped. "The machine picks up on that."

"I can only tell ya what I know." Two solitary tears ran down from each eye.

"Tell us about the other johns," Devlin said. "The one's who went to this other apartment. Was it always Fucci who set it up?"

"Yeah. Either him, or sometimes Paddy Rourke."

"Describe these guys," Grogan ordered.

"Mostly foreigners, ya know? Some South Americans. Some Arabs."

"Any Americans?" Devlin asked.

"Yeah. A couple of others."

"Tell us about them," Grogan said. "Including their first names."

Tina fidgeted, then stopped, afraid she would disengage the wires and throw Grogan into a rage. "Look, Bunny's gonna kill me, he finds out."

"Nobody's gonna find out," Devlin said. "Unless we have to take you in. Then . . ." He ended the sentence with a shrug.

"Tell us," Grogan snapped.

"Well, there was this guy, Walter. Real goofy. Claimed he was a bigshot lawyer. He had this tiny, little thing, ya know?"

"Never mind the size of his fucking lizard," Grogan said. "Who else?"

Tina winced at the rebuke. "There was this other guy. Wouldn't even tell me his first name. But I think he was a cop, 'cause he was wearing a gun in one of those ankle holsters like cops use."

"What'd he look like?" Grogan asked.

"Old," she said. "Like you, except maybe even older."

Grogan felt his heart sink. He jabbed the *beep* key out of pure irritation.

"It's true," Tina pleaded.

"Never mind that. Who else?"

She rattled off a list of first names and descriptions as Devlin jotted them down in his notebook. Later they would compare it with what they already had. What fascinated him now was the revelation of a second apartment, and Fucci's direct involvement. It made him wonder if something might be going on behind Donatello Torelli's back.

When Tina had finished her rogues' gallery of names and descriptions, Devlin leaned forward. "These places—the UN club and this apartment— they did the filming behind two-way mirrors?"

"Yes," she said.

"Who was there—behind the mirrors—when they were doing it?"

Tina twisted in her seat, looked at the wires attached to her wrists and knees, and thought better of it. "At the UN place, it was always Bunny and Rourke," she said.

"Fucci was never there?"

"No."

"What about the apartment?"

"It was always Fucci and Rourke," she said. "Never Bunny. Buster told me I wasn't supposed to tell him. And I didn't. You don't mess with him. Mr. Fucci, I mean. He's . . . well, you know who he is."

"Yeah, I know," Devlin said.

"Look, they ain't gonna find out about this, are they?" She was seeking reassurance again.

"Nobody's going to find out anything unless you open your mouth," Devlin said. He gave her a moment to calm herself. "Did any other women go to this apartment on these special jobs?" he finally asked.

"Just one that I know about," Tina said.

"What was her name?"

"Suzanne. I never knew her last name. She was an English girl, and she was pretty wild. We did a threesome there once, ya know? That's how I know about her."

Suzanne Osborne, Devlin thought. The apartment had to be the final link to the murdered hooker. That, and the fact she had talked to Little Bat.

"Tell me about you and Bunny," Devlin said. "How'd you get tied up with him?"

She looked down at her hands. "He makes movies, ya know. Well, I was in some of them, and he kinda decided he liked me. Got me this apartment and everything."

"When was this?"

"It started about two years ago." She shrugged. "I split from home—back in Columbus, Ohio—and I came here. There was this ad in the paper, and I answered it."

Devlin stared at her, trying to see past the heavy makeup. She had a beautiful face, hidden under it all, and she looked twenty, no more than twenty-one.

"How old are you?" he asked.

Tina stared at her hands again. "Seventeen," she said.

"Fuck," Grogan said. It had been an involuntary response.

"I want the name and address of your parents," Devlin said.

"What for?" Tina's eyes were wide again. Fearful.

"We gotta let them know where you are, kid." It was Grogan this time.

Her head snapped toward him; her eyes were filled with pure hatred. "What for? So my old man can sneak in my room at night? I'm not going back there. You send me, I'll just take off again."

"Look," Devlin said. "We want to put you in protective custody. I'll make the arrangements when I get back to my office." He held up a hand, stopping her objection. "You tell the people who are gonna

talk to you what you told me, they're not going to
send you back to your father. Besides, I want to
show you some more pictures. I'm going to need
you here. Okay?"

Tina stared at him, her eyes filled with suspicion.
She'd run away again no matter where he put her.
There was no question in his mind. But he didn't
have a choice. Christ, she was only seventeen. To
keep her safe he had to ease her into the idea. Make
her want to do it. Otherwise she'd be gone the first
time anyone turned their back. He leaned farther forward, trying to inject trust into the body movement.

"Look, Tina. You put some things together. Nothing that's going to make Bunny suspicious if he
comes back. I'll make the arrangements, and we'll
come get you. You're not going back to your father."

"You sure?" Her eyes still showed suspicion.

"I guarantee it," Devlin said. "But, listen to me."
He raised a cautioning finger. "You take off, and
Bunny's gonna figure it has something to do with
him. Something about this business. And he's gonna
start looking for you. You don't want *that*. You can
hide from us. Maybe. But you can't hide from the
people he works for."

Her eyes widened, and Devlin decided she would
sit and wait. For now. He wanted to leave
Cunningham outside to watch the apartment. But he
knew Rabitto would spot him—that he might panic,
grab Tina, then use his goons to keep Cunningham
at bay while he got away and stashed her someplace
himself. He couldn't risk it. It might just get the kid
killed.

The other possibility—taking her with him now—
wouldn't work either. Word would get out, and
Larry Matz would swoop down. He'd probably even
have authorization from Tina's scumbag father. The
Mafia had arms everywhere, and when they needed
to move on something, it never took long. And they

never had a problem making sure people went along with them.

No. He had to set it up first. Make arrangements with social services. Get the matter of parental abuse on the record. Then find a location only he and Eddie and maybe one other person knew about. Maybe the beach house in Bridgehampton. Bring Adrianna and Phillipa back, then stash the kid there with Sharon Levy.

If he was wrong, she'd run before he had a chance to help her. Then they'd have to start looking for her. But that would be better than doing something that would tip off Rabitto, or Fucci, or Torelli before they had her safely hidden away. That would be like signing the kid's death warrant.

"I feel like shit," Grogan said, as they drove toward the Brooklyn Bridge. "Seventeen fucking years old." He slammed his fist against the dash. "I hate what we did to that kid in there. Jesus Christ on a crutch. Who woulda fucking thought?"

"I bet Judge Rockwell knows," Devlin said. He was behind the wheel, and kept his eyes on the traffic. He felt the same self-disgust at what they had done. Now he wanted to point a finger at someone else. "They probably gave the judge a copy of her birth certificate, along with the tape. You remember how long ago it was, Torelli's ass was sitting in his courtroom."

Eddie stared at him. "I wasn't even thinking about that. It hadda be two and a half years ago, easy. Tina wouldn't of been more than fifteen when they set him up, made those films." He blew out a long breath. "Man, I'm surprised he didn't kiss Torelli's ass right there in his courtroom." He turned in his seat to face Devlin. "You think she'll hang around? It'll be our asses she does a rabbit, and somebody finds out all this, finds out we knew about her being only seventeen—abused and all—and didn't pull her in."

"I don't think we have a choice. And I figure it's the safest bet for her, right now. She runs, we'll find her. We'll set it up with the Department of Social Services, and have her out of there by late tonight. I'll take her straight to Bridgehampton, with Levy as chaperone. And I'll bring Adrianna and Phillipa back."

"Why there?" Grogan asked.

"Because nobody knows about that place, except you. And you I trust." Devlin hesitated. "There's something else that bothers me," he said.

"Like why we don't have any films taken in this apartment?" Grogan asked.

"Yeah," Devlin said. "Makes me wonder if somebody else is running a game on the side, and that there are some other films we haven't found yet."

Outside Tina's apartment, Ralph Federici started his car and drove three blocks to the nearest pay phone. He was free of his IAD shadow for the first time since starting this fucked-up assignment, and he wanted to report in and get Mitchelson off his ass. Then he wanted to get back to the office and wait for Devlin's next move.

"Shit!" Devlin said.

"What's wrong?"

He glared across his desk at Grogan. "Those assholes in Social Services claim they can't do the paperwork we need for a court order until tomorrow morning. They say it's too close to four o'clock. That means no court hearing until day after tomorrow."

"So whadda we do?" Grogan asked.

"We wait. And we send Samuels and Walker out to sit on the apartment. It's a risk, but there's no

choice. Make sure they have some uniforms stashed
around the corner for backup."

"I'll take care of it now," Grogan said.

As Grogan headed for the outer office, Devlin's
telephone rang. He snatched it up and growled into
the receiver. "Yeah. What?"

"Paul? Is that you?"

He recognized Michelle's voice. "Yes. Are you
okay?"

"I'm not sure, Paul. I have to see you. Can you
meet me now?"

"Where are you?"

"At a pay phone, a few blocks from my office."

Devlin glanced at his watch. "Go back to your
apartment. Leave in one hour. I'll follow you."

"Thank you, Paul."

When Michelle had disconnected, Devlin punched
out his number in Bridgehampton. Adrianna answered on the second ring, and he quickly told her
about Tina Grimaldi, and what he wanted to do.

"I know it's a pain in the ass, but it will only be
temporary. Are you okay with it?"

Silence filled the phone. Then Adrianna's voice
came back, harsh and bitter. "Of course I'm not
okay with it, dammit. I'm absolutely stunned you'd
even think about sending her out here."

"Adrianna, she's only a kid. She's only seventeen."

"Paul, I don't care. This is our home, dammit.
And it's the one place where nobody can reach out
to us. The one place where your damned job doesn't
intrude on our lives. And it's safe, dammit. And I
want it to stay safe."

He began to speak, but she cut him off. "Dammit,
Paul, maybe I have to remind you what happened
with the last case. Maybe you've forgotten that the
maniac who was trying to kill me turned on Phillipa
before it was all over. She survived it, Paul, but she
had the living daylights scared out of her, just like I

did. And neither one of us is over it yet. And now, dammit, you're talking about sending someone out here who somebody else wants to kill. You must have lost your mind. If you did that, do you think either one of us would ever feel safe here again? *Do* you?"

Devlin sat in stunned silence. He drew a long breath. "All right," he snapped. "Forget it. Forget I asked."

"I wish I could," she snapped back. "I wish I could forget your willingness to risk the one sane place we have to ourselves—the one place your damned job doesn't crowd us out of."

Devlin waited, ground his teeth. "I'm sorry you feel that way." His voice was cold, unforgiving.

"Oh, screw you, Paul. You knew I felt that way before you asked me to live with you. Don't play *Mr. Abused* with me now, just because I don't want you to dump your shit on our doorstep."

Silence filled both ends of the phone. Adrianna finally broke it. "I have to go, Paul. Good-bye." She put down the phone.

"Shit," Devlin snapped, slamming his own receiver back into place. He marched out of his office, the scar on his cheek glowing white, and stuck his head in Eddie's door.

"Bridgehampton's out," he snapped. "See if you can find someplace else to stash Tina as soon as we get a court order."

Grogan stared at him for a moment, then nodded. He didn't ask why the change was needed. He didn't have to.

Devlin left his office fifteen minutes later, stopped briefly to tell Eddie where he was going, then headed for the elevator.

A minute later, Federici got up from his desk and headed for the door. He could take the stairs and be behind Devlin before he left the elevator and lost himself in sidewalk traffic. He also knew where Devlin parked his department car. He had his own in a loading zone downstairs, so if Devlin headed for his vehicle, he could be in his own and waiting by the time Devlin pulled out of the lot.

As he slipped into his coat, a hand reached out and grabbed his arm.

"Where you goin'?" Grogan asked.

"I was just heading out to check on some things," Federici said.

"Uh-uh," Grogan said. "I got somethin' I want you to do."

Chapter Eighteen

Michelle wasn't in the lobby when he reached the apartment. Devlin had followed her from Fifth Avenue, as usual, making sure there was no other tail. He felt a tightness in his gut as he approached the doorman. The man had seen them come and go now several times.

"The lady I usually come here with?" he asked. "She go upstairs?"

"Yes, sir," the doorman said. "Just a few minutes ago."

"Alone?" Devlin asked.

The doorman looked at him curiously. "Yes, sir. She was alone."

He thanked the man, moved to the elevator, feeling mildly foolish. He had felt a sudden sense of danger for her, just from that minor break in routine. It's the case, he told himself. And because you know how ruthless these bastards really are.

Michelle opened the door as soon as he rang the bell, reached out, and drew him inside. She was very close, and Devlin could feel her body tremble.

"What's wrong?" he asked.

She sank against him, her forehead dropping to his shoulder. "Everything seems to have begun spinning out of control," she said.

"At your club?" he asked.

"Yes. It's been . . . terrifying."

She was wearing a short-sleeved blouse. Devlin

ran his hands along her arms, comforting her. Her skin felt as soft as the silk she normally wore; her subtle, luxuriant scent filled his head.

"Let's sit down. You can tell me about it."

He sat next to her on the living room sofa. She rested her head against the back, closed her eyes. Her long, slender neck seemed exposed and vulnerable. She ran the fingers of one hand through her hair.

"Tell me what happened," he said.

She shook her head, almost imperceptibly. Her eyes remained closed. "A man came to see Paddy today," she said. "He looked like a hoodlum. Very forceful, very intimidating." Her hands played against each other in her lap. "They met privately for about half an hour, and when he left, Paddy was in a rage. He began questioning everyone—interrogating really. Even me."

"What was he after?"

Michelle opened her eyes, turning her face toward him. Her eyes were still frightened. "He wanted to know if anyone had spoken to you, or one of your men. He insisted they knew someone had. He seemed particularly concerned about what might have been said about Bunny Rabitto, and about the films he took away each week." She stared at him. "The things *I* told *you*, Paul." She turned her face away. The gesture felt like an accusation. "He was even physically rough with some of the women," she continued. "They were all terrified."

Devlin's eyes hardened. "Was he rough with you?" he asked.

Michelle shook her head. "No. I thought he was about to be several times. But he seemed to stop himself."

"Describe this man who came to see him."

She turned her head back, still not looking at him fully. "He looked like a well-dressed thug," she said. "Not tall, but large. Middle-aged. With greasy hair and a very thick neck. His face looked ... pushed in."

She had just described half the thugs in New York. "It could have been anybody," Devlin said.

She looked at him now. "What's happened, Paul? Why are they in such a panic? I have to know."

Devlin dropped his eyes momentarily. "We raided Rabitto's film studio this morning. Grabbed all the tapes he's been getting from Rourke."

"Oh, God," she said. She paused, thinking. "I thought it was Ari."

"What do you mean?"

Michelle looked down at her hands; stopped their attack on each other. "When you left me the other day, I went to see him. I told him things were getting out of control. Then I asked him to contact his friends in Washington. To tell them what was happening. To ask them to put a stop to it."

"Why did you do that?"

She looked at him. There was a hint of guilt in her eyes. "Because I'm frightened. And because we're all being dragged into this." She shook her head. "It all started out so innocently. I know that may sound strange to you, but it was. At least initially. The club—the UN itself—was just providing a safe outlet for its diplomats. Protecting them from themselves. Then it all became corrupted when Washington moved in. And now we are being controlled by killers. And no one is safe. And we're all about to be dragged down with them."

"What did Ari say?" Devlin asked.

A rush of breath escaped her. "He told me he wanted Torelli gone as well, but that he'd be killed if he did as I asked. He told me to stop being a fool." She closed her eyes, opened them again. "Then he asked me to get closer to you. To find out what you were doing, so we could protect ourselves."

"And?"

"I told him I wasn't one of his whores. We parted angrily."

"You said he wants Torelli gone. Do you think he might have talked to Little Bat? Fed him information, then panicked when he saw what happened?"

Michelle's eyes blinked. "I don't know. I never considered that. I suppose he could have. I'm sure he met him at one of my parties. He must have spoken with him."

"But you're not sure if he told him anything."

"No."

Devlin mulled it over. "How much do you trust Ari?" he asked at length.

"I don't know. I'm not sure anymore."

He could feel her begin to tremble again, and he reached across and stroked her arm. Her head slid toward him. One hand moved up his chest, then slipped behind his neck.

"You don't have to be afraid," he said. "I won't let anything happen to you." He felt his heartbeat increase as her fingers touched the hair at the base of his head.

She drew his head down; raised her own. Their mouths met—softly, at first—then with a hunger that surprised him; thrilled him. His hands began to play along her body—softly, gently—feeling every nuance, discovering the silky smooth texture of her skin.

They were in the bedroom; their clothes discarded in a long, laborious, pleasurable trail. Devlin ran his hands, his mouth along her body, his senses inhaling her, lost in her soft, smoothly erotic flesh.

He was aware of the perfection of her body, every part like something carved by a master sculptor—no flaw, no tiny blemish visible. Every movement eroticism personified.

Michelle lay back. Her head twisted slowly with pleasure. Her fingers entwined in his hair, roaming to his neck, his shoulders, the fingernails lightly raking his skin; sending chills along his spine. She was like every woman to whom he had ever made love, and like no other, and he felt as though he had fallen into a deep, enfolding chasm, lost in long repressed hedonism and seeking no fast escape.

Somewhere, too, there was guilt, ruthlessly smothered, as he allowed the smell, the feel, the touch of her to overwhelm him. Michelle seemed to sense it, and her own abandon intensified. She gently guided his mouth to new parts of her, telling him with her body the delight she felt with each caress. She guided his mouth to her inner thigh—this softest part of her flesh—and he ran his lips against her, inhaling her essence.

His fingers slid to her vagina, spreading her like the soft petals of a flower, and she let out a low, whispered moan, her fingers tightening in his hair.

"Oh, Paul, let me have your tongue. Softly, softly."

Her back arched as he did her bidding, head thrashing violently now, and he could feel the shudder rising through her legs, moving down her body, plunging to her center. His tongue worked feverishly, eager for the sweet fluid, the taste of her passion.

Then she cried out, and slowly fell back. Still he didn't stop. He wanted even more of her. Gently, she pushed him back, slipped from beneath him, and rose to her knees. Her hands pressed him to the bed, her eyes fixed on his face, her own beautiful face weathered by pleasure taken, but showing a growing wildness for what she now wanted from him.

"And now, you," she whispered.

Her face moved slowly to his chest; her tongue traced the shape of his nipple; her lips suckled him. Fingers moved down his body, barely touching his skin. They tickled the underside of his scrotum, the palm cupping him, then releasing, the fingers moving up, stroking a shaft more steel than flesh now.

She looked at him, a playful smile dancing at the corners of her mouth. Her head joined her hand, fingers supporting him, as her mouth ran along his length, tongue flicking in and out like some serpent of pleasure, his penis throbbing with each subtle touch.

Then her mouth engulfed him, taking nearly all, sucking hungrily, and he fought against the near painful delight of it, afraid he would explode too soon, and lose the rest of her.

She seemed to sense his need, and she rose, eyes wide—even wilder now—in anticipation, and she straddled him, guiding his maleness inside, then thrusting down, gasping once, then again.

Michelle surrendered to abandon and rode him like some wild demon, her hair flying about her head, eyes staring down at him, mouth twisting with every nuance of physical sensation.

Devlin loosed an uncontrollable moan that grew to a guttural roar. It was the sound of an animal lost in rutting frenzy, feeling nothing but the response of his own loins. His seed shot into her, and the muscles of her vagina tightened on him, sucking out every drop, leaving him dry and weak and beaten. His muscles collapsed, his heart beating so fast and hard he thought it might burst, as Michelle's head dropped forward, her cheek against his, lips nibbling against the lobe of his ear—slowly, slowly stopping, replaced now by her shuddering, hot breath.

They lay still, spent. He could feel her heart against his own, and he knew he wanted to keep it there—that he must.

"Paul." Her voice was breathless. "Never, Paul. Never has it been like this."

No. Never, he thought.

The loft was dimly lighted, a soft, spectral glow from a single lamp. Devlin sat in a chair, staring at the telephone some ten feet away. Images of

Michelle plagued his mind, each bout of guilt evaporating in a return to pleasure. He wanted to telephone Adrianna, hear her voice, tell her what he had done, beg her to forgive him. And then to beg her to let him have more and more of the same. He wanted to speak to Phillipa. Ask her to understand her father's madness.

He thought of his conversation with Adrianna only that afternoon—tried to rationalize what had happened with Michelle, blame it on the endless tension his job brought to their lives. But it didn't work. He had wanted it to happen; had wanted *her.* And, worst of all, he still did.

He tried again; thought of his anger when Adrianna had been unwilling to be displaced by a seventeen-year-old hooker, her failure to understand what he had been trying to do. He tried to tell himself *that* was the reason. But it didn't work either. His mind began to assault him, to recall the words in Little Bat's journal, but he fought them off, refusing to hear them. The journal was in his jacket pocket. But he had no intention of ever touching it again. Tomorrow he'd give it to Eddie—let him read it—if for no other reason than to keep it as far away as possible.

Men could throw away the things that were good and right, the very things that made them whole. Everyone in this case had secrets that taunted and threatened them. Sex secrets hidden behind flimsy veils. Secrets they had convinced themselves were buried deep, beyond resurrection. And now, you, too, he thought.

Devlin pushed himself from the chair and moved to the phone. His hand rested on it, then finally lifted the receiver. His fingers poised over the buttons. But now his brain had turned blank. The sequence of numbers he must push, gone. If he took time—thought—they'd return to him. He knew that. He replaced the receiver and returned to the chair.

Fifteen minutes later the sound of the phone startled him. He had been thinking of Michelle again, and guilt flooded back now. It was Adrianna calling him. He was certain of it. Damn your ass, he told himself. How can you tell her—hurt her that way? No. Admit it. How can you risk driving her away? Losing the glue that's made you whole again.

He went to the phone, dreading the sound of her voice—dreading the sound of his even more. She would hear it there. Hear the lie.

"Hello." Devlin heard the hollow sound as his own voice played back at him.

"Christ, I'm glad your there." Blessedly, it was Eddie. "I was afraid I'd have to call that apartment, and blow your thing with the Paoli broad."

Devlin shook his head. What thing? What did Eddie know? "What are you talking about?" He could hear the lie, the hollowness again.

"They hit Bunny Rabitto." Eddie hesitated. "And they hit the kid, too."

"What?" His mind came slowly back.

"They're both dead, Paul. Two guys. They whacked 'em right there in Tina's apartment."

"What about our people? Samuels? Walker?"

"All they saw was two guys going in. They came on foot. Nothing threatening, they said. Then they heard the shots. They start to move, and the two guys are coming out. Samuels and Walker opened up. So did the perps. They got one of 'em. The other got away. There was a third guy in a car down the block. Our guys never saw him. He pulled up as they were bugging out."

"Samuels or Walker hit?"

"No. The perps never touched them. Close but no cigar, Walker said. But they didn't miss inside." He drew a breath. "Walker said it's a mess in there. He sounded a little shaky. Fuck, Paul. We shoulda taken that kid outta there today. I'd like to strangle those cocksuckers at Social Services."

"I'll be there in fifteen minutes," Devlin said.

Mattie "the Snake" Cordino pushed through the side door of the restaurant and started across the parking lot.

These fucking Miami wops, he thought. Wouldn't know how to make a good *osso bucco,* their fucking lives depended on it. And that fried zucchini, Jesus Christ, musta been made last week and fucking frozen.

He strode across the parking lot, headed toward his rented Caddie convertible. Whadda ya expect, he told himself. A fucking Italian restaurant that has fucking Cuban food on the menu. Probably got a fucking spic working in the fucking kitchen.

He stopped at the driver's side of the Caddie. The top was up, and he decided he'd lower it, cruise the area a little.

A lotta fucking good it's done ya so far, he thought. The only pussy you got, you fucking paid for. Probably get fucking AIDS from that spic bitch you had last night.

He opened the door, slid in behind the wheel, and started the engine. He unfastened the latches that held the top in place, hit the button to lower it, and sat back waiting for it to go down.

He barely saw the strand of wire loop over his head; had no time to get his fingers under it before it bit into the soft flesh of his neck. His body was pulled back with tremendous force. Blood poured down his neck as the wire sliced into his throat. He flailed his arms, reached back wildly, but found only air. His feet kicked out, as his body slid from behind the wheel. His body arched farther back, and his shoes drummed on the dashboard. He could hear his own gagging cries, the gurgling sound of blood in his throat. His feet hit the windshield, beating wildly, one finally smashing through the glass, spraying small diamonds on to the car's hood. It was the last thing the Snake saw, the final image to pass through his oxygen-starved brain—tiny pieces of glass sparkling in the artificial light of the parking lot.

The convertible top *klunked* into its retaining well. A hand reached over the seat and hit the button again. Slowly the top began to rise, as the Snake's bladder and bowels released, filling the car with the stench of his last mortal offerings.

Chapter Nineteen

Bunny Rabitto's body lay facedown on the fuzzy, white, living room rug, which had soaked up much of the sticky red pool that surrounded it. Bunny had a hole in his back the size of a baseball, and Devlin knew, when they turned him, the exit wound would be huge, with bits of bone and viscera dangling from the cavity. He looked at the room. Blood and fragments of body matter had sprayed in a wide arc, washing the matching chairs, the chrome tables, the aquamarine sofa, where he and Eddie and Tina had played out their little game that afternoon.

"Shotgun. Probably from no more than six feet away," Michael Blair said. "Makes it look like an explosion in a butcher's shop." The assistant medical examiner had arrived a few minutes after Devlin, and now stood beside him, staring down at the corpse.

"You ever read that old Hemingway story?" Blair asked. "The one starts out with the guy walking across the battlefield? How he can tell the way the fighting went by the way the bodies are positioned?"

"One of the Nick Adams stories, wasn't it?" Devlin said.

"Yeah, that's it," Blair said. "Well, Hemingway was right. Just like here, you can tell." Blair was lecturing again, telling him things he already knew, but Devlin was too bone weary to stop him.

"The way it looks, our victim—who's wearing only a bathrobe—gets out of bed and lets the shooter in. Then he realizes what's coming down. Maybe from the look in the shooter's eye. Who knows?" He shrugged. "He starts to run. Wants to get to his own weapon, or out the back door, or whatever." He jabbed a thumb behind him. "He's running hard, and he knocks over that table. But that's as far as he gets. I figure double-O buckshot. It lifts him up, throws him another six feet forward. Then the shooter goes straight to the bedroom, gets the other one." Blair scratched his head. "Pretty straightforward," he added. "No big secrets here."

Devlin hadn't been in the bedroom yet; hadn't wanted to. Now he would, if only to punish himself. He turned to Blair. "Thanks, Mike," he said. "Give it your best shot, anyway. It's all tied into the other case. I need everything you can come up with."

Blair raised an eyebrow, grunted. "You got it," he said.

Eddie Grogan was standing just inside the bedroom doorway, drawing a crude sketch of the scene in his notebook. Tina Grimaldi, seventeen-year-old child from Columbus, Ohio, was slumped against the headboard. Her body looked small and young and healthy. Except for her head. Most of that was gone. They had shot her in the face, and what had been there, along with the top of her skull, was now splattered against the headboard and the wall.

They didn't have to do that, Devlin thought. They could have shot her with something smaller; pumped as many bullets as they needed into her chest. They could have left her whole for the people who would have to identify her body.

But it was her. There was no doubt. Tina Grimaldi was naked, her arms and legs spread out at awkward angles, the small, carefully groomed, heart-shaped mound of red hair at her center looking sadly innocent and slightly silly. Just a kid, Devlin thought. Somebody, who in another, better life, could have been Phillipa's baby-sitter.

Grogan turned to him. He looked unusually pale. "Blair says they were in bed together before the shooters got here. Says there's fresh semen. I guess Bunny the Fag wasn't after all."

Devlin knew what Grogan was trying to do and knew he was failing.

Grogan shook his head. "She was probably trying to keep him happy until she could get away. Until we came and got her. Goddamn it, Paul." He turned his back on the bed and stared out into the living room. "They could of got that piece of shit anyplace. But they wanted her, too. They knew we had her on film; knew we'd find her."

"Maybe they knew we already had."

Grogan's eyes snapped back. "Whadda ya mean?"

Devlin was still staring at the body. Now he looked away. "They could have picked her up before they did Bunny. They could have said: 'Look, kid, you're being transferred. You're going to turn tricks for us at the casino in Puerto Rico, or Paradise Island.' She would've been thrilled. Her biggest concern would've been whether she needed a new bikini, or not. We'd never have found her. We wouldn't even have looked that hard. She would've been a hooker we had on an old piece of film. We'd check around the city, sure. But that's all. They wouldn't think we even had a name. So they'd know a nationwide search would be out of the question. They'd have to figure it that way."

Devlin turned away now and faced the living room. "The mob's not stupid. They've always had a good sense of public relations. They don't kill women and kids unless they have to, unless there's no other choice. But if they knew we'd already found her; already knew what she could say in court. . . ."

"So you're saying somebody knew we'd been here."

"That's what I'm saying." He looked at Grogan.

"I'm saying we fucked up even worse then we think."

"You think somebody's eyeballing us."

"Me, probably. But, yeah, that's what I think."

"How do you wanna handle it?"

Devlin's eyes were hard, cold. "You know the kind of tail I'm running on Michelle Paoli. How I follow her to the apartment we're using."

"Yeah."

"I want you to do that with me. Starting today."

"One thing," Grogan said. "If you're being followed, how come this scumbag ain't tumbled to the Paoli broad already?"

"Because I think I know who it is, Eddie. And, up 'til now, he hasn't had a chance."

It was well into morning before they finished the work on Henry Street. The report on Mattie the Snake's murder was already on Devlin's desk when they reached the office. It had been forwarded to New York by the Miami P.D. as soon as the body had been identified, then routinely distributed to all detective units. A check with the nationwide NCIC computer had identified the Snake as a member of the Torelli crime family, with a long history of burglary and extortion.

"Could be the guy who broke into Little Bat's apartment. We figure somebody got in pretty clean, and was waiting for him. Could be Torelli's decided to clean house."

"Could be," Devlin said. "I doubt we'll ever know for sure. But we'll have somebody check his old haunts. See if he shot his mouth off to anybody." He tossed the report aside. "I think, maybe, the body count is just starting. And that we better start closing any doors we've left open."

Devlin picked up his phone and dialed Michelle's answering machine. He looked up at Grogan. "If she doesn't call back and change the time, I want you to

leave first and get staked out on Fifth Avenue. Take
Levy with you. I'll park just up from the Met, and I
want you about a block above that. You follow me,
and grab anybody who's bird-dogging my ass."

"You want I should call the apartment and let you
know if we nab somebody?"

Devlin shook his head. "I don't want to spook the
lady. You just bring anybody you collar back here. If
you're not downstairs when I leave, I'll head right
back."

"You got it," Grogan said. He offered Devlin a
small smile. "You know who it is, don't you?"

"We'll see," Devlin said.

"Yeah," Grogan said. He reached down, took a
piece of paper from the desk, jotted a name on it,
and folded the paper in two. He laid it on Devlin's
desk. "We'll open that when you get back," he said.
"See if my aging brain is still hitting on all eight."

Michelle opened the door and slipped her arms
around Devlin's neck before he was even inside.

"Paul," she whispered. "I waited all morning,
hoping you would call."

He pushed her back gently, and closed the door.
"They killed Tina," he said. "And Rabitto. I want
you to think about leaving the city."

Michelle stared at him, eyes wide. Devlin thought
he saw a momentary flash of anger—there, then
gone. "You think Torelli's people know about me?"

"No, I don't. Not yet. But I didn't think they
knew we had found Tina. Now I'm not sure."

"Perhaps she was killed because Rabitto was there
with her. It doesn't mean they knew about her." Fear
seemed to fill her face. "It doesn't mean they know
about me."

Devlin stared at her for several moments. Then he
looked at the floor. "No, it doesn't. I just thought
you should know. That you should consider leaving."

She put her arms around his neck again; raised herself up to him. "I'm safest with you, Paul. It's the only place I do feel safe."

Her face was glowingly beautiful. His hands went to her waist, and he felt the soft, luxuriant flesh beneath his fingers. He felt himself stir, the call of the rut returning. She pressed her mouth against his, slid her tongue deep inside. He wanted very much to forget his newfound fears. He eased her back again.

"I can't," he said. He smiled at her. "Not now. There something I have to do. I want you to stay here, even if it means staying overnight, just to be safe. I'll call later, and let you know when I'll be back."

Michelle looked confused. "Overnight? But . . ."

"I'll have somebody bring you some clothes, an extra toothbrush. I have a woman on the squad who'll know what you need. Give me a key to your apartment, and a note for the doorman."

"But . . . but . . ."

Devlin stroked her arm. "I know I said nobody would know about us meeting. But, after Tina, I can't take any chances. And it's too late to turn back now. So, I don't have a choice. I've gotta take you out of the game." Devlin stared at her. She was so beautiful. There was a cold, ominous feeling in his gut.

She let out a long breath, then smiled. There was a hint of disappointment in her eyes. "Try to come back today," she said. "I want you so much."

"I'll try," he said.

When he left the apartment, Devlin went to a phone booth, called his office, and asked for Cunningham.

"I need you to meet me," he said. He explained the situation. "I've got a little watchdog job for you." He gave him the address.

* * *

Ralph Federici sat on a wooden chair in one corner of Devlin's office. There was sweat on his forehead and upper lip. His jacket was off, and hanging on the back of the chair. The holster on his hip was empty.

Devlin walked over to his desk, eyed Federici's empty revolver, then picked up the note Eddie had written earlier. He opened it, read Federici's name, then looked up at Grogan. He and Levy were standing on either side of the sweating organized-crime detective.

"I guess you're still hitting on all cylinders," Devlin said. He dropped the note and walked toward Federici. The scar on his cheek was a vivid white.

The detective stood. "Look, Inspector, it's like I've been trying to tell these humps—"

Devlin's fist crashed into his jaw, slamming him back against the wall. Federici slid to the floor, overturning the chair. Devlin kicked the chair out of the way, then kicked Federici in the ribs.

Grogan jumped between them, pushing Devlin back. "Hey, whoa. Save some for the rest of us," he said.

Devlin turned and walked away. "Get him up, and sit him down."

Federici slumped in the chair. He wiped blood from his lip with the back of his hand. The hand was trembling. He looked up at Devlin as he walked toward him again. "You got no call to do that," he snapped. "I got fucking rights."

"You got the right to get the shit kicked out of you. You want it right now?" Devlin stared at him. "You know what happened to Tina Grimaldi. And you know that puts you in line for accessory before the fact in a murder rap. We can throw in conspiracy, and a whole lot of shit, right down to grand mopery, you piece of garbage." He pointed a finger at Federici's face. "You play stink finger with me, I promise you, you won't just lose your pension—

you'll do time someplace where there are guys you put away. I'll sell my soul to see to it."

"I just did what Mitchelson told me," Federici snapped. "Since when is it a fucking crime to report to a fucking superior officer?"

"If he's a thief, it's a fucking crime," Grogan snapped. "You're dead meat, asshole. You better talk to us."

"Hey, if he's a thief, how am I supposed to know?" Federici had started to rise from his chair, but thought better of it as Devlin took a step forward.

"If he's a thief, he wouldn't have trusted anybody with this except another fucking thief." It was Levy this time, and the injection of a female voice seemed to throw Federici off. His eyes darted from one to the other.

"We're gonna tie this back to Little Bat's murder," Devlin said. "We're gonna feed it to the newspapers that way. We may not be able to tie that directly to you, but we're gonna hang the label around your neck. A cop who helped get another cop whacked. And, when you get to the joint, even the screws won't help you. There'll be no protective custody. Nothing. You'll be in the general population with all those nice cop-loving pussycats. I give you about a week before they carve your ass like a Christmas goose."

"Hey, maybe they'll take a little longer," Grogan interjected. "See if they can fuck you to death first."

"Look. All right." Federici was pouring sweat now, twisting in his chair. "We followed Little Bat—a couple of us—just to see what he was up to. Mitchelson said it would be like our own little internal affairs investigation."

"But you knew it was more than that, didn't you?" Devlin said.

Federici was breathing heavily now. He was staring at his feet. "Yeah, I knew. But I didn't know he was gonna get whacked. I still don't think it was any of our guys did it."

"But you cleaned out his apartment after you and your buddies found the body, didn't you? You needed to deep-six all the evidence he'd been putting together about the Money Club, and all the people who were being blackmailed."

Federici shook his head. His eyes were wide now. "No. When we called it in—that he was dead—Mitchelson told us to. But there was nothin' there. Everything was fucking gone already. And, yeah, we were worried about this Money Club thing. But I didn't know anything about no blackmail."

"What did you know?" Devlin snapped.

"Just that we were protecting this scam that Torelli was running."

"How many of you were involved?"

"Just me and Mitchelson. And, in the beginning, Battaglia."

"The senator?"

"No. The captain."

"What else?"

"Just that Mitchelson used to meet this guy about once a month, who was involved in it somehow. I figure he's feeding us information, because right after each meeting, we're making these small busts, nibbling away at Torelli's action."

"Who was this guy?"

"This fucking lawyer. You know him. O'Brien." Federici shook his head. "That's when Bat—the captain—went off the deep end. When he found out about this lawyer. All of a sudden he's digging into this Money Club, even though he's not supposed to. Mitchelson tells him to lay off, but we know he's still doing it." He leaned forward, eyes pleading. "Look, I don't know what happened then. Except all of a sudden Bat's dead, and everybody's in a sweat about what evidence might still be out there. But, shit, I thought we were just playing along with some federal scam. Getting a little side action out of it ourselves. And I can't figure what all the sweat's about."

Devlin turned to Grogan. "I want you to get in touch with Jenny Miller and get her over here. I want his deposition on paper. Then I want Samuels and Walker to take him someplace, and baby-sit him until we can bring in somebody from IAD. No charges"—he glanced down at Federici—"unless he fucks with us. If he doesn't, he might just walk. In the meantime, I don't want anything to get out about this until we tie some more ends together."

Grogan stared at him. "You got somethin' else goin', too, don't you?"

"I think so, Eddie. I just need to touch a few more bases first. Then I'll know for sure."

When Grogan had taken Federici into the other room, Levy approached Devlin. "I didn't want to say anything while that piece of shit was here. But something else just came up."

"Like what?"

"First, like that old broad—that neighbor of Little Bat's that we couldn't find. She just got back, found the message we left under her door, and called. And I think somebody oughta talk to her." Levy briefly filled him in.

"You're right," he said. "You do it. Today. She'll be number two on a very short list I've got for you."

"What's number one?"

"First number three. I want you to find our little friend Boardman. Let him know what happened to Tina and Rabitto. Tell him we think he may be next, then squeeze him. Scare the living hell out of him. Take some crime scene photos of Tina's apartment and make him look at them. Then offer him protection. Tell him we'll stash him in a hotel somewhere with a police guard. Tell him, as long as he wasn't the guy who did Little Bat, he can have anything he wants."

"You really think they might whack him?" Levy asked.

"I think they're cleaning house at the Money Club, and Boardman's about to get dusted. You tell him I said that. Tell him I've already got Michelle Paoli stashed away." He glanced toward the door, making sure it was closed. "And that's number one on your short list.

Devlin explained what he needed, then handed her the key to Michelle's apartment and the note for the doorman. "Cunningham's playing watchdog outside the apartment on Seventy-second Street where I've got her stashed," he said. "He knows you're coming. Touch base with him before you go in."

"Where you gonna be if I score with the old lady or Boardman?" Levy asked.

"I've got my own very short list to work," he said. "Just leave word here at the office, and I'll find you."

Number one on Devlin's short list was George Mitchelson. They met, at Devlin's request, in a small bar on Church Street. Mitchelson looked pale and worried when he slid into the rear booth Devlin had chosen. He had good reason to. Word would have already reached him about Bunny Rabitto and Tina Grimaldi, and even Mitchelson would have put things together. Whomever he had reported back to—as Devlin was now sure he had—just may have played a role in getting them killed.

"I asked you to come here, Chief, because I wanted to keep things unofficial. For now." The final words held an ominous note; were intended to. Mitchelson's normally gray complexion became even grayer. "I just had a long talk with your boy, Federici." Devlin added. "I want to tell you about it. But I think you better order a drink first."

There was a tremor in Mitchelson's hand two minutes later as he raised the martini to his lips.

"So Cervone was never really involved," Devlin said.

Mitchelson put the drink down, and shook his head. "He was only following orders from on high. He thought it was this fag thing. That the big brass wanted it squelched." He reached for his glass again, then stopped. "They did, sure. But that wasn't the big thing. Not where the orders were coming from anyways." He closed his eyes momentarily. "It was that fucking Money Club, and what was going on there. We were shit scared that Little Bat had left evidence around, and that you'd find it and start digging into things just the way he had."

"So, when you found out from Federici that we were on to Bunny Rabitto's girlfriend—his little film star—you never passed that on to Cervone."

"I wasn't supposed to. Cervone was just a beard. I passed it to the guy who was giving Cervone orders—Mac Brownell."

Devlin stared at him, allowing his silence to push for more. He wasn't surprised by what Mitchelson had told him. He had already figured that part out.

"Christ, Paul, Brownell knew about this Money Club thing from way back. He was chief of department, remember? He was the guy the feds used as a safety valve to make sure no eager beaver ever tried to bust the joint."

"But then he retired," Devlin said.

"Yeah, but he still had his finger in. He hung on as a consultant to the department. The feds set it up for him. He passed the job of running protection for the club on to me. Since Torelli was involved, any bust anybody wanted to pull would be run by me, and I could stop it. And I kept him posted, kept Brownell up to date on everything." He took a fast gulp of his drink, draining half of it. "Christ, he was my rabbi for a lotta years." He stared into the half-empty glass. "And then he was back as first deputy. I think the feds set that up too."

"So you protected Torelli together."

"Yeah, sure we did. But I thought it was a national security deal. And we were getting paid back with information that let us bust some of Torelli's smaller operations."

"From O'Brien."

Mitchelson stared across the table, his fear palpable now. Devlin knew even more than he had thought. He felt as though he were mired in mud, sinking fast.

"Yeah, from him. But I figured it was really coming from the feds. That they were using him as a conduit. Hell, I knew he worked for Big Bat, and I figured the old war-horse was tied in with the feds, helping them. You know? Once a cop. That sort of thing."

"Then you found out Bat was on the hook, too."

"Yeah. But that was later. After Little Bat went ballistic and started digging into everything. Mac, he told me then how they had Big Bat by the balls, and that we should use it to make his kid back off. I figured, okay, so he isn't helping the feds voluntarily. They scammed him into it. What difference does it make? It's still the same deal. Right? The feds are still feeding us information on Torelli."

"What kind of stuff did they give you?"

Mitchelson told him.

"And you still believed that?"

"Sure. Those federal spooks, they're all alike. They use you and shop you in the same fucking breath. I figured they were just keeping Torelli in check."

But that wasn't it, Devlin thought. Not by a long shot.

"So you never questioned Brownell about it."

"No. I was too fucking stupid to question Brownell. I just went along."

"What set Little Bat off?" Devlin watched his eyes now, looking for a tell.

"It was when he found out about O'Brien. That's when he really started digging. Started looking in places he wasn't supposed to go." He gulped the last of his drink, waved at the waiter for another. "So I laid it out to him. Told him to back off." Mitchelson shook his head. "He lost it. Told me there was more to it than I knew. I told him I didn't give a fuck, the orders were to back off. Later, when he still hadn't, I laid out the stuff about his old man. He just said: 'There's still more than you know.' So, this time I ask him what, but he won't say. Like he couldn't trust me with it."

Mitchelson stopped as the waiter delivered his second drink, then gulped half of it. His eyes followed the waiter away from the table, then he turned back to Devlin.

"Then, for a while, he seemed to back off, and I thought he'd listened to me, saw the sense of it. Then I found out he was still at it. Working on his own."

"How'd you find out?"

"Mac told me." He stared at Devlin, his eyes close to terror now.

"So you went to him again, right?"

"Yeah. But he just denied everything. Said he was out of it. Then he got whacked." He paused, stared down at his trembling hands. "Christ, you don't think Mac had him whacked? Jesus, the man's first deputy commissioner."

"I think Mac did what he was told," Devlin said. "And still is." He studied the fear in Mitchelson's eyes. The man was telling the truth, and the truth scared him shitless.

"Someday I'll let you see a little film I have." Devlin started to slide out of the booth. "A little film staring Mac Brownell." He left Mitchelson with his martini.

Chapter Twenty

Miriam Goldstein had been visiting her daughter in New Jersey since the day of the murder. She had been excited to find the note from the police upon her return, but had agreed to see Levy only on two conditions. First, that she call her Tante Miriam. And second, that Levy escort her the few blocks from her building to Carl Shurz Park.

She was an old woman, well into her seventies, and she walked with the help of a cane. Levy thought she had probably once been strikingly attractive, but the fine lines of her face were covered with other lines now, until the whole resembled not so much a face, but a shattered mirror. But the effect of her age seemed to stop there. Her mind remained quick, her blue eyes bright and alert, and her heavily accented mouth stopped only to gather in needed oxygen.

"So, you see over there?" she said, jabbing with her cane toward Gracie Mansion. "That's vere our mayor lives. A nice Jewish boy. Hah! Every day, I come here to visit him. Does he come out to *schmooz* mit me? Never. Not vonce. Such a big shot he is."

"He's downtown working," Levy said. "At City Hall."

Tante Miriam stared up at her, suspiciously. She was a diminutive woman, had probably shrunk over the years, Levy thought. But her eyes had the gleam of a bird of prey ready to attack. They just looked up at you, instead of down.

"Vot? He doesn't vork here? The president, in Vashington, he has a fancy, schmancy house. He vorks in it. This *meshugenah* mayor, he has to have a fancy office, too. No vonder the city has no money for nothing." She glared at Levy as though she were somehow responsible. Levy shrugged. She knew better than to argue with a Jewish mother. Her defense of Howie Silver, she decided, was finished for the day.

Levy guided the old woman to a park bench, but no sooner was she seated, then she glared across the park and began jabbing her cane again. "You see? You see?"

Levy followed her gaze. A black kid, dressed in tattered jeans, a dirty T-shirt, and a pair of spanking new, ninety-dollar Nikes, was bebopping along one of the paved footpaths. There was a ghetto blaster clamped to his shoulder, undoubtedly killing brain cells with every step. "The kid?" she asked.

"The *schvartzer*," Tante Miriam said. "Here to rob the old people."

"That kid, you saw him rob somebody?"

"They all do it," the old woman snapped. "You should arrest him."

"I have to see him do something first. Or have somebody tell me."

"I'm telling you!"

"But you didn't *see* him do it. I can't arrest him just 'cause he's black."

Tante Miriam threw her hands up in disgust, the cane in one cracking hard against Levy's knee. "No vonder the city isn't safe. Even a nice Jewish girl von't listen to vot's happening in front of her nose."

Levy placed a hand on Tante Miriam's arm, partly to calm her, partly to immobilize the cane. "Tell me about Captain Battaglia," she said.

"Vat's to tell? He's dead." She stared at Levy, ac-

cusation back in her eyes. "See? Even a police captain, he shouldn't be safe in his own house."

Levy waited her out.

"But he vas a nice boy. A *goyim*, but nice. I liked
him. I felt safe he was there, a police captain on my
own floor." She raised her eyebrows, then her hands.
"I should be so safe. He vas the first one they
killed."

"Did you notice any visitors he had? Either the
day he was killed—the day you left to visit your
daughter—or earlier?"

Tante Miriam rocked her head back and forth.
"Some fancy schmancy boys, they came sometimes."

"What do you mean?"

"You know. Fancy schmancy boys. Boys who
don't like girls so much."

Levy fought off a smile. "They came together?
The two men?"

Tante Miriam shook her head. "No. Alvays alone.
Then the *shiksa*, she came sometimes." She held her
nose up, rocked her head back and forth. "Very
fancy, that one. But in a different vey. Sometimes
she came alone, sometimes mit one of the fancy
schmancy boys."

"Can you describe these people?" Levy asked.

"Vot? You think I'm an old lady, I can't remember
nothing no more? Of course I can do that."

Levy listened to her, then asked one final question.
"The day the captain died. Did you see anybody that
day?"

Tante Miriam shook her head. Levy felt her stomach sink. Then the old woman pulled on one ear.

"But I heard," she said.

"What did you hear?"

"Der vas like dis scream." She gave her shoulders
a small shake. "It vas a man. So I go in the hall, and
I put my ear to the nice captain's door. Just to listen
a little. But I don't hear nothing but some people,

they should be having an argument. So, after avile,
I go avay."

"Tell about what you heard. What the people said.
What the voices sounded like," Levy said.

Tante Miriam did.

It was early evening when Devlin climbed the
front steps of the East Sixty-third Street row house.
Judge Oliver Rockwell had refused to see him
earlier at federal court, so he had used Jenny Miller
to dig up the judge's home address, then had staked
out the house, waiting for the jurist to arrive.

It was a moneyed address, sitting quietly among a
row of understated, moneyed addresses. Far more
than Rockwell should be able to afford on a judge's
salary.

The house had a stately brick facade, rising four
stories, and the single bell next to the front door indicated it was entirely for Rockwell's use. The
multipaned windows on each floor were covered by
heavy drapes, denying any view of the interior to
passersby, but even in the fading evening light, the
windows gleamed, speaking of regular cleanings of
the city's grit and grime.

Devlin pressed the polished brass doorbell and
waited. Rockwell answered the door himself, still
dressed in the lightweight gray suit and tie he had
worn home. Devlin flashed his shield and introduced
himself.

Rockwell's eyes hardened, his lips pressed together. He was letting Devlin know he wasn't
amused by the unexpected visit. "I thought I made it
clear I couldn't see you today," he said. "That meant
in my chambers, at my home, or anywhere." His
voice was measured and imperious—almost like a
schoolmaster's, Devlin thought. One who was in-
structing a particularly ignorant child.

"I think you better," Devlin said. He thrust the
manila envelope into Rockwell's hands.

Rockwell glared at him, then at the envelope. Finally, he opened it and withdrew the eight-by-ten photographs inside. His expression changed; the envelope fluttered to the floor, and his hand tightened on the pictures, crinkling the edges.

"I think you better come in here," he said.

Rockwell led Devlin into a room off the foyer, facing the street. It was a small study, lined with rich paneling, with a floor-to-ceiling bookcase taking up one entire wall behind a large mahogany desk. Another wall held a portrait of Oliver Wendell Holmes, illuminated by a small light attached to the top of the frame. The remainder of the room was decorated in rich red leather—a small sofa, two club chairs, and an antique British military drinks table which had probably once occupied some officer's tent in the Afghani desert.

Devlin waited until the judge was seated behind his desk, then took one of the club chairs. Rockwell's face was ashen, but he was visibly struggling for control.

"It's the maid's night off," he said. He inclined his head toward the portable drinks table. "But I can offer you a drink," he added.

"No thanks," Devlin said.

"Mind if I do?"

Devlin shook his head. His eyes never left the judge's face.

Rockwell poured himself four fingers of single malt scotch, then settled back in his chair. "Would you like to tell me where you got these photographs?" he asked.

He was attempting to reassert control in a situation that was already out of control. Now it was Devlin's turn to be unamused. "Let's not play games, Judge. The photographs were made up from some videotapes that were seized in a raid at one of Donatello Torelli's little enterprises. All part of a murder investigation of a police captain named Joseph Battaglia. You may have read about it."

Rockwell's face had collapsed, his jaws slack now. Devlin's sarcasm was lost in his own struggle to find some toehold for self preservation. He took a heavy hit on the scotch.

"As part of that investigation, we've been taking a long look at the UN Committee for Monetary Equality," Devlin continued. "It's not much of a committee. Really just a government-sanctioned whorehouse that I believe you're familiar with."

Rockwell started to speak; thought better of it.

Devlin leaned forward. "That investigation was started by Captain Battaglia, and in addition to him, it's already resulted in the murders of a prostitute named Suzanne Osborne, two of Torelli's thugs—Bunny Rabitto and Mattie Cordino—and Tina Grimaldi, the child in those pictures I gave you."

Rockwell looked as though he'd been slapped, then his eyes dropped to the photographs now spread out on his desk. "I read about those murders in Brooklyn," he said. "But I never recognized her from the photo they ran, and I never connected the name." He shook his head. "I never knew her last name."

A hint of animal cunning suddenly came into Rockwell's eyes. His lawyer's mind had begun working again. Part of the chain of evidence against him had been broken with Tina's death. It made Devlin want to come out of his chair and hit the man.

"Yeah, well you haven't seen her in a couple of years," Devlin said. "Not since sometime before Torelli's last trial in your court. And she was only fifteen back then. Kids change as they grow up. If they grow up." He paused a beat, just for effect, then drew out his next sentence. "Unfortunately . . . for you . . . Tina spoke with us at some length before she was killed." Devlin watched the spark of hope fade from Rockwell's eyes. He seemed to have shrunk in size. His patrician features and bearing had melted away. Now, take away his well-tailored clothes and surroundings, and he would pass for any aging schmuck stumbling along the city's streets. Or maybe even some old fool being pissed on by a teenage whore.

"So, what do you want from me, Inspector? Or are you here to arrest me?" Rockwell's voice was only a croak now.

Devlin shook his head slowly. "No. That's somebody else's job, Judge. Torelli's little blackmail operation, and your acquiescence to it, come under federal jurisdiction. I imagine the FBI will be around in the next couple of days. My only concern is Captain Battaglia's murder."

"Of course," Rockwell said. "And now?"

"Now I need some information, Judge. I want to know about the *other* people who were blackmailing you."

Rockwell sat back in his chair, rested his head against the cushion, and stared at the ceiling. "So you even know about that." He sat forward, eyes staring at something above Devlin's head.

"You see that picture up there, Inspector." Devlin didn't turn to look. "That's Oliver Wendell Holmes, the great hero of my youth. My father named me after him, actually." He served up a faint, rueful smile. "I once had hopes of emulating him in other ways. Of sitting where he sat, on our nation's highest court." He raised his eyebrows, almost as if telling Holmes he was sorry. "My family had the money, and the powerful political connections to make that dream possible," he said. "And I—up until a few years ago—had the spotless, if not distinguished judicial record, to make myself a safe, politically acceptable candidate."

Rockwell stood, went to the drinks table and refilled his glass. He turned to Devlin and raised the glass. "Are you sure, Inspector?"

"I'm sure."

"Of course, I never would have agreed to be nominated," he continued after he had returned to his chair. "Can you imagine the level of blackmail I would have endured if I had?"

Devlin didn't respond. He was growing tired of the man's self-pity.

"Of course, you can," Rockwell said.

"Tell me about the others," Devlin said.

"Yes. The others. I mustn't become maudlin, must I?" He smiled weakly. He looked like a man who had resigned himself to something. "The others were easy. They only wanted money. A great deal of money, but still, only money. I'm sure there would have been other requests later, but I tried not to think about that." The smile returned. "I imagine I shall never have to now. So let me tell you about the others."

A half hour later, when he had seen Devlin out the door, Rockwell returned to his study and opened a desk drawer. Lying there was a thirty-eight-caliber pistol, which he had inherited years ago upon his father's death. Rockwell removed the revolver and sat back in his chair. Then he gave one final look at the portrait of Oliver Wendell Holmes.

Devlin heard the muffled sound of the shot as he slid behind the wheel of his car. He looked up at the study window, then closed the car door. The sonofabitch hadn't even asked if Tina Grimaldi had suffered, he told himself.

Leslie Boardman craned his neck to see across the dance floor. There was a young man seated at a small table. He was blond, lean, maybe twenty, and he was alone.

"Cute, isn't he?"

Leslie glanced at the man standing next to him, who had just spoken. He was a hulking biker whom Leslie had been trying to ignore. There was a red bandanna tied around his head, the color of which almost matched the beard hanging halfway down his chest. His massive, bare arms carried a myriad of tattoos, some of which were distinctly of the home-made, prison variety. The man was rough trade personified, and Leslie wanted no part of him.

"Yes, he is," he said. "And he's definitely my type." He took a step away from the bar, then stopped in midstride. Another man—also young and blond and beautiful—had just slid into a chair at the table.

"Tough luck," the biker said. "But he ain't the only fish in the sea."

Leslie rolled his eyes and returned to the bar. The man was not only Godzilla, he was trite as well. "I'm sorry, I'm too crushed to go on," Leslie said.

The biker shrugged off the rejection, then turned his back in search of new quarry.

Leslie waved at the bartender, and pointed at his glass. The man moved toward him with a mincing, effeminate gait. He was cute, Leslie thought. But too fey. Not at all his type.

"Chivas. Please," he said. He was jostled from behind, pushed up against the bar rail. "God!" he hissed.

"And it's early," the bartender said, commiserating. "By ten o'clock you won't be able to move. Must be a full moon."

Leslie rolled his eyes again. What was this place, cliché city?

He felt a hand on his ass, thought it was the biker again, and turned to confront him.

Paddy Rourke grinned at him. "Just wanted to make sure it was you, sweet cakes. It's so crowded in here. Let's take a little walk." Rourke's eyes failed to match the smile. They were cold, clearly menacing.

Leslie shook his head, pressed himself back against the bar.

"Suit yourself," Rourke said.

Leslie heard a soft click, glanced down, then instinctively shot both hands out, hitting Rourke hard in the chest. Rourke staggered back, nearly fell, but caught hold of the arm of another man, keeping himself up. The knife in his free hand waved wildly.

"No!" Leslie screamed.

Rourke lunged forward, preparing to drive the blade into Leslie's heart. A hand snapped out, grabbing Rourke's wrist. He turned to face his attacker, as the biker's hamlike fist smashed into his face, crushing his nose and loosening several front teeth. Rourke sagged toward the floor, but the biker—still attached to his wrist—held him up and drove a knee squarely against his chin. The knife fell away, and the biker released his grip, allowing Rourke to fall back to the floor.

"Motherfucker," the biker hissed. He raised a heavy, black boot and brought it down on Rourke's face, stomping once, then again.

Leslie Boardman let out a howl of uncontrollable fear, then literally clawed his way through the crowd, and out the front door.

Chapter Twenty-one

Devlin dialed the number his office had given him, then asked the operator for the extension. Sharon Levy picked up on the first ring.

"What the hell are you doing at the Westbury?" Devlin asked without preamble. The Westbury, tucked away on Madison Avenue between Sixty-ninth and Seventieth Streets, was one of New York's more exclusive and unobtrusive hotels—a place favored by many celebrities who preferred not to be easily found. It had a price tag to match its exclusivity.

"I got Boardman stashed here," Levy said.

"The Westbury?"

"Hey, I figure the guys looking for him know that cops are cheap. This place will be way down on their list, if it's on it at all." She paused a moment. "You haven't heard the worst. All I could get is a small suite."

Devlin closed his eyes, shook his head, and smiled. He didn't give a tinker's damn. When the expense report went in to the Puzzle Palace, he'd listen to the bean counters howl; then tell them to go fuck themselves. He was simply overwhelmed by the size of Sharon Levy's cast-iron balls.

"You got some pair on you, kid," he said.

"Hey, what can I tell you. But you're gonna find it money well spent. Our little friend is singing like a canary."

"So you found him."

"I didn't have to. He found me," Levy said. "Paddy Rourke tried to stick a shiv in him tonight at some gay bar in the Village. Our boy called the office, screaming for police protection." She let out a soft snort. "Right now he's in the bedroom, crying himself to sleep. Jesus, sometimes I can't stand faggots," she said.

"What did he give you?"

"I think you better come by and hear this one yourself, boss. You're not gonna believe the tale our little puss 'n boots is spinning."

Devlin thought he would believe it. He thought he knew exactly what song Boardman had to sing. He glanced at his watch. "Okay," he said. "I've got a meeting with Big Bat and his lawyer, O'Brien, in about an hour and a half. I've gotta swing by the office and pick up Eddie, then we'll drop by and see you."

"If you're gonna see Big Bat and O'Brien, you definitely wanna talk to Boardman first," Levy said. "In the meantime, let me tell you what Miriam Goldstein had to say." She told him.

A small smile played across Devlin's lips, then faded. It hadn't been a smile of either pleasure or satisfaction. It had been as sour as the feeling in his gut. "I'll see you in half an hour," he said. He was even more certain now that Leslie Boardman would have no surprises for him.

Devlin put down the phone and looked around the loft that had been his home for almost a year now. He hadn't been back since he'd been called out to the Rabbito/Grimaldi murder scene the previous evening. He had returned to grab a quick shower and a clean shirt before meeting Battaglia and O'Brien. He'd also hoped to wash away some of the filth he'd gotten himself mired in, even though he knew he never really would.

He picked up the phone and punched in another number.

"I miss you," he said, when Adrianna answered.

There was a pause. "Paul," she began, then stopped. "I'm sorry I blew up the other day. I just couldn't do what you wanted. Not after . . ." She let the sentence die.

"It's all right, babe. You were right. I wasn't thinking." And he hadn't been, Devlin told himself. He had been caught up in the need of the moment. The killers had already marked Tina, and nothing was going to stop them from going after her. And it could have been at the beach house. They could have followed her there—followed her to where Phillipa and Adrianna were. They were capable of it—had already proved that, and more. It was a realization that had come to him at the murder scene, and it had chilled him.

"Did you find someplace for her?" Adrianna asked.

"The problem resolved itself. Put it out of your mind. I mean that."

"Are you okay?" Her voice was filled with concern. For him. The sound of it made him feel sick with guilt.

"Yeah, I'm fine. I'd like you to come home."

"Is the case finished?"

"We're tying it all together now. We'll be making arrests tonight and tomorrow. Then a couple of days of paperwork." He paused a moment. "I just need to see you. And talk to you."

"We can leave in the morning."

Devlin hesitated again. "Why don't you see if Phillipa can stay with our next-door neighbor out there. Jean . . ." He tried to find the last name, couldn't. "Whatever her name is. We can head back out in a couple of days." If you still want to, he added to himself.

This time Adrianna hesitated. "All right. I'm sure it will be okay with Jean. And her last name is

Ribicki." Another pause. "Paul, are you sure you're okay? You sound so strange."

"I'm fine, babe. Give me a call at the office when you get back."

"Okay. I love you."

"I love you, too."

As he was slipping on his jacket, the downstairs doorbell rang. He pressed the buzzer that opened that door, then waited for his visitor to make it up to his floor. When the interior doorbell sounded, he looked through the spy hole, then removed his revolver from its holster, and slipped it into his jacket pocket. He opened the door with his hand on the pistol.

The man facing him was average height, average weight, and completely nondescript. He held a credential case in his hand, introducing himself only as "Robinson."

Devlin studied the credentials, then removed his hand from his pocket.

"A spook from Washington," he said. "And it isn't even Halloween."

"Actually, I work here in New York," Robinson said. "We have to talk about this little case you're working on."

The word "little" sent sparks to Devlin's brain. The scar on his cheek became a thin, white line. "You mean the one about a murdered police captain?" he asked.

"That's not the part I'm concerned about," Robinson said.

Devlin had recognized the man from the photos Levy had taken outside Bunny Rabitto's film studio. "It'll have to be another time," he said. He stepped into the hall, forcing the man to move back, then closed the door behind him.

Robinson put a hand up to Devlin's chest. "I think now is better," he said.

Devlin's hand shot out, grabbing his throat, and

propelling him back against the far wall. His other hand went to the man's hip, snatched his revolver from its holster, then threw it down the hall.

"You don't listen too good, asshole," he hissed.

The man's face turned bright red, as he struggled for breath. "Don't make me make things hard for you, Devlin." Robinson's words came out gasping and choking.

Devlin drove his knee up into the man's testicles. Robinson's eyes bulged, then his knees buckled and he slumped to the floor.

"Too bad you don't have a witness," Devlin said. "It's a mandatory two years for hitting a federal officer, right?"

Devlin turned away, and walked off down the hall.

Devlin and Grogan left the Westbury Hotel and headed north to Seventy-second Street. Devlin had spoken to Cunningham earlier by radio, but wanted to touch base again, make sure his instructions were being closely followed. They then headed to John Jay Park near the old Seventy-eighth Street Library.

He had chosen the small, vest-pocket park for several reasons. He would meet Big Bat and O'Brien alone, and he wanted the meeting out in the open where they would feel less threatened. He wanted it there, too, so Eddie and a waiting Stan Samuels could record every word on a directional microphone. And he also wanted to be close to the apartment where Michelle was hidden away, just in case he was needed quickly.

After dropping Eddie off with Samuels a half block away, Devlin left his car at the edge of the park, then moved just inside to an area that held two facing benches. He muttered a senseless phrase, then waited. The lights of Samuels's car blinked twice to let him know they were receiving loud and clear.

Devlin glanced at his watch, then settled back to

wait. It was ten of ten—ten minutes yet to go. Devlin stared into the street. Only the occasional pedestrian scurried by, eager to be off the dimly lighted sidewalks and back to the relative safety of his or her apartment, even though it was cooler here. The lingering day's heat was abated now by a soft breeze coming off the nearby East River. In Europe, Devlin thought, a park like this would be crowded with people well past midnight—neighbors sitting and gossiping about the day's events, or simply enjoying the freedom to escape the heat and boredom of cramped quarters.

Almost as if reading his thoughts, two junkies—one Hispanic, one white—appeared on one of the park's walkways. They spotted Devlin, exchanged whispered words, then parted, one cutting to the sidewalk along the street, the other continuing along the footpath.

Devlin muttered a soft curse, then removed his shield and revolver, and held each up above his head in plain view.

"Turn around, assholes," he shouted. "Or I blow your skinny butts off, then bust you for littering."

The pair stopped, then turned away. The one nearest the street shouted back a terse: "Fuck you, cop," then moved away at a slower, more defiant gait.

Devlin shook his head. He wondered briefly about the poor soul who might later come across that dynamic duo. And get his wallet lifted because three city cops hadn't been able to let them play out their game, then bust their sorry asses for attempted robbery. Couldn't be helped, he told himself. He glanced back at Samuels's car, certain that he and Grogan were gleefully laughing about this latest near application of Murphy's Law.

Big Bat and O'Brien arrived fifteen minutes later in the senator's car. Bat moved straight to Devlin; O'Brien trailed two steps behind, his eyes darting about him—looking for a suspected backup, Devlin thought.

Bat took the seat next to Devlin, leaving the opposite one for O'Brien.

O'Brien remained standing, as though prepared to run. "Why here?" he snapped.

"Tonight's purely informational," Devlin said. "I didn't want to be around too many ears."

O'Brien glanced around, still uncertain. "What is this place?" he demanded.

"John Jay Park," Devlin said. "You remember him. President of the Continental Congress; negotiated the Treaty of Paris that formally ended our little Revolutionary War; first chief justice of the supreme court; and then governor of New York for two terms." He grinned up at the man. "The city fathers wanted to name something after a New York lawyer. He was the only honest one they could find."

Bat snorted amusement. O'Brien glared.

"Very funny, Devlin," he said.

"Sit down, Jim," Bat ordered. "Let's hear what Paul has to say."

"I want to see if he's wearing a wire first," O'Brien snapped.

Devlin stood and spread his suit coat. He noticed Bat didn't object. O'Brien began to pat him down.

"You touch my service revolver, I kick you in the nuts," Devlin warned.

O'Brien ignored him, but did as he was told, then took the opposite bench.

"Okay, Paul," Bat began. "What have you got for us?" Devlin noted that he didn't apologize for the pat down.

He glanced at each man. "I know how and why your son was set up and killed. And I know who all the major players were. If there were others . . ." He paused, offering up a shrug, "Well, we'll get them, when we start to squeeze the the ones we know about." He gave Bat a cold smile. "You know how it works."

"You have this solid, Paul?" Bat asked.

"We have three informants stashed away. Two spilled to us willingly; the other one, kind of inadvertently. But it was all there." He turned to O'Brien. "We had another one, too, one they didn't expect us to get, so they whacked her. But she talked to us first, and everything she said was backed up by video tape."

Devlin turned to face Bat again. "You know about those tapes, right, Bat?"

"You tell me about them, Paul."

Devlin smiled. Once a cop, he thought. "Well, it started maybe five years ago, when some spooks in Washington got nervous about a little honey trap they were running at the UN. So, being the bright guys that they are, they turned the operation over to a private contractor—in this case a certain mob boss named Dapper Dan Torelli." Devlin offered a cold smile. "He was convenient. And he also happened to have his own little film company.

"That's where you came in, Bat," Devlin continued. "Because they gave Torelli a free hand—sort of a quid pro quo. They let him change the rules at this little whorehouse the UN was running, and start bringing in some other talent in addition to the diplomats who were being set up."

He shrugged again. "What the hell, the spooks didn't care. And who knew, Torelli might come up with something they could use some day. So, all of a sudden, some judges, some prosecutors, some D.C. bigshots, started to join some of your buddies in the congress who wanted to get their oil changed. All of it videotaped, of course, and stored for posterity at Torelli's little film studio."

"And probably someplace else, too," Bat said. He shook his head, stared at his shoes for a moment.

"Did you know Torelli offered to give me *my* tapes back?"

Devlin was surprised. "Why didn't you take them?"

"Because I knew he'd have a copy. It's the way a fuck like him works. And I wanted to know who killed my boy. That's what I asked *him* for." He stared hard at Devlin. "Did Torelli have Joe whacked?"

Devlin shook his head. "No," he said. "Some people he thought were working for him might have been involved. But, no. Not Torelli." Devlin considered what he had been told. "This offer, about the tapes, was it made when you met Buster Fucci at that Brooklyn restaurant?" he asked at length.

Bat nodded. "That's when. And it's when I asked them to give me the guy who ... who did that to Joey." He bit down the final words—especially the childhood name he had once used for his son—and Devlin saw his pain again, just as he had in the M.E.'s office all those days ago.

Devlin turned to O'Brien. "Tell me, Jim. What did you advise Bat to do when Buster offered him the tapes?"

O'Brien glared across the ten feet or so, that separated them. "I told him to take them," he snapped. "I wanted the senator protected. I wanted him out from under those bastards."

Devlin turned back to Bat. "You see that's how it all started to turn hinky," he said. "With you, Bat." He paused to let that sink in. "You see the cops Joe worked with in OCC were protecting Torelli—at least the UN part of his operation. But not because they were bent. They were getting some feedback on some of Torelli's other operations. Things they could move on, bust some of his people for. It was never anything big, but good, solid collars anyway. They figured it was coming from the spooks, either because they wanted to keep Torelli in line, or just because they are what they are. Pricks who just can't keep from fucking with people.

"So, anyway, they start getting this stuff. And everybody's happy. But suddenly, something unforeseen drops down on them. Little Bat is seconded to OCC as exec. And when he jumps into this thing, he finds out that the guy feeding them all this shit about Torelli, just happens to be his lover—somebody he's been close to for a lotta years; somebody who's been close to his whole family, especially his father."

Devlin looked across at O'Brien. "Right Jim?" he said.

O'Brien sat stonelike. The only tell was a momentary tic at the corner of one eye.

Bat's eyes were riveted on the man; his whole body suddenly coiled, tense.

"So your son starts digging. He's a good cop, and he's smart. He finds out how you're in Torelli's pocket. He also finds out that your old buddy, the department's new first deputy commissioner, Mac Brownell, is the guy who set up this supposed information trade with the spooks, and that old Mac is in Torelli's pocket, too." Devlin stared at his shoes, shook his head. "Seems like a few years back— before he found out Torelli was running the show— pious, old, straitlaced Mac Brownell needed to get his oil changed, too. But Little Bat's too good to stop there. He knows something doesn't smell right. Some of the stuff they're being fed doesn't make any sense for the spooks to know about. I mean, Torelli's not a fool. He's doing a job for the feds, okay. And he's doing his own little dance on the side. But he's not going to let the feds know what else he's up to."

Devlin looked at O'Brien again. The man was rigid, trying to avoid Big Bat's eyes, which were still fixed on him. "And your son knew that his lover wouldn't know about these things unless they were handed to him. Hell, he's a corporate lawyer.

He couldn't find his dick in a snowstorm out there in mob country."

He turned back to Bat. "So he starts digging deeper. He's concerned about his father. He's concerned that somebody close to him is setting him up a second time, getting him in even deeper than he already is. And he's concerned that the NYPD—and his own unit—are being used with the help of a corrupt first deputy commissioner, who's also supposed to be his old man's friend."

He placed a hand on Bat's now rigid arm, made his voice softer, gentler. "He was a helluva cop, Bat. And a helluva son."

"Go on, Paul." Bat's own voice was a croak.

"So he digs. He works this hooker who plays at this UN whorehouse. He works a guy named Leslie Boardman, who's a male pross there. And he starts piecing it all together. How there's a second little blackmail operation running right under Torelli's nose. He finds out it involves this guy, Paddy Rourke—a Westies clown who's supposed to be working for Torelli. He finds out it involves his lover, little Jimbo over here. And how Mac Brownell is in it up to his teeth. Maybe because this second group promised to give Brownell his film back. Who knows? I'm not sure how deep he goes in it. Deep enough for a few years in the slam, anyway." He sat back. "And then, there are a few other people." He looked at O'Brien again, allowing the man to read what else he knew in his eyes.

"Anyway, they all want one thing, this new group. They're greedy, and they want Torelli out. And now Little Bat is one very big problem for them. So first, at Mac Brownell's suggestion, they try to use your involvement to get him to back off. They send the head of OCC, George Mitchelson—who's not involved, just stupid—to deliver the message. But Little Bat won't bite. He wants you out of it, but he's not willing to sell his soul—or the department's—to

do it. So they try something else. They set him up.
Get film on him, too. With Boardman this time."
Again Devlin stared at O'Brien. "At *Jim*'s sugges-
tion."

He could feel the tension mounting in Bat, and he
turned back to face him, ready to stop him if he went
for O'Brien. "So then they tried to blackmail your
son. They threatened to send the tape to his ex-wife,
fuck up the very tenuous relationship he already had
with her, fuck with his ability to see his kids. But
your son tells them to scratch it. And that's when
they know they have to take him out." He paused.
He wanted to drop the next bit of information all by
itself. "But, you know, Bat, they sent the tape to
Angie anyway. Because that's the kind of vindictive
pricks they are."

Bat's arms were trembling now; his mouth moved
for several seconds before the words came out.
"Who set him up? Who?"

"They all did. But it started with our friend Jim,
here. He passed the word to Brownell that Little Bat
was still working the case. And Brownell dutifully
passed it on to the people behind this second blackmail operation. And that's when they decided Joe
had to be hit. But this second group, they wanted to
use the hit to set Torelli up. They wanted to make it
look like Torelli had caught on to what Little Bat
was up to. They even passed Torelli information
about some computer disks Little Bat had in his
apartment. And they timed the murder so it would
happen just before Torelli's goon got there to steal
them. You see, he was supposed to get caught and
have it all lead back to Torelli. He was supposed to
break in Monday morning, when Little Bat was at
work. But he went Sunday. Who knows, maybe he
had plans to get laid Monday, and figured it didn't
make any difference, so long as he got the stuff. But
he wasn't there when Mac Brownell told Mitchelson
to send out a search party." He paused. "And neither

were the disks. Because the other players—the ones who killed your son—had gotten them first. But they didn't know Bat had put everything on a computer back-up tape, and stashed it in a safety deposit box. We haven't found it yet." He looked across at O'Brien. "But we will. It's only a matter of time."

"So, who was there when my son died?" Bat paused, raised his chin at O'Brien. "Him?" The final word came out with a degree of loathing Devlin had never heard before.

"No. He wasn't there. There's a little old lady, lives across the hall. She's our third informant. Seems she likes to put her ear to people's doors." He placed his hand on Bat's arm again. "When she heard your son scream in pain, she went to the door and listened. Fortunately, she doesn't know what a silenced pistol shot sounds like. So she stayed there, kept listening. And she heard names."

Devlin released Bat's arm. "Paddy Rourke was there." He turned to face O'Brien. "But he wasn't alone." He imitated Bat's gesture, jabbed his chin at O'Brien. "But it wasn't this piece of shit. All he did was set up his boyhood friend, and his lover. That's all he had the guts for."

Bat leaped from the bench with far more speed and agility than Devlin would have imagined. His hands were at O'Brien's throat before Devlin could reach him. Devlin grabbed him from behind and pulled him off.

"You'll never live to get to a fucking court," Bat screamed. "Never! Never, fucking never!"

O'Brien stumbled, then jumped away, out of reach. "You can't prove any of this," he screeched. "None of it."

Devlin continued to hold on to Bat. He smiled at O'Brien over his shoulder. "Sure we can, Jim. You see, you never should of shacked up with Boardman. Pillow talk can be very dangerous. But I guess they don't teach that at Columbia Law."

"You're fucking dead! Dead!" Bat screamed. "Don't worry about court, you sonofabitch! You'll never see one!"

Devlin glared at O'Brien. "Get lost, asshole," he snapped. "We know where to find you."

O'Brien turned and sprinted out of the park. Big Bat struggled against Devlin's hold.

"Why are you letting him get away? Why?"

He pushed Bat back to the bench, and forced him down, then squatted in front of him. "Because I have to see who he reaches out for. It's the last piece of evidence I need." He smiled up at the older man. "Besides, if I'd tried to cuff him now, you would of hit me over the head and killed him. And I didn't want to have to lock you up."

Bat's head sank to his chest. He looked suddenly older and weaker and smaller. Devlin still had one more question for him.

"There's one thing I haven't been able to figure out, Bat. Why didn't Joey come to you, tell you what was going down?"

Bat's chest began to heave, then he started to sob. "We hadn't spoken in over a year," he said, barely able to fight the words out. "The last time I talked to him, I ... I ..." He struggled for control; found it. "I called him a goddamned fag."

After he had put Bat back in his car, Devlin walked over to Samuels and Grogan. He leaned in the window. "You get it all?" he asked.

"Every lousy, fucking word," Grogan said.

"The last part," Devlin said. "From the time he goes after O'Brien. I want you to erase it."

Grogan grinned at him. "You got it," he said.

"With pleasure," Samuels added.

Michelle Paoli put down the phone and stared across the room at Paddy Rourke. Rourke's face was battered, his nose covered by a thick bandage. The sight of him disgusted her.

"That was Jim O'Brien," she said. "Devlin knows everything."

"Then we better get the fuck out of here."

Michelle shook her head. The man's brain was even more disgusting than his face, she told herself. "Jim said he thinks Devlin is trying to protect the senator. And his precious little police department." She raised an eyebrow. "He was alone when he talked to them. I think we still have a few cards to play. Even one Inspector Devlin doesn't know we have."

"So whadda I do?"

Michelle glared at him. "You think you can handle *this* job."

"Look, it wasn't my fault with Boardman. This faggot goon just came out of nowhere."

Michelle offered him a contemptuous smirk. Then her voice softened. "Go to the other apartment, Paddy." And please, use some caution. Don't just walk in the front door. Use the rear entrance. They may be watching us right now. Then wait for my signal." Then she told him what else she wanted.

Chapter Twenty-two

Devlin pulled in behind Cunningham, followed immediately by Samuels and Grogan. The three detectives piled into the first vehicle. Cunningham removed a headset from his crewcut head, then turned a grinning red face to Devlin.

"Just like you figured, Inspector. O'Brien called her, shitting his pants. It's all on the tape. And her little playmate, Rourke, he took off right after. Like his fucking shorts were on fire."

"You see which way he went?" Devlin asked. He was silently cursing himself for not having another man with Cunningham, someone who could have tailed Rourke. They were ready to grab him now; take him out of the game.

Cunningham inclined his head toward York Avenue. "He headed north, hoofing it."

"She make any calls?"

Cunningham shook his head. "Just the ones I told you about before."

"I want to hear the tape," Devlin said. "All of it."

He put on the headset, as Cunningham rewound the small recorder on the seat between them. Michelle's first call went to the answering machine at her Fifth Avenue apartment, changing the outgoing message to leave a new number where she could be reached. Devlin checked the written log of her calls. That first call had been made about two hours after he had left her. Just about the time her nerves would have started to get to her. The call to her machine had been her only option. She couldn't risk calling anyone's office and giving her name.

There was a dead space of time before the next call—well after business hours now. She made three calls. None were answered. Two—from the tone of the push button phone—sounded like same number. The third was different. Later, the lab would be able to identify each number called.

The fourth call, a half hour later, was successful. It was a man—definitely not O'Brien—but one he couldn't quite place. Rourke? Brownell? He couldn't be certain. But it was vaguely familiar. The conversation was terse and to the point. It explained her situation, and where she was. The man suggested she leave, go back to the club. She insisted it would be better if she remained. Her nerves had apparently eased now.

The final call was incoming—from O'Brien—shortly after he had fled the park. He was in full panic, babbling how he, Devlin, knew everything. Michelle snapped at him; ordered him to get control of himself. It was a voice he had never heard her use before—commanding and cruel.

O'Brien did as he was told, went on to tell her about the meeting—how he, Devlin, had come alone; how he was certain the powers that be wanted to protect Battaglia, and the department. He said—voice filled with hope—that they might still strike a deal. Michelle told him to go home and wait; that she would take care of it.

Devlin removed the headset. "When did Rourke show up?"

"About an hour ago," Cunningham said. "He was all bandaged up. Looks like somebody beat the shit out of him."

"Somebody did," Devlin said. "A guy in a gay bar."

Cunningham laughed. "I'd love to hear him explain that one," he said. "Especially to his Westies buddies in one of their Hell's Kitchen hangouts."

Devlin turned to Grogan. "You and I are going up," he said. Then to Samuels and Cunningham: "I want you other guys to stay in place. If you see Rourke heading back, grab him."

Michelle answered the door with a bright, beautiful smile. "Hello, Paul." She turned to Eddie. "And Detective Grogan. How nice to see you again. Come in."

She turned and walked ahead of them toward the living room. She had changed into some of the clothing Sharon Levy had delivered, dressed now in a pale gray, silk blouse and matching pants. All of it flowed with her. She walked like few women he had ever seen, Devlin thought.

Michelle positioned herself before the large window, allowing the night glow of the city to backlight her beauty. She was always on stage, Devlin thought. Always using every edge at her disposal. He wondered why he hadn't noticed it earlier. Or why he'd chosen to ignore it, if he had.

"Why don't you sit, gentlemen. I imagine this will take some time." She gestured toward the large sofa across from her.

"We'll stand," Devlin said. "I don't think it will take that long."

Her smile returned, her fingers toyed with a single strand of pearls at her throat. Real ones, Devlin thought.

"Are you here to arrest me, Paul?" she asked. "Perhaps you're forgetting about diplomatic immunity."

"I'm not forgetting." He returned the smile with an equal absence of warmth. "I thought you might like to cooperate. In your own interests."

Michelle laughed. It was a raucous, harsh sound, a contrast to her oh-so-cultivated image, Devlin thought.

"How so?" she asked.

"You're right. We can't touch you. Not even for murder." Devlin forced another smile. "But old Donatello, Dapper Dan, Torelli? He might feel differently. Especially if a little bird whispered in his ear."

He watched her eyes harden—another first. Then he walked to the telephone on a nearby table, unscrewed the mouthpiece cap, and removed a small transmitter. "Department property," he said. "Torelli gets a copy of the tape, he might find it interesting."

Michelle stared at him in disbelief, then the smile returned. "Your little woman detective?" she asked.

"I imagine, when she dropped off your clothes, she asked for a drink of water. Something."

"A soft drink," Michelle said.

"Gave her enough time while you were getting it," Devlin said. "She's a good cop."

Michelle closed her eyes momentarily, then slowly ran her tongue along her lower lip; smiled again. "My father—sexist old swine that he was—taught me how to play chess when I was just a child. He said the best response to check, was a check of your own." She paused for effect. "But first—please—tell me what led you to me. Was it sweet, little Leslie?"

"Oh, we would have gotten to you eventually," Devlin said. "With Leslie. Oh, by the way, he's stashed away safe and sound. And we also have an old lady, who lives across the hall from Joe Battaglia's apartment. She likes to listen at doors. Has a great memory for names she hears. She's stashed away, too." He paused for effect now. "But, actually, the first tell came from you. Without it, we wouldn't have bugged your apartment; wouldn't have set O'Brien up the way we did; wouldn't have decided to snatch Boardman so fast. You just might have slipped through the cracks. For a while."

Michelle's eyes were hard now, the smile gone. "So, tell me. Please."

"It was this morning. When I told you about Tina Grimaldi. You were trying to be brave—a pretty good act, really. You said her getting whacked didn't mean they were after you, too. You said maybe Tina was killed because she was with Rabitto. In Tina's apartment." He shrugged, affectedly. "You shouldn't have known that. That they were killed together. And where. It hadn't made the papers, or anything, yet." He shrugged again. "Oh, it could have been an assumption. I tried to tell myself that. But it started me thinking. All the information you had. All of it conveniently pointing at Torelli. You, right there in the middle of it, but nobody ever *really* tumbling to you. Then there was the way you lived. Poor little girl from Corsica, surrounded by all those beautiful things. But none of them really yours. Except, maybe, your father's paintings."

"They're fakes," Michelle interrupted. "Good fakes, but fakes all the same."

Devlin smiled again. "Yeah, like I said, none of it really belonging to you. Just a wage slave, living off your diplomatic status." He shrugged. "Still not bad for a whorehouse madam."

"Don't be vulgar, Paul."

"Sure," he said. "But that brought up the greed factor. There it all was for the taking. Hell, once blackmailed, the second time would be easy for those clowns. Especially if you picked the right people. But you were going to get rid of Torelli, anyway. He was too dangerous. And why share?"

"Why, indeed?" Michelle said.

"But then Little Bat came along, and suddenly he was more dangerous than anybody. So you set him up with Boardman. But even that didn't work. He wouldn't bite on the blackmail. So, there was really only one option. And you could even use it to point a bunch of dumb cops right back at Torelli. If you played it right. If you played *me* right." Devlin raised his hands, then let them fall to his sides. "Leslie told us about all that. Your boy, Rourke, really stained Leslie's shorts when he tried to whack him. Now, he just can't stop talking about it." He paused again. "But there's one thing I don't know." His eyes hardened. "Was it you, or Rourke who pulled the trigger on Little Bat?"

"That would be a silly question for me to answer," she said.

Devlin nodded. "Oh, there's one more thing. Maybe you'll tell me that. Your partners in all this. Did they come to you, or did you go to them?"

Michelle laughed again. Again it was harsh and out of character for the woman she'd been playing. "Does it matter?" she asked.

"I suppose not," Devlin said. "And it will come out, eventually. When we start to squeeze these guys."

"But you don't have to do that, Paul. Everyone can still walk away unscathed. Senator Battaglia, all those ridiculous political types, your police department." She paused. "Even you, Paul."

"Me?" It was Devlin's turn to laugh. The sound seemed to anger Michelle. "I'll live with anything you spill."

Michelle walked to a small table, and picked up a videocassette. She turned to Devlin, eyes hard. "Each time we came here, Paul, Paddy Rourke was already here, waiting." She let out a soft laugh. "This really isn't the apartment of some art gallery owner. The committee—or the Money Club, if you prefer—has owned it for years. Technically, Paul, you're on foreign soil again."

She walked back to the window. "I'm sure little Tina told you about the *other* apartment. That was a risk when I told you about her. I knew you'd begin to wonder why you didn't have tapes from that *other* little film studio. And, it was possible that Tina just might remember where it was. But it was *so* long ago, and she was *so* young. I was reasonably certain she wouldn't remember the address." She smiled. "And, of course, telling you also meant you could find Tina for us. It was something Paddy didn't seem capable of doing." She watched Devlin's jaw tighten, then laughed. "And the apartment?" She gestured about the room. "This is it, Paul. And that locked room you saw the first time you were here? That's where Paddy worked. Running our little camera. Right through that lovely antique mirror in the bedroom. You see, only *our* films were made here. Not Torelli's."

Devlin felt his gut tighten. Not at being entrapped, but at having Rourke watch him playing the fool through a two-way mirror. He fought it off.

Michelle studied his face; let out an affected sigh of regret. "He was here, today, too. I thought you might be amorous again," she said. "I was disappointed, of course." She stared at him. "Mildly." She waited several moments, then added: "Check, Paul."

Eddie Grogan moved across the room and took the tape from her hand.

"Of course, it's only a copy," Michelle said.

"Fuck you, lady," Grogan snapped. "And fuck your little checkmate. We'll find the other one. And you'd be fucking amazed how much evidence gets lost in a police department."

Michelle watched Grogan retreat to Devlin's side. "Loyalty is so becoming, Paul," she said. "But, of course, I'd *never* want the police to see that film. It's so damning of me, don't you think?" She ran her hands through her hair, forcing her breasts against the silk of her blouse. Devlin remembered the gesture; remembered his reaction to it.

"But, then, there are other interested parties," Michelle continued. "That lovely woman you live with—the one you spoke so glowingly of. And, of course, there's your young daughter. Phillipa, was it? I'm not sure I remember. I wonder what they'd think if this amusing little tape was quietly placed in their hands?"

Devlin stared at her, jaws grinding. He took the tape from Eddie's hands and tossed it on a nearby chair. "You tried that with Little Bat," he said. "He told you to scratch it. Go scratch it again." He turned and started for the door, Eddie in step behind him.

"Think about it, Paul," Michelle called after him.

Devlin glanced over his shoulder. "I'm too busy," he said. "I've gotta send a little bird down to Mott Street. Let him have a talk with Donatello Torelli."

Eddie was silent until the elevator doors closed behind them. Now he rounded on Devlin. "Where the fuck were your brains?" he snapped. "What's the matter, you ain't got it good enough with what you got?"

"Knock it off, Eddie," Devlin said. His voice was restrained, and he refused to meet Grogan's eyes.

Eddie shoved him, pushing him back against the wall of the elevator. "That an order, Inspector? Well, fuck you, and your orders. You wanna trade lives? Well, I'll trade with you, you fucking asshole. I'll take Adrianna—I'll take my fucking godchild over that piece of French shit. And I'll take Phillipa, too, and the nice, cozy, fucking life you got."

"All right, Eddie." Devlin was staring at his shoes.

"No, it ain't all right. You're gonna call that woman, and tell her we got a deal. Then we're gonna bust every fucking place she coulda stashed that tape—UN property, or no fucking UN property."

"I can't do that, Eddie. I can't fuck up the case that way."

"Yes, you can, Paul." He jabbed a finger into Devlin's chest. "Because the only other option is to fuck up some lives that don't deserve to be fucked up."

Back in the apartment, Michelle turned to face the window. She held up two fingers, then drew the drapes closed.

The man was a fool, she told herself. And that left her only one choice. There would be others in the police department who would be more reasonable. Mac Brownell had assured her of that; assured her he could arrange it. And he would have certain powerful men in Washington behind him.

Michelle walked to a side table and poured herself a glass of wine. Soon all the troublesome men would be gone. She drank to the thought.

Across the street, Paddy Rourke watched Michelle's signal through the telescopic lens of his 8-mm, Czechoslovakian sniper's rifle. Slowly, he repositioned his hands on the stock and trigger guard. He was wearing soft, leather gloves to avoid fingerprints. They had maintained this second apartment to keep watch on their honey trap. The weapon had been a similar precaution. Just in case some enraged victim lost it, and threatened serious mayhem. Or in the event of a raid by a suddenly enlightened Torelli family.

Rourke lowered the rifle, taking steady aim on the glass doors that led to the street. He had done as he was told; entered the building from the rear to avoid the snoops outside. Now he'd follow the other orders. He hoped the damned woman knew what she was doing. Killing two cops, from this distance, with this rifle was easy. He wasn't sure if it was smart.

Chapter Twenty-three

The high velocity, 8-mm. slug took Devlin in the upper left quadrant of his chest, leaving an exit wound the size of a quarter in his back. The impact lifted him and threw him back like a man struck by an overpowering force. His body slammed into the sidewalk seconds after he heard the report of the rifle.

He lay there, breath gone, watching as Eddie began to pull his revolver from its holster. Then Eddie's head exploded, bits of brain and bone spraying out in a dark red wash. Devlin struggled to lift his head, but the sky and buildings above began to spin. Then dark closed in, and he was gone.

Cunningham and Samuels raced into the street. Samuels continuing across and Cunningham stopping midway and emptying his revolver at the open window with the still-protruding rifle barrel.

The rifle fell back, and Cunningham heard Samuels screaming at him. "Officers down! Officers down! Get on the fucking radio." He glanced back, saw Samuels leveling his own revolver toward the now empty window. He turned and raced back to his car.

Devlin awoke hours later in Bellevue Hospital. It was the city's major trauma center—the place all wounded cops were taken, whenever possible.

His eyes focused slowly, finally bringing in the faces of Sharon Levy, Samuels, and Cunningham.

"Your wife and daughter are on the way," Levy said. "Suffolk County cops are bringing them in."

Devlin fought against the unbelievable dryness in his throat. "We're not married," he managed.

Levy grinned at him. "Hey, neither are me and my girlfriend. Who cares?"

Slowly, Devlin's mind began to function. He snapped his eyes toward Samuels. "Eddie?" he asked. "Tell me about Eddie."

Samuels lowered his eyes, shook his head. "He never had a fucking chance."

Devlin closed his eyes. He wanted the room to swallow him, take him away and not bring him back. Eddie's final words to him played again and again in his mind. His red, angry, disillusioned face glared at him as it had in the elevator. Then he saw Eddie's head explode, bone and brain flying out behind him. It was a vision he'd see for the rest of his life. His body began to tremble with the horror of it.

He opened his eyes, found Cunningham. "Michelle Paoli," he croaked.

"We grabbed her," Cunningham said. "The fucking state department had her sprung before her fucking hair was mussed."

His rage grew. "Rourke and O'Brien?" Devlin managed. His chest throbbed all the way through to his back.

"Rourke's among the missing," Samuels said. "But the whole, fucking force is looking for him." He hesitated. "We located O'Brien a couple of hours ago." He paused again, fought off what Devlin thought was the beginning of a smile. "He was in his car," Samuels continued. "A little hole in his right temple. A thirty-eight Smith on the seat next to him. I took the call myself." He inclined his head to one side, then continued, "Funny thing. There was a freshly packed suitcase in the trunk. I figure it was something he always kept there. Just in case he had to travel sudden like. I put it down as a suicide."

Sharon Levy leaned close. "We hit the apartment, when we took the Paoli broad," she said. "State department's not too happy, 'cause we tore it up pretty good." She lowered her voice close to a whisper. "We found a tape in the living room with your name on it. There were two more copies in a safe in this locked-up room. Some guy from Safe and Loft opened it for us. I can't explain it, but the tapes got lost before we could do what the state department said, and put everything back." She shrugged. "I don't think *Ms.* Paoli is gonna bitch too much."

Devlin began to fade out again. He struggled against it at first, wanting to keep his rage alive. He couldn't let them get away with it. Not one of them. He owed Eddie at least that. Finally, he surrendered to his own body. He couldn't help it. Unconsciousness seemed better now. Better than thinking, better than remembering what had happened to Eddie because of him.

Michelle Paoli listened to the news report on CNN. It had been the same all morning. Two New York City police detectives gunned down on New York's posh East Side. One dead, one in grave condition. Names withheld, pending notification of next of kin. Newspapers had been no better. But unless they both died, all she had done was buy some time.

She considered Mac Brownell. He was doing what he could. Badly, as usual. He had directed Mitchelson to arrest Torelli, and through people in Washington, he had put renewed pressure on the mayor. But there was resistance. Mitchelson was dragging his feet. The mayor was subtly stonewalling the Washington intelligence types. And, now, Ari Popolis had ordered her to answer questions from the secretary general's office. There was even the threat her diplomatic immunity might be revoked if the secretary was dissatisfied with her answers.

It was the same. Just as it had been for as long as

she could remember. Men—always at the root of her problems. It had been that way since she was a child living in the houses her mother had run. First in Marseilles, then here in New York. Always taking whatever they wanted. Always lining their own pockets, and leaving only crumbs behind. And always protecting themselves first. Oh, yes, always that. But not anymore. Not ever again. Now it was her's. Now *she* was in control. And she would keep what she had won. No matter what it cost.

She stared at the men seated across from her in her apartment. Perhaps it was time for all of them to cut and run. It had been discussed. But, perhaps not. There were still the tapes she had sent out of the country for safekeeping. As long as she had them, the secretary general and the United States government would allow her to escape. And, perhaps, she could still find a way to stay. There were scapegoats at hand. Male scapegoats this time. She could use them. And she would. If only those fools Devlin and Grogan both ended up dead.

Devlin awoke two hours later. It was late morning, and the sun bathed the room with natural warmth. Adrianna and Phillipa were at his bedside.

He smiled at Phillipa. "Looks like a beautiful day," he said. "You should be on the beach."

Phillipa rushed to him, then pulled up, uncertain where she could safely touch him.

"It's all right" Devlin said. "I won't break."

She leaned down and kissed him. When she raised her head, tears had flooded her eight-year-old's eyes. "You always told me you knew how to duck," she said.

"I forgot," Devlin said.

Adrianna moved next to the child. She placed a comforting hand on her shoulder. With the other, she took Devlin's hand, squeezed it softly. Phillipa rested her head against Adrianna, taking assurance from her maternal warmth. The picture tore at Devlin's heart, filling him with new guilt.

"How do you feel?" Adrianna asked.

"Like I was hit by a truck. But better. A lot better than last night."

"I spoke with your doctor," Adrianna said. Her own eyes started to fill, but she fought it off. For Phillipa's sake, Devlin thought. She shook her head. "He says you were very lucky, that he doesn't expect any complications."

"That's me. Lucky." He was having trouble looking at Adrianna, meeting her eyes. Sooner or later he had to talk to her. But it could wait. He closed his eyes, rested again.

When he came back, Phillipa was gone. He asked Adrianna where she was.

"Sharon Levy came. I asked her to take Phillipa down to the cafeteria," Adrianna said. "This has been hard on her, Paul. You're all she has."

"She has you," he said.

"It's not the same."

Devlin looked toward the window. It was still bright and clear and beautiful. One of those rare, clear days New Yorkers live for. He was still finding it hard to meet Adrianna's eyes.

"Does she know about Eddie?" he asked at length.

"No. I didn't want to tell her. Not yet."

"What about Sharon?"

"I asked her not to," Adrianna said.

He turned back to her. She looked so beautiful. Everything he wanted. Her raven hair was down, lightly caressing her cheeks. Her soft brown eyes were filled with love and concern. Eddie had been right. Only a fool would trade what he had.

"I need you to handle the funeral arrangements for Eddie," he said—guilty he was asking her. "We're the only family he had. I don't think I can do it."

"I've already told the department that," she said. "They're taking care of most of it."

"Tell them, no bagpipes," he said. "Eddie hated them." He heard his voice begin to choke.

"What happened, Paul? Who killed Eddie? Who shot you? The doctor said two inches lower and it would have hit your heart."

"I don't know who pulled the trigger," Devlin said. "But I've got a pretty good idea. The person behind it was a woman named Michelle Paoli. She's a diplomat. Works for the UN." He stopped, fought to catch his breath. His chest was beginning to throb again. "I led us into it," he said. "Right down a garden path. Right from the beginning."

Adrianna lowered her eyes. She was holding his hand again, and she squeezed it now. "Is she beautiful?" she asked.

Devlin looked at her. Now it was she who couldn't look at him. Women's intuition was terrifying, he thought. She knew, but she didn't want to. And he had to tell her. But not now.

"Yes," he said. "The same way a leopard's beautiful. Just enough to make you forget they're always waiting to kill something."

The doctor came in, saving him. He was young and short, painfully thin, haggard, and competent. He probed and prodded; checked the chart. "You're doing amazingly well," he finally said. Devlin thought he looked as though he needed a bed, himself. "Better than I would have thought. There doesn't seem to be any nerve damage, and the wound is healing nicely. We may even be able to get rid of you in a couple of days."

"I was hoping you'd say he had to retire," Adrianna said.

He smiled. The name on his name tag said ROSE. It was a good smile, one that showed an underlying humor. "If it was me, I'd be making reservations for

Florida now," he said. "Life has enough ways to kill you without adding bullets to the equation."

Phillipa and Sharon returned as the doctor was leaving, followed by Howie Silver. The mayor was carrying a bouquet of cut flowers. Devlin was sure his secretary, Ellie Cohen, had bought them, and thrust them in his hand as he left City Hall.

Silver, somewhat sheepishly, asked if he could see Devlin alone. When the others had gone into the hall, he pulled up a chair.

"All hell's coming down," he said. "I've got these intelligence clowns from Washington camped in my office. One of them—Robinson—says you kicked him in the balls." He grinned, shook his head. "And Mac Brownell is pushing to have Torelli arrested, but, apparently, that little assistant D.A. told him to go fuck himself. Also, I got a chief named Mitchelson, who heads up OCC, calling my office, begging to see me. What's going on, Paul? I gotta know."

Devlin told him. The mayor listened; closed his eyes periodically—somewhat painfully, Devlin thought. Then a slow, quiet anger took over.

"I'll fire Brownell this afternoon," he said.

"No, don't," Devlin said. "Don't even suspend him. Just isolate him, but let him think he's making some headway. And tell Jenny Miller to hang tough. Tell her you'll give her a job if she needs one when this is over."

"What about the feds?" Silver asked.

"See Sharon Levy before you leave. Tell her you need some pictures she has. They show that clown Robinson making a film pickup from Bunny Rabitto. Shove it in their faces, and watch them go away."

"Okay," Silver said. He thought a moment. "I'm not sure what we can do about this Paoli woman. I don't want to see her waltz out of here. Not somebody who's killed two of my cops. She's holed up in her apartment, but the state department even forced your people to pull the surveillance there."

Devlin's eyes hardened. "Don't worry about her. She's not going anyplace." He owed that to Eddie Grogan, he told himself. No matter what it cost. "What time is it?" Devlin asked.

Silver looked at his watch. "A little past noon."

"I need you to call Brownell. Tell him you want him in his office between four and five to await word from you. Don't tell him anything else. Just let him stew." Devlin grimaced at the pain in his chest. He had lodged the medication the doctor had given him in his cheek. Then palmed it later. It made him dopey, and he had wanted a clear head more than relief from pain.

"Then I need you to call Brownell back at quarter to five," he said. "Tell him you just got word the UN has revoked Paoli's diplomatic status."

Silver grinned. "Should stir things up."

"Yeah," Devlin said. "Everybody's gonna need new shorts."

After Silver left, Phillipa and Adrianna stayed another hour, before Devlin persuaded them to go home. He said he needed sleep. And so did they. When they had left, he telephoned his office.

Levy returned with Samuels a half hour later. He told them what he wanted.

"You're crazy . . . , *sir*," Levy said. "We can handle this."

"Leave him alone. He knows what he's doing."

They turned to the doorway. Big Bat Battaglia moved up beside them. He held out his hand. There was a small, rectangular cassette in it, about the size of a pack of cigarettes.

"I spoke to my grandchildren," he said. "Their father had given them a key to hold. It was to a safety deposit box in Queens. Joey used his mother's maiden name. Just like I used to." He smiled weakly at the irony of his son's final message to him.

Samuels took the tape.

"Get a uniform to run that down to Boom Boom," Devlin said. He turned back to Bat. "That tape," he said. "There'll be things on it that will hurt you. You know that, right?" Bat's face didn't change. It was stoic and hard, and somehow peaceful.

"I'm resigning from the senate," he said. "For reasons of health." He rolled his head on his shoulders—like an old fighter loosening his neck. "There's nothing indictable in what I did. Nothing anybody can prove, anyway. And I can live with a little embarrassment. Joey gave a lot more for this case."

Devlin noted the use of the childhood name again. And he knew it would be more than a little embarrassment. "You heard about O'Brien?" he said.

"Yes. Terrible thing," Bat said. He and Devlin exchanged looks.

Devlin laid that small devil to rest. The man had deserved his shot. There were times rules didn't matter. Sometimes it was the only way things could turn out right. Like now.

"Help me get out of bed," he said. "I wanna pay a visit to a diplomat."

When he was dressed, Bat placed a hand on his arm. His eyes were clear and hard. There was almost a smile on his lips. He understands what you're going to do, Devlin thought.

"Do it smart, Paul," Bat said. "Cover yourself. Don't let the bastards win by default."

Chapter Twenty-four

Their car pulled up in front of Michelle's Fifth Avenue apartment shortly before five. Devlin had everyone affix their shields to the outside of their clothing. Then he told Samuels to get the car out of sight, and come back to join Levy in front of the building.

"Stay under the canopy," he said. "Make sure you can't be seen from any of the windows upstairs."

"I don't think you should go up alone," Levy said. She had argued with Devlin all the way from the hospital, and was now taking her last shot.

"It's the only way we're going to close this case," Devlin said. "By now she thinks her diplomatic status has been revoked." He looked at each of them, gathering the words for the lie he was about to tell—words he needed to cement it in their minds. "She'll be in a panic. And I think she'll be ready to spill things we still have to know. Just to save as much of her ass as she can. Maybe it'll be enough to make the UN really move against her." He took a shallow breath, fighting off the pain in his chest. "At the very least, she might tell us about people we don't know about yet."

"You're in no shape for this," Levy said. "At least let one of us go with you."

"I'm fine," Devlin snapped. "Too many people, she might pull a clam. She's not stupid. She knows better than to talk in front of a witness. This way, she knows it's my word against hers." He patted his breast pocket; reminding them about the miniature, voice-activated tape recorder he had asked Samuels to bring.

Orders given, and grudgingly taken, Devlin turned to the building's front door. The same doorman—the ex-hose jockey he had encountered on his first visit—was on duty. Devlin approached him, took him by the arm, and led him inside.

"I want your passkey. Now," he said.

The former firefighter looked at him, and let out an amused snort. "Hey, the rules haven't changed since last time," he said. "You know the drill. You got a warrant?"

Devlin shoved him back against the lobby wall. The effort did him more damage than the doorman. "I got a badge, and I got a gun. This is the real thing. Don't fuck with me. Just gimme the key."

The ex-firefighter's lower lip stiffened. Then he thought better of it. He pulled a ring of keys from his belt, and handed one to Devlin. Then he watched sullenly, as Devlin entered the elevator.

Fuck you, blue balls, he told himself. He went into a small alcove, out of view from the front door, picked up the lobby phone, and buzzed Michelle Paoli's apartment.

Devlin touched the small tape recorder in his breast pocket as he stood before Michelle's door. He didn't turn it on. It had just been for show—for Samuels's and Levy's benefit. Later, he'd simply say it had malfunctioned.

Michelle was standing in the small, marble foyer when he opened the door. She smiled at him.

"The doorman called," she said. "The rules here are very strict. But, please, come in."

She turned and walked toward the living room. It reminded Devlin of the last time he had seen her. He and Eddie following her very sensual movements. Today, she was wearing black tights that hugged every inch of her lower body, and a faux leopard silk top. Devlin recalled what he had told Adrianna: that the woman was beautiful the same way a leopard was. Now, she didn't look beautiful to him at all. She looked like the whore she had always been.

Michelle stopped in the middle of the living room. Her arms were folded across her chest. One hip was cocked to the side. Devlin walked to the French doors that led to a small terrace and opened one.

"Is the air conditioning too much for you, Paul?" Michelle asked. She was smiling again, not the jangled bag of nerves he had expected. It didn't matter.

"Have you heard from Brownell?" he asked.

"Oh, yes. He called. Is it true?"

"Yeah, it's true." He wanted the pleasure of lying to her just once. Just once before he threw her off the terrace. And listened to her scream all the way down.

She smiled again. "I told Mac to call his friends in Washington. To pass on a message from me. I think your state department will soon impose upon the secretary general to change his mind. It shouldn't be hard for him. Revoking diplomatic status is quite unprecedented."

Devlin stared her down. "Yeah, you're right. He'd never do it." Now Devlin smiled. "I was lying."

Michelle stared at him, uncertainty flashed across her eyes for the first time. Then she drew herself up. She was a tough woman, Devlin thought.

"But you won't get away with killing two cops," he said.

Devlin withdrew his service revolver and moved toward her. Michelle took in the weapon, then Devlin's face, then the weapon again. The look in her eyes was more disbelief than fear.

"I don't think the secretary general will have to make any decision at all," he said. He placed the barrel of the revolver under her chin and pressed upward. "Let's take a little walk on the terrace," he said.

He guided her around him with the pistol, then turned her away from him and pushed her forward. "This one's for Eddie Grogan," he said.

He felt the blow coming and ducked his head. The lead-filled sap hit his shoulder just above the exit wound. Pain surged through his body, as he crumpled to the floor. A shoe kicked him hard in the ribs, driving away what little breath remained. Then a foot slammed down on his wrist, pinning his hand to the floor.

"Take his gun," Paddy Rourke snapped.

Michelle reached down and yanked the revolver from Devlin's pinioned hand.

"Look out the window. See if there are any cops outside."

Michelle did as asked. "I don't see anyone," she said.

"You sure?"

"Yes, damn it."

"Check the hall. See if anybody's out there."

Michelle returned moments later. "It's empty," she said. Devlin was just coming around. He looked up into Rourke's grinning face.

"You're a bad boy," Rourke sneered. "You wanted to give the lady a flying lesson." He made a reproachful noise with his tongue and teeth.

Behind Rourke, Buster Fucci walked into view. Devlin stared at him. He started to laugh, but it hurt his chest too much.

"I always thought of you as the missing link, Buster," he said. "Now I see it's true."

"Hey, dead men should always go out laughing, Devlin." Buster's voice was pure stoicism, and it made Devlin wonder how many murders the man had presided over.

He looked back at Rourke. He was holding a Glock automatic, fitted now with a silencer. Rourke pulled back the slide, cocking the weapon, then smiled.

"You asked me two questions the other day, Paul." It was Michelle, and he turned his head to her. "Let me answer them now." She walked around to stand over him. She was only a few feet from Rourke now.

"You asked whose idea it all was. Whether I went to them, or if they came to me." She glanced back at Fucci. He was ten feet away, leaning against a wall. "Actually, it was Buster's idea. He doesn't like Mr. Torelli very much. Hasn't for a long time." She smiled. "Not that the thought hadn't already crossed my mind."

Devlin's gun was in her hand, hanging down along her leg. He watched her slowly cock the hammer.

"You also asked who shot Captain Battaglia." She forced a regretful look on to her face. "I'm afraid it was I." She batted her eyes affectedly. "It wasn't very hard. Even a poor, helpless woman could do it. He was all trussed up, with that vibrator sticking out of him." She let out a sigh. "And he simply wouldn't listen to reason. Isn't that what you men always say about *us*?"

Devlin started to respond, but Michelle turned away from him. She was facing Rourke now.

"Paddy?" she said.

Rourke turned to her, and Michelle raised Devlin's revolver and fired one shot into his forehead. A clot of blood and bone and brain matter flew back toward Buster Fucci. Michelle stepped forward and picked up Rourke's automatic. Fucci, momentarily frozen by the human debris, started toward her. Michelle leveled Devlin's revolver at him, freezing him again.

Devlin tried to force himself up. Michelle caught the movement, and pointed Rourke's gun at his face.

She backed slowly away, so she could keep both in view.

"Patience, gentlemen. You'll both get your turn." Her eyes fell on Fucci. "I think you'll be first, Buster. I want to save Paul just a minute longer. You see, I had always intended to get rid of Paddy. He was such a crude person, and not very dependable. It's why I could afford to tell Paul so much about him." She smiled at Fucci. "But you knew that, Buster. You just didn't know I hadn't made up my mind about you. Now I have."

"Hey, wait," Fucci shouted. "We can beat this thing. Don't be stupid. We can still have it all."

"Don't *you* be stupid, Buster. It's over. Here, anyway. I can sit quietly in Europe and collect some handsome royalties. I still have tapes there, and there are some rather wealthy people—even a member of the Saudi royal family who likes little boys—who will pay lovely dollars to keep them locked away."

She glanced at Devlin, making sure he was still immobilized. "And this just tidies things up for your government, doesn't it? Wonderful Paul, here—heroic police officer that he is—has saved me from the real villains, who were about to keep me from telling the truth about them." She let out a sigh. "Unfortunately, he died a hero's death doing it." She smiled. "Yes, I think your government will like it. The secretary general certainly will. And I will gratefully return to Europe. Just *too* frightened to continue my work in this oh, so violent city."

"Sounds good to me, bitch! Now drop the guns!"

Michelle's head snapped to the sound. Sharon Levy was just inside the room, crouched in a combat shooting stance, her weapon held in both hands, leveled and ready.

Instinctively, Michelle swung the Glock up. Devlin lashed out with his foot, making hard contact with Michelle's shin. The effort caused his eyes to lose focus from the pain, but Michelle's only shot went wide.

Levy fired three times, each bullet hitting the center of Michelle's chest in a pattern no bigger than a fist. Her body flew back, hit the floor like wet laundry. Devlin didn't have to look to see she was dead.

Levy swung the weapon on Fucci. "Move once, asshole, and they'll use what's left of you to make pepperoni," Levy snapped.

"I ain't goin' no place. And I ain't carryin' nothin' either," Fucci said. He looked pale, shaken. "Hey, we could make a deal, here," he said.

"Shaddup!" Levy snapped.

Levy patted him down, cuffed him, then pushed him into a chair. The Glock had flown five feet from Michelle's dead body, but Levy kicked it another ten, just for good measure. Then she went to Devlin. There was blood leaking through his shirt. "You been hit?" she asked.

Devlin shook his head, immediately wished he hadn't. "I think the stitches broke. It'll be okay." He let out a breath and grinned up at her. "You don't follow orders too well, Detective."

"Hey, what do they call it? Initiative in the field? Or some shit like that." She motioned back toward the front door. "It hit me, downstairs, that maybe I should ask that asshole doorman if there was anybody else up here."

Devlin's grin returned. "Should have asked it myself."

"Yeah, well, he tells me about these two clowns, so I figure I should come up, just in case. Lucky I still had that key you gave me, when I brought that bitch a change of clothes."

Devlin started to laugh, despite the pain. "She never asked you for it back?" His voice sounded incredulous.

"Oh, yeah. But I had a copy made. Thought we might wanna pull a little burglary here some day."

"You're a piece of work, Levy," Devlin said.

"Yeah. Tell that to those fucks at the Puzzle Palace, who don't want us dykes around."

Epilogue

Devlin stood at the foot of Eddie Grogan's casket, flanked by Adrianna and Phillipa. Sharon Levy and the rest of his unit stood close by. He had asked them to be there, next to him, part of the only family Eddie ever had.

The honor guard stood at attention, as two of its members folded the flag that had draped Eddie's coffin. It was handed to a sergeant, who turned smartly, marched to Adrianna, and placed it in her hands.

"With the respect and love of the department, and his brother officers," the sergeant said.

Adrianna fought back tears as the simultaneous report of seven rifles cracked the silence three successive times. Then came "Taps," played by a lone bugle. They all stepped forward—Devlin, Adrianna, Phillipa, and the members of the unit—and placed individual roses on the coffin.

Sharon Levy slipped her arm around Phillipa's shoulders and guided her away, out of reach of the official department condolence givers, who would now begin to mutter their mundane words.

Devlin brushed most aside with a simple nod of his head. He stopped only to speak with Howie Silver, who looked truly shaken at this, already his second department funeral in his first year in office. He told Devlin to take as much time as he needed. Devlin said he would, and wondered how long he really wanted to stay away. Or if he wanted to go back at all.

The case had resolved itself. Most of the major players were dead. The D.A. was pushing hard for an indictment against Mac Brownell, and would undoubtedly get it. Big Bat Battaglia had resigned from the senate, and was now awaiting the repercussions of his son's investigation. He didn't seem to mind.

Walter Silverberg had been forced out of the attorney general's office, and would probably also face indictment. Ari Popolis had retired back to Greece, and the Money Club, under the order of the secretary general, had closed down. Diplomats would undoubtedly begin getting mugged again.

Everything had been on the backup tape, just as Boom Boom had predicted. Little Bat had been a fortress, just as he had said. The fact he had also been gay had never made it into any of the reports, and Leslie Boardman had been told to keep his mouth shut. In the final analysis, it just didn't matter.

Only Buster Fucci had escaped. If you could call it that. The feds had latched on to him, and Buster had agreed to rat out his boyhood buddy, Donatello Torelli. It would be the first time a mob underboss had agreed to play turncoat for the government, and the feds were convinced that even Larry Matz couldn't save Torelli's butt this time. They had given Fucci full immunity.

But Fucci's time would come. Devlin was certain of it. The Mafia had long memories, and even longer arms. But Devlin hoped it wouldn't come quickly. He liked the idea of Buster looking over his shoulder, knowing what was coming, and waiting. And, if the mob failed, there was always Big Bat. He had a lot of time on his hands, and his tainted heart was still that of a cop.

Still, Devlin wasn't certain if he wanted back in.

Eddie had died because of him—because of his own weakness. And Devlin had discovered some other things about himself—discovered he could kill, coldly and dispassionately, and for the sake of revenge. He wasn't sure he wanted to be anywhere he might fall victim to that sickness. It would take time to figure that one out.

In the meantime, he had another flaw he had to deal with—one he had to sit and talk about with Adrianna.

"It was a beautiful ceremony," Adrianna said, as they reached the limousine that had brought them, and would now take them home.

"Yeah," Devlin said. "No *fooking* bagpipes." He thought Eddie would be smiling. At least about that.

He took Adrianna's arm, as she started to enter the limo. "There are some things I have to talk to you about. Some things I have to tell you," he said.

She looked up at him. She was more beautiful than ever. The sight of her broke his heart.

"I know, Paul," she said. "But I don't want to talk about it. I almost lost you, and now I just want to have you again. Maybe someday. After we've let some time pass."

Phillipa came up beside them. Devlin hung his head; fought the tears that were flooding his eyes. Adrianna took his hand and guided him into the car.

"Let's go home," she said. "Just the three of us."

Now that you've enjoyed
Tarnished Blue,
don't miss these other
bestselling thrillers by
William Heffernan,
all featuring Paul Devlin . . .

Journey down a dark path,
and into the mind of brilliant killer . . .

RITUAL

Her body was strangely and savagely mutilated. She would be the first victim in a series of bizarre murders that share an eerie similarity to an ancient ritual of human sacrifice.

Stanislaus Rolk is a cop they call "the scholar of murder." But he and his partner, Paul Devlin, may have met their match in this insanely brilliant and obsessed murderer. Follow the trail of a madman as he creeps in the street shadows, waiting to stalk his next victim for a sacrifice to a bloodthirsty god. . . .

"Shiver-inducing . . . a spine-tingling chiller that keeps the reader guessing . . . enjoyably creepy."
—*Kansas City Star*

**A small town where secrets lie,
and a killer waits for his prey ...**

BLOOD ROSE

She is found in an open field, her body savaged by wild animals. Within days, a second corpse in discovered, this time visibly defiled by human hands. And now a third victim brings to light the terrifying truth of a relentless executioner. . . .

For former New York Detective Paul Devlin, the new chief of police in a small Vermont town, the safety has suddenly vanished. As he plunges into this desperate search for a killer he can't understand, the next victim is targeted ... and it's the woman Devlin has come to love. . . .

"An electrifying thriller ... Hitchcock would have loved. Devious plots, strong characters ... and suspense from start to finish!"
—*Mystery News*

**Murder was only the climax,
the real fury was in the preparation ...**

SCARRED

A series of successful, beautiful women had become victims of a devious serial killer. First they were hideously disfigured—and only after months of agony, savagely slain.

Detective Paul Devlin was on the case, called out of early retirement by an old sidekick from the NYPD burning to catch the killer and by a lovely ex-love who was the latest target of terror. And while Devlin is only one step behind the killer, it may be not enough to stop him from killing again. . . .

"A clever, well-paced thriller. Heffernan lays out his clues and plot twists with a dark glee that amuses and draws one along in his wake."
—*Publishers Weekly*